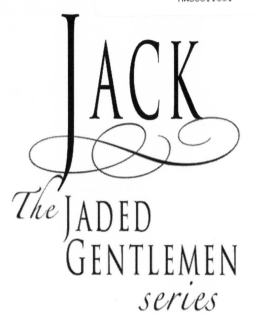

JACK

The JADED GENTLEMEN series

GRACE BURROWES

Published by Grace Burrowes Publishing, 21 Summit Avenue, Hagerstown, MD 21740.

ISBN for Jack—The Jaded Gentlemen Book IV: 978-1941419304

Cover by Wax Creative, Inc.

To the Hon. W. Kennedy Boone, III, (ret.) who knew exactly why, when, and how to apply a dash of mountain law.

CHAPTER ONE

"My poor, wee Charles is all but dead," Mortimer Cotton ranted. "'Tis is the next thing to murder, Sir Jack."

All poor, wee, wooly, twelve-stone of Charles—a ram of indiscriminate breed—lay flat out in the December sunshine as if expired from a surfeit of sexual exertions.

"Thievery has been committed under our very noses," Cotton went on, meaty fists propped on his hips. "That woman stole my tup, bold as brass. Now look at him."

In Sir John Dewey Fanning's estimation, Charles II, as the ram was styled, would recover from his erotic excesses by sundown, if he ran true to his owner's boasts. Based on the contentment radiating from Hattie Hennessey's ewes, Charles had shared his legendary favors with the entire lot of them.

"Mark my words, Sir Jack: Slander is what we have here," Hattie Hennessey retorted. "Mr. Cotton accuses me of stealing yon lazy tup, when he ought to be fined for not keeping his livestock properly confined. Now here his ram is, helping himself to my fodder and to my poor yowes."

Cotton's complexion went from florid to choleric. "Your runty damned yowes haven't been covered by a proper stud since they were born, Hattie Hennessey. Do I hear gratitude for their good fortune? Do I hear a word about compensating me for poor Charles's generosity? No, I hear you blathering on about fines and insults to my integrity as a proper yeoman."

Opinion in the shire was usually divided regarding which injured party—for Hattie and Mortimer were perpetually offending each other—had the true grievance. In this case, Hattie had notified Sir Jack that a stray ram was loose among her ewes.

The very same ram Mortimer would have charged her a fortune to hire for stud services.

"Mr. Cotton, might I have a word between us gentlemen—us human gentlemen?" Sir Jack interjected into the escalating insults.

"I'll give ye as many words as ye like. None of 'em fit for Charles's delicate ears."

While Cotton cast a baleful glance at his exhausted ram, Sir Jack winked at Hattie. She turned her regard on her ewes, the major source of her cash income, and very likely her dearest companions besides her collie and her cat.

Jack paced over to the far side of a hayrick, and Cotton followed a few fuming moments later.

"Hattie Hennessey has not the strength to wrestle your ram over stone walls," Jack said, "much less carry him the distance from your farm to hers." This was not entirely true. Hattie Hennessey had the Hennessey family height and substance, even in old age. She could control a biddable ram over a short distance.

She could not, however, ask for help from anybody under any circumstances, the Hennesseys being notoriously stubborn and independent—much like the Cottons.

"Then she hired this thievery done," Cotton shot back.

"That hypothesis doesn't fit the facts," Sir Jack replied, brushing a wisp of hay from his sleeve. "In the first place, Hattie hasn't a single coin to spare. In the second, I think a certain neighbor, who is too kind for his own good, set the ram down among Hattie's ewes in the dark of night, thus saving a poor widow from begging for aid she desperately needs."

Cotton's bushy white brows beetled into a single line of consternation. "Mr. Belmont, maybe? Or his boys? Boys at that age would consider this a lark. Charles is the friendly sort, when he's not on the job."

Charles was an ovine hedonist. "I'm not accusing the Belmonts of wayward charity, Mr. Cotton."

Those brows shot up, and before Cotton could interrupt, Jack continued his theorizing. He'd learned serving in India that if senior officers were spared having to comment on a report prematurely, matters came to a more sensible conclusion.

"You know Hattie's circumstances would deteriorate if she couldn't replace the ram who died over the summer," Jack said. "You know she can't afford to go a year without a crop of lambs. Rather than affront her dignity with outright charity, somebody with a kind heart concocted this scheme to spare her pride and put her situation to rights. Vicar will likely be impressed with that person's ingenuity."

Vicar had become so weary of the feud between Mortimer Cotton and Hattie Hennessey that he'd taken to preaching successive sermons on the Good Samaritan.

Cotton's backside graced the church pews regularly. His coin was less frequently seen in the poor box.

"You think I *arranged* this, Sir Jack?"

Well, no, Jack thought no such thing, but needs must when the magistrate was at his wit's end. "Such a scheme has your stamp, Cotton, your sense of practicality and dispatch. But if we remain here much longer, congratulating you on your Christian virtues, Hattie will get out her pitchfork and chase that ram from the premises."

"She'll not abuse my Charles when he's spent from his labors. I won't have it. Charles can't know which ewe belongs to which farm."

To Charles, every ewe belonged to him alone, for the span of a few minutes. Jack had known many an officer in His Majesty's army who'd taken a similar view of amatory pursuits.

"I can probably talk Hattie into allowing Charles to recover here for a day or two," Jack said. "I wouldn't want anybody to say that such a fine animal was overtaxed by a small herd." In those two days, Charles would finish the job he'd started—likely finish it several times over.

"My Charlie, *overtaxed?*"

"We're agreed then. If I can talk Hattie around, Charles will rest from his labors, say until Thursday, at which point, I'll get him home to you. If you leave now in a fit of indignation, Hattie will be none the wiser regarding your generosity."

Cotton peered at Jack as if the word *generosity* was among the French phrases tossed about the Quality at fancy dress balls. To Mortimer Cotton, generosity was doubtless another word for foolishness, but he had as much pride as the next man. Jack could almost hear Cotton quoting Vicar's pious admonitions at the next darts tournament.

"You've found me out, Sir Jack," Cotton said, kicking at the dirt. "You'll not breathe a word to anybody? Hattie Hennessey is prouder than any Christian ought to be."

Oh, right. "You may rely on my discretion, Cotton. The plight of poor widows should concern more people in this shire, and I commend you for taking note of that."

"My sentiments exactly. I'll be on my way now, and trust to your, erm, discretion." Cotton bowed smartly and marched off across the barnyard, sparing Hattie the barest tip of his hat.

Hattie watched him go, her faded blue gaze considering. "It's well you sent that bag of wind from my property, Sir Jack, but he forgot to take his rutting tup with him."

"Rutting is what tups do, Hattie." What Jack hadn't done for far too long, come to that.

One of the ewes wandered over to sniff at Charles's recumbent form. Charles rallied enough to touch noses with his caller, then lay back in the straw with a great, masculine sigh. The ewe curled down next to him and began chewing her cud.

"Eloise," Hattie said, shaking a finger at the ewe, "you are a strumpet. Come spring, I'll expect twins from you, my girl."

Charles was known for siring twins and even the occasional batch of triplets.

"Hattie, I must impose on your good offices," Jack said, "for my shepherd won't be available to transport Charles home until Thursday. I went so far as to assure Cotton you'd not charge him board for the ram, nor bring a complaint for failure to properly fence his stock."

Hattie twitched another piece of straw from Jack's sleeve. "Getting airs above your station, Sir Jack, speaking on my behalf to that buffoon."

Jack's station was well above settling barnyard squabbles, but he'd rather have this discussion here than endure successive visits from Cotton and Hattie at Teak House.

"Cotton cannot have it bruited about that his stock is getting loose, Hattie. Show a little pity for a man who likely knows no peace before his own hearth."

Hattie's snort startled the resting ram. "That Perpetua Cotton has a lot of nerve, whining about this, sniffing about that, flouncing hither and yon with a new bonnet every week. Mortimer Cotton needs to take that woman in hand."

How exactly did a prudent man take in hand a grown woman with a wealth of thoroughly articulated opinions and ten children to keep clothed and fed?

"Mortimer Cotton is clearly a man overwhelmed," Jack said, holding a gloved hand out to a curious ewe. "Show him a bit of charity. Let the ram bide among your ewes until I can take the beast home later in the week."

The ewe sniffed delicately, then went about her business. Animals were, in so many ways, better behaved than people.

"Go on wi' ye," Hattie snapped, waving her hand at the ewe. The ewe trotted off a few steps, then took the place on Charles's other side. Sheep were naturally protective of one another, unlike most people.

"I'd take it as a personal favor if you'd allow Charles to stay for a few days, Hattie."

Everything in Jack longed to grab a pitchfork and fill up the hay rack, then top up the water trough, and pound a nail through the loose board tied to the fence post abutting the gate. Hattie would never allow him to set foot on the property again if he presumed to that extent.

"The ram can bide here," Hattie said, marching off to the gate. "Until Thursday morning, no later."

"My thanks." Jack opened the gate for her, and the creaking hinge woke his horse. That fine fellow had been dozing at the hitching post outside Hattie's tiny cottage.

"You'll stay for a cup o' tea," Hattie announced. "Least I can do when you came straight away to deal with that plague against the commonweal."

Did Hattie refer to Mortimer or Charles?

"Perhaps another time, Hattie. I'm expected at Candlewick and have tarried too long as it is. Shall I bring over some hay for Mortimer's ram?"

Hattie stopped short, fists on hips, the same pose Cotton had adopted. "I'll not be taking charity, Sir Jack, if it's all the same to you. Mortimer Cotton has been farming this shire, boy and man, and if he doesn't realize his ram will eat my hay, then don't you be telling him. I'll have a crop of lambs, thanks to Mortimer's incompetence, though they'll likely be contrary and puny."

"I meant no insult," Jack said, taking up his gelding's girth. "I do apologize." He mentally apologized for declining her proffered cup of tea too. Hattie had to be lonely, but Jack had already surpassed his limit of gratuitous socializing and his day wasn't over.

"Apology accepted, this time," Hattie retorted, stroking a hand over the horse's nose. "If you see my little Maddie at Candlewick, tell her to pay a call on her old auntie, you hear?"

On Jack's most daring day, he wouldn't issue an order to Madeline Hennessey, who had not been little for many a year.

"I'll tell Miss Hennessey you miss her."

He swung up on his horse and trotted out of the stable yard, while Charles, apparently recovered, climbed aboard the wayward Eloise and did what rams did best. Jack envied the sheep both his calling and the endless enthusiasm with which he pursued it.

* * *

"Do come sit with us, Madeline," Abigail Belmont said, patting the sofa cushion. "I vow you never rest unless I order you to."

Madeline Hennessey did not want to sit, much less directly across from Sir John Dewey Fanning—Sir Jack, to the locals.

"Please join us," Axel Belmont said, "or I will scandalize my dear wife by consuming more than my share of tea cakes."

The Belmonts were Madeline's employers, and she never overtly disobeyed them. "While I long to preserve Mr. Belmont from disgrace—doomed though such an endeavor must be—I did promise Mr. Chandler that I'd assist him with an inventory of the—"

Sir Jack had risen, as if Madeline were part of the Belmont family rather than a servant. Her post hovered between lady's companion and general factotum these days, which for the most part suited her.

"Please stay a moment, Miss Hennessey," Sir Jack said. "I bring felicitations from your Great-Aunt Hattie, and a reminder that she misses you."

"Thank you, Sir Jack." Aunt Hattie had likely nattered his handsome ear off, complaining about how infrequently her great-niece visited. Madeline called on each of her two widowed aunts every two weeks, weather permitting. It wasn't enough, but with only one half day a week, she couldn't do more.

"Have a seat," Sir Jack said, gesturing to the place beside him on the sofa. "Hattie was in a fine humor, and the tale resulting in that miracle wants telling."

What Madeline wanted was to assist Mr. Chandler with his inventory in the saddle room. Chandler was passionately in love with his horses, unlike the new footman, who fancied himself in love with Madeline—or her bosom.

She took the place next to Sir Jack, though she really ought not. He was one of those men who looked good across the village green or in the churchyard, and he was handsomer still at close range. Also scrupulous about his personal hygiene.

Madeline had to respect a man who was on good terms with soap, water, and a bathtub. If he had sandy hair, brilliant blue eyes, and Sir Jack's fine manners, she could tolerate a few minutes beside him on the sofa—despite his chilly demeanor.

"Did you run across Aunt Hattie in the village?" Madeline asked.Hattie rarely left her smallholding, mostly because the work was far more than one old woman could keep up with. She also had no coin to spend at market, and didn't go visiting, lest friends return the favor and empty her larder.

"Hattie summoned me in my capacity as magistrate," Sir Jack said, holding the plate of tea cakes before Madeline.

She chose the plainest of the lot, which would be delicious because Cook took the honor of the Belmont kitchen seriously. Sir Jack chose the only other cinnamon sweet and passed the plate back to Mrs. Belmont.

"I hope Aunt hasn't been the victim of a crime," Madeline said.

"I'm sure when she recounts the incident, wrongdoing will be involved," Sir Jack replied. "Mortimer Cotton's prize ram, Charles II, came calling on his own initiative. I don't know whether Cotton was more embarrassed that his livestock got loose, or angry that Hattie's ewes had enjoyed Charles's company without Cotton being compensated."

The topic was not exactly genteel, but the Belmonts weren't fussy people, and Candlewick was twelve country miles from Oxford.

"How did you resolve this?" Mr. Belmont asked. "Mortimer and Hattie have been threatening the king's peace ever since her ram died. I was tempted to lend her one of mine, but then Cotton would have been up in arms because I'd deprived him—or Charles—of a potential customer."

Madeline took a bite of her cake rather than ask Mr. Belmont why Cotton's good will was more important than an old woman's livelihood.

"Had you solicited my opinion," Mrs. Belmont said, "I would have told you that Mortimer Cotton is an idiot. If his rams cover every ewe in the shire, every herd will soon be inbred, and Charles will be out of a job."

Mr. Belmont saluted with his tea cup. "Had I been clever enough to think of that argument, I still would have had to deal with Hattie Hennessey's pride. Charles's romantic inclinations have spared us all at least three more sermons on charity and loving kindness."

Madeline would remember the beast in her prayers, for Mr. Belmont was right: Aunt was as proud as she was stubborn as she was poor, much like her sister Theodosia.

"I find I am in need of charity," Sir Jack said. "I have come to solicit Mrs. Belmont's aid, for I've family threatening to visit directly after the Yuletide holidays."

"How I can help?" Mrs. Belmont asked.

Abigail Belmont had the inherent graciousness of a true lady, though she'd been born the daughter of an Oxford shopkeeper. Mr. Belmont was prosperous gentry, and Madeline would have cheerfully murdered any who sought to do the Belmonts or their children harm.

Mrs. Belmont was perhaps thirty, and her husband several years older, but they'd not yet been married a year, and their firstborn was a recent arrival. They glowed with contentment and the sort of glee Madeline associated with happily ever afters and large families.

Sir Jack, by contrast, lived alone but for his servants, and glowed with... well, he didn't glow. At all.

"What you can do," Sir Jack said, "is rescue my household from certain doom. My butler and my cook barely speak, the footmen pretend not to hear or understand the butler's orders, the maids run riot, and my housekeeper threatens to quit regularly. I cannot have my brother, much less my mother, subjected to such tumult."

"Oh dear," Mrs. Belmont said. "Mothers can be quite—"

"Maternal," Mr. Belmont said, kissing his wife's hand and keeping possession of it. Madeline finished her tea cake, which tasted less enticing than it had smelled—not quite sweet enough, a little too dry.

"I realize I'm asking a lot," Sir Jack said, "but there's nobody else upon whom I can impose." To Sir Jack, even soliciting advice would be an imposition.

"You might need to hire a new butler," Mr. Belmont suggested. "Or to clean house, figuratively. Nothing like making an example of a slacker to inspire good effort from those who've taken their posts for granted."

Sir Jack rose and went to the window, which looked out over a drive lined with maples. Though Christmas would soon be upon them, the autumn had been mild. Golden leaves carpeted the grass and clung to the branches, turning the afternoon luminous. One winter storm, one windy morning, and the last of the foliage and its brilliant light would be gone.

Winter, for a man who'd spent nearly a decade in India, would be long and trying. For a woman who thrived on industry, winter in the Belmont household would be a cozy, peaceful, little slice of hell.

"I had hoped Mrs. Belmont might speak to my housekeeper," Sir Jack said. "Perhaps review Cook's menus, organize the maids' schedules, and have a word with Pahdi about the footmen's responsibilities."

"Madeline looks after the menus for me," Mrs. Belmont said.

"And the maids here at Candlewick are on the schedule Madeline devised for them years ago," Mr. Belmont added, the wretch.

For years, Madeline had been Hennessey to him, and he'd been a widower distracted by grief, and by the need to parent two rambunctious boys. Madeline had enjoyed wayward notions where Axel Belmont was concerned—when she'd been young and foolish, and he'd been not quite as young, and devoted to his first wife.

Sir Jack turned a considering eye on Madeline. "One senses Miss Hennessey is competent at all she turns her hand to."

Oh, no, Miss Hennessey was not. In the opinion of her aunts, Madeline had failed utterly to make a good match. Sir Jack was guilty of the same shortcoming, but being a man, nobody would dare chide him for it.

Then too, he was the magistrate. Madeline was not overly fond of the king's justice or those who claimed to enforce it.

"What you need," Mr. Belmont said, "is a second-in-command or aide-de-camp."

Fortunately, Madeline was neither of those things. "Do you mean a house steward, Mr. Belmont?"

Mr. Belmont studied her with the unblinking scrutiny he turned on his botanical specimens, and Madeline abruptly felt like one of those blooms. Torn from the vine, helpless to avoid visual dissection under Mr. Belmont's quizzing glass.

"Not a house steward," Mrs. Belmont said. "Sir Jack, does your mother travel with a companion?"

Sir Jack folded his arms and leaned back against the windowsill. He was indecently handsome in his riding attire. Tall and lean, tending to casual elegance and soft edges that gave him a deceptively comfortable look. Madeline had seen him on darts night, though, with his cuffs turned back, his gaze fixed on the target.

Though a notably retiring man, he was a good neighbor, a conscientious landlord, and a reliable partner for the wallflowers at the local assemblies.

And his darts team *always* won, provided his teammates were at least half-sober.

"My mother does not have a companion that I know of," Sir Jack said. "She has scores of friends in London, and claims they provide her adequate company. One does not argue with my mother and come away unscathed."

One didn't argue with Sir Jack either. Madeline couldn't recall the last time she'd seen somebody even make the attempt.

"The older ladies need to be charmed," Madeline said. "We think because they've lost their youth that they've lost their taste for flattery, and that's not so. They need the silly banter and the sincere compliments all the more for being at a lonelier time of life."

Both men regarded Madeline as if she'd just described how Napoleon might have won the Battle of Waterloo. Mrs. Belmont lifted the lid of the teapot and peered inside.

"I have an idea," Mr. Belmont said, and Madeline stifled the urge to break the teapot over his helpful head. Whatever his idea, it did not bode well for her.

"Mr. Belmont," his wife said, "I believe I will be exceedingly impressed with this idea." She beamed at her husband, and he… Axel Belmont was not capable of simpering. He was well over six feet, blond, muscular, academically bright, and tough as only the father of both adolescent boys and a newborn could be.

He beamed back at his wife, their mutual regard as luminous as the last of the leaves beyond the window, and far more durable.

"Madeline must join your household as a temporary companion to your mother," Mr. Belmont said, sounding pleased with his own genius. "She will have your domestics sorted out, and even you will not grasp quite how she accomplished that miracle."

Madeline choked on the last of her tea cake, only to have Sir Jack return to her side and thump her soundly on the back.

"Belmont, not well done of you," he said, whaling away between Madeline's shoulder blades. "Your henwitted notion has clearly upset Miss Hennessey."

Madeline waved Sir Jack off, though he remained right where he was. "I'm fine," she rasped. "A crumb—something—went down the wrong way."

"Madeline is surprised that I had a good idea, is all," Belmont said. "I haven't come up with a good idea since—"

"This morning," Mrs. Belmont interjected, smiling at her tea service.

An odd silence germinated, then expanded, while all eyes fixed on Madeline, as if she hadn't been sitting on the very same sofa for the past five minutes.

"Mr. Belmont's idea is not henwitted," she said, "but neither is it well thought out. With the holidays approaching, and more Belmont family visiting from Sussex, we'll have much to do here at Candlewick."

"We're not hosting a royal progress," Mrs. Belmont said. "Matthew and the boys consider this their second home. And Sir Jack's mama isn't coming until after Christmas."

Madeline had a sense that a significant shift in household affairs had happened without her noticing. One moment, her praises were being sung, the next, she was being pushed down the drive.

And all the while, Sir Jack studied her as if she were the center ring on a championship dartboard.

"Candlewick is my home," Madeline said, indignation warring with panic. "Are my services no longer required?"

Her services had lately included everything from supervisor of the nursery maids, assistant to the housekeeper, confidante to the cook, and cribbage partner to the butler.

"Of course this is your home," Mrs. Belmont said, in soothing tones that reassured Madeline not one bit. "We would miss you terribly if you accepted another post, but Sir Jack is our dear friend, and he has sought our assistance."

He'd sought *the Belmonts'* assistance, and he was no friend to Madeline.

"The situation would be temporary," Sir Jack said. "My mother has never stayed more than two or three months."

In other words, the daft man was considering this scheme.

"I take it she's managed without a companion in the past," Madeline said. "Might she be insulted at your presumption, choosing a companion for her now, Sir Jack?"

"My mother enjoys a state of chronic affrontedness, probably much like your Aunt Hattie. By selecting a companion for her, I will conveniently indulge her gift for finding insult where only consideration was intended."

"And *I'm* to be the insult you offer her?"

"One of many, I'm sure," Sir Jack replied. "The food, the bed hangings, the placement of the candles on my library mantel, the tone in which I address my servants, or the fact that I address them at all… My ability to disappoint my mother is as limitless as—"

He fell silent, but not soon enough to mask an air of genuine exasperation. Madeline had a premonition of winter evenings in Sir Jack's library. He'd be happily engrossed in some old soldier's literary reminiscences of war, while his poor mama went barmy from boredom.

"Perhaps you should dissuade your mother from visiting at such a dreary time of year," Madeline said. "You might remove to London yourself, and thus have the ability to come and go at the times of your own choosing."

Mr. Belmont poured his wife a second cup of tea and helped himself to a lemon biscuit. "Mothers, in my experience, don't take kindly to attempts to dodge an inspection. If Sir Jack went on evasive maneuvers, she'd redouble her pursuit."

"Quite," Sir Jack said. "Though I suspect Belmont's older sons would attribute the same tenacity to their own dear papa, whose fixity of purpose puts one in mind of a cocklebur. Miss Hennessey, might I tempt you into a position as my mother's temporary companion? You could reconnoiter the situation below stairs, gather intelligence, confer with Mrs. Belmont, and make some suggestions? I would be most grateful."

Madeline did not want Sir Jack's gratitude, nor did she care for his own impersonation of a cocklebur.

"You really must take pity on a clueless bachelor," Mr. Belmont said. "One has a Christian duty, Miss Hennessey, and the members of Sir Jack's staff will thank you for it. A household in disarray is not a happy situation."

Madeline had no use for happy situations, though she did fancy having a roof over her head and a meal or two each day. She did not fancy a post under Sir John Dewey Fanning's roof.

"I am flattered, of course," Madeline said, "but the nursery maids here are both new to their duties, and with colder weather approaching—"

"Nonsense," Mrs. Belmont interjected. "You've trained them wonderfully, and the baby is thriving. You made an excellent ladies' maid when I was widowed, and you were the housekeeper's right hand here at Candlewick before that. Your aunties treasure you, though they hardly have a kind word to say about anybody. A temporary change of scene will do you good."

More beaming went on, while Madeline wanted to pitch this brilliant idea through the window. The Belmonts were good, kind people with whom Madeline could speak her mind. They valued a cheerful staff and yet tolerated no misbehavior toward the female domestics.

Madeline *liked* them. The realization was disconcerting, particularly when she did not like Sir Jack.

Though she didn't *dislike* him, exactly.

"You are not taken with the idea," Sir Jack said, a monumental understatement. "I am prepared to be generous, Miss Hennessey. Desperately generous. You see before you a man with no pride."

Madeline saw before her a man with no scruples and less charm. "Part of the reason your household is at sixes and sevens, Sir Jack, is because you're the magistrate. You hold parlor sessions some weeks, but not others. Your schedule isn't your own, and if a serious matter comes before you, it absorbs all of your attention. Mr. Belmont was the same way when he was the magistrate."

"She's right," Mr. Belmont said, around a mouthful of shortbread. "Damned job wrecks a fellow's peace when folk are naughty. When livestock are naughty too. Your mama won't be keen on you riding off at all hours to investigate the love life of Hattie Hennessey's ewes."

"Belmont," Sir Jack said, "need I remind you from whom I inherited the magistrate's position?"

"And you've never thanked me for stepping down, you ingrate. Miss Hennessey will take pity on you, because she's soft-hearted."

That was the outside of too much. "I'm not—"

"You spoil your aunties rotten," Mr. Belmont went on. "You spoil us rotten, the boys, the baby… Spoil Sir Jack's mama, plant a few ideas in his housekeeper's head, marvel at his cook's syllabub, and inflict your flirtations and lectures on the footmen. Work your magic, and you'll soon have his household running as smoothly as you do Candlewick."

Madeline opened her mouth to scold her employer for that bald overstatement—Candlewick had a superbly competent housekeeper and equally talented cook, though both women were getting on. What they lacked in energy, they made up for in experience.

"You flatter me shamelessly, Mr. Belmont."

"I wouldn't dare."

"I would," Sir Jack said, "if I thought it would inspire you to take this post. You'll have my undying gratitude, a glowing character, the gratification of fulfilling a much-needed office—"

"And his coin," Mr. Belmont said. "Lots of coin, such as no sensible young woman refuses."

Madeline was no longer young. Somewhere between fending off the callow swains in the churchyard—most of them, anyway—and passing every penny she could spare to her aging relatives, she'd made her peace with reality. She worked hard—she'd always work hard—and if she was lucky, she'd have a little coin to see her through when hard work was beyond her.

"I hazard to point out that your aunts would tell you to take the offer." Sir Jack wasn't teasing or exaggerating. He was making the one argument Madeline could not refute. Hattie would wax scathingly eloquent if Madeline turned up her nose at a chance to be the companion of a true lady.

And Sir Jack was offering only a temporary position, nothing more.

Had Aunt Hattie's spring crop of lambs not depended on a wandering ram, Madeline might have refused, but Aunt's situation had been growing dire. Theodosia's finances teetered close to desperate and had for years.

Madeline would not even have a widow's mite to get her by in old age, as her aunts often reminded her.

"I will be your mother's temporary companion," she said, "and if I see problems with how the household is managed, I will bring them to your attention as discreetly as I can."

Sir Jack took her hand in both of his. "My relief beggars description."

Madeline snatched back her hand. "My requirements for taking the position can be articulated fairly easily, if Mr. and Mrs. Belmont would excuse us for a few minutes?"

The Belmonts were on their feet and halfway to the door before Madeline had finished speaking. Their haste put her in mind of parents affording privacy to a young lady and a marriage-minded suitor.

Which analogy was just plain ridiculous.

CHAPTER TWO

Winning a battle was only half a victory, as any soldier knew. The conquered territory must be held when the guns went silent, and the populace brought under the victor's rule, which could be harder than prevailing in combat.

Madeline Hennessey had acquiesced to the scheme Axel and Abigail Belmont had hatched, and so had Jack.

May God have mercy on his soul, for Miss Hennessey radiated discontentment. "What are your terms, Miss Hennessey?"

She rose, and Jack did as well, not only because a gentleman stood when a lady gave up her seat. Madeline Hennessey was tall for a woman, possessed of glorious red hair, a fine figure, and lovely features. Jack wanted to be on his feet when they parlayed.

Her looks were striking, which a plain cap, severe coiffure, and utter lack of adornment only accentuated. Jack was honest enough to admit that in a small way, he enjoyed watching *her*, watching the woman who'd quietly kept a widower's household running while offending none of his more senior retainers. The same woman who'd become a ferocious ally to Mrs. Belmont when her prospective husband had been slow to offer marriage.

Madeline Hennessey was fierce, in other words, and that quality earned Jack's respect as generous curves and winsome smiles never would. That same fierceness put his guard up too, of course.

"I'll want a bedroom on the same floor as your mother," Miss Hennessey said, "though I don't expect to be housed in the family wing. Stairs are the very devil when you must traverse them at all hours of the day and night."

"Easily done. What else?"

"Sunday and a half day off each week, and such other time to myself as your mother allows."

"My entire staff has Sunday and a half day each week. Those who've been with me for more than five years have a guarantee of evenings free as well, provided their assignments are complete."

She left off studying a sketch of some wild rose or other growing by a still pond. Belmont had likely done the drawing himself.

"How does anything get done after sundown, Sir Jack?"

"The junior staff tend to it." As far as he knew. He hadn't asked directly, lest his butler take offense.

"And when your junior staff have all been with you more than five years?"

"The junior staff don't stay a full year of late. Perhaps you'll be able to change that."

"How long will your mother bide with you?"

Too long. "Mama is a force of nature. She comes and goes as she pleases, and one doesn't—that is, *I* do not—presume to interfere with her plans."

Miss Hennessey folded her arms. "The household belongs to you, Sir Jack. Out of respect for you, your family must apprise you of their plans. How else is the staff to accommodate your guests, much less anticipate your needs?"

At least she'd left off studying Belmont's artistry. "Nobody in the entire shire will be left in doubt regarding my mother's needs, wants, opinions, or desires. I joined a regiment bound for India, very much against her wishes, and nearly twenty years on, I'm reminded regularly of what a naughty boy I was."

"You are not a boy."

And Miss Hennessey was not offering him a compliment. "Neither am I quite doddering, madam. What are your other demands?"

He'd meet them, whatever they were. The longer Jack conversed with Miss Hennessey, the more he was convinced she was the answer to his domestic prayers and an able match for Mama.

That Miss Hennessey was reluctant to take the post only attested to her good sense.

"I'll need a wardrobe allowance," she said. "As a lady's companion, I'll be expected to pay calls with your mother, and for that I must be presentable if I'm to endure the ridicule of the local gentry."

"There will be no ridicule." Not to her face, anyway. More than that, Jack could not prevent.

She marched over to Belmont's desk, an enormous article at which many botanical treatises had doubtless been penned. Miss Hennessey extracted paper from a drawer, took up a quill pen, and uncapped a silver ink bottle.

"When shall my half day be?" she asked, putting pen to paper.

"You want a written contract?"

The pen continued its progress across the page. "Of course. Coin is involved, and a woman can never be too careful."

Jack was torn between affront and amusement. "Miss Hennessey, I am a gentleman. My word is my bond."

Still, she scratched away at her document. "Gentlemen are prone to memory lapses, though I'll not hear a word against Mr. Belmont, ever. Your gentlemanly word won't get me very far in court, Sir Jack, and it won't pay for a bolt of cloth from the dry goods store, or buy me new boots before the first snowfall. What is your legal name?"

She would have made a very effective officer, which *was* a compliment. "Sir John Dewey Fanning, though my friends call me Jack."

The pen stopped. "I'm Madeline Hennessey."

How pensive she looked, sitting at the massive desk—and how pretty. "No middle name?" He wanted to know this about her, wanted any detail she'd part with, because information was a form of ammunition.

She resumed writing, and muttered something under her breath.

"I beg your pardon, Miss Hennessey?"

"Madeline Aphrodite Hennessey. I'll thank you not to bruit that about at the Wet Weasel."

"Of course not." Aphrodite was the goddess of love, pleasure, and procreation, if Jack recalled his tutor's maunderings. "Might I inquire as to your other conditions for accepting employment in my home?" The home to which Jack was anxious to return, lest his domestics burn the place to the ground in his absence.

"I will be driven to Sunday services, if your mother chooses not to go."

Jack attended regularly. He wasn't particularly religious in the Anglican sense, but he did want to set a good example for the staff, and socializing in the churchyard aided in his magistrate's duties.

"I will happily drive you to services, madam."

She put down the pen. "*You* will?"

Jack crossed to the desk and peered at what she'd written.

I, Sir John Dewey Fanning, on the date signed below, do take into domestic employment one Madeline A. Hennessey, in the capacity of temporary lady's companion for my mother, upon certain conditions as follows...

"You're a budding solicitor, Miss Hennessey." She had a graceful hand—neat and legible, no schoolgirl flourishes or embellishments.

"I'm a woman without a man to speak for her, unless one relies on Mr. Belmont's overprotective nature—which I do not."

"Hence the severance pay if your employment is terminated in less than thirty days." A considerable sum too, as household wages went.

Beneath her confident manner was a caution Jack had not anticipated. Mama would approve—Mama was all in favor of women looking out for themselves—but Jack did not.

"Miss Hennessey, we are not adversaries. I have an embarrassment of means and need not quibble with my help over contractual details. My objective is that you should enjoy the time spent in my household, to the extent anybody can enjoy time with my mother."

Or with him. Jack had no delusions about the pleasure of his own company.

Miss Hennessey pushed the paper over to him and held the pen out. "A fine speech, sir."

"We aren't to have witnesses to our signatures?"

"The Belmonts can sign it, after I make a second copy."

"Miss Hennessey, you risk insult to your employer before you've begun your duties. I don't need a copy of the contract. The terms are simple, and you'll correct me should I breach them."

"No, I won't." She signed her name in the same flowing, elegant hand.

"You'll allow me to breach the terms of this agreement with impunity?"

"Of course not. If you put a foot wrong, I'll leave."

Belmont would be on Jack's doorstep the next morning, glowering as only Axel Belmont could glower.

"What if *you* put a foot wrong, madam?"

Because Jack had been to war, he'd learned to recognize all forms of bravery, from stoic silence, to a bellowing charge, to an insistence on measured order even amid the chaos of military life.

He'd also learned to recognize fear. The look Miss Hennessey shot him revealed unshakeable determination, but also a hint of uncertainty.

"You're the magistrate," she said. "You excel at catching people in their missteps. Even Mr. Belmont has sung your praises, and he's not a man given to effusions."

Mr. Belmont this, and Mr. Belmont that. Jack considered Axel Belmont a friend. Perhaps prior to his recent marriage, Belmont had been more than a friend to Miss Hennessey. Belmont was merely gentry, not some prancing lord, and winters in Oxfordshire were long and cold.

Did Miss Hennessey not grasp that she deserved better?

"Are you in love with Axel Belmont, Miss Hennessey?" That glimmer of uncertainty had meant something, and Jack's tour in India had disabused him of the need to make moral judgments. "Women likely consider him attractive, and he's not without admirable qualities."

Belmont had many admirable qualities, in fact.

"Who I might fancy matters naught," Miss Hennessey said, rising. "And who fancies me matters even less. I will work hard for my wages, Sir Jack, and you will pay them on time and to the penny. That is what matters."

She was a tall woman, though Jack was taller. They stood nearly eye to eye, that hint of vulnerability lurking in the upraised angle of her chin and the near-glower in her gaze. He could see her great-aunts in her, see the determination and self-reliance, and it… bothered him.

"I will also pay those wages in advance," he said. "I can't expect you to uproot yourself, purchase material, make a new wardrobe, and otherwise take on new employment without a show of good faith on my part. If you can begin immediately after Boxing Day, I'll see that a bank draft arrives here tomorrow."

"Send cash, please. I'd have to apply to Mr. Belmont to deal with a bank draft, and he's a busy man."

Belmont was a man in love with his wife and devoted to his children.

"Cash, it shall be," Jack said, extending his hand.

Because they'd been at the tea tray, he wore no gloves, and neither did Miss Hennessey. She regarded him quizzically, then offered her hand. He bowed over it and kept hold of her fingers.

"I am in your debt, Miss Hennessey, and I thank you for taking on this situation. I rode up the drive, thinking to ask for a fresh perspective on my household situation. I'll ride home grateful to have recruited an ally under my own roof." A fine little speech, if he did say so himself.

"I'll be an employee, sir, not an ally."

She looked so… bewildered and brave and resolute, that Jack let actions speak rather than argue with lady.

"Apply whatever label suits your fancy," he said, brushing his lips across her knuckles. "I'm much relieved that you'll be joining the household." He relinquished her hand and marched away before she could fire off a scold.

* * *

Abigail Belmont had been raised more or less in a bookshop, and she didn't put on airs, though Madeline would rather her employer did go on with a little more decorum. Instead, in the week since Sir Jack's call, Abigail had assisted in the creation of three new dresses, and was intent on passing along several more from her own wardrobe.

"You can carry off the brighter colors," Abigail said, draping a maroon velvet carriage dress on the bed. "I am a mother now. I need fabrics that wash easily, and don't take stains."

"I won't have any occasion to wear such finery," Madeline protested, smoothing a hand over the soft material. "And this color looks good on most women."

"On you, it looks better than good," Abigail replied, laying a cream-colored shawl on top of the dress. "This remove to Sir Jack's could be very advantageous,

Madeline. Why are you so reluctant to go?"

Because a new household meant teaching a whole new crop of footmen that Madeline would not be ogled, groped, disrespected, or underestimated. Because Sir Jack had as much as admitted he was at daggers drawn with his mother.

"I consider Candlewick my home," Madeline said, as a beaded reticule joined the pile on the bed. "The staff here are like family to me. At Sir Jack's, I will be an intruder with airs above my station."

Abigail tossed a pair of cream slippers onto the heap of finery. "Your version of family consists of a pair of crotchety old women, and the staff here rely upon you to solve every difficulty and smooth all rough patches. That's not the same as being your friends. Have you a watch?"

"No." Any jewelry in the Hennessey family had been sold ten years ago.

"A lady's companion needs a time-keeping device," Abigail said, crossing to her vanity and opening a jewelry box. "This will do."

She pitched—pitched!—a golden brooch at Madeline that turned out to be a lady's watch pin.

"You must not do this," Madeline said, though she didn't dare throw the jewelry back. "I'm not a soldier marching into battle, that you should polish my weapons and stock my haversack. I'll be back here by spring, and then what will I do with all of this, this… treasure?"

Abigail's look was pitying, before she mercifully returned to sorting through her jewelry. "These are cast-offs, Madeline Hennessey. I would have given them to you before—that's one of the perquisites of being a lady's maid—but you'd have sold them to support your elders. I am a scandalously wealthy woman, and you must resign yourself to enduring my whims. Thwart me, and I'll take the matter to Mr. Belmont."

Madeline sat on the Belmonts' enormous canopied bed, then realized what she'd done and bounced to her feet.

"That's not fair, ma'am. Mr. Belmont is ruthless when it comes to… well, he's ruthless in defense of your whims. I'll need a baggage wain to carry my effects to Sir Jack's if you involve Mr. Belmont in this discussion."

Abigail's smile was sweet. "So don't force my hand. Take the clothing—though we'll need to let out a few of the bodice seams—and wear it in good health. Sir Jack is wealthy too, you know."

Madeline busied herself folding the clothing scattered across the bed. Abigail had selected a half-dozen dresses, more than Madeline had owned since going into service at the age of fifteen. She picked up the maroon velvet, the feel of it making her heart sing.

Once, all of her clothes had been this fine, when she'd been too young to realize her good fortune.

"You have given up arguing with me," Abigail said. "I'm not fooled,

Madeline. You excel at the tactical retreat, which is half the reason Candlewick runs as well as it does. Cook and Mrs. Turnbull are fast friends because of you. Not every household enjoys such cooperation."

"Cook and Mrs. T have much in common," Madeline said, folding the dress into a soft heap. "Sometimes, they need to be reminded of that. Not the earrings too, ma'am. I draw the line at fripperies."

Abigail remained before her, a pair of simple gold earrings and a thin gold bracelet in her palm.

"A lack of vanity becomes you, Madeline, but a lack of sense does not. Take these."

"You sound like your husband."

"Take them, or you'll be displaying this stubbornness for his entertainment."

Madeline held out her hand, and Abigail passed her the jewelry. The sunlight pouring through the window turned the plainest of adornments into luminous magic.

"I'm grateful, ma'am. Don't think I'm not."

Abigail was back at her vanity, sorting through the box that held her combs, hairpins, and ribbons.

"If you're so grateful, Madeline, why would you rather be anywhere else right now, when most women in your position would be trying on those dresses? You are joining a wealthy man's household and must look the part."

Madeline was grateful—and uneasy, the same way she'd been uneasy when Mama had explained, years ago, that big girls did not need governesses, and they didn't ride ponies either. The next day, her beloved little steed, Gideon, had been led away from the stable, and the promised horse to replace him had never materialized.

"I'm a simple housemaid, not a thespian," Madeline said, picking up a blue merino walking dress. "I'm not interested in looking a part. I'm interested in doing a good day's work for my coin. You cannot give me those combs."

"Yes, I can. You have never been a simple housemaid. Mr. Belmont says you were the civilizing influence his boys needed growing up, and Madeline, I will miss you awfully. Mr. Belmont attributes all manner of virtues to you, and he's not a loquacious sort. I will call at Sir Jack's frequently once we get through the holidays, and if he's in any way not up to standards, you will let me know."

The concern in Abigail's eyes was genuine, but so was the lurking guilt. Abruptly, Madeline considered that she truly had become excess baggage under the Candlewick roof. During the years of Axel Belmont's widowhood, the house had needed an organizing hand, but Axel Belmont had finally remarried, his boys were off at university, and Candlewick ran like a top now—a happy top.

"Sir Jack will be up to standards. He is the pattern card for gentlemanly behavior," Madeline said—he was also bereft of charm. "You need not concern yourself in that regard."

"Oh, he stands up with the wallflowers, arrives punctually at services, does his bit on darts night, but men can be so... we *all* can be so oblivious to what's before our noses. It's time Sir Jack settled down, and I'm sure his mother is making this visit to see to that very priority."

Madeline dropped into the reading chair by the fireplace. Of course, Abigail was correct. Mothers did not leave the gaiety and luxury of London to spend the winter ruralizing with bachelor sons for the pleasures of the country air.

Oh, joy. The skirmishes between mother and son would doubtless erupt into pitched battle.

"I will aid Mrs. Fanning to see her son settled," Madeline said. "Though my efforts might see me turned off without a character."

Would she be welcome back at Candlewick in that case, or would she be shuffled from aunt to aunt, until one of the local yeomen decided a wife with domestic experience would do well enough despite a bit of wear?

"Madeline, you are an idiot," Abigail said, in tones only a mother could achieve. Kindly, ruthless, chiding, and admonitory, all at once. "Sir Jack is not a royal prince. He isn't the sort to go up to Town for half the year. He is the sort to appreciate a woman of integrity and brains."

Appreciate? "As long as he pays me on time and keeps to the letter of our agreement, I will appreciate his integrity and brains as well. I'd best find trunks to transport all of this. Sir Jack will think he's being invaded."

While Madeline felt as if she were being cast out of her home, again.

* * *

The day was unseasonably mild, and the landscape wore the peaceful mantle of early winter after a good harvest. Miss Hennessey sat beside Jack on the seat of the dog cart as he—a man who'd been entertained by rajas and the Regent—cast about for a conversational gambit.

He and Miss Hennessey were to share a household, after all, and what Jack knew of companions suggested Miss Hennessey would be underfoot as much as Mama would.

"Will you miss your post at Candlewick?" Belmont had been quite clear that his sons—the two attending Oxford twelve miles away and the little tyrant in the nursery—were in a collective decline over Miss Hennessey's departure.

"I don't know."

"How can you not know if you'll miss people you've worked for and with for years?" Discreet inquiries had confirmed that Miss Hennessey had been employed at Candlewick for nearly a decade.

"Because we're barely a mile from the foot of the drive. Tell me about your mother."

Not a request. "She's a terror. You'll get on famously."

The first hint of a glance slid in Jack's direction.

"I mean that as a compliment, madam. Did you toil away for Belmont year after year without ever hearing a compliment?"

The cart hit a rut, autumn having brought ample rain to the shire. Miss Hennessey was pitched against Jack's side, and because he was holding the reins, he could do nothing to assist her. She pushed herself upright by bracing a hand on his thigh, but the dratted horse barreled through a puddle that hid yet another rut, and Miss Hennessey's hand *slipped*.

"Heavenly choruses," she said, scooting several inches away. "I'm not usually clumsy. I'm sorry. I didn't mean—"

She blushed magnificently, as only a redhead could.

"One wonders what our taxes pay for," Jack said. "Upkeep of the roads must not be high on the list. You asked about my mother. Her proper name is Florentia Hammerschmidt Fanning, formerly of the Hampshire Hammerschmidts of Carstairs Keep. She was a noted beauty in her day, and still prides herself on her looks. Here, take the reins."

"What makes you think I can drive?" Miss Hennessey asked, accepting the ribbons.

The gelding in the traces, Beauregard, was a former coach horse. A child could drive him through a thunderstorm, and Beau would see that the vehicle arrived safely to its destination.

"Belmont claims you are up to any challenge. This is a good likeness of my mother, though it's about five years out of date."

He held a miniature before Miss Hennessey, the likeness of an older woman with portrait-blue eyes and a kindly smile. Some artistic license had been taken with the smile, but the features were Mama to the life.

"She's quite handsome," Miss Hennessey said. "Though I don't see much of a likeness to you."

Implying exactly *what*? "I take after my late father," Jack said, pocketing the miniature and taking over the reins. That maneuver necessitated a brush of his gloves against Miss Hennessey's, after which, she again retreated several inches.

"I bathed last night," he said.

"I *beg* your pardon?"

"Slide any farther to the left, and you'll fall from the cart, Miss Hennessey. If we're to share a household, see each other at meals, and otherwise cohabit at Teak House, you'll have to deal with a certain proximity to my person."

While Jack would have to deal with proximity to hers. Today she wore a brown velvet day dress with a cloak of black wool. Tooling along in the cart, even a mild day felt nippy, and the fresh air had tinged Miss Hennessey's cheeks not with roses, but with… passion flowers of the soft, creamy pink Jack had often admired in India.

Madeline Hennessey was attractive, which was a pity. Mama did not easily tolerate pretty young women in her ambit.

An oncoming gig distracted Jack from his gloomy musings. When the other driver pulled up, Jack did likewise, so the occupants of the two vehicles were facing each other at a conversational distance.

"Mr. McArdle, good day."

"Sir Jack, Miss... *Hennessey*?" Hector McArdle's rising inflection suggested he'd taken note of Miss Hennessey's fetching ensemble, and possibly her passion flower complexion too.

Randy old goat.

"Mr. McArdle," Miss Hennessey replied, offering McArdle a pretty smile that didn't quite reach her eyes. "How fare you?"

"Well, you might ask, miss, and well I found our magistrate. I was on my way to see you, sir, and my business was not entirely social."

Of course not. Jack's neighbors invited him to their gatherings when they needed a bachelor to make up the numbers—another duty he'd inherited from Belmont—and they called on him only rarely, thank heavens, unless they had matters of a legal nature to discuss.

"If Miss Hennessey can spare a moment," Jack said, "I'll happily listen to your concerns now." *Happily* being gentlemanly hyperbole. McArdle was the local coal merchant, and had a successful businessman's gift for jovial inanities.

"I can walk the rest of the way," Miss Hennessey offered, gathering her skirts as if to climb down.

"No need for that, miss," McArdle said. "Mrs. McArdle brought the matter to my notice, and if she mentions it to her quilting friends, it will soon be all over the shire."

"Say on, Mr. McArdle," Jack said, "and I will offer whatever assistance I can."

McArdle glanced about, as if highwaymen were lurking behind the hedges, hoping to hear word of buried treasure.

"The entire neighborhood relies on me to keep them in coal," McArdle said, as if this state of affairs were an eleemosynary undertaking on his part. "I am conscientious about my duties, and always keep plenty of coal in my yard. Winter weather will pounce upon us any day, and nobody in this shire will suffer the cold because Hector McArdle let his inventory run low."

"We are all grateful for your sound business practices," Jack said, because McArdle clearly expected praise for maintaining a supply of the only product he sold.

Miss Hennessey admired the surrounding landscape. Beauregard swished his tail. Jack mentally cursed Axel Belmont for stepping down as magistrate, and Squire Rutland—the only other candidate for the magistrate's job—for removing permanently to the coast.

"Somebody has helped himself to my coal," McArdle said. "Waltzed right up to my loading shed, and scooped up the loose bits left over from the week's work."

Loose bits, given McArdle's notions of tidiness about his yard, probably amounted to several hundred pounds of coal from the loading shed alone. But for the efforts of an enterprising thief, that coal would have sat about until it became too damp and disintegrated to properly burn.

"I'll come by and have a look as soon as Miss Hennessey's effects have been unloaded at Teak House."

McArdle's pale blue eyes darted from Jack to the woman sitting silently at his side.

The quilting gatherings had nothing on the darts teams for spreading gossip. "Miss Hennessey will bide at Teak House in the capacity of companion to my mother, who should arrive from London forthwith."

"Your mother, you say?"

"And my brother, Jeremy. Will you excuse us, McArdle? The sooner we're on our way, the sooner I can inspect the scene of the crime."

Jack nodded, his hands being on the reins, and gave Beauregard the office to walk on. The cart was soon bouncing along, while McArdle sped off in the opposite direction.

"Such are the criminal activities flung at the king's tireless man," Jack said. "But you know that, having dwelled at Candlewick." She'd been *in service* at Candlewick, not quite the same thing.

"Mr. Belmont was only a substitute magistrate," Miss Hennessey said, "and for the most part, the little crimes and pranks he investigated gave him a reason to leave the property and socialize, such as he's able to socialize."

"Do I hear a criticism of the venerable Axel Belmont, Miss Hennessey? I thought he walked on water in the eyes of his staff and family." Jack esteemed Belmont greatly as well—the man had prodigious common sense and was honorable to his bones.

"Many a country squire grows lonely tending his acres, Sir John Dewey Fanning."

Belmont was more interested in tending to his roses—and his wife, from what Jack had seen. "My friends call me Jack, or Sir Jack." He hadn't been called plain Jack since he'd left India.

Miss Hennessey maintained a pointed silence.

"So what do you think happened to McArdle's coal?" Jack asked a quarter mile later.

"Somebody took it."

"*Which* somebody?"

Miss Hennessey twitched at her skirts. "Somebody who did not want to freeze to death this winter."

Oh, she'd get along with Mama famously. "You don't think it was taken to be sold?"

"If the missing coal was the orts and leavings strewn about the loading shed, then it's not good enough quality to sell, and the thief isn't very good at stealing. Selling a quantity of stolen coal quietly would take some doing in a place where gossip moves on the slightest breeze."

This was why Jack didn't shove the magistrate's job off on some other unsuspecting fool: He liked puzzles, whether they dealt with how to get supplies to a garrison on the other side of a flooded river, or how to find the culprit who'd stolen Nancy Yoder's fancy tablecloth from the honeysuckle hedge outside her laundry.

"Why do you say the culprit was stupid?" Given the current state of England's criminal laws, any thief was either stupid, desperate, or perilously prone to adventure. In the not too distant past, mere children had been hung for stealing a spoon.

"The thief was not stupid," Miss Hennessey said, "but inept. He or she took both the lowest-quality coal and possibly the only coal McArdle would notice was missing."

She was… right. The coal yard was an enormous dirty expanse, with great black heaps enclosed by a single fence. Much of the coal was under tin roofs, none of it particularly secured. McArdle would not have noticed a few hundred pounds missing from among tons and tons of inventory.

His wife, however, had noticed that somebody had essentially tidied up one corner of the coal yard.

"The thief wasn't lacking in sense," Jack said, mentally moving facts and suppositions around. "He took only as much as he could make off with in an hour or two, and he chose a time when nobody would notice his activities." The days were at their shortest, Christmas having just passed, and that meant long evenings when most were snug in their beds.

"To somebody with a family to keep warm," Miss Hennessey said, "that two hours of larceny might make a very great difference."

Jack turned the cart up the lane to Teak House. "If I catch that person, he'll be in a very great deal of trouble." Though McArdle would not have sold the stray bits and piles of coal littering his loading shed. Civil damages would be difficult to prove as a result. "McArdle will be wringing his hands over what amounts to coal dust for the next six months."

He'd also be strutting around the Wet Weasel every Friday night, asking Jack when the thief would be brought to justice.

"Tell McArdle to get a dog," Miss Hennessey said. "Even a friendly dog will set up a racket if a stranger comes on the premises. The cost of a large dog and the expense of feeding it will likely exceed the value of the stolen coal over the dog's lifetime, but McArdle can well afford the expense. He cannot afford for a more ambitious thief to take advantage of his sloppy business practices."

"A dog. I should tell McArdle to get a dog?" Jack brought the cart to a halt in the stable yard, but made no move to climb down. He would never have thought to suggest McArdle purchase a dog.

"My Aunt Theodosia's bitch whelped almost two months ago," Miss Hennessey said. "Mastiff-collie crosses from the looks of them. Enormous creatures, but quite friendly. Your mother might fancy one."

Mama would never be caught with anything less than a purebred, though Jack had always liked dogs.

"I'll consider it." He set the brake and leaped to the ground, then came around to assist the lady from her perch.

The instant Miss Hennessey's feet touched solid earth, she stepped back, her gaze fixed over Jack's shoulder in the direction of the manor house.

"What's wrong?" he asked.

"Nothing is wrong. I believe your mother has arrived."

Jack turned to find no less than his porter and three footmen unloading a sizeable baggage coach under the manor's porte-cochère.

"Something is, indeed, quite wrong. Mama wasn't supposed to be here for another three days at least."

CHAPTER THREE

"You are fretting," Axel Belmont said. He stood in the doorway to the nursery, a fundamentally shy man with hidden stores of perception and consideration Abigail was still learning to appreciate.

"Come in, husband. His Highness is almost asleep."

They had a pair of nursery maids, but neither Abigail nor her husband believed in turning their children over to paid help for the entirety of their infancy. The baby was tiny, having come a few weeks early by Abigail's calculations. What he lacked in size, he made up for in vigor.

"The hour is not late, and yet I am almost asleep," Axel said, settling into the reading chair near the hearth. "How you manage, when your sleep is interrupted at all hours by our son, I do not know." He got up to toss a log onto the fire, for in the nursery, wood was burned. "Jack and Madeline will be fine."

Axel was worried, in other words. "You will miss her," Abigail said. "I do too, already."

Axel had lost his first wife years ago; Abigail's first husband was also deceased. This marriage, the second for them both, was characterized by an intimacy of the heart as well as of the body. Nonetheless, Axel's children from his first marriage were a pair of high-spirited university boys, and the infant was male as well.

For Abigail, Madeline Hennessey had been good, *female* company.

"I do miss her," Axel said, "and yes, if you're wondering, Madeline was a pleasure to behold when mourning finally eased its grip on me, but she knew better than to take advantage."

"Then I am in her debt even more than I knew," Abigail said, "because she was your friend, whether or not you recognized her as such. Would you like to hold the baby?"

Axel took the sleepy bundle and cradled the child against his chest. "Jack still hasn't come right."

Because Axel's passion—after his wife and family—was botany, he was prone to observation. Because he was ferociously intelligent, he ruminated on his observations.

"He might never," Abigail said, gently. "We don't know the whole of what transpired in India, but he did ask for our help, and that's… that's unprecedented. He seems to like being magistrate."

Axel nuzzled the baby's crown. "Like is… a euphemism. It's a duty, and any former soldier rises to duty like a healthy vine climbs to the sun. Duty makes a cold bedfellow."

"I never considered marrying him," Abigail said, for she could sense the question lurking at the periphery of this discussion. "I enjoyed his company when he came to call at Stoneleigh Manor, but I enjoyed passing the time of day when Mr. McArdle brought a load of coal. I was that isolated. Has that child fallen asleep?"

"Yes."

They sat for a long moment before a peacefully crackling fire.

"Tuesday," Axel said. "Assuming the mild weather continues, I'll pay a call on Sir Jack on Tuesday."

"Madeline will need time to reconnoiter, and neither one of them will want us hovering. Friday, I think. They really are well-suited."

Abigail could trust Axel to reconnoiter on her behalf.

"They don't know they're well-suited," Axel replied, "and they'll fight any inclination toward each other's company. Madeline will tell herself that Sir John Dewey Fanning is above her touch, and Jack will tell himself that a gentleman does not importune the help. I must have been daft to suggest this scheme."

Abagail had been the one to put forth particulars. "What do we know of Madeline's upbringing?"

The baby sighed, as if the last vestige of consciousness had finally slipped from his grasp.

"She joined this household as a scullery maid and was soon Cook's right hand. From there, Mrs. Turnbull took over, and when Caroline fell ill, Madeline stepped in to make decisions I was too… I could not make. I've always had the sense my dear Hennessey was not what she seemed, though."

And for Axel Belmont, observations had to add up to conclusions.

"In what regard?"

"The yeomanry are not given to great height," Axel said. "A specimen deprived of good soil, adequate water, and sunlight is usually a runty individual, whether in the greenhouse or the cottage. Madeline's aunts are both in penurious circumstances, and yet they are robust women."

"Sometimes, adversity strengthens us." Axel's love had strengthened Abigail, and she hoped she'd done as much for him.

"Madeline knows French, though she never speaks it."

"How would a scullery maid learn French? Unless in a former post, her employers spoke it at home?"

"I don't know. I caught her dusting a Latin grammar one day too, and her expression was rapt and... homesick, is the only way I can describe it."

Abigail rose and took the baby from her husband. "Where we come from matters not half so much as who we are today and where we'd like to go. I'd like to go down to dinner with my husband." In truth, Abigail would rather have gone straight to bed, but the body needed sustenance.

They hadn't yet resumed relations after the birth of the baby, and the lack made Abigail desperate for her husband's affection. This was his third child. He knew the parental terrain and had a confidence about his parenting Abigail lacked.

Axel accompanied Abigail to the next room, where a nursery maid dozed in a rocker by the fire.

"Evening, ma'am, sir," the maid said, pushing to her feet. She glanced at the ormolu clock on the mantel, for Madeline had established the notion that the nursery should, within reason, run on a schedule. "The baby's asleep?"

"For now," Abigail said, passing the child into the nursemaid's arms. "I'll stop back before retiring."

Axel held the door and took Abigail's hand when they'd gained the corridor. "You'd never let the child out of your sight if you had your way."

For two weeks after giving birth, Abigail hadn't let the baby out of her sight, and Axel had barely let Abigail out of his.

"Neither would you," Abigail said, kissing her husband's cheek. "But you tell me that fifteen years from now, I'll be glad to send the boy off to Oxford—glad. I can't imagine that."

Nor could Abigail grasp what it must be like for a woman to come of age in service, doing hard physical work every day and having no dream of a home and family of her own.

"Cease fretting," Axel said, as they descended the stairs. "I'll go visiting on Thursday."

"Thursday will suit."

"Thursday it is. Madeline will have either slain the gallant knight by then, or become smitten. I'm thinking she'll start with putting out his lights."

* * *

"You waited dinner for me," Sir Jack said.

He ought to be Sir John, but the less formal name suited his energy and lack of pretensions. He was as dignified as a man of his means should be, but he wasn't... he wasn't a prig. Madeline had been curiously relieved to learn that his staff doted on him, and was fiercely loyal too.

She'd also been relieved that Mrs. Fanning had sent her luggage on ahead—a warning shot fired across the bow of the Teak House domestic frigate. When the lady herself would arrive was anybody's guess.

"The kitchen waited dinner on you," Madeline said, keeping to her place at the table. "A curry is easy to keep hot. How did you leave Mr. McArdle?"

"Ready to accept ownership of a dog," Sir Jack replied, peering at the offerings on the sideboard. "Was it also the staff's decision that you should sit at my right hand, rather than four yards away?"

Madeline had moved her place setting after the footman had withdrawn. "This end of the room is warmer, owing to the fireplace behind you."

"I watched my parents dine at a distance from each other for years. Struck me as lonely, when they spent other years separated by oceans and continents. Shall I serve for you?"

The habit of the household was to put the serving dishes on the sideboard, so Sir Jack could take as much or as little as he pleased, buffet style. This approach was unusual and informal, but the food was kept hot in chafing dishes, and nobody was made to stand about in livery waiting on a man detained by missing coal or a loose ram.

"I can serve myself," Madeline said, getting to her feet. "Do you often enjoy foreign cuisine?"

Sir Jack lifted the lid of a chafing dish, and the fragrance of spices too numerous to name filled the dining room.

"Ladies first."

"What is it? I don't want to be rude, but neither do I want food to go to waste because my eyes were more adventurous than my belly." And heaven knew, spicy food was not an English cook's first choice.

"Chicken, mostly, with lentils, potatoes, and a sauce involving turmeric, curry, saffron... If you don't care for it, you needn't eat it. The curry is usually eaten over the rice."

He stood holding the silver lid, steam rising from the food, his gaze watchful. This was the fare he'd chosen for himself, his preference, when spices were expensive and an undercooked beefsteak the staple offering at every gentleman's club worth the name.

Madeline spooned a generous portion onto her plate. "One is consigned to bland fare below stairs. The monotony alone jeopardizes the appetite."

She held the lid for Sir Jack and let him put a pastry-pocket sort of thing he called a samosa on her plate. He took three, along with a heap of the curry and two round, flat servings of a bread that smelled of garlicky, buttery heaven.

"Perhaps I'll try the bread too," Madeline said.

Sir Jack obliged, adding to the feast on her plate. "Naan, is the term for the bread. When one lacks utensils, the bread can serve as a platter."

"And yet we use silver tongs to move it from the basket to the plate."

When they returned to the table, Sir Jack held Madeline's chair for her. Nobody had held her chair since her fourteenth birthday, unless it was some footman trying to peer down her bodice in the servants' hall. The courtesy was disconcerting, but like the exotic food, not unwelcome.

"Do we say grace?" Madeline asked.

Sir Jack took his seat and flourished his serviette across his lap. Madeline did likewise, wondering if he'd intended to prompt her into recalling her manners.

"We are good old Church of England in this household, and damned glad to have hot food on such a chilly, blustery night. We say grace. For what we are about to receive, we thank Thee. Amen. Will that do?"

"You might have embellished a bit," Madeline said, as Sir Jack poured her a glass of wine. "Mr. Belmont uses grace as a means of lecturing his offspring, expressing his gratitude that their various peccadilloes and blunders haven't cost him his sons, and so forth. Are you waiting for something?"

"Try the wine. If it's not suitable, we'll send it back."

A dim memory stirred, of Madeline's papa observing the same ritual with the first footman. Madeline took a cautious sip, fruity fragrance blending with a slight sweetness on her tongue.

"That is... To be honest, I wouldn't know if it was good or poor, but I find this wine very appealing."

Sir Jack filled both of their glasses. "I'm not much of a wine connoisseur, but Pahdi tries hard to run my household as if a gentleman bides here. The wine is likely quite good. Mama will inform us when it's not, and delight in doing so."

The mountain of baggage that had arrived in anticipation of his mama's visit suggested she'd be gracing Sir Jack's household for several years at least.

"Then ask her to take over the ordering of the wine," Madeline said, picking up her fork. "You rely on her good sense and experience, and thank her for putting the wine cellar to rights. One hesitates to point out the obvious, but you *are* a gentleman." He'd accounted himself such when it came to contractual matters, why wouldn't he be one in other regards?

"I like a good, light ale," he said. "Gentlemen don't admit as much. Mama would be scandalized. Does the curry agree with you?"

"The curry is delectable."

"Not too spicy?"

The meal was a test. Between one bite of exotic fare and the next, Madeline realized that her host—her employer—was monitoring her reactions, opinions, and decisions as if she were taking an oral examination.

"Not too spicy," she said. "Too much heat, and the flavors fade. This is perfection."

Sir Jack tucked into his food, nothing diffident or languid about his appetite. "Did you get Mama's worldly goods situated?"

"I started the maids and footmen on that task, and if madam says we did it all wrong, we'll wink and smile at each other, and put every last slipper and fan exactly where she wants it to be. You have a good staff, Sir Jack. They care for you, and for their work."

One of the footmen was deaf, but what he lacked in hearing, he made up for in willingness to work hard, and in a quick ability to perceive what was needed.

"While Mr. McArdle cares only for his coal," Sir Jack said, pausing for a sip of wine. "Was McArdle's family poor a generation or three ago, that he's so focused on his precious coin?"

"That far back, I wouldn't know. I came to this area only when I went into service. McArdle has likely been the victim of much theft prior to this. He simply didn't realize it. He has a large family and ought to take better care of the business that keeps them all fed."

Sir Jack's fork halted mid-air, a bit of samosa steaming before him. "He hadn't even a lock on the gate in the fence surrounding his yard. If my children were freezing, I'd have been tempted to help myself to a few sacks of coal."

"Have you children?" Many wealthy bachelors did, and most acknowledged their offspring, if not the relationships from which they sprang.

"I do not. Do you?"

She'd asked for that. "No, sir."

Though what did Sir Jack do for female companionship? He was attractive, well-to-do, and healthy. As he consumed his supper with the systematic focus of a fit, hungry man, Madeline assessed him for the first time from the perspective of a woman who lacked for male companionship.

He'd know what he was about *in bed*. He might not be the most romantic fellow, but he'd hold up his end of the bargain, so to speak.

"Eat your dinner, Miss Hennessey. I've been known to raid the larder late at night and help myself to cold fare, but curry is best consumed hot."

Madeline complied, because she was hungry, because the food was lovely, and because capitulating on small matters meant more latitude on large ones.

"I've seen your senior servants at Sunday services," Madeline said. "How does that work?"

Sir Jack crossed his knife and fork over his plate, and tore off a bite of naan with his fingers.

"I call for the coach to be readied, the servants don their Sunday best, and off they go. I prefer to take the dog cart, myself, or the vis-à-vis. You and Mama will join me, if the weather is fine. If not, we can take a coach."

Madeline's imagination boggled at the idea that a single man might own five different conveyances—or more. A sleigh, a fine coach, an older version for the servants or transporting goods, a dog cart, a vis-à-vis... Sir Jack probably had a traveling coach as well, and a phaeton for trips down to London.

"I meant, your butler was very likely not born on English soil. What of his native religion? I don't mean to be rude, but I wouldn't want to offend him. The butler is the head of the household staff, and if I put a foot wrong with him, it can't be fixed."

The butler was a good-looking fellow too, in a dark-eyed, slender way.

"Pahdi is a tolerant, kind-hearted sort. He joined the Church prior to leaving India. I do not regard his spiritual well-being as my business, though maintaining at least the appearance of Anglican sensibilities makes the life of a native of India easier here in England. Might I have the butter?"

Madeline passed the butter, which was molded into pats in the shape of fleur-de-lis. "I asked him for a tour of the house today, and he said you were better situated to oblige me."

Sir Jack applied a good quantity of butter to his warm bread. "And you could not tell, because Pahdi is the soul of deference, whether he was being stubborn or modest. Pahdi delights in being cordially unreadable. I'll show you around tomorrow. You'd be well advised to send a note to Candlewick assuring the Belmonts of your safe arrival."

"I'm but a few miles away."

Sir Jack patted her hand. "When others care about us, they assume the privilege of worrying about us. You either send the Belmonts a note, or your former employer will be here before sundown bearing a pair of gloves you left behind, recipes, or some other polite excuse to assure himself I haven't ravished you."

The wine was quite good, and Madeline might have drunk hers a bit too fast. "Perhaps he'll make sure I haven't ravished you, sir."

Sir Jack passed her the butter. "You're welcome to try. Mama would likely wish you the joy of such a thankless undertaking. I believe I'll have another samosa."

* * *

"How did Miss Hennessey occupy herself in my absence?" Jack asked.

Pahdi turned down the lamps on the library's back wall before answering. Jack's butler was a great believer in routine, order, and making his employer wait for useful information.

"Miss Hennessey unpacked your mother's trunks so that all will be in readiness when that good lady graces us with her presence. Miss Hennessey also unpacked her own trunk, inspected the rooms we've prepared for your esteemed mother, declined a tea tray, and requested that we wait supper until your horse was seen coming up the drive. She also asked me for a list of which servants are assigned to which tasks—the better to learn their names, she said—and for a tour of the premises."

"Provide her the list, and while you're at it, please make a copy for me. Why didn't you show her around the house?"

And why had Jack made that asinine comment about *ravishing* her, then all but invited her to try ravishing him? She'd think him a barbarian, and she wouldn't be far wrong.

Pahdi had perfected smiling inscrutably long before he'd reached his majority, but Jack had learned to read the subtler signs—tension in the shoulders, silences that went on a moment too long, lashes lowered to shield thoughts.

Miss Hennessey's arrival had disquieted Pahdi.

"The house belongs to you," Pahdi said. "You should decide what parts of it she sees, what parts she doesn't. She asked for fresh flowers in your mother's quarters. We have the heartsease and the chrysanthemums."

"Heartsease for Mama," Jack said, propping his boots on the corner of the desk.

"Your mother will chide you for abusing the furniture, esteemed hero of Parrakan."

"Thank the household gods *you* would never be so presuming. Have you taken Miss Hennessey into dislike?" The peace of Jack's domicile was in tatters, for all dinner had been a good showing from the kitchen. If Pahdi and Miss Hennessey began feuding, the winter would be very long indeed.

Though… interesting.

"Miss Hennessey seems a very competent female," Pahdi said, checking the mantel clock against a gold pocket watch. "But she is a female."

A magnificent female, when viewed by candlelight. She didn't suffer from the timidity of the typical English palate, maunder on inanely about the weather, or expect a constant stream of flattery.

None of which explained Jack's suggestion that she might ravish her host.

"The last time I checked," Jack said, "the maids in this household were all female. Cook is a female, both laundresses are female, and while the conclusion must be regarded as tentative, Mrs. Abernathy also qualifies as female. We will leave the question of her species for another time."

Mrs. Abernathy was the housekeeper, and regarded Pahdi as little more than a savage. She'd been hired through an agency when the previous housekeeper had retired a year ago, and Teak House had hovered near civil war ever since.

"Mrs. Abernathy is proof that in a past life, I was the scourge of the seven villages, so great are the afflictions I must bear in this present incarnation."

Pahdi added fresh coal to the flames in the hearth, though Jack would be retiring shortly.

"I can't let Mrs. Abernathy go until my mother has retreated to London, and you'd best not mention past lives and incarnations in Mrs. Abernathy's presence."

Madeline Hennessey would likely shrug off such talk as exactly what it was—talk.

"I say as little as possible to Mrs. Abernathy," Pahdi replied. "She makes me long for the jungles of home, where tigers, cobras, and diseases were all a boy had to worry about."

"Your chattering makes me long for the peace and quiet of my bed," Jack said, getting to his feet. "See us through my mother's visit, and then I'll be about replacing Mrs. Abernathy. You never did tell me what your objection is to Miss Hennessey."

Pahdi placed the quill pens in the standish, along with the bottle of ink, and tidied the stack of writing paper Jack kept to one side of the blotter.

"I do not object to Miss Hennessey," Pahdi said. "She studied that Bible at great length."

Well, damn. Jack had not taken Madeline Hennessey for the scriptural sort. "She read the Bible?" The family Bible sat in pride of place at a reading table, though a good dusting was about all the attention the book had received under Jack's roof.

"Not that I would presume to monitor the behavior of a woman brought into this household by your revered and brilliant self, but no, she did not read the Bible. She studied your family tree."

A spindly little bush, more like.

"Then she doubtless saw that Uncle John—long may he live—and his title grace a branch higher than my own. If you're determined to be cryptic, I'm for bed. You are not to stay up late making Miss Hennessey's list of servants and duties. We must all rest while we can, for when Mama arrives, even Mrs. Abernathy won't have time for brewing mischief."

"A consummation devoutly to be wished," Pahdi said, bowing gracefully. "Pleasant dreams, estimable sir."

Jack left Pahdi to his feigned obsequies, which tended to grow more effusive the more disgruntled Pahdi became. For Mrs. Abernathy, only satirical panegyrics would do, and for English winters, Pahdi could produce entire rhapsodies of irony.

Regarding Miss Hennessey, Pahdi had been oddly reticent. Jack chose to be encouraged by that, and by another detail from his conversation with his butler.

Miss Hennessey had said the *staff* had set dinner back to await Jack's arrival. She'd lied—he liked knowing that she could be convincingly dishonest. *She* had been the one to see that Jack had arrived home to a hot meal with some refreshingly intelligent company, and she'd dodged all responsibility for that bit of consideration.

Miss Hennessey of the flaming-red hair, fearless riposte, and domestic competence, was shy.

The winter would be interesting, indeed.

Though Jack would apologize for the ravishing comments, at the proper place, and in the proper time, assuming he could find same.

* * *

"Call me Sir Jack, if you must use the honorific," said Madeline's temporary employer. "I was plain Jack Fanning for more than twenty years. I rather liked old Jack, while this Sir John Dewey Fanning fellow seems a useless sort."

For a useless sort, he fairly flew through the house, which in Madeline's estimation was larger than Candlewick by a good dozen rooms on each floor.

"In what way is Sir John Dewey Fanning different from Jack Fanning?" Madeline asked, as they descended from attics much in need of dusting and organization.

"Jack was a soldier. He knew his duty, and while he might not have enjoyed every aspect of it, he thrived on knowing what was expected of him, and how to get it done. Sir John Dewey Fanning spends his time chasing errant rams, presiding over domestic feuds, and preparing for a siege of maternal devotion that won't break until spring."

The house was lovely. Oak paneling was meticulously maintained with lemon oil and beeswax, not a speck of dust dared mar a bannister or window ledge, and the carpets were lush and lustrous—and yet, the house was not *loved*. At Candlewick, the doorjamb of the butler's pantry was marked with pencil slashes delineating the height of each Belmont boy on his birthday.

A framed letter from the Empress Josephine to Axel Belmont on the subject of propagating roses hung in the Candlewick library. Late at night, Mr. Belmont would play his violin, and the melody reached even to the servants' hall below stairs and the maids' quarters on the third floor.

Here, the staff was at daggers drawn, and not a single bouquet graced a sideboard. No wonder Sir Jack's mama fretted over him.

"Be glad you have a mother to besiege you, Sir Jack."

He paused on a landing that enjoyed little natural light. "You don't?"

He'd ask the Belmonts about her family, if Madeline was unforthcoming. "My mama died when I was fourteen. My father sent me to my great aunts, and I went into service shortly thereafter."

What an awful year that had been. Madeline's schoolroom education had come to an abrupt end, and her education about life—and disappointment—had begun in earnest.

"You miss them," Sir Jack said. "I'm sorry. I barely knew my father. He was in India more than England, and my mother refused to raise us children anywhere but Merry Olde." He resumed his progress down the steps at a brisk pace. "I could never understand what a man might crave more than the company of his own family."

"So off to India you went, to see for yourself."

They'd reached the floor of the house where the maids slept. No gleaming pier glasses, thick carpets, or handsome sideboards to see here, but neither was the ceiling leaking, or the window at the end of the corridor cracked.

No smiles from Sir Jack either. "Why is it so cold up here?" he asked. "Feels as if somebody has left a window open."

"It's cold up here because the maids are on this floor for only the few hours they have to sleep," Madeline said. "The upper servants—the butler, housekeeper, first footman, and house steward—if you have one—have rooms on the kitchen level because it's warm in winter and cool in summer."

How could he not know this? But then, he was a former soldier who'd apparently grown wealthy in service to the crown. Why should he know how the maids suffered?

"That is a damned silly arrangement," Sir Jack said. "The infantry do the fighting and marching, they should be the first ones fed and provisioned."

"You'll move Mrs. Abernathy up under the attics?" Mrs. Abernathy enjoyed her station far too much, and for all the wrong reasons. Madeline had met her like before and learned to stay well away.

"I'd like to move Mrs. Abernathy out of my house, but needs must for now. You have a smudge…" Sir Jack rubbed the pad of his thumb along the curve of Madeline's jaw. Unlike his brusque speech and brisk pace, his touch was gentle, unhurried, easy.

Ye gods. Madeline endured what felt like caresses, until Sir Jack had un-smudged her to his satisfaction.

"You must not be so familiar, sir." Her stern warning came out more like a plea. "Familiarity with your staff can cause much discord below stairs. You must be seen as fair, proper, and even-handed."

"Spending the day with soot on your cheek would mean *you* were seen as untidy, careless, and oblivious to decorum."

How Madeline wished she were oblivious to *him*. Sir Jack stood improperly close, his expression daring her to argue with him.

"You might have told me I needed to use my handkerchief, pointed to the exact spot on your own countenance, and kept your hands to yourself."

He was off down the corridor. "You take after your aunts. Very fierce, very principled. There's little I admire more than courage and honor. Let's use the servants' stairs." He opened a paneled door Madeline would have missed entirely, and went jogging down into a gloomy stairwell. The air here was colder even than on the floor above and the light more limited.

On the next landing, Sir Jack lifted a door latch, but the door refused to open.

"What in blazes?" he muttered, jiggling the latch. "Mrs. Abernathy will hear about this." Louder rattling and more colorful muttering followed.

"Let me," Madeline said, extracting a hairpin from her chignon. "Sometimes, rust or dust can wreak havoc with the mechanism, and a little coaxing is all that's wanted."

She wedged her hairpin into the latch and tickled and twisted, then tried the latch again. A second try was also fruitless.

"Hang this," Sir Jack said, climbing the stairs two at a time. Madeline followed at a slower pace, for her employer's tone was more unsettled than the situation called for. They emerged back onto the maids' dormitory floor, where the light revealed that Sir Jack was pale and nearly panting.

"Are you all right, sir?"

"No, I am not. I do not care for dark, enclosed spaces. I loathe them, in fact. The only aggravation that bothers me worse is a lack of solitude."

The man Madeline beheld was not afraid, but he was... unnerved. "I don't care for crowds either," she said, taking his arm. "I'll ask Pahdi to oil the latch, or have it replaced if the mechanism is worn. Have you given any thought to entertainments you might host during your mother's visit, or holiday appointments we should put up to mark her arrival?"

Teak House was spotless, beautifully appointed, and entirely lacking in holiday decorations. Twelfth Night was still a good week off, and not so much as a cloved orange suggested the holiday season was in progress. No decorations graced the public rooms, no greenery swathed the front entrance.

"The holidays must be endured, Miss Hennessey, whether we hang a wreath on the door or not."

They took the main stairs arm in arm, which meant their pace remained decorous. "I see. You are awaiting your mother's guidance because she has a much firmer grasp of how socializing over the winter months ought to go on, and you don't want to offend her. Wise of you, Sir Jack."

When they reached the bottom of the steps, Sir Jack did not release Madeline's arm, but stood peering at her, his expression disgruntled.

"I was held prisoner in a cell so small I could neither stand up nor lie down. I'm told I was there for several months, but I had no way of knowing at the time. This was years ago, and I don't often speak of it."

He *likely* never spoke of it. The words *I'm sorry* begged to be spoken, but he'd hate hearing that.

"I was beaten almost daily my first year in service," Madeline said, something she didn't mention either. "Then the first Mrs. Belmont ascertained what was afoot and offered me a position at Candlewick."

Sir Jack escorted Madeline to an opulently appointed parlor, a fire crackling merrily in the hearth.

"Why would anybody beat a young girl daily?"

Madeline remained silent. The reality of a life in service for an attractive, clueless girl was unattractive indeed, unless she landed in a household like Candlewick, where treating the help decently was a matter of family pride.

"Whatever the reason for your ill usage, it wasn't justified," Sir Jack concluded. "I won't interrogate you. You asked for flowers to be put in Mama's bedroom, though I see we have a bouquet in her sitting room as well. What do you think of the heartsease?"

"A cheerful flower, sir, and hardier than most."

"You needn't aspire to cheerfulness with me," Sir Jack said, drawing the curtain back from the window. "Tend to Mama, smooth what ruffled feathers you can among the staff, leave me in peace, and I'll reward you handsomely. It is goddamned snowing."

Autumn had hung on and on, with only the occasional bitter day or frigid morning even as the official start of winter had approached. The holidays had begun mildly as well, but winter was apparently intent on making up for lost time, for snow was pouring from the sky.

"I love how snow makes everything clean and new," Madeline said, joining Sir Jack at the window. "The first snowfall especially."

"You will not love how snow makes Pahdi mutter and grumble, though this weather might delay Mama's arrival."

"What of you?" Madeline asked. "Do you enjoy the snow, resent it, long for spring?"

Her question—small talk, and about the weather of all the uninspired topics—resulted in a flicker of amusement in Sir Jack's eyes.

"Belmont won't be as likely to come nosing about if the snow keeps up. I hope you wrote a convincingly sanguine note to him and his lady?"

"I did, sir. Shall we move on? I've seen your mother's chambers, and if she doesn't appreciate the appointments, she's a fool."

"Tell her that, why don't you? I enjoy seeing Mama at a loss for words, though the experience is ever fleeting. The rest of the guest rooms are similarly commodious. My own apartment is around the corner and down the corridor."

He started for the door, and Madeline followed, because they still had most of the house to inspect. Sir Jack stopped short before leaving the parlor, so she nearly ran into him.

"It's not right," he said. "Not right that your first year away from home was hellish."

He'd left the drapes open in his mother's sitting room, which admitted light, true, though it also made the room colder. Madeline unlatched the door and preceded him into the corridor without closing the drapes.

"It was only a year, and I survived, and now I'd like to see your apartment." He'd survived too, though like Madeline, he'd doubtless been changed by his experience in captivity.

"You'd like to see my apartment? I assure you that will not be necessary. Pahdi himself looks after my rooms, and his efforts are more than adequate to ensure my comfort."

Madeline marched along, because she knew where Sir Jack's rooms were, and knew that neither maid nor footman, nor even Mrs. Abernathy, set foot therein.

"Will you manage to keep your mother out of your rooms, Sir Jack?"

"If Mama dares to intrude upon my privacy, I'll..."

"Yes?"

"One can't court-martial one's mother."

"Nor can one send her packing back to London when the lane is filling up with snow."

They came to a halt where the corridors intersected.

"Mama means well," Sir Jack said. "But I cannot abide the notion she might barge into the one part of the house that I consider my own."

Barging about uninvited was the singular province of older female relations. "Consider what the staff must think about only Pahdi seeing your chambers."

"That I like my privacy and treasure my solitude?"

"That you either have an unnatural relationship with your butler, or you're keeping lurid secrets." Madeline suspected neither to be true.

"Unnatural—*unnatural* relationship? Lurid secrets? Miss Hennessey, you have a prodigious imagination. If I laid a hand on Pahdi with any prurient intent whatsoever, James would slay me where I stood."

James was the deaf footman. "James—?"

Sir Jack examined his reflection in a gilt-framed mirror and ran his hand through his hair. "James. And Pahdi. They are fast friends, and that's all anybody—or I—need know."

He studied Madeline, not directly, but in the mirror. This was another test, but far be it from Madeline to criticize people for their friendships. Life, especially life in service, was a challenging proposition.

"Let's have a look at the other guest rooms," she said.

"You will not collude with Mama in her attempts to inspect my private chambers?"

"Have Pahdi install a lock on the door, sir, and be sure that he and you are the only people to have keys. Mrs. Abernathy will not dare confront you on such a personal matter. If she does, you will have grounds for turning her off."

"A lock. First, a dog, now a lock. Miss Hennessey, you are a marvel of common sense. Belmont is doubtless ruing the day he allowed you to stray from his household."

Sir Jack strode on down the corridor, leaving Madeline to puzzle out why she felt like smiling. He'd complimented her—sincerely and honestly, more than once—and he also apparently intended to heed her suggestions.

To be respected, listened to, and appreciated was…. lovely. That Sir Jack would not begrudge his staff their friendships was lovely too, and yet, Madeline's smile faded.

In this entire house, Sir Jack considered only a few rooms his own, and he dreaded the arrival of his closest family members, suggesting that he was… lonely.

And loneliness could be a form of captivity, as cold, cramped, and miserable as any prison cell.

CHAPTER FOUR

"This wretched weather is your fault, Jeremy Fanning. But for your dithering about in London, we'd be safe at Teak House now."

Jeremy Fanning considered himself a man of peace, the Fannings having followed the usual arrangement among the better families. When one son went for a soldier, another went for the Church, as if the celestial scales balanced on a simple nose count. One son marched to battle, another marched up the church aisle each Sunday. All very tidy, though it didn't leave brothers with much to discuss on the rare occasion when their paths crossed.

"I do apologize, Mama." For the fortieth time. "The whims of the bishop are beyond my control. At least the snow is pretty, and we're safe and snug at wonderfully commodious lodgings."

The snow had started the previous afternoon, great torrents of white whipped along by stinging wind that created drifts such as could send a coach sliding into a ditch all too easily.

Sometimes prayers were answered, though in Jeremy's experience, the Almighty's sense of humor was not to be trusted.

"You call this commodious?" Mama harrumphed. "I've seen broom closets larger than this parlor."

Florentia Fanning had last seen a broom closet when she'd hid in one as a child, if then.

"The innkeeper has been generous with the coal and the tea tray, and for that we should be grateful," Jeremy replied, letting the window curtain fall back into place. The innkeeper had been so generous with the coal that the parlor was beyond cozy and approaching stifling, hence Jeremy's post by the window.

Mama excelled at the rotating complaint. She'd chided the innkeeper for his drafty parlor, and now she'd chide him for a lack of ventilation. When that volley of criticisms palled, she'd call an objectionable odor to his attention, or a draft. The tea would be too weak or too strong, the sheets too cold or over-warmed.

Mama was creative and tireless in her efforts to point out the shortcomings of her situation. Though she lacked a title, she'd married an earl's younger son, and Papa had left her well-fixed. She thus commanded significant social consequence, and had become like that crotchety wealthy uncle nobody dared snub.

"What is that creature doing in here?" she asked, as a marmalade tabby emerged from behind the sofa. "If this parlor is plagued with mice, I'll not pay for our lodging."

Jack had sent Jeremy ample coin to ensure Mama's journey up from Town was conducted with all the comfort of a royal progress.

"I'd say that cat is showing great good sense," Jeremy replied. "He prefers our company to that available in the stables."

The cat was a healthy specimen, and the generous dimensions of its head suggested it was a tom. The beast leaped up onto the sofa and sniffed at Mama's sleeve.

"Presuming wretch," Mama said, stroking a hand over the cat's back. "You'll shed all over the furniture. Put him out, Jeremy."

"He's not my cat to put in or put out, Mama. Would you really see a helpless creature tossed into the snow?"

The cat stepped into Mama's lap, circled once, and curled down onto her skirts. Helpless, indeed.

"Why is it doing this?" She scowled at the cat, even as she scratched its cheek. "Cat, you are in sore want of manners."

The cat yawned, then set its chin on its paws. Manners, it might lack; confidence, it did not.

"He knows a kind soul when he sees one," Jeremy said, and this was—oddly—not pure flattery. When Mama could pry her attention from her own situation, she generally meant well. Her entertainments saw likely couples paired for the first time on the dance floor. If a young lady was gaining a reputation for unkind gossip, Mama would put the woman in her place before anybody was ruined, including the young lady herself.

Only with family was Mama so relentlessly critical.

"The cat simply favors a roaring fire. Make it stop snowing, Jeremy. You're a parson, and one expects you to have influence with the heavenly authorities."

"One doesn't have influence with the heavenly authorities, Mama. You know better."

The cat had commenced purring loudly enough to be heard across the room.

"You will never become a bishop if you don't learn to hurl your brimstone a bit more convincingly, my boy. One wants conviction about one's scolds. You are the henchman of the Deity himself, after all. Do you suppose this beast has a name?"

"I'll ask the innkeeper the next time I see him. Shall I fetch you a book, Mama?" For clearly, Mama was going nowhere in the immediate future. She had a fresh tea tray, a cozy parlor more or less to herself, and an adoring familiar in her lap.

"I suppose a book will do. Knitting with this dratted feline in the room is out of the question. He'll pounce on my yarn and destroy weeks of work."

The cat would have to wake up to pounce. "A book, then, and if you like I'll read to you."

"Some Wordsworth. He's insipid enough to put a saint to sleep, regardless of the frustrations she might face."

Jeremy opened the parlor door and nearly ran into Miss Lucy Anne DeWitt.

"Reverend! Oh, I do beg your pardon. I was coming to check on Mrs. Fanning."

Brave of her, but Lucy Anne was the cheerful, practical sort who knew what was afoot without having it spelled out for her.

And she was endlessly pretty in a blond, blue-eyed, smiling sort of way.

"I was about to fetch Mama her Wordsworth. If you'd like to join us, I can read to you ladies."

Lucy Anne beamed at him. In two days of sitting across from her in the traveling coach, Jeremy should have grown inured to that smile, but it was so warm and genuine that verbs like *bask* and *wallow* came to mind.

"I'd love that above all things," Lucy Anne said, moving past him into the parlor. "And oh, look! A kitty! I adore a handsome feline, almost as much as I adore a bite of shortbread on a chilly afternoon."

"Jeremy, for pity's sake, close the door," Mama snapped. "You'll let out all the warm air, and tempt the cat to chance the elements."

Jeremy slipped through the door and left the ladies—and the cat—to the parlor's warmth. He collected Wordsworth from his mother's apartment, the finest the inn had to offer, and took a minute to enjoy the solitude of his own chamber.

Lucy Anne had the knack of charming Mama, and very likely of charming everybody. Mama had spent most of the Season culling the crop of marriageable young ladies, and Lucy Anne had apparently been her choice for the honor of charming—and marrying—Sir Jack Fanning.

Jeremy took himself down the steps, pausing in a shaft of sharp winter sunlight on the landing.

In the time he'd taken to retrieve some poetry, the weather had shifted, from the storm's last squall to relentless sunshine on a painfully brilliant white landscape. Mama would have the team in the traces at first light tomorrow, and Jack's fate would be sealed.

Jeremy sent up a prayer for his brother—who'd had enough captivity to last a lifetime—and prepared to be scolded for how quickly or slowly he read, which selections he passed over, and which ones he chose to read for the ladies.

At least Lucy Anne provided Mama with agreeable companionship. Despite many prayers for patience and fortitude, Jeremy would have pitched Mama into the snow by now, but for the good humor Lucy Anne conveyed with her smiles.

* * *

Miss Madeline Hennessey had a gift for deception.

Jack had been prepared to enjoy his last proper dinner before Mama turned every menu to consommé, beefsteak, and potatoes, when Miss Hennessey had brought up the topic of holiday decorations. Christmas Day having passed, nothing would do but a supply of greenery and mistletoe must be laid in before Mama's arrival. Per custom, however belatedly observed, the entrance hall and front door were to be swathed in pine boughs, lest Mama think Jack had spent his holidays without benefit of pine needles all over his carpets.

"I hope you're satisfied," Jack said, stomping snow from his boots. "I am frozen from my toes to my ears, Pahdi will not speak to me for a week, and the footmen are all too chilled to hang the blasted stuff they spent most of the morning collecting."

"Order the footmen a round of toddies," Miss Hennessey shot back. "We're preparing for the arrival visitors, not a forced march to Moscow. A bit of good cheer, and the footmen will be fetching ladders and ambushing the maids."

She unwound a scarf from Jack's neck and shook the length of gray lamb's-wool, showering the foyer with snow and damp.

"You appear all docile and biddable," Jack said, unbuttoning his greatcoat. "But then you set an objective, and heaven help the sensible fellow who suggests your course requires further thought. You might have warned me you're as stubborn as a mud-stuck mule."

Miss Hennessey whisked off Jack's hat and set it on the sideboard. "Your mother is *on her way*, Sir Jack. If you do not make her feel welcome, you will suffer for your lack of consideration the entire winter. While you might deserve such a fate, your staff does not."

Here was another bit of dissembling. Miss Hennessey appeared to be a domestic servant who'd done well in the household of generous and open-minded employers. She was, in fact, quite shrewd, having a grasp of strategy many a general would envy.

"My staff is complicit in your foolishness, and when they all come down with an ague, I will blame you."

The sideboard sported a pile of mistletoe, and on the steps outside, the footmen had left an abundance of greenery to make into swags. The air in the foyer was fresher as a result, and the outing had put color in Miss Hennessey's cheeks.

"When your footmen come down with an ague, I will show Cook how to make a tisane that will bring them right in a day or two. Where shall we hang this mistletoe?"

Sir Jack undid the frogs of Miss Hennessey's cloak, lest she forget she even wore one in her haste to direct the next phase of this holiday invasion.

"Hang it anywhere you damned please, and don't expect me to—hold still, madam."

She tipped her chin up and let him finish unfastening her cloak, then turned so he could peel it from her shoulders.

"You need a new cloak, Miss Hennessey." Her scarf was a bit tattered as well, and a surreptitious glance suggested her boots weren't adequate to the challenge of a fresh snowfall. Her feet had to be even colder than Jack's.

Miss Hennessey passed him her gloves, as if he were the first footman or the porter. "This cloak was a gift from my Aunt Theodosia, who is nearly as tall as I am. It was her best, at the time, and is my only cloak. Insult my cloak at your peril."

"I meant to remark a simple fact. You there—" Jack raised his voice to get the attention of a maid scurrying past with a feather-duster in hand. "Please ask the kitchen to serve a round of toddies in the servants' hall, and have mulled wine brought for Miss Hennessey and myself in the library. I'd also like mulligatawny soup with naan for our luncheon, and that can be served in the library as well."

Where a roaring fire stood a prayer of thawing Miss Hennessey's toes—and Jack's temper.

He tossed her gloves onto the sideboard.

"You must decide where the mistletoe and greenery go," Miss Hennessey said, as if instructing a dim little scholar. "The butler would typically direct the footmen, and Pahdi might lack the familiarity with our traditions to do so knowledgeably."

"One hangs mistletoe from the rafters," Jack said, mostly for the pleasure of arguing with her. "Pahdi will figure that much out."

Miss Hennessey took her gloves from among the mistletoe and stuffed them into the pockets of her cloak, which Jack had hung on a hook.

"Pahdi is dealing with a staff trying to anticipate your mother's every need. Will she bring a lady's maid, and where will that worthy sleep? Does she travel with footmen and grooms, as well as a coachman, or has she hired a conveyance that will turn around and leave upon arrival?"

"She'll take her traveling coach, which is nearly the size of Prinny's pavilion," Jack said, though why hadn't anybody bothered to ask *him* these questions previously? "She prefers to impose on her host rather than bring along footmen, though her coachman and head groom have been with her for years. As for a lady's maid… we can recruit a maid for that function."

Miss Hennessey stepped closer, so she was nearly toe to toe with Jack. "Which maid? Do any of them have experience being a lady's maid? Will the other maids be jealous? What if your mother finds fault with the person chosen, and the others find out about it? Mrs. Abernathy ought to have foreseen these difficulties, but she's too busy criticizing the work of the footmen."

"Come with me," Jack said, taking Miss Hennessey by one cold hand. "If you're reporting a mutiny, then at least do so in the privacy of the library."

Privacy, *and warmth*.

She came along peacefully enough—more deception, for Jack could feel her cocking and aiming sharp retorts as an archer knocks her arrows.

"I will now breach all decorum," Jack said, when they'd reached the sanctuary of the library, "and remove my boots, lest my toes become permanently cramped by the cold. I suggest you do likewise."

"One does not remove—"

Jack took the chair closest to the fire and yanked off his right boot. "I have seen a woman's feet before, Miss Hennessey. In India, bare feet are common, for a certain class." The left boot followed, and Jack placed them beside his desk.

Miss Hennessey regarded his boots with something like puzzlement. "This is not India."

"The problem in a nutshell. If we were in India, my mother would not be planning a protracted raid on the garrison. Shall you remove your boots?"

Miss Hennessey's hems were damp, though they'd dry quickly enough if she remained near the fire. "I don't suppose it could hurt."

Jack toed on the slippers beneath his desk and busied himself with building up the fire. The library was kept cozy at all hours, which took some doing when the draperies were also routinely tied back.

"I'll take your boots," he said, gesturing with his fingers, when she'd removed her footwear.

"And do what with them?" Miss Hennessey asked, rising from the sofa.

"Put them beside mine, where the heat of the flames won't damage the leather."

Miss Hennessey tended to that task herself. "About the mistletoe."

Jack was saved from the impending skirmish by a soft triple-tap on the door. Pahdi entered bearing a large silver tray laden with soup, naan, a porcelain teapot, and two glasses of steaming wine.

The scents were luscious, all complicated spices and good food.

"Thank you, Pahdi," Jack said, taking the tray from his butler. "When the footmen are half drunk from their toddies, I'll direct them in the hanging of the mistletoe. Tying the greenery into swags is usually done in the servants' hall, and today is a fine day to undertake that task. The maids are welcome to a seasonal tot, given the nature of the afternoon's activities."

Once Mama arrived, they'd all be kept busy with far less enjoyable work.

"Meaning no disrespect to ancient British traditions," Pahdi said, "but being a simple Indian butler, I do not understand why poisonous shrubs are a required part of holiday celebrations. I'll send you James and William when your meal is complete, sir. Their superior English brains can doubtless manage the challenge of decorating the inside of a house with shrubbery usually found only outside of that dwelling."

"They'll need a ladder," Miss Hennessey said. "And part of that ancient British tradition is that couples who meet beneath the mistletoe offer one another a kiss in the spirit of the joyous season. You shouldn't reprimand those who adhere to the tradition, as odd as it might seem."

"I had heard of this tradition, but did not know whether to believe such a decorous and worthy culture would indulge in frivolous behavior."

"Believe it," Miss Hennessey said, "and avoid standing beneath the mistletoe lest you be accosted by Mrs. Abernathy."

"Miss Hennessey is teasing you," Jack said, at Pahdi's horrified expression. "Mostly. The kissing bit is a silly tradition, not a general order. Be off with you, before there's a riot below stairs."

Pahdi withdrew with a swift bow.

"How long has he been in England?" Miss Hennessey asked from her place before the fire. "Kissing beneath the mistletoe is hardly an arcane practice."

"He's been with me since I came home," Jack said. "But my household has done little to observe the holidays in past years. Are your stockings also wet?"

Miss Hennessey had turned before the fire, her skirts brushing the fender, and a bare toe had briefly peeked from a holey stocking.

She adjusted her skirts. "A gentleman wouldn't notice."

"A lady would be left in avoidable discomfort as a result of the gentleman's feigned blindness. Give me your stockings."

"Sir Jack Fanning, if you think for one instant that I will remove an article of apparel simply to avoid a slight damp—"

Jack was on one knee, his hands under her skirts in the next moment. "I hate the cold, do you hear me? India was marvelously hot. Burning. Heat so thick it pressed on your very mind. These stockings are soaked, and you'll have chilblains and an ague and lung fever just as I need you to keep my mother from—"

He'd untied her garter by feel and peeled the stocking from her calf. He held up the wet wool like a limp pelt.

"Now the other one, Miss Hennessey. Our soup is growing cold, and your feet will not get warm until you do as I say."

She took the wet stocking from him and hung it over the fireplace screen. "You are daft. The heat of India has scorched the manners right out of you."

"Probably," Jack said, untying the second garter and retrieving another sopping-wet stocking. He wasn't taking liberties, but neither could he ignore the fact that he was touching a woman under her skirts for the first time in years.

And enjoying himself, which was such a relief, Jack didn't bother apologizing for his presumption.

"Here," Jack said, shuffling off his slippers. "Put these on, and you might be spared the lung fever part."

"What about the mortification part?" Miss Hennessey donned his slippers, though they were a bit too big for her. "These are wonderfully warm."

"You're welcome. Let's eat."

Jack nearly missed it as he arranged her second stocking over the screen—the first was already steaming—but Miss Hennessey was smiling at her feet.

Her expression included pleasure, self-consciousness, and a touch of bewilderment, and Jack wanted to lecture her about employers who allowed their help to go about poorly shod and badly cloaked.

He settled instead for serving her hot, spicy soup and fresh buttery naan, then enjoying a large portion of the same himself. The wine was hot and spicy as well, and the result was one of the most satisfying repasts Jack could recall since leaving India.

"About the mistletoe," Miss Hennessey said when her bowl was empty.

"Hang the mistle—bother the mistletoe, rather. What difference does it make where the damned stuff is?" And why hadn't Pahdi sent up any extra wine?

Miss Hennessey took a dainty sip of her drink. "You want to hang some in the places the staff frequent, a little private, but not dangerously private, and in the front foyer, of course."

"Perhaps the libation has muddled me, but what is dangerously private?"

She peered at him over her drink. Such a way with a silence, she had.

"Miss Hennessey, if any fellow in my employment takes liberties beyond those freely offered, he's turned off without a character."

"Freely offered is subject to a world of interpretation, Sir Jack, and the interpreting is done by footmen eager for any kiss. Mrs. Abernathy is not the sort to inspire confidence in the women working for her."

Miss Hennessey had been beaten daily her first year in service, probably for *not* offering her kisses—or more—freely. Somebody needed to be flogged in public for that, likely her first employer. Had she let Belmont know what a hell she'd endured before coming to his household?

"I take your point." Taking her point was becoming a habit. Miss Hennessey was uncommonly sensible, and wearing Jack's favorite slippers, she'd acquired a touch of the adorable too.

Perhaps one glass of wine had been sufficient after all.

"Let's put the footmen out of their misery, shall we?" Jack asked, extending a hand down to her.

She took it—her fingers were warm now—and rose as if the wine might have unsteadied her a bit too.

"My thanks, Sir Jack."

He kept hold of her hand, and what he did next was a result of pure instinct. Miss Hennessey stood close enough that a whiff of lavender came to Jack over the scent of the fire in the hearth and the damp wool drying on the screen. Without her boots, she was not quite as statuesque, not quite as formidable.

Perhaps that was what inspired Jack to bend his head and kiss her. Not her cheek, which would have been a better way to convey the simple liking he felt for her, but right on her full, sensible, rarely smiling mouth.

Her hands rested gently on his biceps, and he and she remained thus, mouths touching, nobody moving, until Miss Hennessey's grip on his sleeves tightened, and she stepped nearer.

Whatever Jack had intended—holiday gesture, a moment of affection, or even flirtation—he had no explanation for why he gathered her closer and let the kiss blossom into intimacy. When Miss Hennessey ought to have slapped him, she looped her arms around his neck and pressed the luscious abundance of her curves closer.

Desire charged forth at a dead gallop to ambush Jack's self-restraint. He'd forgotten how intense the sensations associated with erotic yearning could be, or perhaps his body meant to make up for years of sexual indifference at the worst possible time.

He *wanted* this woman, and that absolutely would not do.

Miss Hennessey recovered first, resting her forehead on Jack's shoulder. She was the tallest woman he'd kissed, and the fit of their bodies was marvelous.

She was utterly unlike Saras, who'd been so diminutive Jack had at first mistaken her for delicate.

"I'm sorry," Jack said, though he was apparently not sorry enough to turn loose of the lady.

"For kissing me?"

She would ask that, and she'd know if he was anything less than honest.

"For kissing you without permission. You are under my protection, and I am the last man who should impose on you."

Belmont would kill Jack for imposing, if imposing it had been.

Miss Hennessey stepped back and downed the last of her wine, though it would no longer be hot.

"You would not know how to impose on a woman if your life depended on it. Will you send me back to the Belmonts' now?"

Jack probably should. His reaction to her had taken him by surprise. No warning shouts had gone out from his breeding organs to his thinking brain, and he had no explanation for an arguably ungentlemanly impulse.

"Do you want to return to the Belmonts' household? I wouldn't blame you."

But he would... miss her. In a few short days, Miss Hennessey had opened his eyes to aspects of owning and managing a large domicile he'd been oblivious to. And she kissed... she knew how to kiss, how to hold a man, how to communicate bodily delight in his overtures.

"Do you want me to go?" she countered, gathering up her stockings from the screen.

Jack hesitated to say yes—the sensible answer—and yet admitting he did not want her to go was a risky alternative.

Pahdi's characteristic triple tap sounded at the door.

"Come in," Jack bellowed.

"I beg your pardon, Sir Jack, Miss Hennessey, but a large coach is coming up the drive. I thought you would want to know."

"Battle stations, Pahdi," Jack said, sitting at his desk to tug on his boots. "Alert Mrs. Abernathy that I'll be introducing her to Mama and remove the damned pile of mistletoe from the sideboard in the foyer. Be sure the fires in Mama's apartments are roaring, and get a tea tray with shortbread and biscuits ready to go—the best everyday china, and nothing that tastes of lemon. Mama cannot abide lemons."

"Have someone gather up these dishes," Miss Hennessey added, "and the head footman should also be introduced to Mrs. Fanning along with you, Mrs. Abernathy, and Cook. The maids will need clean aprons and tidy caps, and the footmen should have on their best gloves."

Pahdi bowed and nearly ran from the room.

"Your slippers," Miss Hennessey said, bracing herself on Jack's desk to scuff out of his footwear.

"Keep them," Jack said. "And in answer to your question, I would not let you leave this household now if Axel Belmont crawled through the snow to beg you to rejoin his staff at Candlewick. The invasion has begun."

To emphasize that point, or perhaps to demonstrate his complete loss of sense, he kissed her again, a proper smack on the lips.

"No more of that with your mother nearly at the door," Miss Hennessey said. "We'll finish this discussion later."

Jack decided on a tactical retreat rather than argue details with Miss Hennessey, because *later* might mean spring, or summer, or next Christmas. At the very least, they were agreed she ought to remain under his roof for the present, and that felt damnably like a victory.

* * *

A buxom redhead in domestic service got kissed, fondled, teased, and flirted with, until she learned to handle herself and the men who would presume on her person. Madeline had grasped the basics by the time she was sixteen.

Dress like a shabby nun, which wasn't difficult. Never look a man in the eye, especially not when angry—and Madeline had been angry a great deal. Pretend gross stupidity, while keeping a sharp lookout in all directions. Never mistake a man's desire for respect, regardless of his sweet words or fervent promises.

By the time she'd turned seventeen, she'd permitted the occasional liberty— on her terms or not at all—but a sampling of male charms confirmed that nothing a man had to offer compared with the security of a position in a household like Candlewick.

Jack Fanning wouldn't jeopardize Madeline's position, but he had very much upended her reason.

As Madeline changed into her best pair of house slippers, and an enormous coach came jingling up the snowy drive, she struggled to make sense of Sir Jack's kiss.

His kiss, his embrace, his presumption with her stockings, and her own acquiescence in all of it.

"Not mere acquiescence," Madeline admitted to the room at large, "participation. Enthusiastic participation born of wanton inclinations and sheer loneliness."

She'd been lonely all of her adult life, that wasn't news. The problem was, Sir Jack was lonely too, and worse, Madeline was attracted to him.

He was well regarded in the neighborhood and among the staff, for all he didn't go out of his way to be liked. He was his own person, and in a gruff, charmless way, perceptive about what mattered.

Madeline checked her appearance in the cheval mirror, and saw a woman who could never be mistaken for a shabby nun. In Abigail Belmont's discarded finery, the hopeful, happy girl Madeline had been shone through, a girl Madeline had never thought to see again.

Not simply a buxom redhead, but a woman with a sparkle in her eye—a woman who'd been kissed without being presumed upon. Her dress was amethyst velvet with blue trim, and Abigail had given her a peacock paisley shawl to match the shade of the trim.

Madeline wrapped the shawl about her shoulders, decided against a cap, and left her room no more settled than she'd arrived.

Which was another part of the problem. She was unsettled, and in her bones, she knew that Sir Jack had been unsettled too. He hadn't planned that kiss, hadn't stepped back with smug satisfaction in his eyes while he adjusted himself behind his falls.

He'd been as surprised as Madeline, and a long winter loomed ahead of them both.

"Please come down to the library, miss," Pahdi said, when Madeline encountered him at the top of the steps. "Sir Jack would like to introduce you to his respected, lovely, most gracious mother."

"One adjective will do, Pahdi. You wouldn't want anybody to think you're less than confident of your station."

Pahdi's dark brows rose. "Excellent point, Miss Hennessey."

"Mrs. Fanning will order you about, trying to provoke a reaction from you," Madeline continued as they descended at a pace far slower than Pahdi would likely have set. "You make a game of it. The more she goads you, the more polite and solicitous you become."

He silently repeated the word *solicitous*. "Have you been to India, Miss Hennessey?"

"No, though I hear it's lovely and fascinating, if something of a challenge to the average Englishman. When you bring in the tea tray, don't let Sir Jack take it from you. Wait for him to tell you where he'd like you to set it down."

"Of course. Sir Jack forgets."

"They all forget, and then they scold us for their lapses. Or worse, they don't scold and then we wish they would so we could muster a little resentment."

Pahdi's eyes began to dance, though his countenance remained as smooth as Mr. Belmont's farm pond on a cloudless day.

"India would be no challenge for you, Miss Hennessey, provided you took care with the brilliant sun."

He tapped on the door of the library.

"How do I look?" Madeline asked, for Pahdi was the only person she could ask.

"Lovely, but not too lovely," Pahdi said with a wink. "The mother will find you pretty, and Miss DeWitt will want to make a friend of you."

He opened the door before Madeline could ask, *Who's Miss DeWitt?*

* * *

In Jack's experience, the ambush was a tactic preferred by native forces when outgunned by the British army. His Majesty's armed services were too brave for such a craven approach to combat, and that courage—or blundering on the part of their officers—often earned His Majesty's soldiers an early grave.

Mama had the instincts of a maharani protecting an imperiled throne when it came to ambushing her eldest son.

"You might have warned me," Jack muttered to his younger brother as Miss Hennessey swept into the library.

"Mama didn't let on Miss DeWitt was joining the party," Jeremy replied. "I climbed into the coach and found not one lady but two on the front-facing seat. Who is this?"

Yes, who was this? Gone was the field marshal of mistletoe-gathering missions, and in her place was a demure, shyly smiling young lady who wore lavender and blue quite well.

"Mama, Miss DeWitt, may I present Miss Madeline Hennessey, who has graciously joined the household to ensure you ladies have some agreeable female companionship while enduring the dreary months of winter in Oxfordshire. Miss Hennessey, my estimable mother, Florentia Fanning, and Miss Lucy Anne DeWitt, of the Dorset DeWitts."

Miss Hennessey's curtsey was interesting. She didn't bob with the nervous deference of a maid meeting a new employer. She dipped with relaxed grace, first to Mama, then to Miss DeWitt, who had apparently misplaced her smile.

"A pleasure to meet you both," Miss Hennessey said. "May I enquire as to your journey? The weather has abruptly become disobliging, hasn't it?"

"We managed," Miss DeWitt said. "Reverend Jeremy found us the loveliest inn, and Mrs. Fanning's coach is a marvel of comfort."

Jeremy cleared his throat, which was probably a vicar's equivalent of elbowing his brother in the gut. Jack battled a reluctance to introduce Miss Hennessey to his brother, based mostly on the ridiculous thought that they'd like each other.

And make a beautiful couple.

Jeremy was nearly as tall as Jack—handsomely tall in Jeremy's case, not awkwardly tall—and his hair tended more to auburn than Jack's nondescript sandy blond. Then too, Jeremy was nine years Jack's junior, and had never subjected himself to tropical sun and wind, much less to torture, captivity, and army rations.

"Miss Hennessey," Jeremy said, bowing over the lady's hand. "Very kind of you to join us. I'm sure we'll make a lively foursome at whist, if nothing else."

That foursome apparently did not include Jack.

"Miss Hennessey, you shall pour out," Mama said, taking the chair nearest the fire as Pahdi entered the library bearing yet another enormous silver tray.

"I would be happy to, ma'am," Miss Hennessey replied, and that was a mistake.

One didn't graciously consent to Mama's directions. One submitted in meek silence. Miss DeWitt took the place between Jack and Jeremy on the sofa, while

Miss Hennessey took the second wing chair near the hearth.

When Jack would have risen to take the tray from Pahdi, his butler shot him a warning glance.

"Miss Hennessey will do the honors," Jack said, gesturing to the low table. "Thank you, Pahdi."

Without so much as a tinkle of china, Pahdi set the tray before Miss Hennessey.

Heaven defend her if she didn't know how to preside over a tea service.

Miss Hennessey picked up the lid to the teapot, checked the strength of the tea, and prepared the first cup for Mama—a dash of sugar, a splash of milk—then went smoothly around the circle dispensing tea and small talk.

When she came to Jack, he made sure their fingers brushed at the exchange of the tea cup, which was juvenile of him. Miss Hennessey served herself last, taking her tea as Mama did—a dash and a splash—but looking ever so much more elegant than Mama managed to.

Florentia Fanning was not a young woman, and though Jack had made his duty-visit to London in the spring, she'd aged even in the few months since he'd seen her. She was blond, so the graying of her hair was an ongoing subtle change, but the lines on either side of her mouth were deeper, and her complexion bordered on sallow. Jack rummaged around in his emotions, trying to find some reaction to this development, and found only a vague wish that his mother's later years be filled with contentment.

"Have you a parish of your own, Reverend Jeremy?" Miss Hennessey asked.

"I am between posts, but the bishop assures me he's finding me a congregation. At present I'm on his staff, which I'm told is a necessary step in gaining advancement in the Church."

"Quite necessary," Mama said, a bit too fiercely for somebody who had no grasp of Church politics. "And when Jack insists on rusticating for the entirety of the year, it's just as well you're in London, Jeremy."

Jack had shipped out for India when Jeremy had been a small child, and thus did not know his brother well. He suspected Jeremy's vocation was genuine, however, and trotting around at the heels of some bishop was not in keeping with that vocation.

"I'm glad Jeremy's in London," Miss DeWitt said. "Else he should not have been available to escort us up here to Oxford, would he?" Her smile was different from Miss Hennessey's, at once harder and more gay.

"I'm glad I was able to come along," Jeremy said, "for many reasons."

"Mrs. Fanning, would you care for more tea?" Miss Hennessey asked, just as the smiles became blinding.

"No, thank you. Jack, when will you send that native boy back from whence he came?"

Mama had fortified herself with a cup of tea, and the civilities were apparently over.

"Pahdi does an excellent job as butler," Jack said, mildly, lest Mama have the satisfaction of knowing she'd drawn blood. "I'm happy with his services and would miss him if he abandoned Teak House." If he abandoned *Jack*, though, Jack had nearly pitched Pahdi overboard when they'd sailed from India.

Saras's dying wish had been that Pahdi see Jack safely back to England. Pahdi would have swum the distance behind the ship rather than ignore his sister's command.

"I will find you another butler who doesn't resemble one of those Indian assassins," Mama said. "You needn't worry on that score. When the holidays have concluded, you send him off with a character and a bit of coin. That's how it's done, and the rest of the staff will thank you for it. They cannot possibly enjoy taking orders from this Patty creature."

The smiles had winked out on all sides. Jack set his tea cup down rather forcefully.

"Now there you would be mistaken, Mrs. Fanning," Miss Hennessey said. "Are you sure you don't care for more tea?"

"Of course I'm sure, and I'm never mistaken."

"Pahdi is not the typical English butler," Miss Hennessey went on. "This makes him something of a mystery to the rest of the staff, though they attend services with him every week, and take their orders from him gladly. He's not in the ordinary way, and you know how servants are—they take pride in their households, and an exotic butler sets Teak House apart. Sir Jack has a neighbor whose staff boast of their employer's roses, of all things. Miss DeWitt, more tea?"

"Half a cup, if you please."

Mama's expression was equal parts surprise, indignation, and confusion.

The mistress of the ambush had been ambushed, and Jack wanted to laugh and point like a naughty boy. Jeremy was studying his tea cup, and Miss DeWitt was deliberating over the choice of a tea cake or shortbread.

"You say he goes to services?" Mama managed.

"Every week, without fail," Miss Hennessey replied. "Sir Jack runs a proper household, and Sunday is often the only time the help can socialize between estates. Don't you find that staff morale benefits from a Sunday outing, weather permitting?"

Deftly done. Mama could not resist giving her opinion, no matter how ill-informed she might be on the subject. She nattered on about setting an example, community standing, and lapses in decorum, while Jack pondered a question from the magistrate's portion of his mind.

How was Madeline Hennessey, who'd spent a decade in service, impersonating a lady of the manor so convincingly? True, she'd observed Abigail Belmont at close range, but Abigail Belmont had come from a well-to-do merchant family, not gentry, and Candlewick was not a pretentious household.

Miss Hennessey presided over the tea tray, deflected Mama's usual ration of bile, and flattered a woman who delighted in managing everything in her immediate environs, all without appearing to do more than sip her tea and pass the plate of tea cakes.

Who was Madeline Hennessey? Who was she *really*, and when could Jack kiss her again?

CHAPTER FIVE

"This is your half day," Sir Jack said, as Madeline sat down to breakfast.

For Madeline, the routine of eating with the family was frankly onerous. A maid didn't have to stop in the middle of a task, change her attire, fix her hair, and sit down for a meal that took far longer to consume for being a social occasion. She ate her meals—if she ate at all during the day—when her work permitted, and without liberal servings of small talk and family contention.

"Today would normally be my half day," Madeline replied, taking the seat at Sir Jack's right elbow. Nobody else had come down yet nor would they likely bestir themselves for an hour or two, if yesterday had been any indication.

"I see no reason to deviate from established custom," Sir Jack said, pouring her a cup of tea. "Belmont would complain on your behalf if he got wind that I'd failed to abide by the letter of our contract."

The tea was ambrosial. The leaves were used fresh for each pot, and Sir Jack, having spent time in Asia, was something of a tea connoisseur.

"I have been in your household less than a week," Madeline said, adding sugar—more luxury—and milk to her cup. "We have yet to establish a custom, and the ground being covered with a foot of snow, I'm unable to use my half day."

She could walk to Aunt Hattie's, the nearer of her aunts' properties, but that would be almost three miles of frigid going each way, and her boots were simply not up to it. Then too, this week was more properly Theodosia's turn for a visit—a shade more than six miles roundtrip—and disturbing the schedule would have consequences.

"Well, I can use your half day," Sir Jack said, topping up his own cup. "You will please accept my invitation to take you calling upon your aunts, or to Candlewick, or to any damned where my mother is not hovering with critical comments about everything from my cravat to my footmen to my use of a wrought-iron poker to arrange the logs in the hearth."

Mrs. Fanning was a force of nature, determined to bend her sons into her notion of manly paragons.

"Your mother also compliments you."

"No, she does not. She appraises my features, as if she were an auctioneer at Tatt's, tempting buyers to bid on a questionable specimen. I no longer have a sizeable nose, I have a rugged countenance. I'm not lacking in conversation, I'm a man who can keep my own counsel. According to Mama, thwarting a few small native rebellions was tantamount to saving the realm. Miss DeWitt's opinion of me is likely the worse for Mama's efforts. Please pass the butter."

"Are you to be inspecting Miss DeWitt?" None of Madeline's business, really, but Miss DeWitt was lovely.

Sir Jack sat back, the butter knife in his hand gleaming silver in the morning sunshine. "Oh, of course. Mama has been parading potential wives before me since I came home. This is the first time she's inveigled a young lady into impersonating a houseguest, though. Miss DeWitt is barely half my age, and all she wants is a solid fellow with ten thousand pounds a year to devote to her care and cosseting. Where's the jam?"

Madeline retrieved the jam from the sideboard and plunked it down by her host's elbow. "You are a solid fellow with the requisite attributes."

Sir Jack's version of cosseting was unconventional—such as lending Madeline his slippers, which she'd yet to return—and he was worth much more than ten thousand pounds a year, if gossip was to be believed.

"I am not a solid fellow, Miss Hennessey. Do not mistake me for such. Eat your eggs, lest they get cold."

Not simply eggs, but a fluffy, cheesy, omelet served with golden buttered toast. "You might be in a hurry to avoid breakfast with your mother, but my occupation at present is to provide her and Miss DeWitt companionship. Why don't you and the reverend go shooting or something?"

Mr. Belmont wasn't much of a sportsman, though he rode to hounds on occasion. He'd been more likely to disappear into the home wood or the fields looking for botany specimens. He would return hours later in a fine humor, his boots muddy, his specimen bag full, and his belly empty.

Sir Jack, by contrast, apparently relied on his magistrate's duties to roust him from his manor house on occasion. That and darts night.

"I do not engage in blood sports," Sir Jack said. "If Mama were back in London, where she belongs, you would see far less beef served at my table as well. How soon can you be ready to leave?"

Common sense said racketing about the countryside with Sir Jack was ill-advised. He hadn't made any opportunities to kiss Madeline again, but she'd lost sleep recalling his initial overture.

A lot of sleep.

"Give me ten minutes," she said, finishing her tea. "I'll meet you at the back door."

He rose as she got to her feet. "Make it five."

* * *

The house had become like a prison, with Mama or Miss DeWitt lurking in the locations where Jack usually sought solitude—the library, the estate office, the family parlor. Mama claimed the estate office had the best light, the library the coziest hearth, the family parlor the softest sofa cushions.

Worse, Jack would catch Jeremy studying him, as if some sort of brotherly pronouncement ought to be forthcoming because Jack was the elder by nine years. Those nine years, a few Continents, and an ocean or two meant Jack had nothing of substance to discuss with a sibling he barely knew.

"You are punctual," Jack said, as Miss Hennessey came down the back steps. She'd donned the worn boots and the black cloak, though her scarf was a sturdy brown wool article. Her gloves had been mended, but had no apparent holes.

"A half day is a half day," Miss Hennessey said. "If I'm not back shortly after luncheon, your mother will have grounds to rebuke me."

"Can't have that," Jack said, tossing a scarf around his neck. "Come along, the sleigh should be ready."

"We're taking the sleigh?"

All Jack could see of Miss Hennessey's face was her eyes peeking over her scarf. She had beautiful eyes, luminous blue, intelligent, and expressive.

Right now those eyes were wary, which was a rebuke in itself.

"We're taking the sleigh," Jack said. "*Now*, if you please, before Mama appears with yet another lecture on familial duty and the joys of married life." He opened the back door, and led Miss Hennessey into a painfully brilliant winter morning. A slow drip from the eaves was counterpointed by a bitter wind, and the path to the drive was already dusted over with drifted snow. For an instant, homesickness swamped him—for the heat, color, and noise of India—which was ridiculous.

India had never been home. His worst memories were of India, and he had no desire to return.

A groom led the team up from the carriage house, the boy muffled in wool cap, scarf, gloves, and coat.

"I'll drive," Jack said. "Get you back to the stables, and we should be home by mid-afternoon."

The boy tugged his cap and scampered off with a salute. Miss Hennessey sprang into the sleigh with little help from Jack, and they were soon trotting down the drive.

"Why not marry Miss DeWitt?" Miss Hennessey asked.

A question Jack had put to himself more than once. "You are Mama's minion now?"

Jack had kissed Miss Hennessey, well and truly kissed her as a man kisses a woman he desires. That she'd bring up his marital prospects was lowering in the extreme.

Had his kiss been that unremarkable?

"You are heir to a title, according to your family bible," Miss Hennessey said, tucking the lap robe around Jack's knees. "That means you bear the burden of ensuring the succession. Your brother is unmarried, and clearly, your mother is concerned for you."

Because Jack held the reins, he could not see to the lap robe. Miss Hennessey had the knack of making all snug and cozy, and she was no longer missish about proximity to Jack's person. The bricks at their feet were toasty, while the wind whipping at Jack's nose and cheeks was bitter.

"My mother is... she means well." Of that, Jack had had no doubt. "My father all but abandoned her to go adventuring in the king's name. Not well done of him."

"Men do that," Miss Hennessey said. "They hare off, spouting some noble excuse for their selfishness, and come home when the frolic pales."

Her tone was not bitter so much as bleak—past the point where she could be disappointed.

"Has somebody abandoned you, Miss Hennessey?"

"Not recently. May we stop at the Weasel? I'd like to purchase a small keg of ale for my aunt."

Not recently. *What the hell did that mean?*

Jack was happy to go to the Weasel, in part because he'd take any excuse to remain in the fresh air, away from his family, but also because the local publican was the best source of gossip. No magistrate worth his salt ignored local gossip when a coal-snatching thief was on the loose.

"We can certainly stop by the Weasel. When you were at Candlewick, did Belmont put a conveyance at your disposal for these weekly visits?"

"I had the use of the dog cart, or a horse if I preferred. The grooms do not relish riding sidesaddle to keep the ladies' mounts in exercise."

Miss Hennessey scooted about, tucking the lap robe around herself. Jack would soon lose all feeling in his face, but he was very aware of sitting hip to hip under the blanket with the lady.

"How is it a housemaid knows how to ride and drive, Miss Hennessey?"

The scooting stopped. "Neither activity is complicated when the horse is well trained. The Candlewick stables have only well-trained stock. Have you purchased your mother's Christmas token yet?"

Jack steered the horses in the direction of the village, which took them past the Candlewick drive. At Miss Hennessey's so-helpful suggestion, the family would exchange Christmas tokens on Twelfth Night, a few days hence.

"I was under the impression, madam, that companions were to be cheerful at all times, and there you go, reminding me of yet another shortcoming on my endless list of shortcomings. I know not what to give Mama. She abhors all things Indian and is determined to give me the sort of wife I'm disinclined to choose for myself. Perhaps I'll find her a husband."

"My aunts could advise you," Miss Hennessey said. "They have assessed the attributes of every mature single male in the shire, and some of the immature ones as well."

"Did they find all the fellows lacking?"

Miss Hennessey's gaze was fixed on the Candlewick manor house a quarter of a mile away. Did she miss her home? Would she have preferred to visit there instead of with her crotchety aunts?

Jack, oddly, looked forward to seeing her with her relations.

"The gentlemen were not interested in older women who lacked means," she said. "I'm warned frequently that I'm likely to end up in the same situation—older and without means. My aunts have a plan for when that time comes."

"Female relations tend to be full of plans." Jack did not like to think of Miss Hennessey impoverished and alone. Over the past few days, he'd found himself thinking of her in his bed, though, which was… a problem.

Ladies who found their way to a man's bed quite reasonably expected a place in his life, in Jack's experience, and in that direction lay misery for all concerned.

"The aunties have made their wills," Miss Hennessey explained. "Each leaves her property to me, with a life estate to her sister. When the last auntie dies, I inherit from them both. I'll have either a small dowry as a result or the equivalent of a widow's mite to see me through my dotage. I have no earthly idea how to manage a small holding, but some inheritance is better than none."

In the time needed to drive from Teak House to the village, clouds had moved in, turning the day gray and bleak. The Wet Weasel was still sporting seasonal swags of pine roping on the front posts, wreaths on each window, and a bright red bow on the door, but the oppressive weather rendered those gestures futile rather than welcoming.

"Your dotage is decades away," Jack said, while his own felt imminent. "It must be nice to know that your family has your best interests at heart and a plan for safeguarding your future." A plan with which Miss Hennessey was in agreement.

He pulled up the team before the tavern, and a boy came out to lead the horses around to the coaching yard.

"Keep them moving," Jack said, tossing the child a coin. "We won't be long." He climbed down and came around to assist Miss Hennessey from her perch, though the lady was looking anywhere but at him. "Have I offended, Miss Hennessey?"

She hopped down and remained standing before him, the wind whipping loose strands of her hair against her jaw.

"You do not offend, but neither do you understand. My aunts have almost nothing, and to inherit from them, I must lose the only people I can call family. A bitter trade, is it not?"

She walked around him and up the steps into the Weasel, leaving Jack feeling cold, vaguely ashamed, and yet, puzzled too. He'd asked her how she'd learned to ride and drive, and been prepared to hear that the first Mrs. Belmont had shown her, or a doting uncle had given her a pony in her girlhood.

Instead, Miss Hennessey had prevaricated. Riding and driving were skills, neither one acquired quickly or easily. Horses were prohibitively expensive for most households, and the meanest conveyance was an extravagance for many.

Who was Madeline Hennessey, and when—and why—had she given up on the traditional notion that holy matrimony would see her future secured?

* * *

Nothing would do but Aunt Theo had to put on the kettle and offer Sir Jack weak tea and stale bread with butter before allowing him to escape back out into the elements. He'd graciously tolerated Aunt's hospitality, then he'd excused himself to "see to the horses." Madeline heard an ax rhythmically applied to wood, suggesting he was splitting logs Theodosia had been too weak to manage on her own.

Cold weather made the splitting go easier, but Theodosia's lungs did not tolerate cold well.

Aunt was parsimonious with her coal and had even bragged in Sir Jack's hearing about knowing how to stretch a delivery from McArdle far longer than her neighbors could.

A bad moment, that.

"Sir Jack would do nicely as a husband," Theodosia said, wrapping the bread in a towel and returning it to the bread box. She carefully swept the crumbs onto a plate, saving them for her precious biddies. If not for her puppies and laying hens, Theodosia would have very little income indeed.

"You're considering marriage to Sir Jack?" Madeline had been considering Sir Jack too, though she knew better than to dream of marriage where he was concerned.

"Don't be a goose. He'd do for you. He's not an idiot."

Not an idiot was high praise for a man, coming from Theodosia. She'd married an idiot, because her parents had selected one for her. Those parents had been long gone when she'd learned the idiot had squandered most of her dowry. He'd died without male heirs though, so Theo owned her small property free and clear.

"Sir Jack is a gentleman," Madeline said, dumping her plain tea back into the pot. "When Mr. Tavis maundered on for ten minutes about the darts tournament and the winter assembly, Sir Jack was all polite attention."

Outside, the ax blows fell in a slow, regular rhythm. Aunt would have no need to hoard her coal if Sir Jack came by regularly.

"Tavis is not half so enthusiastic about darts or dancing as he is about the money they bring him," Aunt retorted. "If there were anywhere else to procure ale, I wouldn't let you buy from him."

Mr. Tavis was one of those older, single men of means who hadn't the sense to take a wife.

"I've brought you biscuits," Madeline said, rather than let Aunt start on the tavern owner's faults. "These would go to waste at Teak House, and my clothes soon won't fit, I've eaten so many myself."

She withdrew a wrapped parcel that held a dozen biscuits as well as a few pieces of shortbread and two plain tea cakes.

"Does Sir Jack's cook know you have these?" Aunt asked, not touching a single one.

Cook had put them on the tray or plate from which Madeline had taken them, so Madeline could answer honestly.

"Of course. She sent them up to me with a morning tray or an afternoon tea tray. Sir Jack isn't a pinchpenny, and his staff eat well. I'm sure he'd like knowing you were enjoying a small treat from his kitchen."

Aunt's hand hovered over the lot, as if the sweets might dodge off as soon as she chose one. "Sir Jack looks at you."

Madeline looked at him too, at his mouth, at his gloved hands on the reins, at his shoulders filling out the many-caped greatcoat. In her dreams, she did more than look.

"Sir Jack is the observant type. A fine quality in a magistrate. Take the shortbread. You know you adore it."

"It's best enjoyed with hot tea. I'll save it." Aunt turned away to cough delicately into a tattered scrap of a handkerchief.

She would feed the lot to her damned chickens on the theory that happy chickens laid more eggs, and more eggs meant more money.

"Take one now," Madeline said. "Please."

Theodosia had been a beauty in her day. Hattie frequently said as much, with a sibling's peculiar talent for wounding with a compliment. Theo was still a handsome woman, but her blue eyes were sad, her manner timid. Timidity on a tall, handsome woman of mature years was heartbreaking.

The ax had fallen silent, meaning Madeline was out of time.

"I'll save the sweets," Theo said, smiling brightly. "You'll bring some to Hattie too, won't you?"

"Of course. Is there anything else you need?" Madeline asked, though she knew the answer. Neither Theodosia nor Hattie ever admitted to needing anything, and yet, the cottage was frigid and stank of dog, the slices of bread had been pathetically thin, and Theodosia's gloves were more darning than weaving.

"I'm fine, dear. You must not keep Sir Jack waiting."

Sir Jack would have driven home by way of Yorkshire to prolong the outing, the poor man. "Then I'm on my way, and I'll see you in two weeks."

Aunt knew better than to walk to services in this weather.

"My love goes with you, Madeline… and about Sir Jack."

Madeline looped her scarf around her neck, though she wanted to wrap it over her aunt's mouth.

"Whatever you're going to say, Aunt Theo, don't—"

"Money is important, but it isn't everything or even the most important thing," Theo said, which was about the last admonition Madeline would have predicted. "Jack Fanning isn't frivolous, and his people speak well of him. He's… good, if somewhat out of the common way. He wouldn't steal your dowry and drink the rents."

Oh, she meant well. The aunties always meant well. "He also won't marry me. His own dear

mama has brought him nothing less than a bride to cheer him past winter's gloom. Don't feed all the biscuits to your hens."

Aunt looked chagrined, but when Madeline bent closer to kiss her cheek, Theodosia grabbed the ends of Madeline's scarf.

"So he won't marry you. He's a bachelor for now, and a lonely one. Show him some attention, and see where it leads. Many a woman has been happy and well-cared-for outside of marriage."

Aunt was not among them. "You are being scandalous, Theodosia Hickman. Shame on you, and enjoy the biscuits."

Madeline escaped into the bitter weather and found Sir Jack and the sleigh waiting for her on the lane. She climbed in beside him and scrambled under the lap robe before he could tie up the reins and assist her.

"Are we to wait here until spring?" Madeline asked.

"You are as bad as I am," he said, clucking to the horses. "She's half your extant family, and you charged out of there as if a press gang were after you. Did she upset you?"

Lately, everything upset Madeline, including the concern in Sir Jack's eyes, and Aunt's cough.

"I've been saving the biscuits off my tea tray for her, and she'll just feed them to her biddies." And worse, Madeline could look forward to the same future, if she was lucky.

"There is no stubbornness like the stubbornness rooted in aspirations toward self-sufficiency. Among the Hindu, a beggar's blessing is a coveted treasure."

What had that to do with anything, and why must it be so blasted cold? "My aunts are not beggars." Not yet.

"The beggar's blessing is coveted, because a blessing is all he has to give, the equivalent of a rich man's entire fortune. Your aunt can be generous with her chickens. Mr. Tavis can boast of his darts tournament, though it's simply one noisy if profitable night out of the year. We're all beggars, viewed in a certain light, and we all have our fortunes to bestow."

Some might say Sir Jack's musing was the result of having spent too much time in the tropical sun, but Madeline found comfort in his words. Theodosia was not eccentric for pampering her chickens, she was... human.

"Thank you," Madeline said. "For splitting the wood too."

"Exertion is a way to stay warm."

He said nothing more, but when he'd turned the sleigh onto the road that would take them back to Teak House, he shifted the reins to one hand, and wrapped his other arm around Madeline's shoulders.

She bundled into his warmth, grateful for his generosity, but wishing he'd ask the horses for a slower pace.

* * *

"Jack is just like your father," Mama said.

Even to Jeremy's professionally charitable ears, this was not a compliment. "In what sense, Mama?"

"Jack uses duty to do as he dashed well pleases," Mama retorted. "Pass the salt. Lucy Anne, don't you care for the soup?"

The soup was a peppery version of chicken stew, the recipe suited to one who enjoyed Indian cuisine. Jeremy had finished his out of politeness, but Lucy Anne—Miss DeWitt, rather—was mostly staring at hers.

"I'm afraid my digestion isn't up to the robust spices," she said, pushing the bowl an inch away. "It's quite delicious, though, quite... interesting, really."

"It's not to my taste either," Jeremy said. "Give me good English cooking, and don't spare the salt."

Mama set down her soup spoon. "Where can Jack be? And in this weather, as if I don't have enough to worry about."

Jeremy was ordained in part because he enjoyed the study of Scripture. A snippet of a parable would get stuck in his mind, and he'd wring from it every possible significance, going back to the Hebrew, Latin, or Aramaic to appease his curiosity. Unfortunately, he was prone to the same habit with remnants of conversation, such as his mother's claim to have worries.

Jack had outwitted native assassins, army politics, matchmakers, and stupid generals. He would handle himself well enough on a winter day in his own backyard.

"Sir Jack is escorting Miss Hennessey," Lucy Anne said. "I saw them take the sleigh out as I came down to breakfast. I'm told it's half day for some of the staff, and assume that includes Miss Hennessey."

Mama dragged the salt spoon through the cellar. "They went sleigh-riding in this cold?"

Sleigh-riding generally worked best in brisk weather. "If you ladies would like some fresh air, I'll be happy to take you out when Jack returns."

Mama waved a dismissive hand over her cooling soup, which inspired the footman to remove the bowl to the sideboard. He followed with Lucy Anne's and Jeremy's bowls, and placed the serving trays on the table. Ham, potatoes, turnips, bread, and butter soon graced the table.

"Thank you," Mama said. "That will be all."

The footman hovered at the sideboard, his expression uncertain.

"He can't hear you," Lucy Anne said. "He's deaf, from being a soldier. Mr. Pahdi explained it to me. The guns were loud, apparently."

Of course the guns had been loud, but Lucy Anne was so sweet, so kind. "You're excused," Jeremy said, slowly. He pointed to the door for emphasis.

The footman bowed and withdrew.

"I hope you see what I mean," Mama said to Lucy Anne. "Sir Jack left a portion of his reason in India. Out running about in the snow, employing footmen who cannot hear the simplest commands, leaving the house only half-decorated when guests are due any day and the holidays not half through. He's a good man, but he's not… He'll be a good husband, and all husbands have shortcomings. A woman must be realistic."

Jeremy was abruptly embarrassed for his brother, and for his mother. No handy line of Scripture came to mind, no witty quip.

"I like Jack," Jeremy said. "He's brave, honorable, and kind."

"Kind?" Lucy Anne muttered, slanting a glance at the empty seat at the head of the table.

"Of course he's kind. Why else would he have taken Miss Hennessey to see her aging relations on her half day? At least, that's what he told me he was about when our paths crossed this morning. Miss Hennessey would never ask him, so he must have been motivated by kindness."

"Miss Hennessey has aging relations?" Lucy Anne asked.

"Doubtless, she does," Mama said, taking Lucy Anne's plate, and scooping a heap of turnips onto it. "All paid companions have aging relations. One feels sorry for the woman, to have a pair of doughty aunts and that unfortunate red hair too. Then the poor thing is cursed with excessive height. Jeremy should remember Miss Hennessey in his prayers, considering the crosses she has to bear."

Lucy Anne's expression went from adorably confused, to pleased, to dismayed. "Mrs. Fanning, you must leave some turnips for everybody else."

"Nonsense. Turnips promote regularity. Trust me on this. If we're to remain cooped up in this house, we'll all need frequent servings of turnips, for inactivity does not promote regularity. Jeremy, you shall carve the ham because your brother is detained elsewhere by his charitable nature."

Mama went off onto one of her diatribes about her own charitable exploits, many of which Jeremy suspected were years in the past, if not outright fictitious.

He took Lucy Anne's plate to serve her a portion of ham, and just happened to tip half her turnips onto his own plate while Mama was busy buttering her potatoes.

The smile Lucy Anne aimed at Jeremy, however fleeting, was as real as the scent of turnips perfuming the parlor's warmth.

* * *

When a man refused to participate in blood sports, he became an object of conjecture among those who did ride to hounds, shoot, hunt grouse, and otherwise comport themselves like normal landed Englishmen.

Jack compensated for a lack of bloodthirstiness by honing his abilities as a darts player, and for his efforts, was captain of a team. Axel Belmont captained another team, though the primary activities on any given darts night consisted of trading ribald insults and drinking rather than hitting the bull's-eye.

"For this, I left the company of my darling wife and beloved offspring," Belmont muttered, beneath the roar of the assemblage at a comment regarding Vicar Weekes's imperfect aim.

"I'm investigating the theft of a few bags of coal," Jack replied, passing Belmont a tankard of ale and taking one from the bar for himself. "Or that's what I told my guests I was about. Shall we sit?"

Belmont led the way to a table beside the snug, and Jack followed. They would be ignored so long as the ale was kept flowing, and Tavis ensured it flowed like a spring tide.

"The pot gets richer each year," Belmont said. "His Majesty will soon get wind of our little tournament, and dip the royal fingers into the winnings."

The tournament stakes were the result of the shilling-apiece entry fees paid by each member of a team for each contest during the year. The teams that progressed to final rounds paid considerably more, it typically being the captain's obligation to cover his team's entry fees.

"Tavis would do better to have this tournament during the summer," Jack replied. "The stink in here is prodigious."

The Wet Weasel had an *English* stink, composed of damp wool, sweat, ale, tobacco, coal smoke, muddy floorboards, plus fresh bread, and a beef stew contributed by the kitchen.

"The stink in here has been prodigious for two hundred years," Belmont said. "How fares Miss Hennessey?"

"Belmont, your small talk must be the despair of your lady wife."

"My lady wife treasures my ability to communicate without words, or she did before the infant appeared. If Madeline Hennessey is anything less than well content, you will please return her to me."

The ale was on the bitter side, too dark for Jack's tastes. He set the tankard aside, though the potation wouldn't go to waste. Children of various ages made a game of helping themselves to undefended drinks.

"Miss Hennessey is not a possession, that you should consider her on loan like a breeding ram, or a spare saddle."

Belmont took a sip of his ale. Since marrying his Abigail, he'd become a more peaceful man, quiet rather than taciturn.

"Neither is Miss Hennessey without a champion, Fanning. Abigail ordered me to accost you for a report, my scheduled sortie to Teak House having been rendered impossible by the weather. She worries over Madeline, and thus I worry over Madeline."

While Madeline worried for two aging relations, both of whom lived in severe penury. "Why worry about a comely and supremely competent woman?"

Belmont signaled a tavern maid watching Vicar's turn at the darts. She nodded and disappeared into the kitchen.

"You're not finished with the drink before you." In fact, Belmont had set his tankard beside Jack's, as if the brew didn't agree with him either.

"I'm not ordering another ale, and you will not avoid my question."

"Miss Hennessey has succeeded in earning my mother's approval, to the extent my mother approves of anybody. Miss DeWitt also enjoys Miss Hennessey's company, and my brother, Jeremy, is probably half in love with her."

Belmont, of course, pounced on the aspect of Jack's recitation that had no relevance whatsoever. "*Miss* DeWitt?"

"Lucy Anne DeWitt, of the Dorset DeWitts. Her papa is the younger son of some viscount or other. My mother is choosing her moment, and will soon apprise me of the lady's financial situation, regardless of my lack of interest in same."

"My condolences on the imminent loss of your bachelorhood, but you still haven't answered my question."

"Miss Hennessey is…" Madeline was a problem. "Exactly what the household needs. She has the knack of explaining to my butler situations I have no idea he's befuddled over. She keeps peace between my mother and the staff, and has even found ways to make it seem that my mother is complimenting the maids and footmen."

Madeline had also orchestrated matters so that Mama and Mrs. Abernathy had not run afoul of each other, though any day, Jack expected that truce to be broken.

Another roar rose up, along with a round of applause. Somebody had hit a bull's-eye, or come close.

"Madeline is indeed a domestic paragon," Belmont said. "Have you proposed yet?"

"Belmont, imagine how uncomfortable you'll be, riding home through a frigid December evening after I've accidentally spilled a tankard of ale in your lap."

"You've thought about proposing," Belmont said. "Or thought about considering it. The tropical sun doubtless left your mental processes less than nimble. Take heart. Madeline's the patient sort. Witness, she put up with my boys for years and only threatened to quit once a week or so."

"She put up with you."

"And somehow managed to tear herself away from my household at the first opportunity. My pride is in tatters."

Belmont's wife had presented him with a son less than nine months after the nuptials. His pride enjoyed insufferably good repair.

"I've directed the stable to keep both a cart and a lady's mount available to her at all times," Jack said. "She's free to visit Candlewick whenever she pleases. What do you make of McArdle's coal thief?"

Belmont, having also served the occasional turn as magistrate, might have some useful ideas on this topic.

"I think if Madeline will have you, you'd be damned lucky to marry her. If the issue is a dowry—"

"Two tankards," Jack said. "Both of them nearly full. Hate to ruin a fine pair of riding boots, but I can be lamentably clumsy."

They fell silent while the tavern maid brought over a tray of cheese toast. Belmont helped himself to a slice and bit off a corner, the melted cheese turning the undertaking untidy.

"Have some," Belmont said. "We both have another round to play before we can return to our cozy beds—in your case, a lonely cozy bed."

The cheese toast, like everything else Jack could see, hear, smell, taste, or touch, was unequivocally English. Once upon a time, to return to such a setting had loomed like a pipe dream, a fantasy of fevered imagination.

Now all Jack wanted was peace and solitude, and perhaps another kiss or three from Madeline Hennessey.

"I want some damned caraway on this cheese toast," Jack said. "Some cardamom, or pepper, or a touch of curry. Not boring old bread toasted to hide how stale it has become and boring old cheddar."

Belmont's hand paused halfway to the tray. "You do know how dearly Tavis holds his coin? Spices such as those would cost him the entire year's darts revenue."

That revenue sat in a large glass jar on the shelf behind the bar. The winning team would get three-quarters of the haul, split among all the players. Tavis would keep the rest.

Jack selected a piece of toast, tore it in half, and took a bite. "What about McArdle's missing coal? Any ideas?"

"Coal has gone missing from McArdle's yard since the first winter his father set up shop. Whoever took this lot did him a favor."

Not the first time Jack had heard that sentiment. "Why do you say that?"

"A family in need might pinch a bit here or there on a moonless night, because McArdle's yard is a mare's nest of disorganization. Whoever stole from him this time called his attention to how much inventory he's losing because of his poor management. You do know that if you break Madeline's heart, I will call you out?"

"Belmont, has marriage made you daft?"

"Marriage has made me sane, also happy." More cheese toast was munched into oblivion. "Marriage done properly is a lovely institution. You should try it."

"I did."

Well, damn. Jack hadn't had enough ale to blame his slip on Tavis's drink.

"I'm sorry," Belmont said, quietly.

"For?"

"The lady is not at your side; therefore, she must have gone to her reward, leaving you a widower. No wonder your mother is concerned for you."

The sound of coins hitting glass over the noise of the crowd signaled the end of the game of darts, though Jack's turn was still two games away. The jar behind the bar was almost full of money, but after the upcoming tournament, it would be empty again.

"I married a woman in India," Jack said. "She did not... a fever took her. Her brother is my butler. My family has no idea, but when I escaped from captivity, I would have perished but for my wife's devotion." Jack had married Saras because an officer's continued existence had been tenuous even in times of peace, and Saras had deserved every legal protection he could fashion for her.

To Belmont's credit, he merely continued to consume his cheese toast, as if hearing confessions was all in the day's socializing for him. Jack would never have had this conversation with Vicar, but Belmont was a widower.

Perhaps that explained a silence broken for the first time in years.

"As my first wife lay dying, she did me a great service," Belmont said. "She ordered me not to wallow in my grief. Said our children needed to see that I had not climbed into the coffin with her. I never loved her more than I did at that moment—such wisdom and selflessness—and I was never more angry with her. She knew me so well."

Jack tucked his hand under his thigh rather than knock the tankards from the table. "You wallowed anyway."

"For a few years. Life moves us forward, and then we catch a glimmer of our own demise on a distant horizon—a lung fever, a friend our age dies—and moving forward becomes a purposeful undertaking. I wouldn't waste time looking for McArdle's thief. The lesson was cheap at twice the price, and now I hear McArdle is keeping dogs on the premises after hours."

He'd not purchased a puppy from Madeline's aunt, though. He'd gone to a "breeder," meaning a yeoman farmer, rather than an older woman who desperately needed his coin.

"What did you get Mrs. Belmont for her holiday token?" Jack asked.

Belmont's expression was a cross between devilish and bashful. "I have it on the best authority that the gift of my handsome company from day to day is all Abigail requires by way of a boon."

"You'll look very handsome wearing a plate of cheese toast on your head," Jack said. "You are no help whatsoever, Belmont."

"The child in my nursery suggests your definition of help diverges from my lovely wife's. Somebody needs to tell Vicar to aim left. He makes the same mistake over and over."

"His mistake is in his appreciation for Tavis's ale. My mother has everything she needs, and any gift to Miss DeWitt will encourage the wrong notions."

"I see your dilemma. Ask Madeline, she'll know exactly what to give them. You will please tell my dear Madeline that we miss her abominably, Mrs. Turnbull has gone into a decline, and Cook hasn't made her signature scones since Madeline abandoned us. The footmen are beyond all hope, which is why the Candlewick team is making such a dismal showing tonight. At this rate, Tavis will need a larger winnings jar."

Belmont took the last two slices of cheese toast and put them together into a sandwich.

"What do you know about Madeline Hennessey, Belmont? About her past."

Nearly half the sandwich disappeared before Jack had an answer. "Not much. Caroline, my late wife, added Madeline to the staff. I didn't really notice Madeline until after I became a widower, and by then, she was nearly running the household. I assume she's a local girl, because both of her aunts live here, but you might ask Vicar… once he's recovered from his evening among the flock."

Madeline Hennessey was not a girl, and Jack's ear, which had grown sensitive to dialects in India, would not have placed her as local. She spoke, now that he considered the matter, with the same genteel elocution as Miss DeWitt.

"Miss Hennessey was your employee for nearly a decade, and yet, you know nothing about her. If she weren't religious about visiting her aunties, you'd know less than nothing."

Belmont finished his sandwich and dusted his hands over the empty plate. "I know you are smitten, and my wife will be pleased to learn of it. You will bring your guests to supper tomorrow evening at six of the clock. If your womenfolk are very well behaved, Abigail might permit them to coo over my youngest while you, the reverend, and I swill brandy in the library."

Belmont's wife wanted to assess matters firsthand, in other words, and confirm whatever reports Belmont brought her.

"I will ask your wife what manner of Christmas token she would have appreciated," Jack said, rising. "If you serve decent brandy, I might share her reply with you before next winter."

"Madeline needs a new cloak," Belmont said, getting to his feet, "and I must uphold the honor of Candlewick at the dartboard. Until tomorrow."

He sauntered off, while Jack passed his ale to the same small boy who'd driven the team around to the yard earlier in the day.

"Don't suppose you know anything about McArdle's missing coal?" Jack asked the lad.

The boy's eyes grew huge, and he shook his head.

So the criminal was a local fellow, possibly even Tavis, who was known to pinch a penny until it howled for mercy. Tavis also complained loudly about the cost of coal, but wasn't about to send a team into Oxford to buy from one of McArdle's competitors. Perhaps Belmont was right. The thief had done McArdle a favor.

Though Jack was not, contrary to Belmont's pronouncement, smitten.

Yet.

CHAPTER SIX

The Teak House library was kept toasty warm at all hours, and thus Madeline read there rather than in her bedroom. The bedroom was lovely, uncomfortably so, for a woman who'd been in service for nearly a decade.

The library, by contrast, had a personality all its own. Some of the appointments were standard for the home of wealthy gentry. The lovely piano, sizeable desk, globe, reading table, and shelves of books would have gone nicely with Candlewick's decor.

The scent of sandalwood incense, however, which Pahdi burned in an effort to discourage damp and vermin from plaguing the books, was unique. The teak sideboard was both exotic and more costly than the usual furnishings in a country house library, and the gleaming samovar was still more evidence of wealth and worldly sophistication.

And yet, Madeline felt less out of place here than in the bedroom she'd been assigned in the family wing.

Reading for an hour anywhere before retiring was a guilty pleasure, because a servant's candles were rationed, while a lady's companion could squander candles, lamp oil, coal, and even firewood without comment.

"What absorbs you so thoroughly?" Sir Jack asked.

He stood near the closed door, though Madeline hadn't heard him come in. "How long have you been spying on me?"

"Since I started attending the quarterly assemblies. I suspect you've been spying on me for nearly as long, espionage being the primary purpose for such gatherings. Would you care for a brandy to ward off the evening's chill?"

He was in riding attire, the toes of his boots damp from the snow, his hair tousled by the wind. Doubtless he'd come to the library to get warm, much as Madeline had.

"No brandy, thank you. I'll bid you good night." A servant would wait to be dismissed. So much about being a lady's companion was at once odd and familiar.

"No need to run off, Miss Hennessey," he said, crossing to the sideboard. "I see my absence was not an occasion for idleness here at Teak House."

By the standards of a chambermaid, Madeline had been scandalously indolent since returning from Aunt Theo's.

"I mean the decorations," Sir Jack said, leaning back against the sideboard and crossing his arms. "You've hung mistletoe in my front entrance among other places, though the holidays are all but behind us, thank the benevolent powers."

"We had extra mistletoe," Madeline said, closing her book and rising. She should go. She should stop gawking at Sir Jack, stop wondering what he was thinking.

"Mr. Belmont was at the Weasel, defending the honor of Candlewick's darts team. He said he'd call me out if you're unhappy here." Sir Jack pushed away from the sideboard. "Nonetheless, I could not answer him, because I must first inquire of you directly: Are you happy?"

"I'm a paid companion, Sir Jack. My happiness is of no moment."

"Your happiness matters to me."

Based on his disgruntled expression, he was not pleased by this development, while Madeline was more flattered than she should have been.

"I'm well-fed, comfortably housed, and luxuriously clothed." For now. "Why wouldn't I be happy?"

He stalked closer and picked up Madeline's book. "Miss Austen?"

"Miss DeWitt didn't care for it, so I was intrigued." What a pleasure, to sink into a world of elegant prose, deft irony, and merciless honesty.

"You were missed at the Weasel. Belmont sends his regards. We're to dine with him tomorrow at Candlewick."

That would be… awkward. "How is Mr. Belmont?"

"Bearing up under the strain of new fatherhood. His team won't win the tournament if he continues to play so indifferently."

Many a night, Madeline had watched the coins piling up in the winnings jar, while Tavis couldn't pull the pints fast enough. He'd close the tavern early tomorrow night, just so he'd have time to reorganize his inventory and tap a fresh set of kegs. Vicar Weekes considerately scheduled Bible studies for the evenings the Weasel closed early.

"The championship is next week?" The championship was always the first

Saturday after Twelfth Night, a consolation for the conclusion of the holiday season. The winter assembly was intended to serve the same function, lifting spirits when winter was at its worst.

Sir Jack set her book on the desk. "You never answered my question. Are you happy here?"

No employer would ever pester a maid with such a question. "I am content. I'm grateful." And in the most luxurious bed Madeline had enjoyed in years, she was dreaming of Sir Jack Fanning.

"I'm grateful as well," Sir Jack said, propping a hip on the desk. "I am living the life I longed for when I was locked in a prison cell. My fervent prayers have been granted, for the most part, and yet… I am not content."

This was also Madeline's fault, apparently. "Perhaps you're tired."

"Weary to the bone. Kiss me, Madeline."

She wanted to, trumpeting winged cherubs, she wanted to. "A gentleman does *not* order a lady to participate in such an undertaking. In fact, no employer should presume on an employee's compliance with unsolicited overtures, and I would rather be beaten than coerced—"

Sir Jack touched a finger to Madeline's lips, then pointed straight overhead.

A sheaf of wilted mistletoe hung from the crossbeam, white berries peeking from between pale green leaves.

"If you ever tell me who your first employer was," Sir Jack said, "I will have him bound over for the assizes on as many charges as imagination and a shred of gossip will support. I mean you no disrespect, Madeline."

Madeline.

For years, at Candlewick, she'd been Hennessey.

Hennessey, where did I put my spectacles? Hennessey, can you pop out to the stables and remind Mr. Chandler it's time to eat? Hennessey, could you finish mixing the biscuits while I rest my old bones?

And occasionally, when Mr. Belmont was being particularly dunderheaded, *Hennessey, you forget your station.*

He'd been mistaken. Madeline never forgot her station, but standing beneath the mistletoe with Sir Jack using her Christian name, she forgot for a moment why she must not encourage his interest.

Sir Jack gave her every opportunity to dash away, to snatch up her book and dodge off to her lovely bedroom. He rested his hands on either side of her neck, brushing his thumbs over her cheeks. Her common sense might as well have gone wafting up the chimney, as Madeline's mind became boggled by sensations.

Sir Jack's hands, warm and calloused, gently angling her head. His scent, fresh night air, along with a whiff of horse and pine. The muted roar of the fire, and the lovely warmth of the library, and then…

A soft brush of his mouth over hers. Madeline's eyes drifted closed on a plea. *Do that again.*

He obliged, the wretch, twice more. Three warnings, and then his mouth settled over hers.

Madeline had been kissed, rather a lot. Footmen, farm lads, grooms, the occasional blushing son of the local gentry, a curate two summers ago, and she'd allowed a few men more than kisses. Her experience had been in aid of gathering information.

What could possibly transpire between a man and a woman that resulted in lifelong devotion, poetry, scandal, dynasties, battles, babies, contented old age, or endless regret? Proper young ladies were not permitted to know, but within reason, and with appropriate caution, women in service could ask.

Madeline had asked, and been disappointed every time. The kissing and cuddling was fine as far as it went. The swiving afforded momentary pleasure amid a lot of awkwardness and false promises, but on the whole…

On the whole, she'd been conducting her investigations with the wrong men.

Jack Fanning could cherish a woman with his mouth, could imbue his kisses with such slow wonder, a lady's knees went fluttery and her whole focus became *him*. His warmth, his taste, his textures.

Silky fine hair, a little cool and damp from the elements. Chin a long day away from contact with a razor. Lean muscles wrapped on long bones, fine tailoring covering the lot. His arms came around her, and everything inside Madeline rearranged itself into a more comfortable configuration.

Sir Jack was growing aroused, and was unselfconscious about letting Madeline know it. At the same time, she felt no compulsion to quell his desire, nor to explore its potential.

She'd been kissed. She'd finally, finally been well and truly kissed.

Sir Jack's hand settled at her nape and kneaded gently. "You're not running off."

"Neither are you."

He stepped back, taking Madeline by the hand and leading her to the sofa. "We must come to an understanding."

Madeline would rather indulge in more kisses, because an understanding sounded damnably close to a disappointment. She took a seat on the sofa, and Sir Jack came down beside her.

He looped an arm around her shoulders and drew her close. "Your kisses leave a man muddled. I do not muddle easily."

Madeline muddled more easily than she'd realized. "You needn't make any stirring declarations, Sir Jack. I'm a housemaid playing at paid companion.

When your mother goes back to London, I'll put off my borrowed finery and return to Candlewick, assuming they still need me."

Sir Jack was as accomplished at cuddling as he was at kissing, which was beyond unfair. "I was a prisoner once. I didn't care for it."

"I'm sorry." Worse than that, Madeline wanted to hunt down the scoundrels who'd mistreat a man so egregiously, even given the indignities attendant to all war.

"What I mean, Madeline, is that I cannot abide the thought that my attentions… You must tell me if I'm imposing. Don't humor me, tolerate me, or otherwise accede to overtures contrary to your own preferences. You are not chattel, no matter what the law says. Your wishes do not simply matter, they will control the course of our dealings."

He meant this. From a different man, these lofty words might be just so many false promises, quickly tossed aside behind the door of some empty pantry.

"We're to have dealings?" she asked.

"That is entirely up to you."

She should kiss him one last time—a parting kiss—and scamper off to bed to dream of him. He was Sir John Dewey Fanning, in line for an earldom, decorated veteran, and the chosen, if unenthusiastic, future fiancé of Miss Lucy Anne DeWitt of the Dorset DeWitts.

Also the magistrate.

"I am not looking for a husband."

"I am not looking for a mistress, much less looking to impose on a woman in my employ."

What did that leave? Lovers, possibly. Much to think about, definitely. This kiss, unlike its predecessor, had made matters too complicated to untangle in the space of a late-night cuddle.

"Your kiss…" Madeline wasn't sure she ought to confess what his kiss had done to her.

"Yes?"

Sir Jack was smiling, the first true smile Madeline had seen from him, and it was every bit as potent as his kisses. Charming, shy, mischievous, male, male, and male… He knew what his kisses did to her, and was pleased with himself for it.

"You should smile more often, Jack Fanning."

"I should kiss you more often, but right now, I'll light you up to your bedroom instead."

A prudent plan. Sir Jack pulled Madeline to her feet, fetched a carrying candle from the mantel, and escorted her straight up to her bedroom door. When she might have risked another kiss, Sir Jack instead pressed his lips to her forehead, bowed, and withdrew.

Leaving Madeline standing in the dark, chilly corridor, trying to recall where else in the house she'd told Pahdi to hang mistletoe.

* * *

"Did I, or did I not, tell you Sir Jack's darts game was off?" Axel Belmont asked, climbing into bed beside his wife.

The baby slept in a bassinet in the nursery across the corridor, which was Abigail's scheme for maximizing parental sleep in the face of a newborn's schedule. When a nursery maid tapped on the bedroom door, Axel would bring the baby to Abigail. At the conclusion of the pantry raid, he burped the child and returned him to his slumbers. Axel had even acquired the skill of changing the baby's linen, much to his wife's amusement.

"Sir Jack was notably quiet at dinner," Abigail said, tucking close.

Her shape had changed with pregnancy, and so had Axel's regard for her. Love had turned to something so vast and tender, words failed. In his first marriage, he'd loved with the joy, tenacity, and conscientiousness of a young man. This time, love owned him, heart, mind, soul, and body.

"Sir Jack was allowing the voluble Miss DeWitt to have the floor," Axel said. "I'd forgotten how young women chatter."

"Are you calling me old?"

"You are sensible. I fear the young lady was nervous. Mrs. Belmont, mind your hands."

They had agreed that marital relations would not resume until after the assembly, and Axel was determined that their children would be reasonably spaced.

Abigail was determined to turn him into a lunatic. "Reverend Jeremy Fanning was something of a surprise."

"A handsome, if rather innocent, surprise. Madam, if you keep that up—"

Abigail had a bold touch where Axel very much enjoyed being touched.

"You were saying, Mr. Belmont?"

"I was saying that I did not take our Hennessey for a coward." Madeline had declined to join the dinner party, which was troubling.

"Madeline is shy, and being a guest in a house where she's been in service would be a challenge for anybody."

"Abigail…"

"Hmm?"

She'd developed a rhythm, slow and sweet, her grip on Axel that perfect blend of relaxed and snug that made a fellow give thanks for a cozy bed and a generous wife—also for a sleeping baby.

"Candlewick is not a formal household," Axel managed. "Madeline has friends here, and they miss her."

Abigail's caresses slowed. "I miss her. You do too, as do Mrs. Turnbull, Cook, Mr. Chandler…"

Axel covered Abigail's hand with his own, though whether he was urging her on, or simply participating in his own torment, he could not have said.

"Our staff has grown elderly," Axel said. "I hadn't noticed until Madeline left us to take Sir Jack in—to organize Sir Jack's household."

"Maybe she'll take him in hand too," Abigail said, kissing Axel's cheek. "If I see the right moment, I'll explore the notion of retirement with Mrs. Turnbull."

For long sweet minutes, Axel let go of whatever important, sensible point he'd been about to make, and instead held on to his wife. The next weeks could not pass quickly enough, though Axel withstood satisfaction as long as he could.

"I tell myself I'm not a rutting university boy anymore," he said, taking his wife in his arms several blissful moments later. "I tell myself that with maturity comes a certain self-restraint. I tell myself all manner of fairy tales."

"Not too long from now, you can test my self-restraint to the breaking point," Abigail said. "You are worried about Madeline?"

Grown men with vast stores of self-restraint did not worry over errant domestics. "What do we know of her, Abigail? One day I looked up, and there was this tall, pretty girl sweeping the ashes out of the library hearth. When Caroline fell ill, that girl had become a young woman, and kept the household together despite the owner's determination to work all night and drink all day. Madeline has been at Candlewick for nearly ten years, and yet…"

"I know," Abigail said, turning over to nestle her backside against Axel's hip. He turned on his side too, and spooned himself around his wife. "She was my lady's maid for a short time, and yet, I have no idea who her people are—beyond a pair of difficult aunts—or how she learned to do such fine embroidery. If you rub my back like that, I will fall asleep."

The infant would wake her up at least twice during the night. Sometimes the little fiend was at his mother more than he was in his bassinet, and yet, Abigail never complained.

"Go to sleep, Mrs. Belmont. Dream of spring." Axel certainly did.

"I believe I shall, but soon you must call on Sir Jack. He needs reinforcements."

Already, Abigail's tone had become sleepy. Axel kneaded her shoulders in a slow, soothing rhythm. "You think Miss DeWitt is besieging Sir Jack's bachelorhood."

His widowerhood, in truth. That revelation had explained a few things.

"If so, she's armed with nothing more than a pea-shooter. I suspect Madeline's artillery has turned Sir Jack so quiet and thoughtful."

Good for Madeline, good for Jack Fanning.

"Go to sleep. I'll gather intelligence for you later in the week, even if I must listen to more chattering in service to my queen."

Abigail fell silent, her breathing slowing to the regular pattern of well-deserved sleep. Axel remained awake for a few moments more, rubbing his wife's back, and wondering what, besides Madeline Hennessey's artillery, might have wrecked the hero of Parrakan's legendary skill with darts.

* * *

Madeline sat at Jack's desk, a pair of gold, wire-rimmed glasses perched on her nose. The sight was both scholarly and… erotic, damn it. No matter where Jack laid eyes on her—over a hand of whist, or waving good-bye to the party last night as they'd departed for Candlewick—she called to the part of him he'd successfully ignored since leaving India.

"You have recovered from your megrim," Jack said. He'd wondered, when she hadn't come down to breakfast that morning.

She jumped to her feet, a hand at her throat. "You surprised me." Her expression was both flustered and self-conscious, possibly even guilty.

"Obviously." Surprising her was only fair, when she surprised him at every turn. "Are you prone to headaches?"

"Yes, though they aren't usually as severe as the one I had last night. I trust the evening at Candlewick was enjoyable?"

Jack let the change of subject pass, for the lady did seem truly unnerved. "Dinner was good, English fare. Beef done to a turn, potatoes whipped with butter, green beans in sauce, and so on. Mrs. Belmont was disappointed that you did not join us."

Jack had been disappointed at Madeline's last-minute excuse too.

She resumed her seat—Jack's seat, come to that. "I will visit them on my half day."

"Whom did you visit last night?" Bad of him, to ambush her like this, but she'd taken the dog cart out after making excuses for the dinner engagement. A small, pestilentially insecure part of him wondered if she'd gone to meet a beau.

"I dropped in on Aunt Hattie," she said. "I'd only been able to see Aunt Theo on my half day, and I had another hoard of biscuits to share. The fresh air helped clear my head, and a full moon on snow is so pretty."

Madeline Hennessey was pretty. She wore a burgundy velvet day dress that showed off her figure to a distracting degree.

"You were naughty," Jack said, leaning a hip on the corner of the desk. "You deprived me of the pleasure of driving you to visit your aunt on your next half day. Instead, I will be forced to endure yet more rounds of whist and the latest London gossip about people I hope never to meet. Were you writing a letter, Miss Hennessey?"

Jack was being naughty, leaning closer as if to peer at her work, when he was in fact breathing in lavender and memories. Her hands on his arms, her shape resting against him, her kisses….

"I was making a list," she said. "Comparing Pahdi's version of who does what with the tasks as I've observed them done."

"What does your list reveal?"

"Pahdi can't very well oversee tasks happening throughout the house if he's expected to open the front door."

Her handwriting was the lovely, flowing script of an educated lady, and notably legible. "The sharpest set of eyes should be posted as lookout."

"We are not a garrison in some distant jungle, Sir Jack."

And yet, Jack felt as if he'd lost his bearings. Miss Hennessey had freckles across the backs of her hands. He'd like to kiss each one, and that sentiment put him in mind of life after captivity. Sentiments and sensations were too sharp, bright, pungent, and distracting where Madeline Hennessey was involved, and nothing quite made sense.

"How do you suggest the front door be managed?" he asked.

"Assign a footman to the post, the oldest and most distinguished of the lot. If he does well, then consider naming his post that of under-butler. Give Pahdi the freedom to inspect work as it's being performed and to look after the house in the manner of a steward."

Eminently sensible. The best commanding officers knew how to earn the trust of their subordinates without fraternizing. That often meant wandering through the stables, the mess, or the parade ground at the odd hour.

"Does Mrs. Abernathy inspect the work as it's being performed?"

"Mrs. Abernathy sets the maids against each other, expecting them to tattle on one another."

"Bad form," Jack said, scooting closer and squinting at the paper. "Informants destroy *esprit de corps*. What's this?"

She'd put his name on the page as well, though no duties were listed below Sir John Dewey Fanning.

Pahdi's tap-tap-tap sounded on the door, and Jack rose. "Come in."

Pahdi opened the door, a red-faced Bartholomew Tavis beside him. "Mr. Tavis has come on urgent business, sir."

"I don't need no Hindu lackey to announce me," Tavis said, elbowing past Pahdi's slighter form. "I've come to see the king's man about a serious matter."

Pahdi's profile could have been carved in mahogany.

"Remove your cap, Tavis," Jack said, as Pahdi withdrew. "You are in the presence of a lady."

The tone of command had Tavis yanking off his cap, despite the confusion in his eyes. "Miss Hennessey?"

She rose and bobbed a curtsey. "I'll leave you gentlemen to your discussion."

Tavis was a great hulking fellow with more brawn than brains, and the opinion among the local populace was that his late mother had done a better job of running the Wet Weasel than Tavis did. Tavis worked hard—everybody agreed he was a hard worker—but he was also a hard man, according to his employees and patrons.

Tavis followed Miss Hennessey's progress across the library, his gaze not exactly respectful, though neither was he plainly leering.

"She reminds me of somebody," he said. "In that finery, she reminds me of somebody. A figure like that could sell a lot of ale."

A comment like that could get a man called out, despite Jack's distaste for violence.

"Shall we sit, and may I offer you a drink?"

"Not much of a drinker," Tavis said, looking anywhere but at Jack. "I fancy a cup of good black tea, if you must know."

"So do I," Jack replied, tugging the bell-pull twice. "While we're waiting for the tray, perhaps you can acquaint me with the reason for your call?"

"You have a mighty lot of books."

Libraries were supposed to have a mighty lot of books. Jack did not have a mighty lot of patience.

"I enjoy reading." He took the seat Madeline had vacated, in hopes Tavis would light in one of the chairs before the desk.

"You don't worry about light-fingered help?"

The question was another slur aimed at Pahdi. Jack wasn't surprised, though he was disappointed.

"If you refer to my butler, the answer is no. I have no concerns regarding theft of my property. I have trusted Pahdi with my life. When my own stout English recruits had fled to a man, Pahdi remained by my side, appropriated my gun, and aimed straight for the tiger. I was too weak to flee and had to be carried by native bearers on a stretcher. They too, refused to abandon me."

Pahdi had missed the dratted tiger, but the noise of the gunshot had driven the beast off. Jack's men had been unable to look him in the eye the rest of the way back to the garrison.

"A tiger?"

"Sitting no farther from me than you are from that piano. Few men live to tell of such an encounter, but this has little to do with your visit, I'm sure."

Tavis put his cap back on, tugged it off again, then wedged his bulk into one of the chairs facing Jack's desk. The stink of coal smoke, ale, damp wool, and darts night cut across the library's sandalwood scent.

"The darts money is gone," Tavis said. "All of it. Somebody took the whole winnings jar, and the championship is coming up next week."

The winnings jar would weigh a good deal, and moving that many coins in a glass container would be a noisy proposition.

As the first footman arrived with the tea tray, Jack set aside Miss Hennessey's lists and began one of his own. "When did you notice the jar was missing?"

Tavis had closed early the previous night, as was his custom following a darts night. A few guests had been staying on the premises, and they'd all taken the morning stage for London. Tavis had been seeing to his own breakfast, when he'd noticed the jar was missing.

"Did your guests have luggage?"

"They did. One gent was very particular about how his trunks was lashed to the boot. You think my winnings are on their way to London?"

"It's possible. I'll have a look around and talk to your help, nonetheless. Have you any idea how much money was in that jar?"

Tavis knew to the penny. "It's not the money," he said, finishing his third cup of tea. "It's the notion that somebody could take that jar, when it sits above my bar all through the year. Stealing is a crime."

Punishable by death, under some circumstances. The law took no issue with the free exercise of stupidity, however.

"Stealing is a crime, and I'm sorry you've been the victim of a thief. You were right to bring this to my attention." The thief had stolen coin, but more to the point, Tavis's dignity as a proprietor had been affronted. That, rather than the amount taken, had Jack asking more questions.

"You've said you left the storeroom door unlocked, so the tradesmen could make deliveries from Oxford without you having to tend the back door throughout the day. When do you lock the premises at night?"

Tavis peered at his empty tea cup, the delicate Japanese porcelain incongruously dainty in his enormous grip.

"I don't lock up. A wayfarer can arrive at any hour, and if they have to stand about, banging on the front door, they'll wake every guest I have. The front door is never locked, same as the church. Always open for business."

His smile was sad, proud, and worried.

"The Weasel's reputation for hospitality is well earned," Jack said, though that reputation had been built by Tavis's mother, rather than the present owner. "But if you're in the storeroom, back in the kitchen, down in the cellars, and the front and back doors are unlocked, then anybody could have waltzed in and taken that jar of money. Did they take any other funds? Any inventory?"

Tavis rose and tugged down his waistcoat. "Nothing that I could see. I have a question, if you don't mind."

Jack stood, mentally rearranging his day to make time for a trip to the Weasel. "I'll answer, if I have anything useful to contribute."

"Where was your butler last night?"

Oh, for God's sake. "Why do you ask?"

Tavis studied the books lining the library's many shelves. "He wouldn't dare steal from you, but his kind don't approve of the drinking of spirits. That's a fact."

The leaps of bigotry Tavis had demonstrated—no logic involved whatsoever—were prodigious. Jack escorted his guest to the door, while trying to fashion a civil riposte.

"Pahdi is Church of England, Tavis. If you accuse every teetotaler of theft, many a widowed auntie will be charged without evidence. The Crown frowns on accusations without evidence, as do I. Such accusations, if patently false, can give rise to suits for defamation of character."

Jack opened the library door and found Madeline Hennessey and Miss DeWitt coming down the stairs.

"Ah, Miss Hennessey, you can put Mr. Tavis's mind at ease on a small matter."

Madeline smiled graciously, while Miss DeWitt's expression was uncertain. Bartholomew Tavis had not exactly donned his Sunday finest before calling at Teak House.

"I'm happy to help," Madeline said.

"Where was Pahdi last evening?" Jack asked. "I cannot vouch for him, because I was enjoying Candlewick's hospitality. You, however, declined to join the outing, so you can tell us if Pahdi remained at home as well."

"In this household," Madeline said, rearranging her cream wool shawl, "the butler tends the front door, and we knew you and your guests had been invited to Candlewick for dinner. As far as I know, Pahdi remained at his post for the evening, right by the front door. I passed by several times, and he was in the porter's nook each time. I believe he welcomed the party home upon your return from the evening with the Belmonts."

"So he did," Jack said. "Tavis, if you have no more questions, I'll join you at the Weasel after luncheon."

Tavis bobbed awkwardly toward the ladies and took his leave.

"What interesting callers you have," Miss DeWitt remarked, a bit too brightly. "But oh, look! You are standing in a most fortunate location, Sir Jack!"

Her glee boded ill for Jack's future, and his mood. "I'm standing on my own two feet. My preferred location, when upright. Tavis has been the victim of a minor theft, and called upon me in my capacity as magistrate."

Miss DeWitt's smile dimmed as Jeremy appeared at the top of the steps with Mama.

"A minor theft?" Madeline asked.

"The winnings jar from the darts tournament has gone missing. Not a lordly sum, but far more than a pittance. I suspect one of the passengers on the morning stage helped himself to funds all but orphaned in the common. Tavis takes not the smallest measure to discourage theft. One hopes he'll accept a few gentle suggestions when I hare off after luncheon to have a look at the scene of the crime."

"Hare off after I've kissed you," Miss DeWitt said. "For you are directly under an enormous sheaf of mistletoe!"

She stepped closer, braced a hand on Jack's shoulder, and aimed a pair of pink, puckered lips in his direction. She tasted of lemon drops, and her kiss was cool and damp like a granny's. She'd also aimed for Jack's mouth, not his cheek, and only partially connected with her target.

"Happy Christmas!" Miss DeWitt said. "And Happy New Year!"

Miss DeWitt's expression was quite pleased, Mama looked triumphant, while Jeremy's gaze was… disappointed?

And Madeline Hennessey was smirking at her worn boots.

CHAPTER SEVEN

"I'll come with you, Jack," Jeremy announced to the table at large, and he wasn't about to take no for an answer. "Vicars do this. We call on each other as a courtesy when we're traveling. You can investigate your crime, and I'll chat up Vicar Weekes about Proverbs."

As the household had sat down to lunch, Miss Hennessey had suggested Jack talk to the people who'd attended the weekly Bible study, to see if any of them had noticed unusual activity about the posting inn the previous evening. She'd also put forth the notion that most business establishments hung bells on their doors to notify the proprietor of a customer's arrival.

"We can all go into the village with you," Lucy Anne said, clapping her hands. "We'll take the sleigh and have a merry time."

"I'm sure Miss Hennessey will be happy to take the sleigh out," Jack said, "if you ladies are in need of fresh air. When I'm investigating a crime, I try to maintain my focus on the matter at hand."

Lucy Anne's smile faltered, then glowed anew. "We'll make biscuits, then. I brought my mama's recipe, and by the time you've caught the scoundrels, we'll have fresh warm biscuits waiting."

Jeremy nearly pointed out that Lucy Anne's estimate of the effort necessary to catch thieves was hopelessly optimistic, but he didn't want to make Jack look incompetent.

"Biscuits are bad for your teeth," Mama said, stirring a second spoonful of sugar into her tea. "If Jack is determined to racket about the countryside in the dead of winter, searching for some pig farmer's lost gambling stakes, then all I can say is I hope his affairs are in order."

Such a comment would have had Jeremy on his knees before his mother, asking absolution for his every filial shortcoming. Mama's mood all through luncheon had been sour, but that remark came close to meanness.

"Please have patience with the publican, Mrs. Fanning." Miss Hennessey set the cream pot by Mama's tea cup. "Mr. Tavis's mother passed away two winters ago during the holiday season, and he labors under the certain knowledge that he'll never be her equal. She had the knack of profitable hospitality, and the Weasel hasn't been the same without her."

"The trades do fret over the least coin," Mama said. "Most unbecoming, but I suppose Jack *is* the magistrate. For now."

"Precisely," Jack said, rising. "I bid you ladies farewell. Jeremy, let's be off."

"We'll look forward to those biscuits," Jeremy said, snatching a last roll from the basket in the middle of the table. "Cinnamon is my favorite."

Jack hauled him out the door by the elbow. "Do you truly want to call on Vicar, or are you simply in need of respite from the company of the ladies?"

"Respite?"

"From the cooing and twittering, the tittering and beaming. Drives me daft. Get into your boots, and I'll meet you in the stable."

"You sound like Mama," Jeremy said, around a mouthful of roll. "She's old, and her joints ache, and we've neither of us given her babies to dandle and spoil. What's your excuse for such a foul humor?"

Jack took the rest of the roll from Jeremy. "You think her joints ache?"

"Her knees especially. Mostly, I think her heart aches."

Jack tore off a hunk of fresh bread, passed the rest back, and regarded Jeremy with a look that on a governess would suggest somebody had misplaced her charge and left some other little fellow in his place. A fellow with jam stains on his shirt.

"Mama's heart aches, as in, she's not long for this earth, or she needs a beau?"

Jeremy had left his riding boots by the back door, and before Jack could pilfer more of a most excellent, fresh roll, he took off in that direction.

"The two are related, don't you think? Sadness is a burden on the spirit that could easily weaken the heart. Mama worries for you. She blames herself for letting you go out to India. She blames herself for every horror that befell you there."

They clomped down the stairs, earning a glower from a tabby cat who hissed at them as they passed on the landing.

"Mama told you this?" Jack asked.

"She doesn't have to spell it out. I can see how she looks at you. Don't suppose you stole this money just so you have a reason to leave the house?"

Jack stopped at the foot of the steps. "That is a brilliant notion. Are you sure the Church is the best use of your talents?"

"Yes. I'm not a hero like you. I'm just a nice fellow who wants everybody to be happy. You stopped wars—"

"Don't be daft. I nearly started a war when I got myself captured, and that was nobody's fault but mine."

Jeremy crammed the last of the roll into his mouth. "Tell Mama that."

Jack paused to let a serving girl go by with one of the beautiful tea trays that seemed to circulate about the house endlessly.

"You're serious," Jack said, leading the way to the back door. "I'm not about to tell a gently bred older lady about the misery that can befall an arrogant English officer in the jungles of India. The tale involves dirt, itching, vermin, vile odors, and foul language."

"And that was before you were taken prisoner, I'll wager. You've captured Miss DeWitt's heart, if that's any consolation."

On either side of the corridor, cloaks, capes, and coats hung on pegs. Boots were lined up in pairs along the wall; caps, scarves, and mittens sat on a shelf above the outerwear. The sight put Jeremy in mind of the church vestibule in changeable weather.

An entire congregation lived and worked at this house, and this was the magnitude of the domicile Miss DeWitt should expect to call her own.

The thought was lowering to an un-Christian degree.

"My brother is barmy," Jack said, tossing Jeremy a scarf. "Miss DeWitt has had exactly no private conversations with me, and her assault under the mistletoe was her first overture of an affectionate nature. One doesn't want to hurt the young lady's feelings, but her technique wants practice. I hope you have gloves."

"Of course I have gloves. You're not interested in Miss DeWitt?" For the lady's sake, Jeremy wanted Jack to notice what a lovely, sweet, gentle maiden was being paraded before him as a marital prospect. For Jack's sake, Jeremy wished Mama had not been quite so presuming.

For his own sake... He wished being a nice fellow wasn't such a dashed nuisance sometimes.

Jack swung a greatcoat over his shoulders, and even that simple, quotidian activity was executed with a sort of manly panache. The coat settled about broad shoulders, the wool hugging a figure every lady must find worth an extra look.

"You are right that I endured horrors in India," Jack said, tapping a hat onto his head at the perfect angle between rakish and dapper.

Debonair was the word for that angle. Vicars were never debonair.

"Is there a but?" Jeremy asked, stuffing his arms into the sleeves of his own coat.

"I'm coming to believe there is," Jack said, tugging on gloves. "I got myself into a lot of trouble, and I got out of it, eventually, with the help of those who by rights should have left me in the ditch to die."

"Your native butler?"

"And his… family. When my own commanding officers had conveniently given up on me, rather than let my capture create awkwardness for them, Pahdi and his relatives kept looking for me. They posted a ransom, without which, I would never have been able to bribe a guard and eventually escape. I had adventures, Jeremy. India was for the most part an adventure, rather than a horror, and some of it was…"

Miss DeWitt had best not see the smile Jack wore just then. She'd melt into a womanly puddle of tenderheartedness, because whatever Jack was recalling, he was recalling it with buckets of handsome wistfulness.

"We're racing into the village," Jeremy said. "I'm smaller, younger, lighter, and I will beat you on a good horse, even if you are a hero and an adventurer, and everything a young lady could wish for in a husband."

With a flick of Jack's wrist, Jeremy's hat came spinning through the air, straight at Jeremy's middle. Jeremy caught it with his left hand and jammed it onto his head.

"Beat me to the village if you must," Jack said, opening the door and letting a blast of cold air into the house. "I'd rather you bested my performance beneath the mistletoe the next time Miss DeWitt becomes determined to observe quaint holiday customs."

He sauntered out into the chilly day, leaving Jeremy to debate whether Jack, the great adventurer and hero *who'd nearly caused a war*, was teasing—or issuing a challenge.

* * *

"Mrs. Weekes claims it was sitting there when she came in to dust the altar this morning," Vicar Weekes said. "I have no notion how it got here, and was on my way to fetch you when you met me on the road."

The winnings jar, nearly overflowing with coins and bills, sat on a shelf in the church vestibule. To Jack, the slotted wooden poor box perched atop the jar looked worn and small by comparison.

"I can't help but think somebody was offering the congregation a reproach," he said.

"A metaphor," Vicar murmured, regarding the arrangement as if it were a work of art.

Jeremy lifted the little wooden box and shook it. "Not much in the poor box, and this being the needy time of year." He set the poor box back atop the winnings. "If I were a widow or an orphan, I might find another parish to be poor in."

Except, affiliation with a parish required residency for a certain duration, and without residency, no entitlement arose to charitable benefits. The poor moved to better their lot—in search of a job, family connections, or an easier climate—at their peril.

"Has a crime been committed?" Vicar asked. "The winnings jar was on one side of the street earlier in the week, now it sits on the other side."

The jar was the size of a small keg, and doubtless weighed a fair amount. No child had effected this mischief, particularly not with a foot of snow on the ground.

Bartholomew Tavis came through the church's front door, a dingy white apron dangling to his knees beneath his coat.

"You found it!" His smile transformed his countenance from hard man to amiable publican. "You found the winnings and the very same day. Well done, Sir Jack."

Well done, somebody.

"I did nothing," Jack said. "Vicar's wife came upon the jar just as you see it now, with the poor box crowning the lot. Somebody wanted to make a point."

Tavis's smile faltered. "I should lock up the Weasel, I know. Ma never did, but times are different now. The custom from London and the north can't be trusted."

Vicar was being no help at all.

"Your mother was very much respected, wasn't she?" Jeremy asked. "I've been in the area only a short time, and already I've been told what a fine establishment the Weasel is."

Thank you, baby brother.

"Ma was a saint," Tavis said. "She never turned away a customer, never let a body go hungry. I hold the darts tournament in her honor."

Mrs. Tavis had raised a man prone to self-deception, if not lying. The darts tournament was in honor of the Weasel's profitability.

"I have spent time in the East," Jack said, walking up to the winnings jar, but not touching it. "I have seen many odd and wonderful things that science cannot explain. I had not thought to see such goings-on in dear old England, but then, it's a special time of year."

Vicar cleared his throat.

"What's odd?" Tavis asked, lumbering across the vestibule. "That's my winnings jar, and it looks full up to the brim, same as it was last I saw it. I'll just be returning it to its rightful—"

"Your mother passed away over the holidays not two years ago," Jack said, shaking the nearly empty poor box. "She was a widow, noted for her hospitality and kindness, and now you've memorialized her legacy with a tournament that's the talk of the shire. I am not convinced a thief moved your winnings jar, Mr. Tavis."

Vicar finally got into the spirit of the drama. "Mrs. Weekes remarked just the other day that our poor box is a disgrace. Your own mother, Tavis, was nothing if not generous, and without her good example, I regret to say that we're forgetting the needs of the less fortunate. They have nowhere to go for a meal in the middle of a hard week, nowhere to warm their feet when their own coal bin is empty."

The Weasel had served both needs, up to a point, but under Tavis's management, the policy had become "pay to stay."

"Everybody misses Ma," Tavis said. "But a man has to make a living too."

Jack said nothing. He tithed generously and probably more conscientiously than other wealthy landowners *or merchants* in the parish. That wasn't the point.

"You would certainly know more than I about running a tavern," Jeremy said, "but did your mother's approach gain custom that might otherwise have passed the Weasel by? The ladies can be very shrewd about such things."

"Good will has ever been part of a prudent business strategy," Jack observed, handing Vicar the poor box.

"Charity is part of our Christian duty," Vicar added. "I cannot believe…." He opened the little box and upended three coins into his palm.

"That won't exactly buy a Sunday ham," Jeremy muttered. "Much less coal or a new pair of wool stockings."

"I have a suggestion," Jack said, after a suitably unhappy silence. "Tavis, if you announce an intention to donate your portion of the winnings to the Widows and Orphans Fund, the rest of the darts teams might follow your example. The tournament would become even more of a tribute to your late mother, and a fine testament to the Weasel's role in the community as a beacon of kindness and generosity."

The Weasel was best known for its indifferent winter ale. Nobody remarked as much, for Tavis appeared to be considering Jack's suggestion.

"You don't think the money was stolen?"

Vicar set the empty poor box on the shelf and dropped the three pathetic coins inside. "Very odd sort of thief that moves a jar of coins from the tavern to the church without taking a single penny. I've certainly never heard the like."

"I think your mother was also warning you," Jack said. "You can run a fine, hospitable, gracious establishment, and set a shining example of charity for the rest of us, but lock up at night, hang a bell on the doors, and mind who has a key."

"Aye," Tavis said. "A bell is a fine idea. That's quite a large jar."

Jack thought of Theodosia Hennessey's weak tea and stale bread, her sister's fallow ewes and sagging gates.

"If your example inspires the entire contents to be placed at Vicar's disposal for charitable purposes," Jack said, "the Weasel could start a holiday tradition that spreads to coaching inns throughout the realm. Your mother would be very proud to know that her good influence did so much for so many."

That was true, if a bit... ambitious.

"You'd be an inspiration," Jeremy said. "I'll certainly tell this tale to my bishop when I return to London. I've witnessed a miracle right here in Oxfordshire."

"I'll tell our bishop as well," Vicar said. "You're a fine man, Bartholomew. Your own mother often said as much."

Tavis's sigh should have shook the rafters. "I was never one to argue with Ma. Nobody with any sense did. I'll make the announcement at the championship. I'd like to take the jar back to the Weasel though."

"Of course," Vicar said. "The better for all to admire the magnitude of your generosity and your good mother's wonderful example. Happy New Year, Bartholomew."

Tavis looked anything but happy as he cradled the jar in his arms and left the church.

"That part about the beacon," Jeremy said in the ensuing silence. "That was inspired. Perhaps you should consider a career in the Church, Jack."

"Somebody should," Vicar muttered. "I mention charity as often as I dare in my sermons, but after having importuned the more fortunate parishioners for a new roof last year, I dare not over-emphasize my pleas for the widows and orphans. The day Matilda Tavis earned her wings was not a good day for the poor of the parish."

Because feeding widows and orphans mattered less than putting a few buckets under the eaves?

"My team will agree to give up any winnings," Jack said. "Belmont's team will as well. That ought to get the momentum going."

"The widows and orphans thank you," Vicar said, "as do I."

"I'm not the one who should be thanked," Jack said, leading Jeremy to the door. "This is the most creative bit of thievery I've seen on three continents."

"Or the most creative miracle," Jeremy said. "Happy New Year, Vicar, and may the best team win."

They left the Vicar in the empty church, smiling despite his nearly-empty poor box.

* * *

"I caught him stealing her boots, bold as a pirate!" Mrs. Abernathy brandished Madeline's boots under Sir Jack's nose.

Pahdi stood before the library hearth, radiating indignation.

"Mrs. Abernathy, you will please lower your voice," Sir Jack said, wresting the boots from her. "What use would Pahdi have for a pair of lady's boots?"

A pair of worn lady's boots much in need of new heels. Madeline felt awful for the butler, and ashamed for herself too.

"Miss Hennessey's boots have plenty of wear left in them," Mrs. Abernathy said. "They can be sold in Oxford at any number of shops."

Madeline was under no delusions about why Sir Jack had asked her to vouch for Pahdi's whereabouts earlier in the week. Bartholomew Tavis had doubtless accused Pahdi of stealing the darts winnings. In what passed for Tavis's reasoning, a man surrounded every day by expensive silver, spices, crystal, and porcelain would of course tramp through deep snow on a winter night to steal money on public display.

"When was Pahdi to travel the more than ten miles to Oxford to negotiate this sale?" Sir Jack asked. "Half-day is not enough time for such a journey in this weather, and the shops are closed on Sunday."

Mrs. Abernathy looked to Madeline, apparently expecting support on the basis of gender—support that would not be forthcoming.

"He had the boots, sir," Mrs. Abernathy insisted. "I saw him with my own eyes, sneaking down the corridor with the boots in his hand. If you doubt my word, I will turn in my resignation this very day."

Please let her turn in her resignation. Madeline sent up that silent prayer on behalf of the entire household.

"I do not doubt your word," Sir Jack said. "I doubt your judgment. Pahdi, what have you to say?"

Surely the blood of princes flowed through Pahdi's veins. He shot such a glower at Mrs. Abernathy, she ought to have gone up in flames on the spot. The glance he gave Madeline was apologetic.

"Miss Hennessey does not leave her boots out each night for the boot boy to clean, and yet, in this weather, footwear needs attention if it is to keep the feet warm and dry. I thought to bring the boots to the kitchen for the boot boy, and have them back in Miss Hennessey's room before she noticed they were missing. In Teak House, we care for each other's well-being, and Miss Hennessey is deserving of every kindness."

He spoke with gentle deliberation, as if explaining basic concepts to somebody of limited understanding.

Mrs. Abernathy's complexion turned nearly the same shade as the holiday ribbons festooning the tall candles on the library mantel.

"A fine and clever story," she snapped. "Sir Jack won't listen to that taradiddle if he wants me keeping house for him. You, Mr. Pahdi, may take your lying, stealing, disrespectful—"

Sir Jack had cocked his head, as if curious to learn how badly Mrs. Abernathy had misjudged the situation.

"Tell him, Sir Jack," Mrs. Abernathy said. "Tell him his kind aren't welcome here. I don't care what Bartholomew Tavis puts about regarding angels and miracles, we've a thief in our midst, and I know who it is. You show these people an ounce of kindness, and they take endless advantage. It's not your fault you've a kind heart. Many a good man has gone out to India and come back addled."

In Madeline's opinion, Mrs. Abernathy was the one who was daft. But then, she mostly lurked below stairs. She'd never known Sir Jack to chop wood for an old woman living alone, hadn't seen him patiently partnering his mother at whist, didn't know how conscientiously he took his duties as magistrate.

And had no idea how deep his loyalties ran. Mrs. Abernathy took Sir Jack's coin and bullied his maids, which she probably considered a fair exchange.

Jack set the boots on the desk blotter. They were pathetic, as boots went, though they didn't give Madeline blisters anymore.

"Only a fool would steal boots such as these," Sir Jack said, "and I know for a fact that Pahdi is not a fool. Mrs. Abernathy, I understand that you are no longer comfortable with employment at Teak House. I will regretfully accept your resignation and provide you with a character suited to the service you've rendered. I'm sure you have family who would delight in your company. In the morning, you will be paid generous severance and conveyed to the Weasel along with your effects."

Like Pahdi, Jack did not raise his voice, and yet, Madeline wanted to cover her ears and run from the room. Mrs. Abernathy beat her to the door, after an enormous sniff, and the merest twitch of a curtsey.

The housekeeper slammed the library door closed just as Sir Jack murmured, "Happy New Year, Mrs. Abernathy."

"Miss Hennessey, I apologize." Pahdi bowed to Madeline. "I should have asked your permission before appropriating your boots."

"No, you should not," Sir Jack replied. "Permission would have been denied, as we all know. You were being thoughtful, and Mrs. Abernathy is a disgrace. I am in your debt, in fact, because I should have let her go long ago."

The two men exchanged a look, one communicating volumes of resignation, understanding, and—if Madeline wasn't mistaken—some humor.

"I will see to my own boots," Madeline said, "though I thank you for your thoughtfulness, Pahdi."

She reached for her boots, but Sir Jack stopped her with a hand around her wrist.

"Pahdi, if you'd excuse us?"

Madeline slipped her hand free of Sir Jack's. Pahdi bowed and withdrew.

The boots sat on the desk blotter, the knotted laces and worn heels a testament to years in service, and more years of service to come.

"Teak House is without a housekeeper," Jack said. "The holidays are barely behind us, we have company underfoot, and I'm sure Mrs. Abernathy will not leave without sowing a few seeds of discord. I am trying without success to find a sense of alarm over these developments."

Madeline was alarmed. She'd been a fool to kiss Jack Fanning before, but a lonely fool was allowed a few missteps. She had no excuses now, and yet all she could think of was the mistletoe dangling a few feet away.

Jack Fanning was the very last man she ought to be alone with, and under no circumstances—

"Madeline?"

"Pahdi could not possibly have been stealing my boots," she said. "Mrs. Abernathy was a lazy, mean-spirited, bigoted old fool."

"A fool?"

"Anybody can see that Pahdi is devoted to you. He's far from home, has no family, no mates, and he's the butt of endless unkind speculation. I would not remain by your side under such circumstances unless I loved you dearly. Even if Pahdi were stealing boots, you ought not to dismiss him."

Sir Jack set the boots on the floor. "If he was engaging in wrongful acts, I might not have a choice, my dear. I am the magistrate, and stealing is stealing."

And Jack Fanning was a former soldier, and a gentleman, and he was… right. Stealing was a crime, in the eyes of the idiot, damned, stupid, perishing law.

"It's fortunate I'm not stealing boots, then."

"You ought to consider it, at least once," he said, taking her by the hand and drawing her down beside him on the sofa. "Your footwear is barely recognizable as such. Belmont should be ashamed."

"Do not malign Axel Belmont in my hearing, Jack Fanning."

He leveled the smile at her, the bashful, brash, mischievous, delicious smile. "Will you rescue me from my own folly, Madeline? I know you are here on temporary assignment as a lady's companion, and Mama has yet to express a single complaint regarding you. Now I have rendered us without a housekeeper at a highly social time of year. This was not well done of me, when, as Mrs. Abernathy so helpfully pointed out, a thief is on the loose."

"You are intent on catching the thief—or thieves?"

Jack sat back, crossing his feet at the ankles. "Something about the purloined coal and the mysterious levitating coin jar smacks of the same hand."

"What about Mr. Cotton's errant ram?"

"That might have been an innocent case of wandering livestock."

Madeline rose, the topic far less interesting than kisses, though just as fraught. "It might not. In all three cases, somebody benefitted without costing the victim much of anything."

"True, and in the cases of McArdle and Tavis, one could even say the victims themselves benefitted from the thief's visit. Cotton's ram is certainly none the worse for his outing either."

The habits of service offered Madeline a distraction from watching Jack Fanning's mouth form words. She wandered the room, straightening an afghan over the sofa, tidying a stack of books on the reading table, closing the cover over the piano keys. She was arranging music in alphabetical order by composer when a pair of strong arms encircled her waist from behind.

"Madeline Hennessey, you have been avoiding me."

"Trying to."

Jack dropped his arms and turned her by the shoulders. "Why?"

"You should marry Miss DeWitt."

He took the music Madeline held—a piece by Clementi in F major that she'd spent a month memorizing when she'd been eleven—and set it aside.

"I should marry Miss DeWitt? And here I thought you the sensible, observant type."

"Miss DeWitt would be the perfect wife for a knight of the realm. She's pretty and cheerful, and would never impose on you. She'd make a good mother, and she'd know exactly how to seat a group of thirty, even if the numbers weren't perfect."

"Do you know how often I've entertained thirty people at dinner?"

He had the silver to seat twice that number, as well as the crystal and the china. "Not as often as you should."

"Never, Madeline, nor do I intend to start now. I do, however, intend to kiss you."

* * *

Jack's thoughts were leaping about like March hares. One moment, he was grasping for the common thread connecting the thefts from Tavis and McArdle, the next he was admiring the curve of Madeline Hennessey's mouth. Then he'd recall that his household was without a housekeeper, and be assailed by both relief and chagrin.

He ought to have turned Mrs. Abernathy off months ago.

And he ought to resolve his situation with Madeline Hennessey, though not when she was regarding him as if she'd like to flee straight out the nearest window.

"Unless, of course, you'd rather I didn't kiss you," Jack said, stepping back. "The choice is yours."

"The kissing isn't the problem."

Kissing wasn't entirely a solution either. *Jack's* problem was that after years of cordial indifference on the subject of the fairer sex—or the next thing to it—his breeding organs had chosen *now* to recall their intended use.

Happy New Year, indeed.

On the one hand, the timing was awful. Miss Hennessey was arguably in Jack's employ, and thus under his protection in the gentlemanly sense. He ought to leave her in peace on that ground alone. Then too, his mother was underfoot, to say nothing of the dimpled Miss DeWitt, as well as Saint Jeremy.

And thieves were loose in the shire who would not surrender themselves to the king's man without conscientious investigation on Jack's part.

The timing, the setting, the person—wrong, wrong, all wrong.

On the other hand, Jack was bloody grateful that his interest in women hadn't deserted him permanently. Madeline Hennessey knew what she was about, and would plant him a facer if he overstepped.

And should Jack fail to heed that warning, Belmont would finish the thrashing Madeline started.

"If kissing isn't the problem," Jack said, "then what is?"

Miss Hennessey sat at the piano and pushed the cover off the keys. "If a woman marries, she becomes her husband's property."

Jack sat beside her on the piano bench, an agreeably crowded arrangement, even though the m-word had entered the conversation.

"Your great-aunts did not choose well, I take it."

"They did not choose at all," Madeline said, starting on a competent rendition of some lively bagatelle—without benefit of the written music. "Their parents chose for them, and my aunts dared not disobey. I hate that."

"The times were different." Jack watched her hands and wondered where a housemaid found time to learn, much less memorize, parlor music.

"The times weren't that different," she said. "You really should court Miss DeWitt. You need a wife, not a passing fancy. That's all I'd be to you, and I can assure you, that's all you'd be to me."

She brought the piece to a cadence, leaving a ringing silence.

"I've never been a passing fancy before." Nor did Jack care for that status now.

The slipper was supposed to go on the other, daintier foot. The male of the species bestowed his favors on ladies of easy virtue—note the plural—and they were the passing fancies, often very passing. Jack had never been particularly free with his favors, but prior to his marriage, he'd not been a monk either.

"I've been a passing fancy a time or two," Miss Hennessey said. "I don't recommend it. The promise of pleasure is seldom kept, the affection superficial. Then there's the bother of being discreet, and extricating oneself when interest wanes or is caught by another passing fancy. All quite... tedious."

She was right, in the normal course. Flirtations became affairs that all too often became petty dramas in the mess hall.

Though Jack did not anticipate another passing fancy catching his interest. Not in the foreseeable future, and discretion under the present circumstances wouldn't be that great a challenge. If he had to choose a woman who was not given to histrionics, it would be Madeline Hennessey.

"You disdain marriage," Jack said, "and you're not interested in a dalliance, and yet, you haven't flown off in high dudgeon. Should I be encouraged?"

Madeline rested her forehead on his shoulder, as if he'd delivered bad news. "You should be married, and I'm assuring you that if any such daft notion afflicts you where I am concerned, I will refuse you."

"Refusal is the lady's prerogative. I was married once before, years ago. You should know that. I know well what marriage entails." Though he didn't know what marriage *to Madeline* would entail, nor did the idea alarm him as it ought.

"Did you love her?"

"Passionately, to the point of foolishness, as young men are wont to do. She was half-English, lovely, and very stubborn. Saras was the reason I didn't die when I escaped from captivity with only the most tenuous grip on my reason. Pahdi is her brother, and she charged him on her deathbed with looking after me."

Jack knew not why he was telling Madeline this, unless it was in an effort to convince her that they weren't so different. He'd been weary and lost, far from home, and not at all himself. His financial means had been ample, but emotionally, he'd been beggared by his ordeals.

"That's the sadness in you," Madeline said, folding her hands in her lap. "You smile so seldom, and you never refuse a duty. You're trying to live up to her memory."

Or was Jack trying to escape his memories of India? "I like to be busy, much as you do. The devil finds work for idle hands, witness, our rash of thefts. There's something else you should know, Madeline."

"You don't like guns. Mrs. Belmont told me, but any fool can see your house has no weaponry on display. You don't ride to hounds, you don't go shooting. The footmen at Candlewick decided you'd seen too much of war."

The conversation was unusual, but also like kissing. Intimate, novel, risky, and lovely. Jack took Madeline's hand and pressed his lips to her knuckles.

"I abused opium. Took me forever to get free of it. Pahdi and Saras went through hell with me, and I still… It's not something I will ever be able to joke about or discuss lightly."

"My aunts tipple. I shudder to think what they'd do if they could afford regular access to spirits."

The aunts were Madeline's cross to bear, or the sadness in her, to use her words. Jack would think about how to solve that problem later.

"Your aunts would never do anything to disgrace you," he said, though they might help themselves to loose coal, or wrestle a jar of coins from the tavern to the vicarage.

Well, damn and blast.

Madeline retrieved her hand. "You are so confident of that, and yet, you barely know them. Your mother will be waking from her nap, and I should be above stairs if she wants me."

Jack rose from the piano bench and scooted aside so Madeline could get to her feet. "If you enjoy playing the piano, you should feel free to use this instrument. It gets little enough use, and yet, it's a fine, handsome specimen." *Like the gentleman standing before you.*

"Now you're flirting with me," Madeline said, circling around him. "If you must flirt with me, I cannot stop you, but I ask that you do so with utmost discretion. You'd be much better off with Miss DeWitt."

Jack stepped closer. "I'd be bored to tears, and you, Madeline Hennessey, are standing beneath the mistletoe. Again."

* * *

Madeline kissed Jack as if he were leaving for India on the next tide, as if she were the one passionately, foolishly in love.

Because she was. The more she learned about Jack Fanning, the more she admired him, and the more she wished she wasn't a former housemaid stealing biscuits for her aging relatives.

He kissed her back, not with the abandon with which Madeline flung herself at him, but with a relentlessly gentle thoroughness that had Madeline sighing against his mouth.

"You drive me daft, Jack Fanning."

His clothing drove her daft. Madeline wanted to touch *him*, not the soft wool of his jacket, the silk of his waistcoat, or the fine linen of his shirt. She did not dare, because of all men, Jack Fanning was not for her.

He was above her touch, which didn't bother her as much as it ought to. He was heartbreak personified, regret wearing breeches, and all she wanted was to get those breeches off of him.

The next thing she knew, she was sitting on his desk, watching as Jack crossed the library to lock the door.

Think, Madeline. "Your mother will awaken—"

"Five minutes," he said, stalking right up to the desk and positioning himself between Madeline's knees. "Give me five minutes, Madeline, and then you may retreat into your impersonation of a lady's demure companion. We deserve five minutes, and then you can consider whether the pleasure I promise you is worth the tedium involved."

Surely even Madeline in her overwrought state could get into only a little trouble in five minutes?

Jack recommended the kissing, while Madeline managed to tug his shirt free of his breeches so she could go exploring. The skin of his back was warm and covered with what had to be scars. She learned the contours of his mistreatment by touch as he insinuated a hand under her skirts.

"You are a bold man, Jack Fanning."

"I'm a determined lover, very determined."

His touch was both knowing and delicate, tracing the shape of her knee, then drifting higher.

"What are you about, Jack?"

"Looking for treasure. Lie back on the desk, Madeline."

She yanked his hair, hard.

"I beg your pardon. Madeline, may I invite you to lie back, while I spend the next three and a half minutes..." His caresses glossed over her sex, and Madeline subsided onto the blotter.

The position was undignified, with her legs sprawled over the side of the desk, her skirts in a wrinkled heap about her. One of her slippers slid off her foot and hit the carpet. She kicked the second one free as well.

"My slippers," Jack said. "They're too big for you."

"Not too big," Madeline retorted.

Jack was splendidly adventurous. He touched her between her legs, intimately and with far more skill than Madeline had known a man could possess.

More skill than she possessed, certainly.

Madeline had been aroused on occasion and found coupling with a considerate man a pleasant indulgence, but Jack's fingers teased, stroked, and tempted her beyond the bounds of mere pleasance. Desire escalated to need, and from there to a dark, mad, clawing sense of frustration.

Jack's free hand closed about Madeline's breast, and she arched up into his touch.

"Let go, Madeline. I want to see you soar."

The part of her mind still capable of thought heard the plea inside the command, and her body must have heard the invitation as well, for in the next moments, incandescent sensation coalesced where only frustrated desire had been. Madeline's breath caught as her body endured more sheer glory than she'd experienced in all of her previous encounters together.

When she opened her eyes several dazed eternities later, Jack was bent over her, brushing her hair back from her brow, and looking like a worried Viking prince.

"I mussed your hair, Sir Jack." Madeline ought to put him to rights, smooth his hair back to order, but all she could do was smile.

He smiled back, beatific and rascally, both. "You indeed mussed my hair, while I'm sure your skirts have become a bit wrinkled." He helped Madeline to a sitting position, and she wrapped her arms around his waist.

"Is that a trick you learned in India?"

His heart beat in a steady rhythm beneath Madeline's cheek. She'd pay for these five minutes, probably for the rest of her life, but she needed a few more moments in Jack's arms.

"It's a trick you can do for yourself, universal to the species. The experience can be repeated too."

Wicked, wonderful man. How would she ever give him up, much less to the vapid charms of Miss DeWitt?

"Your five minutes are over, Sir Jack." Madeline wanted nothing so much as to fall asleep in his arms amid the joyous glow of a fading pleasure.

"Shall I carry you upstairs?"

He could do it, and he would do it. Madeline drew back and ran her fingers through his hair. "No, thank you. You need a comb and some tidying."

"I don't think that's what I need, and I'll spend the next weeks convincing you that's not what you need either. I think we've both had enough of tidying." He kissed Madeline on the mouth, but mercifully refrained from elaborating on his point. When he stepped back, she scooted off the desk and slid her feet back into the discarded slippers.

Jack was fabulously wealthy and had the respect of the entire shire. He did not need her—would never need her—her common sense insisted.

He wanted her, though.

She wanted him too, even now, with satisfaction thrumming through her veins. "You may try to convince me that some discreet, friendly untidying would be enjoyable," she said, mustering a smile. "When you're not otherwise occupied with catching thieves or dodging Miss DeWitt."

"I thrive on duty and challenge," Jack replied, his smile nowhere in evidence. "And my five minutes are over… for now."

He reached overhead, plucked a white berry from the mistletoe, and pitched it into the ash can by the hearth.

Madeline kissed him on the cheek and hurried up to her room, though the oversized slippers made a hasty retreat somewhat perilous.

CHAPTER EIGHT

Jeremy started his morning studies in the Teak House family parlor, brushing up on Proverbs, among his favorite books of the Old Testament. Pithy biblical phrases were a handy way to establish ecclesiastical credentials, which Jeremy had apparently failed to do with Vicar Weekes.

"A friend loveth at all times, and a brother is born for a time of adversity." The difficulty was, a snippet of Scripture didn't tell a fellow which brother was the one born to be of aid in the time of adversity—Jack or Jeremy?

"Oh," Miss DeWitt said, "it's you. I heard your voice and thought Sir Jack was in here."

She stepped into the parlor and closed the door behind her. "I don't suppose you know where he's got off to now?"

Jack had taken Miss Hennessey to visit her aged aunties, it again being half day.

"He's probably racketing about the shire in search of a thief or two, which leaves me entirely dependent on your good offices, Miss DeWitt."

"Lucy Anne, please," she said, taking a seat beside Jeremy on the sofa. "How can I be of assistance, Reverend Jeremy?"

She was a valiant little creature, hiding her disappointment in Jack's absence. Jeremy could not blame Jack for investigating crimes, but this business of becoming Miss Hennessey's personal coachman rapidly approached poor hospitality to Jack's other guests.

"I'm not feeling very reverend, so you must call me Jeremy. I had hoped the local vicar might allow me to preach a sermon or two as a guest while I'm in the area, but he has yet to oblige me with an invitation. We do that, you know. We vicars. We share our pulpits."

Except Jeremey hadn't had a living of his own for more than a year, since the bishop had recalled him from Sussex, where he'd been happily preaching away to a flock more elderly than devout. He missed his congregation, and worse, missed the sense of providing a contribution simply by being a cheerful presence.

A cheerful heart is good medicine, but a crushed spirit drieth up the bones.

"I heard about the darts money," Miss DeWitt said, patting Jeremy's hand. "The vicar must be a bit at sixes and sevens, don't you think? The thief has preached a sermon to the local flock without taking the pulpit at all."

"Do you suppose that's the problem?"

"Or perhaps the vicar doesn't want to impose on you when you're enjoying time with your family. I get the sense you and Sir Jack do not have many interests in common."

Another pat to Jeremy's hand softened that delicate observation.

"Jack is nearly ten years my senior, and he was off to India before I even went to public school. I beat him when we raced into the village the other day, though. We're neither of us good at being idle for long."

Perhaps Jack had allowed Jeremy that victory?

"I remarked to your dear mama just this morning that you're a very robust specimen for a vicar, Jeremy Fanning. I'm sure all the young ladies enjoy coming to services when you're preaching."

None of Jeremy's flock had been exactly young, but the ladies had done a good job of remaining awake during his sermons. The old fellows… not so much.

"Would you like to go riding with me?" Jeremy ventured. "A robust specimen can absorb only so much Scripture at a sitting, and the weather has turned agreeable."

For the dead of winter the morning was mild, meaning the sun was out and the wind wasn't too bad. Very little of the snow had melted.

"Perhaps later," Miss DeWitt said.

She was stroking Jeremy's hand now, probably out of nerves, for clearly something weighed on the young lady's mind.

"You must tell me how I might be of service, Lucy Anne. I know Miss Hennessey is good company for Mama, but that leaves little company for you."

Miss Hennessey was a saint when Mama fell prey to one of her restless moods. No request was unreasonable, no riposte too acerbic to dislodge Miss Hennessey's equanimity. Even Lucy Anne occasionally retreated to compose letters to her sisters, while Jeremy retired to pray, and Jack… Jack went off on the king's business.

Or something.

"I don't want to impose," Lucy Anne said, "but lately, I have become concerned."

She was very pretty when she was concerned, with her fine blond brows drawn down, her blue eyes filled with anxiety. She had a firm, concerned grip on Jeremy's hand too.

"My calling is to bear the worries of others, Lucy Anne. It's no good to listen to the bishop grumble in his palace, or Mama fret about misplacing her third silk shawl of the day, when somebody else suffers in meek silence with a genuine problem."

Most of being a vicar was common sense. Be kind, set a good example, don't put on airs, and in this regard, Jeremy would put his depth of vocation up against the most learned scholars and devout archbishops.

"I fear I do have a problem," Lucy Anne said, worrying a nail between rosebud lips. "A very personal problem, but I don't know to whom else I might turn."

Jeremy patted her knuckles, for she seemed to be the sort of female who was comforted by tactile measures.

"You may confide in me, Lucy Anne, and I will never betray your trust."

Jeremy had heard many confessions, another part of vicaring that came easily. People talked to a man who had no expectations of them other than that they try their best to be decent to each other. All the brimstone and hellfire tactics did was make folk quick to judge one another and slow to admit their own shortcomings.

Lucy Anne beamed at Jeremy as if he'd waved his hand and brought spring to the shire. "I knew I could trust you. You're such a *good* man."

Even a good man was allowed to notice what a fine figure the Almighty had bestowed on a lady. In fact, temptation was a part of life, and a good man welcomed the opportunity to practice restraint… or some such rot.

Jeremy's focus was not on a recollection of the bishop's complicated theological contortions, but rather, on how Lucy Anne's eyes shimmered when she was in the grip of strong emotion.

"I am a man pleased to be of aid to a lady in need." That sounded about right, not too preachy, and not like a fellow flirting with his brother's intended.

Though Jack didn't flirt with Lucy Anne *at all* that Jeremy could see. Puzzling, that.

"My need is personal," Lucy Anne said, her lashes drifting down. "Very personal."

"Trust me, Lucy Anne," Jeremy said, despite the warning bells chiming in the belfry of his gentlemanly honor. He was alone, sitting quite close to, and holding hands with, the woman Mama had chosen for Jack.

And Jeremy was enjoying himself far too much.

"I fear I have ruined my chances with Sir Jack," Lucy Anne said. "Your mother all but ordered me to accost him beneath the mistletoe, but, well… you were there. It didn't go well."

The great hero had botched that encounter entirely. "You must be patient with Jack. I don't think he's had much practice kissing lovely women."

For an instant, Lucy Anne's gaze reflected incredulity, but only an instant. Perhaps Jeremy had misread her expression, or worse, perhaps nobody had told her she was lovely.

"I rather think the problem is he's had too much experience," she said. "One hears things, about the *conditions* in India."

Indeed, one did. British Army officers had been known to intermarry with the local women—sometimes more than one local woman at the same time—wear native dress, and adopt native customs if posted far from civilization. Jack had doubtless departed on occasion from the strictest dictates of his upbringing, but that had all been years ago in a land far away. An exotically different land.

"Jack endured a lot of bad treatment in India, Lucy Anne. He doesn't say much about it, and it is all very much in his past. You must be patient with him. He really is a splendid fellow."

The impatience in her gaze was unmistakable, though she was trying mightily not to show it. Jeremy didn't blame her for being exasperated, and much of the blame belonged at Mama's feet for presuming to matchmake under Jack's very roof.

"What if the problem isn't Jack?" Lucy Anne wailed softly. "What if it's me?"

An immediate show of manly sense was in order, lest the poor dear dissolve into tears. From thence would follow concern about her nose turning red, or her eyes being puffy, and all manner of related horrors for a fellow who grasped that neither the truth nor a kindly meant prevarication would untangle the lady from her upset.

"Lucy Anne, Jack is a bumbling, gormless bachelor." All bachelors were bumbling and gormless, to hear Mama tell it, as were most married men. "If he fails to appreciate a woman as lovely, kind, delightful, and sweet-natured as you, then the fault is not yours."

"You really think I am lovely, kind, delightful, and sweet-natured?"

"Most assuredly." Also pretty, and—Jeremy accounted himself an honest fellow in the privacy of his thoughts—well-endowed.

"Then you won't mind kissing me, will you?"

She was appallingly hopeful about her conclusion—also entirely in the right.

"Kissing you?"

"Of course. You saw that incident beneath the mistletoe. I swear Sir Jack would rather have been kissed by a hedgehog. He's a man of experience; therefore, the problem must lie with my *in*experience. I have concluded that I must apply to you for kissing lessons."

"That's quite… quite logical." Also utterly daft, though Jeremy wasn't about to tell her that when she was beaming at him so hopefully.

"I knew you'd oblige me, Jeremy. With a little practice, I'm sure I can do better next time."

A brother was born for a time of adversity. Jeremey would check his sources, because it might well be that Proverbs was a warning that a brother was born to *cause* a time of adversity.

He rose and locked the door. "Let's come away from the window, Lucy Anne, and take this slowly, step by step."

* * *

"I heard you sent that Abernathy woman packing," Hattie Hennessey said to Jack. "What took you so long?"

Jack had to admit the question was fair, if rude.

"Aunt," Madeline muttered from across the room that served as Hattie's kitchen, parlor, and dining room.

"One doesn't discharge an employee on a whim," Jack said, shifting on the hard chair at Hattie's table. "To do so invites employees to quit on a whim, and the entire household suffers from the resulting chaos."

Hattie's cottage was neat as pin, and unlike her sister's dwelling, free of the smell of dog. A spinning wheel sat near the hearth, dried flowers hung in bunches from the exposed rafters, and a braided rug covered the middle of the plank floor.

And yet, the cottage was frigid, and Hattie's teapot was a small jasper-ware version with a chipped spout. The chair Jack occupied was missing a slat, the table did not sit evenly on the plank floor. Her tea cups did not match each other or their saucers. Over the mantel, however, was a portrait of a lovely young girl in the garb of the past century.

The girl was willowy, with auburn hair peeking out from a lacy cap. Her bodice was decorated with fanciful embroidered flowers. Her hair was unpowdered and adorned with strings of pearls, and her pose exposed an amount of bosom that the present day would consider daring, if not scandalous, for such a young woman. She bore a girlish resemblance to Madeline, though her eyes lacked Madeline's sharp intelligence.

"I know all about discharging employees," Hattie said. "When I was in service, finding housemaids and footmen willing to work for their pay and remain sober on their half day was as much effort as tending to the laundry. Mr. McArdle tolerated no slacking, and his butler was worse than he was."

As both a magistrate, and as an officer of the crown in India, Jack had learned to listen to the prompting of instinct. Why had Madeline chosen to visit Hattie, after purportedly dropping in on her on earlier in the week?

And why hadn't Jack asked Madeline's aunts about the Hennessey family history?

"Have a biscuit," Madeline said, setting the tray before Jack. "Aunt's favorites are ginger, while I prefer the shortbread."

Jack took a cinnamon biscuit, but he wasn't about to be distracted from Hattie's disclosures.

"You worked for Hector McArdle?" he asked, holding the plate out to Hattie.

Hattie deliberated, though Jack counted four ginger biscuits among the dozen left on the tray.

"Not Hector," she said, taking a piece of shortbread. "His father, Abner McArdle. I was his housekeeper, until he turned me off without a character. This is the best shortbread I've had in ages."

Very likely, the only shortbread she'd had in ages, unless Madeline had included some on a previous visit.

Madeline poured the tea all around, though there was no question of adding sugar or milk, for Hattie apparently hadn't either. The irony of wealth had impressed Jack during his first year abroad. The poor would graciously share what little they had, while the nabobs hoarded treasures untold, and made elaborate provisions to protect silver, gold, jewels, and art that would never see the light of day.

"Why would Abner McArdle turn you off without a character?" Jack asked.

"Perhaps we might discuss that another time?" Madeline murmured.

"Nonsense," Hattie retorted. "Sir Jack isn't an unbreeched lad, unwise to the ways of the world. Hector's youngest brother, Caleb, couldn't keep his hands to himself. One of the maids wasn't of a mind to accommodate him, and I intervened. Two weeks later, Caleb accused me of stealing a spoon, and it was found in my bedroom, right under my pillow. Now I ask you, how did Caleb know where to look for that spoon, and what fool keeps a stolen spoon under her pillow?"

Madeline took a biscuit for herself. "Let's not bore Sir Jack with the details, Aunt."

"I am ever interested in the workings of the law," Jack said, and these were by no means details. "If the spoon was found in your quarters, why weren't you charged?"

"Because rape is a crime too," Hattie said, dunking her shortbread in her tea, "and that's exactly what would have happened had I not boxed young Caleb's ears. Abner had spoiled the boy for years, and knew his youngest son well. Hector was paying a call on his papa that day and saw the whole little drama, but he knew better than to peach on his baby brother. I was loudly denounced as a thief, though Abner sent me on my way with a packet of cash too."

She ate her shortbread in philosophical silence, while Jack wanted to break something. This tale was likely enacted in households all over the realm, when the reputation of a strutting boy was threatened by the dictates of common decency.

"You never sought employment again?" Jack asked.

"What would have been the point?" Madeline replied, before Hattie could speak up. "A domestic dismissed without a character has no hope of finding decent employment. Doubtless, Caleb would claim the maid enticed him, and more spoons would have turned up in curious locations. This is how the world works for those in service. More tea, Aunt?"

"No, thank you. Madeline, you mustn't be disagreeable, or Sir Jack will think you don't appreciate your position."

"What I think," Jack said, "is that Caleb McArdle ought to be charged with attempted rape, provided I can find the maid in question. Hector might not have spoken up before his father, but to dissemble under oath is perjury. The statute of limitations on felonies is twenty-one years, and rape is a felony."

Madeline's tea cup hit her saucer. "You would charge a man ten years after the offense occurred?"

She looked dismayed rather than impressed with Jack's suggestion.

"The law is the law, Miss Hennessey. A young woman was taken advantage of, and when your aunt tried to intervene, the retaliation was severe."

"The notion of seeing Caleb McArdle bound over for the assizes is lovely," Hattie said, "but it won't happen. He went off to university and died after consuming bad fish, if you can believe the gossip. The boy's death sent old man McArdle into a decline, and he soon followed his son into the grave. Hector inherited the entire coal yard, which is fortunate when the man has ten children."

Hector, whose coal thief Jack would likely never catch. Much to ponder regarding Hattie Hennessey's past, and wrong done her by the late coal man.

"Is that your portrait over the mantel?" Jack asked.

"Yes," Hattie said, not even glancing at the painting. "I wasn't a beauty, like Theodosia, but then, my husband was unlucky in business rather than a fool, God rest him. I married a third cousin, which is often the best sort of husband. Madeline, you will please wrap up these lovely biscuits, unless Sir Jack would like another?"

The biscuits were already slightly stale, but Hattie would probably make them last another week.

"I could not possibly eat another," Jack said, rising. "Miss Hennessey, I will see to the horses, but you are not to rush away. Give me a few minutes to offer the beasts water, while you catch your aunt up on the news from the village."

He bowed to both ladies and withdrew to the chilly yard between Hattie's sheep byre and her cottage.

His first task was to fill up the water trough for the sheep from the cistern beside the house. Hattie's wooden bucket leaked, and the cistern was frozen over, so the undertaking was cold and time-consuming. Next, he used a shovel standing beside the door of the cottage to dig a path through the snow between the byre and the cottage, and when those necessities had been tended to, he forked hay to the sheep from the thatched hay rick beside their pen.

"If that's you, Eloise," he said to an inquisitive ewe, "I'll pass along your regards to Charles when next he and I meet."

The gate still sagged, a length of rusty tin flapped against the roof of the byre, and the hay was far from good quality. If Hattie's story could be believed, this desperate existence was her thanks for presuming to hold a young man accountable for his actions.

Jack was wrestling a sizeable rock onto the loose tin by virtue of standing on the sleigh bench, when Madeline emerged from the cottage, pulling the door closed behind her.

"You've watered the horses?" she asked.

"The horses are all of three miles from home," Jack said, leaping to the ground. "They didn't need watering." Hattie Hennessey needed help, though. Jack didn't point out the obvious, lest he find himself facedown in the snow.

"I've told her to sell that portrait," Madeline said, stalking off to the sleigh. "I think she keeps it to torment herself."

"Perhaps she keeps it to recall a happier time?" Jack suggested, handing Madeline up into the sleigh.

"What is the point of recalling a happier time? That happier time is lost, and it can't be brought back by staring at a picture. Hattie would be better off selling the damned thing and buying sugar for her tea."

Or paying Mortimer Cotton for the services of his ram?

"Teak House will send Hattie a belated Christmas box," Jack said, "and she'll have a crop of lambs in the spring." Those measures were not adequate to address the penury Hattie endured. "All of the money from this year's darts tournament should be donated to the Widows and Orphans Fund. Hattie will see a share of that, as will Theodosia."

He gave the horses leave to walk on, and soon had them trotting smartly in the direction of Teak House. The sun did nothing to moderate the cold. If anything, the temperature was dropping as the morning wore on.

"Madeline, say something."

She wiped her eyes with the end of her scarf and sniffed. "If you hadn't watered the sheep, I would have. Breaking the ice out of the cistern and scooping the ice from the trough makes Aunt's hands ache awfully, and she has no laudanum—" Madeline turned on the seat and braced her forehead against Jack's shoulder. "I am awful. I've wished my aunts would die rather than see them endure another winter. They never have enough to eat. Theo has lately developed a cough. They're always cold, and they worry so, about the sheep, the chickens…"

While Madeline worried about them.

Jack had abundant coin with which to address Hattie's and Theo's poverty, and he'd make every effort to do that, though he suspected they'd rebuff anything resembling charity.

"Madeline, Hattie's situation is not your fault."

She made an odd noise, and her shoulders hitched.

Jack pulled the horses up right in the middle of the lane. "It's not your fault," he said again, fishing a handkerchief from his pocket. "Please don't cry, love."

Madeline pressed his handkerchief to her eyes, like a blindfold. "You don't understand. It *is* my fault. Every bit of it. It's all my fault."

* * *

To say those words aloud—*It's all my fault*—only made audible the defining misery of Madeline's existence, and yet, her admission unloosed a torrent of tears.

And in front of Jack Fanning, of all people.

"Such a dire pronouncement," Jack said, wrapping his scarf around Madeline's neck. Unlike her scarf, which was coarse wool, his was soft and bore the fragrance of sandalwood.

"It's the truth," Madeline said. "I hate to cry. That's true as well." Unfortunately, every word Hattie had spoken had also been factual.

"When you can look upon injustice and undeserved poverty and feel nothing, then you should be concerned. Your tears are evidence of a caring heart."

He faced straight ahead, the wind ruffling his hair. His tone was severely reproving.

"You don't say what I expect you to say," Madeline replied. "I do care about my aunts, and their situation is my fault."

The offside gelding stomped a hoof in the snow. Jack took up the reins and asked the horses to walk on.

"You are at fault, because you did not allow young McArdle to lift your skirts?"

"Yes." No sense prevaricating about this when Madeline was withholding information in so many other regards.

"I take it you sought another position?"

Jack was very much the magistrate, interrogating rather than conversing, and that helped Madeline put aside her tears—for now.

"Without a solid character reference, a girl who has only a few weeks' experience in service would never find another position. Aunt was let go for stealing, and the new housekeeper regarded me suspiciously as a result. Caleb was determined to make me regret my *stubbornness*—his word—and thus I was frequently disciplined for offenses I did not commit."

"Beaten," Jack said. "To encourage you to look more favorably on rape by comparison. Why haven't you delivered a few stout blows between my legs, Madeline?"

"I beg your pardon?"

"How am I different from Caleb McArdle?"

And men accused women of going off on queer flights. "You're alive, for one thing, and you mean me no disrespect, for another."

"I want under your skirts, and I'm not offering marriage."

He'd already been under her skirts, and Madeline's entire view of erotic intimacy had undergone a sea change. If she had any sense, she'd tell him their dalliance was over before it had begun.

Madeline had no sense, not where Jack Fanning was concerned. If her lot was to grow old fretting over hens and ewes, she wanted one experience of passion with a man who knew what he was about.

"If you did offer marriage, I'd turn you down, sir. To become invisible in the eyes of the law, lose all authority over myself, and subject myself to the dubious guidance of a man holds no appeal. Am I a strumpet?"

"Don't be ridiculous. You are a mature, healthy woman who harbors no romantic illusions."

"I'll take that for a no. Let's agree you're a mature, healthy man who also harbors no romantic illusions. Caleb was a rutting, spoiled little bore to whom a new maid was simply a toy to be played with until it broke or got with child."

The sleigh flew along, the horses' breath puffing white in the winter air. Jack turned the vehicle up the Teak House drive and was soon assisting Madeline to alight.

"He didn't, did he?" Jack asked, quietly.

As the groom led the team around to the carriage house, Madeline stood in the drive, her hands on Jack's shoulders, his at her waist.

"I beg your pardon?"

"McArdle—nothing broken, I hope?"

What was he asking? "Aunt intervened before I'd suffered more than bruises and a bad fright."

"And thereafter? You said you'd endured a year at your first post, before you removed to Candlewick."

What did that matter? Madeline had left the McArdle household nearly ten years ago, far wiser at sixteen than she'd been at fifteen, and yet, Jack was apparently... concerned.

"Nothing broken, Jack. A bad patch, we all have them. The other maids and footmen looked after me when the king's justice did not. I came right, as you did."

He offered his arm and escorted her to the house by way of the side garden. Madeline thanked him for the outing, did *not* kiss his cheek, and repaired to her bedroom to trade her boots for his house slippers.

* * *

Axel Belmont wished he could rouse his dearest wife from her nap, but a new mother needed her rest, and Sir Jack Fanning needed a sympathetic ear—this instant.

"Madeline was new to service," Jack said, pacing the length of Axel's larger glass house. "Little more than a girl, recently bereaved of both parents."

Madeline, not Miss Hennessey. Certainly not Hennessey, as Axel had addressed the young lady for years.

"I hadn't known she was an orphan," Axel said, gently transferring a seedling to its own pot. "And new to service. Have you been in Hattie Hennessey's cottage, Belmont?"

Axel straightened and braced his hands on his lower back. The worktable was low enough that the plants upon it were away from floor drafts, but still had room to grow. Having a newborn in the house had prompted Axel to a frenzy of propagation among his plants, for after winter, came the spring.

Sir Jack was looking at him expectantly, so Axel cast back over the remnants of the conversation.

"I have not had the pleasure of being a guest at Hattie Hennessey's hearth."

"Hattie has a painting over her fireplace," Jack said, taking a sniff of a white rose blooming on a lovely specimen at the end of the table. "A portrait rather than the usual pastoral scene. It's skillfully done, and the subject is a young Hattie Hennessey."

Axel preferred botanical prints and floral still lifes. "What is the significance of the painting?"

Sir Jack paced along between the rows of plants, and Axel wished he'd received his guest in the library. Twenty-four hours after visiting Hattie's cottage, Jack Fanning was still in a taking, and plants—roses especially—did not thrive in the presence of human acrimony and strife. Axel would not admit that sentiment to any save his wife, who could be trusted not to laugh at him for such fancies.

"Have you had any portraits done, Belmont?"

Axel transferred another seedling to its own pot. "I will have one done of my wife, when she's not as preoccupied with an infant." Abigail might want a portrait of her husband, and Axel would indulge her, despite his loathing for inactivity.

Jack shot him an assessing over-the-shoulder glance. "You will pay handsomely for a professional painting. Poor families have no portraiture, unless somebody has an aptitude for sketching. This was an oil, beautifully framed, of a young lady with pearls in her hair."

Six more fledglings to go, roses all. "So Madeline's people had money at one point."

"A great deal of money, and then they lost everything."

"Fanning, you cannot—half the banks in Scotland failed because of the Darien scheme. Many a family has come to grief with bad investments, gambling, intemperate spending. Hattie and Theodosia are nearing their three score and ten. What do the family's circumstances half a century ago matter?"

Sir Jack came marching down the aisle so quickly his passing stirred the foliage on either side of him.

"You don't know when they lost their money. I've been asking about at the Weasel and elsewhere. Both sisters came to this area as a result of matrimony. First Theo, then Hattie, when their parents got wind that Theo's husband was neighbors with a distant Hennessey cousin. The ladies had dowries."

Four more left. "Most families try to set aside a portion for their daughters. What is your point?" For Sir Jack was leading up to some conclusion, some hypothesis that had him more animated than Axel had ever seen him.

"The ladies live one step above dire poverty now," Sir Jack said, peering at the seedlings Axel had planted. "Theo's husband squandered her portion. Hattie, being the younger sister, had less to begin with. She went into service with the McArdle family when she was widowed some twenty years ago, and when Madeline needed work, Hattie vouched for her."

To gather up this kind of detail, Sir Jack had probably spoken with half of Vicar's prayer group, a notably venerable gathering.

"Now comes the part I don't want to hear," Axel said, patting dirt around the roots of a tender little specimen. Not all seedlings survived transplanting, and there was no telling which would fare well and which would wither.

"Hector McArdle's brother, Caleb, made a nuisance of himself to young Madeline. Hattie put a stop to it, and Caleb saw Hattie accused of theft. Hattie lost her post, for which Madeline blames herself. Instead of having a housekeeper's salary plus the rent from the freeholding, Hattie had neither. I gather Hattie was all but supporting Theo by then."

"And so the house of cards came down." Having occasionally served as magistrate, Axel had a nodding acquaintance with the law. As a man who might someday be raising a daughter, he did not much respect the legal treatment of women in England.

The realm had prospered spectacularly under a female sovereign, one who'd disdained to take a spouse, and maintained control over her throne as a result.

How long were the women of England to be punished for the slight Elizabeth had dealt to English manhood?

"Shouldn't you water the transplants?" Sir Jack asked.

Everybody was an amateur botanist. "My hands are dirty, and I'm not done here. You are welcome to wield the watering can, but drown my posies and—"

"Yes, yes. You'll call me out. Reluctantly, of course, but with deadly intent. What are these plants?"

"Roses."

Sir Jack used a light hand, not too much water, not too little. "One arrogant young cock sends three women into penury. If you were one of those women, what would you do, Belmont?"

Axel gave the matter some thought as he transferred the last seedlings.

A life in ruins, all because a man's casual pleasure had been thwarted by a girl with the backbone to reject his unsolicited advances. The topic did not make for happy contemplation.

"I might set a streetwalker upon him who'd give him an incurable disease."

"Remind me not to cross you, Belmont." Jack finished with the watering can and set it on the floor. "You see my point though, don't you?"

Axel saw that in allowing a guest into his glass house, he'd been able to keep working, so the plants had the benefit of sunlight throughout the transplanting process. Grafts were best done at night, while—

"I beg your pardon, Fanning. What is your point?"

"When I took Madeline calling on Theodosia, Mrs. Hickman all but bragged about being able to make a coal delivery last longer than her neighbors could."

"Coal." The same commodity stolen from Hector McArdle's yard. "Not good, Fanning. Old women aren't supposed to lark about, committing crimes by the full moon."

"And Hattie Hennessey has every reason to ameliorate her circumstances by stealing coal from the McArdle family business."

Axel wiped his hands on a rag, though rich, black dirt remained under his fingernails. "Hattie and Theo will benefit from the darts revenue too, and between the two of them, they could easily have moved that money to the church."

Sir Jack paced back to the end of the table, where the white blossom peeked from between lush foliage.

"Both of them keep livestock, Belmont, and they are quite hale. Either of them could have pulled that prank with the darts jar, simply to aggravate Bartholomew Tavis."

The poor of the shire would applaud that notion. Axel rather admired whoever had moved that money too.

"What will you do?" he asked. "You can dismiss the miracle of the darts jar as a prank, but taking coal from Hector McArdle is thievery, plain and simple."

"And I am the king's man," Sir Jack said. "Which is your fault."

Axel used his penknife to clean the fingernails of his left hand. "Squire Rutland had a hand in matters." An incompetent hand, which was how both Axel and Jack Fanning had been press-ganged into taking the job.

"Don't blame a man who had the sense to remove to Bath permanently. As I see it, you are the reason this problem has landed in the middle of my family's visit, so you must help resolve it."

"As I see it, you haven't any evidence with which to make arrests. All you have is supposition and coincidence." Damned convincing though they might be.

"Mrs. Abernathy saw my butler carrying Madeline's boots to the kitchen for a cleaning. She concluded he was stealing these boots, though they are the most disgraceful excuse for footwear I've ever seen. Without even talking to Pahdi or to Madeline, Mrs. Abernathy, as judge, jury, and executioner, expected me to turn Pahdi off without a character on her word alone. You'll cut yourself if you keep that up."

"I will not. You're saying, if these antics don't stop immediately, public opinion will convict two old women of wrongdoing whether you bring charges or not."

"Precisely, and Madeline would never forgive—*I* would not forgive myself, if that happened, which is why you will assist me to resolve the situation before recourse to the law is unavoidable."

"*Ouch*—damn it."

Sir Jack had the sense to remain silent while Axel tucked the penknife away.

CHAPTER NINE

Somebody—or some*thing*—was in the kitchen.

Madeline knew that Teak House had a pantry mouser, a gray tabby more interested in dreaming of mice than snacking on them. Few cats would take on prey larger than a mouse, though, and the rustling down the corridor was larger-than-a-mouse in nature.

She set aside her list of medicinals, despite her reluctance to leave the herbal. The space was cozy, private, and peaceful. The winter moon beamed through the mullioned window, and dried plants and flowers hung from the rafters.

The noise came again, a scrape, a bump... Unlike some households, nobody slept in the Teak House kitchen, except possibly the cat.

Mrs. Abernathy's departure had resulted in a general lightening of household morale, though the tweenie was feuding with the scullery maid, both of whom were enamored of the head stable lad.

He—a young, black-haired behemoth burdened with the name Apollo—was flirting with both girls every chance he got, and a deserted kitchen was an excellent place to flirt on a winter night. Madeline took a last whiff of rosemary—the herb for remembrance—picked up her carrying candle, and blew out the flames in both mirrored sconces.

She made her way down the corridor to the kitchen quietly, but not stealthily. She who had behaved scandalously in the library had no wish to embarrass others in the kitchen.

"Where is the damned butter?" Jack pulled out one drawer after another, then started opening cupboards.

"In the window box."

He ceased his plundering. "I thought you were Pahdi. You're nearly as quiet, though you're more fragrant than he."

"Thank you."

"That was an observation, not a compliment. Belmont passed along his regards when I called upon him this afternoon, by the way. What brings you to the bowels of the house at such a late hour?" Jack was in shirt-sleeves and waistcoat, his cuffs turned back. An ink stain on the heel of his right hand suggested he'd been at his ledgers or his correspondence.

Madeline was in her nightclothes, covered in several layers from neck to ankles, and upon her feet she wore the warmest footwear she had—Jack's house slippers.

"I'm organizing the herbal," she said, fetching the butter. "Mrs. Abernathy neglected the medicinals, and somebody had best set them to rights before illness visits the house. Shall I put together a tray?"

"I'm not hungry," Jack said. "I was tending the fire when a log fell, and the resulting mess gave me a singed knuckle."

Hence, his search for the butter.

"You'd be better off with a cold cloth."

He held up his left hand, which sported a red third knuckle. "You won't kiss my mishap better?"

"I might—if you do as I tell you."

The narrowing of his eyes said he liked that, liked that Madeline would put him in his place.

"Wait here," she said, retrieving a clean towel from the stack on the counter and retreating down the corridor. Outside the back door, Madeline scooped a handful of snow into the towel.

"Use this," she said, passing Jack the towel full of snow. "It will take the heat out more effectively than the butter would, and save the kitchen stores."

He wrapped the towel around his left hand. "Better, of course. Your endless competence never fails to impress me."

"I like you more when you're comparing my scent to the butler's."

"You admit to liking me. I'm flattered. Can you spare me a few minutes of your time?"

Madeline adored that he'd ask her for her time. Jack paid her salary, though Madeline answered to his mother. All of Madeline's minutes were his to command, though if she'd declined his request, he would have obliged her.

And in the past few days, as he'd been riding about the neighborhood in search of thieves and pranksters, Madeline had missed him.

"My task in the herbal is not urgent. Shall we talk in there?"

He gestured with his right hand, and Madeline preceded him down the corridor. The house was quiet, as a well-built edifice would be on a calm winter night.

The herbal was about eight feet square, the dimensions of a dressing closet or linen closet, though it had a sizeable window that faced the back gardens, and a hearth that took up most of one wall.

Jack closed the door, which only made sense on a cold evening. "You have organized this place."

"What good are medicinals if nobody can find them?" Madeline took an armchair by the fire. "What did you wish to discuss?"

Jack propped a hip against the work table. "Not a what, but a who. I've been freezing my ballocks off, dashing all over the shire to ask people about your family's past, and it occurred to me—just as my nose had come to resemble an icicle—that I could simply ask you a few questions."

Madeline scuffed out of her slippers—Jack's slippers—and tucked her feet under her. "Why ask questions about the Hennessey womenfolk?" For that was all that remained of her family. Three women without means, none of whom needed the magistrate asking questions.

"Because you're a puzzle, confound you, and I like solving puzzles." He frowned at the discarded slippers. "I like you."

Liking was... permissible. Madeline had liked every man to whom she'd granted a kiss or a cuddle. That Jack Fanning liked her, and would say so, was still a problem. He was to be her discreet frolic outside the bounds of propriety, her revenge on haphazardly upheld standards of decency.

Her calculated risk. "I like you too."

"Then tell me who you are, Madeline Hennessey. You arrived in this area at the age of fourteen, joined your Aunt Hattie in service at age fifteen. That leaves more than half of your life unaccounted for."

As well it should be. "I had parents, one of each, in the usual fashion. They were fond of each other, and of me, as best I could tell. My father was also fond of gin."

Jack twiddled a sprig of rosemary, the piney scent perfuming the herbal. "Opium by another name."

"For some," Madeline said, trying to ignore how firelight cast Jack's features into planes and shadows. He'd be attractive into old age, drat him. "Papa drank to excess and gambled, and that's a fine way to go on for those who are either titled or blessed with infinite wealth. He was a well-born commoner who lived beyond his means on a good day. When my mother died, he sent me to my aunts, assuring them he'd mail regular sums for my expenses."

"And the regular sums never arrived," Jack said, "while a need for decent boots and the onset of winter are painfully predictable. One can see why you're reluctant to repose your trust in the male of the species."

What was he—?

Well. Madeline considered Jack's reasoning, because in her efforts to earn her wages, look after her aunts, manage presuming footmen, and favor the occasional sore knee, she hadn't made time to reflect much on her upbringing.

Why invite misery? "Papa wasn't a bad man, but he was weak. He ended up in the Marshalsea prison, where he was beloved by all despite his enormous debts. Consumption took him, and that was a mercy. My aunts had nothing good to say about him."

"And yet," Jack said, "he was charming, handsome, witty, well-liked, and he adored your mother and you. You couldn't even resent him very effectively when he broke promise after promise."

Had Jack tossed the cold, wet towel at her, Madeline could not have been more surprised at his observation.

"We worried for him. When Papa was ill from his excesses, when he'd disappear for days at a time, when we found him asleep in the stable, we worried for him."

And now, years later, in a quiet little herbal, Madeline could resent her papa like blazes.

And resent her poor mother, and the stupid English laws that required a woman to cleave to her husband even when he was wrecking the futures of all concerned.

Madeline had been five years old the first time she'd found her papa asleep in the garden before breakfast. Seven when she'd realized nobody worked for them very long. Eight when she'd lost her pony.

"This discussion makes me want to break something," Madeline said. "Something delicate and valuable." The herbal was full of glass jars, crockery, mixing bowls... She clutched her shawl lest her hands find something fragile to hurl against the hearthstones.

Jack rose and knelt before her. "I'm not delicate, and I'm not asking for your trust, except in so far as I'm willing to give you mine."

He kissed her, and that... that helped. Madeline could refocus disproportionate upset over old business onto the new passion of kissing Jack Fanning. He tasted of mint tea, and kneeling as he was, Madeline could wrap her arms around him and control the progress of the kiss.

She needed to be the one to say when teasing escalated to a dare—*taste me back*—and when she opened her knees so Jack could wedge himself between them. She winnowed her hands through his hair and scooted closer, caught in the grip of both physical desire and rampaging emotion.

"Your damned clothes—" Jack muttered, rearranging bunches of fabric.

"Lock the damned door," Madeline shot back, even as she clutched at his shoulders.

Jack sat back, his hair disheveled, his grin diabolical. "You can think at a time like this. Truly, I am in the presence of a formidable woman."

He levered to his feet and crossed the room, while Madeline wallowed in the pleasure of watching him move.

Jack paused at the door. "I want a bed for this."

"I don't. Maids, footmen, your brother, anybody could see us going upstairs."

Miss DeWitt might see them, or Jack's own mother.

Worse, Madeline might lose her nerve somewhere between the cozy understory and the drafty upper floors. Bringing up the past, with all its heartache and betrayal, had set loose in her a determination to have her pleasure of Jack Fanning. If she was given even five minutes to consider the folly of what she contemplated, she might never have that pleasure.

Jack fastened the lock, a quiet click of metal on metal that made Madeline want to shout with triumph.

"We do it your way, then," he said. "This time."

"Enough talk," Madeline retorted, rising from the chair and dragging the curtain across the window. "And you'd better have more than chatter to offer, Jack Fanning, or there won't be a next time."

There ought not to be a next time. There shouldn't be a *this* time either.

"I adore a challenge," Jack said, unbuttoning his waistcoat. "I suspect you do too."

"You'll know soon enough, if you cease prattling and get your falls—"

He was on her in the next instant, his arms around her, his mouth covering hers, and that was exactly, precisely, gloriously where Madeline needed him to be.

* * *

In India, erotic pleasure was a respected and celebrated aspect of married life—and of unmarried life. Jack had sampled as broadly of the local customs as the next bachelor officer, and yet, he'd never come across a woman quite as sure of her objectives as Madeline Hennessey.

She gave him orders—with her hands, with her mouth, and with her body insinuated against his.

Like that.

Again.

Closer.

Madeline set the pace, urgent but not frantic.

She got half the buttons of Jack's falls undone, lest there be any mistaking what all of this privacy was in aid of.

And she towed Jack by his cravat across the room, then scooted up onto the table, occupying the spot where Jack had perched earlier.

Jack heeded her commands willingly—*like that, again, closer*. He adopted the pace she set, and he tucked himself up against her heat when she spread her knees and tugged him within kissing range. He capitulated to Madeline's whims and commands not because she demonstrated great confidence about her desires and how Jack ought to fulfill them.

Just the opposite. Jack suspected—would have bet his best team, in fact—that Madeline Hennessey was a woman desperate to avoid yet another occasion of disappointment.

In her kisses, her caresses, her muttered directions, and restless shifting, Jack sensed bitterness and hope warring for the upper hand, resignation and rejoicing battling for control of the lady's heart.

"Now," she whispered against Jack's mouth. "I want you now. Enough fumbling about, enough teasing—"

Fumbling about?

"Madeline Hennessey, I have not yet begun to tease you."

Fine words, and bravely muttered, but coming from a man who'd spent ten years pretending sexual indifference was *just fine*, those words were balderdash. Jack wanted Madeline Hennessey with the same passionate craving he'd once reserved for his pipe of opium, and that—that honest, terrifying truth—gave him some self-restraint.

He gentled their kiss and stroked a hand over Madeline's hair. "There is no hurry, Madeline. We have all night if you want all night."

She pulled back, her expression wary. "Five minutes ought to suffice."

Hell hath no tragedy like a woman inured to disappointment. "I will swive you until your bum wears that table smooth. I will kiss you until you taste nothing but desire. I will pleasure you until you ache with satisfaction."

Jack spent the next five minutes elaborating on his promises. He began the kissing all over again, but delicately this time, patiently, tenderly. He kissed Madeline as if she were his every dream incarnate, his secret wishes come to life. When she was tucked against his chest, sighing gently, he acquainted her with the delights his hands could wreak on her breasts.

Her nightclothes were unadorned with embroidery or bows, but Jack imbued his caresses with every grace note and flourish he could muster.

And Madeline Hennessey bloomed for him, with as many nuances and hues as the passion flowers Jack had first seen in India. Breath by breath, sigh by sigh, she exchanged desperation for surrender, and hurry for wonder.

"You excel—" she murmured.

"*We* excel."

As the fire burned down in the hearth, Jack built a conflagration. He took eternities to insinuate a hand under Madeline's skirt, and treated himself to every curve and contour of her limbs at a pace intended to aid memorization.

Sturdy, feminine, graceful, strong, warm, interesting—between Madeline's ankle and knee, Jack mentally applied a dozen adjectives to the territory he explored.

New territory, and that occasioned both pride and sorrow. The sorrow was an acknowledgment that the love won in India had been lost there too. The pride was Madeline's gift to him.

Despite herself, despite all the disappointment she'd endured previously, she was trusting Jack now as a lover, if nothing else.

He shifted, so the only place he touched Madeline was the seat of her pleasure. She leaned back, bracing herself on her hands. Her hair had come loose, a cascade of russet curls rioting over her shoulders and down her back.

Madeline rocked minutely into his touch. "When you do that…."

Jack pushed her skirts up, so he could see where he caressed. The candles and firelight didn't illuminate much, but that she'd let him look at her meant worlds.

"When I do this, it makes me want to be inside you," Jack said, illustrating his words with a single finger. "Like that."

"Wicked," Madeline said. "Wickedly lovely."

Jack made it lovelier still, and very, very wicked, though his cock was clamoring to finish what his fingers had started. Madeline allowed the pleasure and let herself find satisfaction when she might have resisted. As Jack let her skirts fall over her knees, and held her panting against his shoulder for a drowsy moment, he realized she might not know how to delay her own gratification.

"I don't want to let you go," Madeline said. "I can't move."

"Good."

Jack finished undoing his falls and took himself in his hand. He used his cock to nudge and tease at Madeline's sex, and at first, she remained passive. Then she began to move, to anticipate Jack's explorations, and reverse the cat and mouse.

Jack dipped, Madeline scooted, and before he'd maneuvered the requisite quantity of self-control into place, they were… joined.

"Yes," Madeline whispered. "Don't just stand there now."

"I need a moment." A moment for the jolt of pleasure to fade to a throb. Madeline was heaven—like coming home, and like waking up in an exotic paradise, both.

"You need—?"

Jack felt comprehension suffuse her—her kiss tasted of smugness.

"Take as long as you like," she said, stroking his bum. "We have all night if you need it."

He'd never last all night. At some point, his shirt had come off, along with his cravat and his waistcoat. Madeline entertained herself by applying her tongue to Jack's nipples, which entirely defeated his efforts to regain his composure.

"Madeline, I'm trying not to disappoint you."

She goddamned wiggled. "You taste like sandalwood and"—more torment, counterclockwise—"fruit, or clove maybe. You're delicious."

I am doomed. "I will not remain like this, all but buried inside you, and discuss my bath soap."

Madeline shimmied, so her robe and chemise fell off her shoulders.

"Madeline Hennessey."

"You can call me Maddie," she said, taking more of him.

Jack had promised himself that Madeline's dictates would determine the details of their joining. She'd set the pace, the tone, the tempo. *Now*, not disappointing her wasn't enough. He needed to please her, to recalibrate her grasp of how much pleasure was possible when two people set about indulging their passion.

A fine plan.

Jack's plan went up in flames as Madeline urged him deeper and locked her ankles at the small of his back. He tried to hold back and managed to send Madeline through the fire once more, but that was the limit of his endurance. When she re-established a tempo, Jack let go.

He wrapped his arms about her, moved in close, and gave her the short, hard strokes that sent pleasure ricocheting through him. Madeline's nails dug into his back, and he gloried in the intensity of the sensation.

She shuddered and gasped and might even have called his name. When Jack was sure he'd done right by his lady, he withdrew, and spilled his seed against her belly.

As they held each other in a loose embrace, breathing in counterpoint, Jack thanked the gods of disporting widowers that he'd been *able* to withdraw—the timing had been a near thing, indeed.

And now came a pleasure Jack had forgotten—the blend of relaxation and invincibility that a good swiving bestowed in its wake. His legs and back burned as if he'd run halfway to London, and yet, his mind was utterly tranquil.

Jack groped about on the table behind Madeline and drew her chemise and robe up over her shoulders, for protectiveness had edged its way onto his emotional agenda along with... humility.

Madeline Hennessey had chosen to take him as her lover, and Jack could only hope he hadn't disappointed her, because he very much—very much—hoped there would be a next time.

Many next times. Preferably in a nice, big, comfortable bed.

* * *

"Managing a household like this would be a challenge for any woman." Mrs. Fanning ran a finger down the length of the family parlor's mantel. "The problem is not the size of the dwelling, of course."

Was she disappointed that not a speck of dust was to be found?

Madeline pretended to focus on her embroidery, a pair of doves cooing amid a leafy bower on the corner of her Sunday handkerchief. Mrs. Fanning would find no soot on the mantel, no andirons that wanted for blacking, no rugs in need of beating, though not for lack of searching on her part.

"I'm sure you'll tell us what the difficulty is," Miss DeWitt said.

Mrs. Fanning paused directly in front of the hearth, blocking some of the light and heat the fire cast in Madeline's direction. The evening was chilly, the wind having picked up as the sun had set.

"My dear Lucy Anne," Mrs. Fanning said, "can you imagine introducing a woman's touch to a household that has not only been deprived of a lady's guiding hand for years, but has also been managed by that foreign fellow Jack seems to treasure so dearly?"

This again.

"Mr. Pahdi seems quite competent." Miss DeWitt held up her cutwork, which was more holes than paper, so diligently had she been snipping away.

"That is the very problem," Mrs. Fanning retorted, smacking her hand on the mantel. "Mr. Patty *seems* competent. Jack will forgive him anything, witness Mrs. Abernathy's unfortunate situation. That's very pretty, Lucy Anne. Can you make another to match it?"

"I can certainly try."

Lucy Anne DeWitt was good at trying, at persisting in the face of obstacles, at dealing constructively with the cards fate handed her. Madeline would have hated her for that, except she respected Lucy Anne, and knew all too well the burden of being an attractive female of marriageable age.

"I think a little variation in a pattern can make the results more interesting," Madeline said, knotting off the gold thread. "Mrs. Abernathy will likely be happier in a new position."

Lucy Anne shot Madeline an incredulous look, for Madeline's observation came close to arguing with Mrs. Fanning.

Which was just too damned bad. Since making love with Jack in the herbal two nights ago, Madeline had become a different person. How blind she'd been—how ignorant. All the men she'd permitted intimacies previously had been bumblers at best, and inconsiderate louts more likely.

When Jack Fanning made love with a woman, she was cherished, pleasured, cosseted, and ruined for anything less than unfailing consideration from her partner.

What a cruel irony that Madeline should learn this lesson from him, whose attentions she ought to have discouraged at every turn.

"Mrs. Abernathy was a fool," Mrs. Fanning sniffed. "Doubtless the butler was stealing, but he's the head of the domestic staff and has Jack's loyalty. Only a daft woman risks confrontation under such situations."

Madeline tucked her hoop back into her workbox and closed the lid.

Mrs. Abernathy had been a bigot, a martinet, lazy, and unkind. And yet, she'd thought she was calling her employer's attention to wrongdoing, much as Aunt Hattie had. When a man spoke the truth, he was credited with integrity and courage. When a woman spoke the truth…

"Oh, piffle!" Miss DeWitt set aside the tiny scissors she'd been using to fashion her creations. "I'm so clumsy." She tucked the pad of her index finger against her lips. "One wants the scissors to be sharp, but then one fails to exercise adequate care."

Madeline passed her a scrap of cloth from her workbox. "I've done the same thing countless times. Wrap it snugly, and the bleeding will soon stop." Madeline's mishaps had been with kitchen knives, not parlor scissors.

"The woman who takes this house in hand will have a great challenge before her," Mrs. Fanning said, resting a hand on the mantel as if starting over on a scene at a theatrical rehearsal. "Jack must be made to see that his bachelor ways no longer serve him. He should be entertaining, riding out to the local meets, spending the Season in London, and donating to the Oxford charities. The lady of the house will have to guide him in these undertakings without being seen to influence his choices."

Lucy Anne's cutwork lay in her lap, a spot of blood marring the white paper she'd been snipping at.

No help from that quarter, but then, Lucy Anne was shrewd.

"Why not simply explain to your son that he's neglecting the responsibilities of his station?" Madeline asked.

She respected Jack for choosing the magistrate's responsibilities over weeks of waltzing in London. She understood why a soldier who'd seen too much violence would eschew fox hunting, and she grasped why lavish meals intended to impress the local gentry would hold no appeal for Jack.

Jack Fanning was not a boy, not a lordling playing at life. He was a man who'd spent months with death as his cellmate, and he need not impress anybody by appeasing appearances.

"Do you think I haven't tried to show Jack the error of his ways, Miss Hennessey?" On an indignant swish of skirts, Mrs. Fanning took the place on the sofa beside Lucy Anne. "He's as stubborn as his father. Thank God for Jeremy, who has become my sole comfort, despite his unimpressive demeanor."

Madeline leaned across the low table, plucked Lucy Anne's ruined attempt from her lap, and pitched it into the fire.

"I enjoy Reverend Fanning's company very much," Madeline said. "He is cheerful, kind, honest, and a credit to you in every way, Mrs. Fanning." Also a very attractive man, who like Jack, had not a vain bone in his body.

"I quite agree," Lucy Anne said, examining her injured finger. "You have two fine sons, Mrs. Fanning. Very different, but both remarkable gentlemen."

Lucy Anne shot Madeline a glance from beneath lowered lashes. *Let the old besom argue with that*, her expression seemed to say.

Madeline winked at her, while Mrs. Fanning marched off to the escritoire by the window. "I have tried so hard with those boys, and what thanks do I get? Jeremy can't be bothered to curry favor with the bishop. Jack insists on keeping relics of his Indian adventures under my very nose. It's endlessly trying, if you must know. A mother has hopes, and can endure only so much."

Jack and Jeremy were sons to be proud of. Each man, in his way, was making a meaningful contribution to society, while Mrs. Fanning...

Mrs. Fanning was what every young woman should aspire to be. Well-provided-for, socially secure, respected by her family... also bored to tears, lonely, and meddlesome as a result.

"I hate to add to your burdens," Madeline said, "but Mrs. Abernathy's decision to leave her post has created a problem that ought not to be overlooked, one I'm sure neither Sir Jack nor Pahdi can address."

Mrs. Abernathy had *chosen* to leave her post, a point Madeline wanted to emphasize.

"I will never deny my boys what aid I can give them," Mrs. Fanning said, gazing out into the night. "Ungrateful though they might be."

Nagged though they might be.

"The herbal was in disarray," Madeline said, "and I've organized it as best I can, but I have no store of recipes for tisanes, poultices, or decoctions. Mrs. Abernathy either took them with her, or relied exclusively on memory and the efforts of the staff."

"That's not good," Lucy Anne said. "My mama has a book—a whole shelf of books—for home remedies, stain removers, cleaning mixtures, and so forth. If somebody should fall ill..."

"Precisely," Madeline said. "Then it will be too late to assemble the knowledge that should be guarded in any household, but so often isn't."

Mrs. Fanning perched on the gilt chair at the escritoire. "You've looked about for the simples and tisanes and found nothing?"

"I've looked. I've asked Cook and Pahdi, and they refer me to the stable master, who has excellent recipes for liniments."

"Horse liniment won't aid a putrid sore throat." Lucy Anne had begun another creation, using the tiny scissors on a round of paper.

"That it will not," Mrs. Fanning said, taking a sheet of foolscap from a drawer. "We must make a list, ladies. The health of the household is imperiled, and it's up to us to repair the oversight."

For another hour, while Lucy Anne littered paper trimmings all over the carpet, and Madeline painstakingly added flowers to her doves' bower, Mrs. Fanning made her list.

The evening tea tray with biscuits arrived at ten of the clock, and the footman tarried long enough to build up the fire. All was snug and cozy, and Mrs. Fanning was gleefully absorbed in her task.

Madeline took a moment to appreciate the sheer luxury she enjoyed on a cold winter night.

Not far away, her aunts were likely shivering and hungry in their beds. How did a woman who had neither Mrs. Fanning's security of station, nor Lucy Anne's determination to find a good match, save two lonely old women from a fate they'd done nothing to deserve?

CHAPTER TEN

"Forgive the interruption, most esteemed sir," Pahdi said with a bow. "I must report an irregular occurrence."

Jack put aside his pen, because Pahdi determined on a report would not be deterred, and an afternoon with the Teak House ledgers had left Jack irritable.

"Out with it. If Apollo has got the tweenie with child, you needn't pretty it up. They'll be married by St. David's Day, if I have to have Jeremy perform the service at gunpoint."

Pahdi lifted the lid of the teapot growing cold at Jack's elbow. "I do not pretend to fathom the subtleties of courting among the sophisticated Englishmen whom it is my honor to serve, but what purpose does a firearm serve at a celebration of nuptial love?"

"I spoke figuratively. I would inspire Apollo to a responsible attitude toward his offspring by any means necessary."

"Of course. Inspiration about parental duties is ever wise, and in a tangential fashion, it's about that very topic upon which I must report."

Pahdi had been a youth when Jack had come home to England, but the late-afternoon light slanting through the windows showed him to be a man in his prime—a damned good-looking man.

What did he do for female companionship, or was his friendship with James his sole source of affection? Why, in ten years, had Jack never pondered this mystery about the person he'd known longest among his staff, somebody was family to him by marriage?

"Say your piece," Jack replied, rising from his cushions. That Pahdi would make this report in the privacy of Jack's chambers suggested the matter was delicate.

"I am the butler of Teak House," Pahdi said, setting the tea tray on the sideboard. "The security of the premises and its people are my first concerns, because worrying about the owner of this handsome establishment is a cause lost to all sentient beings."

"Your ability to deliver a sermon is entirely wasted outside the church."

"In your unending generosity, you have conveyed that sentiment to me previously." Pahdi took a spill from the jar on the mantel, used the fire in the hearth to light it, and lit the wall sconces one by one. "The matter I must bring to your attention concerns the morale and conduct of the household, and yet at least one of the parties involved does not answer to me. Your guidance is therefore required, lest I misstep in my ignorance of—"

"I will petition the crown to add circumlocution to the already impressive list of felonies under English law."

"Several nights ago I was making my final tour of the premises before seeking my bed," Pahdi said, tossing the burning taper into the fireplace. "Every night, I secure each lock and walk each floor with an eye toward an unlatched window, a candle set too close to the holiday greenery."

Everything Pahdi did, he did quietly, and yet, trouble lurked at the end of the recitation as obviously as a lovesick elephant called to his mate.

"My gratitude for your vigilance is without limit. I don't tell you that often enough."

Pahdi's glance was fleeting and disapproving. His notions of proper English behavior could fill a book, most of it based on Jack's disappointing example.

"I perform duties for which I am generously compensated. My nightly inspection finishes up below stairs. I ensure the pantries are locked, the main kitchen fire banked, and that all is secure. The herbal is typically left unlocked, however, because anybody can wake with a need for a cup of chamomile tea, or a ginger tisane to settle the belly."

Well, damn.

"Has somebody plundered the stores in the herbal?" Jack's wits had been plundered there. Thoroughly, generously, repeatedly.

"Are you aware that Miss Hennessey took it upon herself to organize the herbal after the departure of that disgrace to domestic service whom it was your great misfortune to employ as a housekeeper?"

Pahdi was a gentleman. That he'd refer to Mrs. Abernathy so disparagingly was proof that the situation had been worse than Jack knew.

"My mother has decided to take up where Miss Hennessey left off," Jack said. "She's writing a recipe book for the herbal, which is a complete waste of time. Axel Belmont is among the most learned botanical authorities in the realm, and I need only—"

Pahdi gave him another disapproving look, though the butler had an entire arsenal of sighs, silences, and glances intended to reprove without a word.

"What?" Jack said, for this reproach included a hint of exasperation.

"Your mother will know remedies of which the learned and much-respected Mr. Belmont will have never heard."

Possibly true. Mama's memory was prodigious. "Then I'm glad she's decided to memorialize her knowledge."

"I was doubtless a robber of temples in a past life; a despoiler of shy, pious virgins; a sorrow to my mother and her mother too, for your response tempts me to imprudent speech."

"And in the next life, you will be butler to Old Scratch if you don't get 'round to your point."

"Old—?"

"You will be a butler in hell," Jack said. "Shy, pious Anglican fellow that you are."

"Those who disrespect their mothers can look forward to emptying chamber pots during cholera epidemics in many subsequent lives. My own sainted father assured me of this, and he would not lie to his beloved son."

"Pahdi, *what is the problem*? I'm the magistrate, you'll recall, and the essence of that dubious honor is that I solve problems, such as the law allows."

Pahdi picked up the quilt at the foot of Jack's bed and refolded it so the edges matched exactly.

"I have reason to believe somebody was making in appropriate use of the privacy afforded by the herbal several nights ago. Miss Hennessey had been working in there, and thus the fire was lit. I included the herbal on my final inspection as a result. The door was locked, so the identities of the happy couple remain unknown to me, and while my personal opinion is of no moment whatsoever, Mrs. Fanning would likely frown on copulation among the medicinals."

Mama would have eighteen varieties of hysterics. Thank God that Madeline had reminded Jack to lock the door.

"You have no idea who might have been enjoying themselves at such an hour of the night?"

Pahdi rarely made eye contact with his social superiors, and yet, he missed nothing. Jack admired the red brilliance of the sun setting beyond the window rather than meet Pahdi's gaze.

"I have no idea, honored sir, who would so disrespect your household with such goings-on."

"If you did know," Jack said, rearranging the tassel holding the curtain back, "what would you tell the wayward couple?"

Pahdi *knew*. He knew very well who'd been behind that locked door, and he'd taken several days to consider how he'd raise the matter with the male half of that couple.

"The couple is not wayward," Pahdi said. "The fellow involved is the wayward party. First, he does not bother to pleasure his lady in one of the many beds in this fine house, or even to favor her with a bed of fragrant hay in a private corner of the stable. Second, he avails himself of the lady's charms at an hour when the servants are not all abed, thus jeopardizing her good name among the help. Third, there being no married men on this property, the fellow is in a position to offer the lady the protection of his name, but he instead plucks for himself the momentary pleasure of a blossom that ought to be cultivated as the rarest of blooms —"

This was the sermon Jack had been flagellating himself through long, sleepless nights. The pleasure of making love with Madeline Hennessey had been remarkable, like visiting a scene from memory and finding it even lovelier than he'd recalled.

But the guilt... Jack had forgotten the corrosive, half-acknowledged abrasion of guilt that scraped the chains of conscience across even beautiful memories when a man strayed from the rules. A young man could drink, fight, or march that guilt away.

A mature man dealt in honesty. "She doesn't want me, Pahdi."

"Then you are to be severely condemned," Pahdi said, taking a stray tea cup from the desk and adding it to the tray. "A woman's willingness is hers alone to give. You taught me that."

"She was willing," Jack said. "She was ferociously willing—insistent, even—but my hand in marriage was not her objective."

And that was... bewildering, annoying, baffling. For the first time in Jack's life, he grasped the frustration women experienced unrelentingly. They waited for a man to propose, waited for him to tire of the charms of foreign shores, waited for him to take an interest in his own children, waited for him to decide on which night he'd pay a call to their bedroom.

How did the ladies endure such powerlessness? The notion that a fellow was worth waiting for paled compared to the actual experience of being... disregarded.

Marrying Madeline Hennessey would be problematic, but that Jack was prohibited from even considering the idea bothered him. He—the knighted hero of Parrakan, master of the house, the king's man, and all-around decent-if-charmless fellow—wasn't worth marrying.

"The lady does not regard you as a suitable party?" Pahdi asked, oh so carefully.

"Apparently not."

"Why?"

"Because I've allowed an impertinent rascal the position of butler."

The joke fell flat. Pahdi's expression shuttered. He bowed and lifted the tray.

"Pahdi, Madeline defends you at every turn. She's the last woman who'd take exception to my choice of butler. The problem is me."

Pahdi set the tray back down. "She is a wise woman, for you are a problem, if I might speak honestly without risking durance vile."

Thank God, Pahdi always managed to speak honestly—in his way. "If you have wisdom to share, you must not withhold it."

"The lady does not regard you as a suitable party. You must change her mind. Did Saras teach you nothing?"

Saras had taught Jack a great deal, some of it involving feathers, potions, toys…. "She taught me to listen to her brother, when that worthy deigns to speak in something clearer than Delphic mutterings."

"You have great wealth. Bah, many have wealth. You have a knighthood. Your Regent has created hundreds of knights. Why should Miss Hennessey look with favor on your suit?"

Jack sat on the windowsill, putting cold air at his back, the better to force the gears of his mind to turn.

"Because being my wife should be preferable for Madeline to a life of stepping and fetching, waiting on others, and doing as she's told."

"Should it? Should it really? The uncompensated and unending joys of matrimony, with the attendant risk of death in childbed, the surrender of all of a woman's possessions to her husband, the loss of a right to spend even her own wages or hire her own servants, is preferable to earning a salary and the occasional half-day off in service?"

The questions were rhetorical and maddening as hell. "Or course marriage is preferable to service." If the woman married a good fellow.

A very good fellow. A rarity among fellows. A damned saint with a fortune to spare.

Maybe. Childbirth killed women every day, and it was an awful death.

Pahdi cast forth a sigh that would have done God proud on the occasion of Adam and Eve dooming humanity to life outside the garden.

"I leave you to reflect on your faultless convictions," Pahdi said, bowing, then taking up the tray.

He closed the door quietly—a trick, that, when a heavy tray had to be balanced—and Jack made himself count to ten before he snatched the nearest pillow from the bed and hurled it against the wall.

* * *

"Excuse me, Pahdi," Madeline said. "I'm looking for Sir Jack."

The butler held a silver tea tray, which had to be heavy. Though he was a slight fellow, the weight didn't seem to burden him.

"Sir Jack has sought the privacy of his chambers to review ledgers, Miss Hennessey. If you like, I can send a footman—"

"No need," Madeline said. "I'll find him myself."

Pahdi's expression never wavered. In his eyes, Madeline saw unspoken warning nonetheless.

"I know," she said. "Nobody disturbs the brave knight when he's polishing his sword, or whatever he gets up to of an idle afternoon, but this is urgent."

She patted Pahdi's arm and marched off, though she'd managed to surprise the unflappable butler, and that was a small satisfaction.

Madeline rapped three times on Jack's door in the exact rhythm Pahdi typically used, and she was bid enter.

"If you must flagellate me again so soon, at least have—oh, it's you."

Not a cheerful realization, apparently. "You were expecting somebody to beat you?"

Madeline had heard of such goings-on. The Candlewick library had a number of texts that depicted exotic sexual practices in detail. Dusting the books had not allowed for more than the occasional, furtive peek, much to Madeline's frustration.

"I was expecting more torment from my butler," Jack said, picking up a cushion from the floor and tossing it onto the bed. "Come in."

He wore a robe, pajama pants, and nothing else. His feet were bare, and behind him was a large four-poster bed. No hangings hid the bed from view or distracted from the soft expanse where Jack slept nightly.

The scent of the room was exotic—not the soothing sandalwood of the library, but more complex fragrances, as if incense was often burned here. Stepping into this room was to cross a cultural threshold as well as a physical one, and to leave Madeline in the position of the foreigner.

"Perhaps your butler would be happier in India," Madeline said.

The furnishings were unusual. The bed was carved teak. A folding screen in the corner had been painted to depict tigers amid lush foliage. A brilliant peacock-feather fan was displayed over the clothes press, and the desk—more teak—was so low, the floor was the only possible seat from which to work.

Perhaps *Jack* would be happier in India?

"My mother would delight to see Pahdi repatriated to his homeland," Jack said. "I hadn't thought you shared her prejudices."

Madeline did not have time to fence with the man who'd occupied her waking and sleeping thoughts for three days.

"Your mother is jealous of your butler," Madeline said. "He has more of your time and your regard than she does. I hope I am not prejudiced where Pahdi is concerned, but I didn't come here to discuss your mother's loneliness."

For Madeline to be in this room alone with Jack was scandal waiting to happen—again.

Jack unknotted his robe and opened the wardrobe, another massive teak creation. "I could ask you to step out and receive me fifteen minutes hence in the family parlor, but that strikes me as ridiculous. What can I do for you?"

They hadn't exactly avoided each other in the past few days, but Jack had been busy trying to track down the darts thief and the coal thief. Madeline wasn't sure he intended to prosecute either miscreant, and hoped she'd never find out.

"My Aunt Theodosia is ill. One of the Candlewick maids stopped in to visit her on the way to the village, and found Theo battling a lung fever."

"I hate lung fever," Jack said, tossing his robe onto a hook inside the wardrobe. "I hate anything that smacks of illness and suffering. You aren't thinking of risking contagion by going to her yourself?"

That's exactly what Madeline had been thinking, but when she would have replied to that effect, Jack plucked a shirt from his wardrobe.

In so doing, he turned enough that his back was visible, a part of him Madeline had never seen. She'd touched the scars writhing across his flesh. The marks were old, pale, and far too numerous.

"You don't want your mother to know," Madeline said.

Jack pulled the shirt over his head. "I beg your pardon?"

"You don't want your mother to know how close she came to losing you in India, and so you keep a distance. The distance hurts her."

"The distance protects her too, as you must remain protected from your aunt's illness. I'll send a note around to Dr. Higgans. He can have a look and let you know how your aunt fares."

"You will do no such thing," Madeline said, stalking up to Jack. "Higgans won't bestir himself to see to a sick old woman until his every other patient is in the pink of health. Theo can't pay him, and he'll say she's too elderly and nothing can be done. That's exactly what he said when she fell ill two years ago."

Madeline saw in Jack's eyes that he wanted to argue—to *reason* with her, in male parlance.

"I will go to her without your blighted *permission*, Jack Fanning, and you can call it breach of contract and toss me out into the snow."

"Madeline, I would never—"

"But you'll consign an old woman to suffering alone? She'll try to feed her chickens, Jack, in this miserable cold. She'll worry over those damned dogs, and neglect herself, assuming she can get out of bed at all. She'll cough herself to death because nobody could spare her a toddy or find warm stockings for her feet. Bedamned to you if that's your idea of Christian charity."

Jack brandished a handkerchief, which made no sense.

"Your cheek," he said, touching his own face. "You've tears…"

She snatched the handkerchief from him. "Thank you. I'll likely miss supper, and don't expect me back tomorrow. I'll make my excuses to your mother if I return, and I'm sure the Belmonts will retrieve my things if I'm not welcome back."

"I'm sending a note to Higgans," Jack said.

He was a decent, honorable Englishman, and protecting the women of his household was his duty. Sending for the doctor was generous—Jack would see that Higgans was paid—also pointless.

"My aunts are all I have. You can't stop me from going to Theo now."

He took the handkerchief from Madeline, and when she expected him to toss it aside, he instead dabbed gently at her cheeks.

"Meet me downstairs in a quarter hour. We'll need the medicinals, clean sheets, a basket of provisions, and some spirits. If you must charge unarmed at dragons ten times your size, at least ride into battle with a trusty squire at your side."

Jack wasn't a willing squire—she had no delusions about that—but in this instance, he was *her* squire, and she very much needed the aid.

Madeline pitched into him, reveling in the succor of his embrace. "Thank you. Thank you, Jack."

"Thank me when Theodosia has been returned to good health, and your own well-being hasn't been imperiled."

Madeline held on to him for another long moment, because that feeling—of riding into battle unarmed, against dragons ten times her size—was all too familiar.

The privilege of having a trusty squire at her side was all too rare.

* * *

Jack clucked to the horse the instant Pahdi set the bag of provisions beside Madeline on the bench of the sleigh. The evening air was brutally cold, and Madeline's silence conveyed loads of worry.

While Jack's emotions veered close to anger.

Saras had been as stubborn as Madeline, unwilling to leave Jack's side as he'd thrashed his way through days and nights of fever and nightmares. He'd had three weeks to gradually mend and regain his strength, and then she'd fallen ill.

Idiot woman. Dear, precious, unique, bold, lovely, *dead,* idiot woman. And then Jack's temper lurched toward sorrow because he missed his late wife, though the missing at some point had become more nostalgic than bereft.

When had that happened?

"Does Pahdi want to return to India?" Madeline asked.

Jack could feel her shivering in her plain cloak. He switched the reins to one hand, pulled the lap robe up to her shoulders, and wrapped an arm about her.

"If you catch your death, I will haunt you through your next seven lives."

She tucked in close. "If you catch yours, I will never forgive myself."

"Yes, you will," Jack said. "It might take ten years, but you will. I've never asked Pahdi if he'd like to return to India. He has family there and writes to them regularly."

Jack still had a few friends in India as well, such as old military associations qualified as friendships.

"If you don't ask him what his preferences are, he'll never tell you," Madeline said.

"Pahdi can be blazingly articulate when he's of a mind to be. I honestly don't think he'd leave James."

Good God, the night was arctic. Jack urged the horse to a canter, because the sooner they were out of the frigid air, the better.

"Pahdi won't leave you," Madeline retorted. "People in service are loyal to their employers in the misguided hope the loyalty will be reciprocated. For the employer, the transaction involves coin, room, and board, for services rendered. Loyalty from a domestic is our way of insisting that we're not slaves for a wage."

Jack let that provocative insult remain unchallenged. Madeline was terrified for her aunt, and she spoke from bitter experience.

"I sent a note to Higgans," Jack said. "I expect he'll come by this evening or tomorrow morning."

"Thank you."

They didn't speak again until the sleigh pulled up in Theodosia's yard. Barking started up within the cottage. No candles glowed in the windows, and Jack could detect no scent of smoke on the night air.

"See to the horse," Madeline said, leaping to the ground and grabbing the bag from the seat.

"The horse can stand for a moment," Jack said, but in this cold, only for a moment. "Let's unload the supplies first."

Madeline was already halfway to the door. Jack followed, carrying blankets and what felt like a bag of coal. No paths had been shoveled across the snowy yard. No chickens perched on the fence boards.

Madeline rapped on the door, then pushed it open.

The stench hit Jack before he'd crossed the threshold. Confined dogs, sickness, boiled cabbage, and despair. The fire in the hearth was down to coals, giving off only meager light. Heat would doubtless intensify the stink, but Jack could see his breath clouding before him in the front room.

"Aunt Theo!" Madeline called over the barking and whining of the dogs. "Aunt?"

The puppies and their mother occupied a boarded-off corner of the front room, and from the stink, they'd been there for some time.

"Tend to the fire," Jack said, setting the blankets on the kitchen table. "I'll see to Theodosia."

See if she was still alive, which required lighting the tallow candle before Jack could make out anything in the bedroom.

Theo lay curled in a box bed, nothing but her face peeking out from the covers. A nightcap covered her hair, and though she was a tall woman, illness had made her small and frail.

"Theodosia," Jack said, sitting on the bed.

Madeline stood in the doorway, still in her cloak and scarf.

"Theodosia, wake up." He gently shook her shoulder. "Theodosia Hickman, you've company. Your Madeline has come to call, and she's upset to find you abed at such an hour." Theo very likely sought her bed as soon as the sun went down, to conserve candles and coal, if nothing else.

"Maddie?"

"She's brought beef tea," Jack said. "You will swallow every drop."

"Martha."

"Martha may have some as well."

"Her hound," Madeline said, from the end of the bed. "We'll look after Martha, and the chickens, and you, Aunt Theo." She spread an extra blanket over her aunt, a thick wool afghan brought from Teak House.

"My feet," Theo said. "So cold."

"I'll heat some bricks." Madeline patted her aunt's shoulder and whisked off again.

"I've horses to see to," Jack said. "You are not to run off, Theo Hickman. Be good for your Maddie, or you'll get the sharp edge of my tongue and hers too."

Jack left the bedroom door open and found Madeline adding coal to the meager glow in the hearth. The fireplace hadn't been swept clean in some time, and the bed of ash was probably the only reason the coals still held some heat.

Had the fire gone out...

"I'll put up the horses," Jack said. "I'd get some beef tea into her as soon as you can. It should still be warm, as many towels as Cook wrapped it in. The dogs have to go. This stench is intolerable."

Madeline rose, the wrought-iron poker in her hands. "Theo loves these dogs. The puppies are worth money, and they belong to her. You can't just toss them in the river because we've hit a bad patch."

Jack set both hands on Madeline's shoulders. "I meant, I will remove them to the byre, where the sheep and goats give off some warmth. The bitch is doubtless famished too. If there's enough beef tea, give the hound a serving."

Besides, the river was frozen solid, much like Jack's toes, nose, ears, and chin.

He kissed Madeline's forehead, risked a quick hug, and then forced himself back out into cold and darkness.

* * *

Madeline was numb, though the numbness was born of fatigue rather than cold.

Theo's cottage was snug, the dogs ensconced in the byre. A pot of soup steamed on the pot swing, and late-morning sun streamed through the windows.

The doctor had not come, of course. Madeline hadn't expected him to, though Jack clearly had. Theo's cough had quieted with regular applications of whisky toddies, though low fevers had come and gone throughout the night.

Jack had come and gone too. He'd dealt with the chickens, sheep, goats, and the dogs; brought in a quantity of wood for the wood box; then taken the sleigh back to Teak House. Around midnight, he'd returned with more coal; food for canines, livestock, and people alike; incense to chase the stink of dog away; three books; a change of clothing for Madeline; and several pairs of thick wool socks.

Through the rest of the night, he'd taken turns with Madeline sitting with Theo, and dozing in the front room. At first light, he'd left again, promising to return before noon.

"Maddie?"

"Coming, Aunt." Madeline pushed up from her chair before the hearth, hips and knees protesting mightily. Being a housemaid was particularly hard on the joints, and cold and fatigue didn't help.

"You are here," Theo said, pushing herself to a sitting position. "I wasn't sure if I was dreaming or awake. Very odd to dream about being snug and warm when you're not, though. I don't hear the puppies."

"Jack moved them to the byre—Sir Jack," Madeline said. "He also brought kitchen scraps for Martha, milk porridge for the puppies, and corn for the chickens. We owe him much, Aunt."

Theo plucked at the covers, most of which had been brought over from Teak House.

"He was here too," Theo said. "I remember that."

Madeline would never forget how it had felt to have Jack's company throughout a long night. "Would you like some porridge? We haves honey and even cinnamon, and milk to go with it. I had some earlier."

Sometime in the night, Jack had set the oats soaking so a hot breakfast had been a possibility. Madeline had been too preoccupied to think of breakfast, but oh, that first meal of the day had been sublime.

Also solitary.

"Cinnamon... Sir Jack is a man of parts, Madeline. You did well to join his household."

Madeline pushed back the drapes, for the fire had had hours to chase the chill from the cottage. "How do you feel, Aunt?"

"Old, grateful, worried about you. You do know I'm going to die, Madeline?"

Madeline kept her back to her aunt. "Must you?" This announcement had begun to find its way into conversations two years ago, when Theo had last fallen ill.

"You'll die too," Theo went on. "I notice your own demise doesn't particularly concern you." She coughed delicately, though Madeline suspected the cough was at least partly manufactured.

The interrogation and exhortation would go on until spring if Madeline allowed that. "Aunt, I have feelings for him. I don't know what to do."

Jack had known what to do, and he'd not made a fuss about it either. Madeline had emerged from a round of spooning beef tea into her aunt to find Jack on his knees scrubbing the corner of the cottage where the dogs had been penned.

Like a housemaid, but with more muscle and determination. Madeline had been so upset at the sight she'd nearly run from the cottage.

She'd had flowery speeches and flattering toasts from men of lesser station. She'd had promises and even a stray proposal or two. She'd seen men on their knees spouting ridiculous poetry, but she'd never thought to see a man—much less a knight of the realm—on his knees beside a bucket with a scrub brush in his hands.

She had wanted to cry, but had instead reminded him that the walls could hold the stink as much as the floor could.

He'd scrubbed the walls too.

On the counter sat oranges, bread, butter, jam, the three books, Madeline's work basket, a tin of black tea, and a sack containing a loaf of sugar. The window box held butter, milk, and cheese.

Madeline wanted to cry all over again. "Pity the poor dragon, attacked by a knight who has Jack Fanning for her squire."

"Don't mutter, dear. Do I hear horses?"

Yes, thank God. "Jack's returned, and he has somebody with him."

"Not that dreadful Ralph Higgans, I hope. That man couldn't quack a healthy piglet."

"A woman," Madeline said, leaving the window. "You'll not talk of dying before company, Theodosia Hickman." Madeline might start to cry again, and she'd already endured that mortification twice with Jack Fanning as a witness.

"I'm old and sick," Theodosia said. "I can say whatever I please, and I say you could do a lot worse than Jack Fanning."

"You are old and scandalous."

Madeline did a creditable flounce from the bedroom, but came to an abrupt halt in the kitchen as Florentia Fanning entered the cottage, Jack at her heels.

"Oranges are all well and good, but lemons quiet a cough much more effectively," she was saying. "A bit of lemon juice with honey and whisky, heated to steaming with a dash of cinnamon and nutmeg. Miss Hennessey, you poor thing. You look a wreck. How you must be worrying for your dear aunt. You did the right thing to send for me. I know Jack must have protested awfully, but I'm here now despite Jack's grumbling, and all will be well."

CHAPTER ELEVEN

Jack had overseen many a troop movement in India, and transferring Theodosia Hickman to Teak House required the same skills—patience and a talent for heavy lifting. The traveling coach had been pressed into service for Mama, Theodosia, Martha and the pups, while a quantity of clothing and personal effects had been packed into the boot. Jack and Madeline had remained behind, tidying up the provisions brought over from Teak House, making the bed, and banking the fire.

"I'll establish one of the grooms here temporarily," Jack said, "and if Theo's recovery is prolonged, I'll find a tenant's son ready to try his hand at running a smallholding."

Madeline was moving slowly, wrapping up perishables, organizing staples in the cupboards.

"Theo's recovery might be… she might not recover entirely," Madeline said. "When your mother departs for London, I might have to move in with my aunt."

And Jack might lose his temper in the next instant. "Your aunts need the coin you earn in service." Though Madeline had a point as well. Theo had been barely keeping up, clearly putting off tasks that mattered—scrubbing the water trough, mucking out the byre, periodically draining and cleaning the cistern, among others.

One good spring storm, and Jack suspected the roof would start leaking, which spelled doom for a small, elderly domicile.

"I like my position at Candlewick, but selfishness on my part won't solve what's amiss here, Jack."

Coin would solve what was amiss, but instinct warned Jack not to point out the obvious. He had coin, and the Hennessey females had enough pride to tell him to keep every penny of it.

"Vicar Weekes needs a puppy," Jack said. "The pups are certainly old enough to leave their mother."

Madeline closed the cupboard and eyed Jack as if he'd spoken in Urdu. "Vicar Weekes, who's seldom seen outside his study or the church, needs a puppy?"

"Certainly. Mrs. Weekes is occasionally alone at night when her husband must comfort a family dealing with illness or the death of a loved one. A dog provides both company and safety, and those pups will be enormous."

They'd eat enormous amounts too, and Theo had barely been feeding herself.

"I'm sure you must be right," Madeline said. "But I'm tired and out of sorts. I've never known Vicar to have a pet."

She was asleep on her feet, while Jack felt the roiling energy he associated with anticipation of a battle. For Madeline to move to this mean, tiny cottage would be wrong, and for Jack to tell her what she must do or not do would be wrong as well.

Also stupid.

"If you're through here," Jack said, putting the tin of tea in the cupboard, "then I'll take you back to Teak House."

Jack stood immediately beside Madeline, close enough to see the fatigue leaving shadows beneath her eyes. Her hair had been tidily pinned earlier in the day, but beating rugs, remaking the bed, and dusting every inch of the cottage had imperiled her coiffure.

This was what love looked like—tired, anxious, disheveled, but willing to soldier on indefinitely.

Jack tugged loose a pin threatening to abandon her coiffure entirely and handed it to her. "I sent Higgans a note last evening before we set off."

"I know."

"I had a note delivered to Hattie this morning, alerting her to the situation as well. You haven't received a reply from Higgans, have you?"

"He'd reply to you, wouldn't he?"

Jack turned Madeline by the shoulders and drew her into his embrace. "I signed the note with your initials: *Aunt Theo quite ill. Please come.* I didn't want to explain why a neighbor three miles distant from this cottage would be notifying the physician, and we were in a hurry."

Madeline rested against him, which helped quell the anger building inside Jack.

"I never expected him to come, Jack. The last time Aunt was ill, it took us three months to pay Higgans' fee, and all he did was glance at her and suggest we send for the surgeon to bleed her."

Nowhere in this cottage could two people sit side by side except on the freshly made bed, so Jack remained in the front room, arms around Madeline.

"I am the king's man, and Higgans's cavalier disregard for a helpless old woman should be a crime. I can do nothing to hold him accountable though." The groom who'd delivered last night's note to Higgans had assured Jack that the doctor had been home preparing to sit down to a hot, hearty supper.

Madeline slipped from Jack's embrace. "This is when Vicar would tell you to leave Higgans's fate in God's hands."

"Vicar Weekes's living is generous, his manse snug, and his duties congenial. When Mrs. Weekes is ill, Higgans will come at a smart pace. I like Weekes generally, but he's lazy, and in this case, his guidance is ridiculous."

Ah, finally. A small, tired smile. Madeline kissed Jack's cheek and surveyed the cottage. "Weekes is lazy, but not mean, and you are fierce. I've done what I can here. If you'd take me back to Teak House, I'd appreciate it."

The emergency of Theodosia's illness had passed, and for Jack to be alone with Madeline under these circumstances—no family under the same roof, no servants hovering, no exigent circumstances—was courting scandal.

Jack would rather court *her*.

Life was just full of frustrations lately. Take, for example, the positive loathing Jack had developed for Madeline's cloak and boots, about which he could also do little.

"The damned darts tournament is tonight," Jack said when he'd assisted Madeline into the sleigh and turned the horses onto the lane. "Will you attend?"

"Of course not."

"Half of Belmont's staff will be on hand to cheer their team along. Your presence wouldn't be unusual." His request came not from any male need for her to admire his prowess at the dartboard—if any prowess he still had, after the past twenty-four hours—but rather, from a need for Madeline to put down her burdens for a few hours and cast off her responsibilities.

Madeline twitched at the lap robe and pulled up the collar of her worn cloak.

"You told your mother that I begged for her to attend Aunt Theo, and made it sound as if you loathed the idea. Why?"

Even tired, Madeline would not have neglected to explore this topic. "Mama might have refused me a direct request, and I couldn't have that. She is toweringly competent in the sickroom, and her presence at the cottage provided chaperonage, of sorts. The woman is endlessly contrary, though. If I'd asked, she would have told me I was presuming, interfering, and otherwise neglected to use sense."

Jack had been terrified his mother would refuse to help.

"Thank you for interfering," Madeline said. "My aunt could well be dead or dying if you'd been less willing to interfere. Your mother simply wants you to appreciate her, to notice her, and all she's learned in life."

Madeline's perspective bore the unmistakable odor of unwelcome truth. "I notice and appreciate that my mother, like present company, can be stubborn and contrary. If Mama hadn't been willing to come, Jeremy would have accompanied me without a second thought."

Because Jeremy was a good man. Jack had reason to hope that Jeremy was an accomplished kisser as well.

Madeline yawned behind her gloved hand. "I like your family, Jack Fanning. You ought to get to know them sometime. Your mother isn't the only one who's stubborn and contrary."

That was the last thing she said before falling asleep with her head on Jack's shoulder. The better to spare her from the bitter wind, Jack slowed the horse to a walk, and took the roads home, rather than the shortcuts across the farm lanes.

* * *

"Well?"

Jack Fanning had a way of making a single syllable into an entire interrogation. Too bad the king's man hadn't any children—yet—who'd show him the futility of that imperious tone and arched eyebrow.

"Well, have a seat," Axel said, beneath the noise of the Weasel's championship-night crowd. "I vow, Fanning, this is the last year I'm leading a team. I will sponsor entire legions, but when a man hasn't had a decent night's sleep in weeks, this nonsense pales. My attendance at the assembly is looking none to assured either."

Fanning slid onto the bench on the opposite side of the table, the same table they'd occupied the last time they'd endured the Weasel's hospitality. Nothing wrong with allowing a little comfortable predictability to creep into life.

Axel and Jack Fanning weren't old, after all. They were merely… mature.

"Half the damned shire must be here tonight," Fanning said, as the foam on his ale gradually settled. "Would that Vicar's Bible studies gathered as much support. How is Mrs. Belmont?"

Mrs. Belmont was counting the days—or nights—until the assembly, much like her husband. "Abigail thrives on motherhood. The child will want for nothing, and it's as if with that baby in her arms, Abigail doesn't either. A man can feel…"

"Extraneous," Fanning said. "Surplus to requirements. As when not five people are available for a game of whist, but six, and the poor fellow who owns the premises is told to go bring his ledgers up to date, or write to some old chum in India. I am the host at Teak House, in theory at least, but abruptly my earthly sanctuary has become overrun with chattering females abetted by my brother. He knows more bawdy jokes than both Mama and Theodosia Hickman combined."

A tavern maid hurried by, and at the next table, some half-drunken smallholder stuck out a booted foot and tripped her. She landed more or less in Jack Fanning's lap, which resulted in much laughter from those nearby, and a saucy smile for Fanning from the woman.

Fanning rose with the lady in his arms, set her on her feet, and kept hold of her by the wrist. He turned a ferocious glower on the neighboring table.

"Battery," he snapped, "consists of a harmful or offensive touching of another's person. Apologize to the lady or be given an opportunity to admire my formal parlor on Monday morning, when I will have you bound over for the assizes."

One did not interfere with the magistrate when he was about the king's business—particularly not when his tone conjured images of a growling tiger, complete with a switching tail. Axel kept his mouth shut, as did the lady.

"I meant no harm," the young fellow grumbled.

"Had Miss Tansy fallen and struck her head against this post,"—Fanning delivered a hearty blow to solid wood—"she would have suffered grievous injury, to say nothing of lost wages and humiliation. Whether you meant to cause harm or not is immaterial. You meant to trip her."

The entire table looked sheepish, and Tansy's detractor suffered a punch on the arm from the man next to him. "Apologize, Wyatt. The lady coulda smacked her gob. My cousin lost a tooth that way."

"I'm sor—"

Jack Fanning grew three inches taller on a single in-drawn breath. "When a gentleman tenders an apology to a lady, he does so *on his feet*."

The crowd had not yet noticed this exchange, which was fortunate. Over the years, the Weasel had been the scene of a few mills in conjunction with the darts championship, and Axel had no desire to explain to his lady how the king's man—a sober, reasonable fellow, when not falling in love—had started a general donnybrook.

The batterer scrambled to his feet and swiped a hand over unkempt hair. "Miss Tansy, I do apologize. I meant no harm."

Tansy's blush was most becoming.

"*And?*" Fanning added.

"And I won't do it again."

"*Ever*," Fanning said, letting go of Tansy's wrist. "If I were you, Miss Tansy, I'd serve the occupants of this table last on every occasion."

She bobbed a curtsey and scampered off, casting a smirk over her shoulder at Wyatt. The young men vacated their table and shuffled away in the direction of the dartboard.

"They'll be engaged by the time the assembly rolls around," Axel said, when he wanted instead to knock Fanning's head against the post. "Well done. Was that a demonstration of the legendary diplomacy you exhibited in India?"

Fanning took his seat, gaze on the young men now lounging against the bar and trying to look adult.

"Do you know, I dropped my butler at the lending library this evening, and from thence he is walking back to Teak House. Despite this weather, I could do with about twenty miles of forced march myself right now, in any direction away from this nonsense."

Axel remained silent, for the king's man wasn't finished.

"In India," Fanning said, "I didn't exercise diplomacy so much as I translated. My domestics taught me the local languages, and I was able to prevent some misunderstandings. I caused a few as well."

The subject would do as a change in topic when Fanning was spoiling for a fight. "Is that how you were taken captive? In the midst of translation duties?"

"That's one way to look at it. Another is that I became entangled in local politics, and my simple, straightforward English mind wasn't capable of foreseeing cause and effect as they would play out in the vastly more complicated arena of Indian society."

"Like a debutante at a ball," Axel said. "But like most of the young ladies, you eventually came right?"

The man staring at his ale across from Axel was not *right*. He was tired, irritable, and very likely besotted. About damned time he came home from the jungles of memory.

"I came right eventually. My colonel had had me declared dead—attacked by a tiger, drowned, waylaid by brigands. In India, misfortune comes in many fatal guises. The lady I married had third cousins who took exception to the behavior of some junior officers toward the local merchants. My capture was intended to make a point. Because the colonel had no control over his men, the underlying offenses toward the merchants had gone unpunished, and thus by way of retaliation—it's complicated."

"When you tried to atone for the ineptitude of your superior officers, you were instead made an example of."

"Until I inconveniently escaped, and then the only course open to my colonel was to pretend he was overjoyed to see me alive."

"Though doubtless, surplus to requirements."

"Shut your mouth, Belmont."

Axel lifted his tankard in a toast. "How's Madeline?"

Fanning's scowl deepened, which ought not to have been possible. "Madeline is exhausted. Theodosia Hickman has removed to Teak House. She became dangerously ill with a lung fever, and Madeline was up most of the night caring for her."

How would Jack Fanning know Madeline Hennessey's whereabouts in the wee hours unless—?

"How fares Theodosia?"

"Well enough. She will be cosseted past all bearing, until she recovers in defense of her wits. I didn't realize Higgans participated in these gatherings."

The good doctor was at the bar next to Vicar Weekes, engaged in deep discussion.

"Everybody will stop by at some point this evening," Axel said. "Because you're here, they're more likely to behave themselves for the duration of the tournament. After that, Tavis is on his own."

"When can you take a puppy?"

The course of true love must be running quite amok. "Fanning, I despair of your conversation."

"The beasts are in my stable, consuming several times more than grown men in good health. You promised, Belmont."

Axel had promised he'd discuss with his wife the prospect of adding a dog to the Candlewick household, among other items.

"I can take the dog tomorrow, assuming your head isn't too sore. Bring a puppy by, and Madeline as well. I miss her."

Fanning left off glowering at the physician and the vicar. "*You* miss her?"

"Terribly. The secret to Cook's delicious scones was that Madeline beat the batter just so. The footmen were cheerful because Madeline scolded them and flirted with them in equal measure. Mrs. Turnbull has accused the maids of being forgetful, when in fact, my housekeeper is the one who can no longer recall which task she gave to whom because Madeline managed the assignments. Even my stable master misses the only person who could suggest to him how the saddle room should be organized. My wife, alas, is concerned with a newborn, and thus—in defense of my entire demesne, I *miss Madeline terribly*, as does the rest of my household."

Fanning's expression traveled an interesting spectrum, from thunderous, to curious, to commiserating.

"Too bad, old man. You can't have her back. Madeline is threatening to move in with Theodosia when my mother returns to London."

Hence the scowls, frowns, and threats of arrest.

"That won't do, Fanning. The senior Hennessey women are a problem, and woe to the man who oversteps when he tries to effect a solution. Having Madeline give up a salaried position to feed chickens with Theo won't solve a thing."

"Of course it won't."

"So what will you do?" *Propose, you damn fool. Get down on your handsome knees and ask the woman for her hand in marriage.*

"For starters, I shall sell the rest of those puppies, cash in advance."

* * *

"You should give Miss DeWitt a puppy," Jack said.

Jeremy did not consider himself a gifted intellect, but neither was he daft. "*I* should give Miss DeWitt one of those mongrels impersonating carnivorous elephants in your stable?"

"Of course," Jack said, pacing around the estate office's desk. Jack's path was clockwise, relative to Jeremy's seat at the desk. "If I give the woman anything—a single blossom—Mama will get ideas. Miss DeWitt is a charming young lady, but Mama's ideas are not always well-thought-out."

True enough. Mama had ideas enough to restart the Napoleonic Wars. Abetted by Mrs. Theodosia Hickman, all manner of plots were possible.

"A puppy is a rather personal gift," Jeremy replied. "That is to say…" Puppies were adorable. All paws and ears, wiggling tails, and bright, happy puppy-eyes. "I see your problem, Jack. The ladies do tend to read significance where there is none and take odd notions."

Jeremy was taking an odd notion, a not-very-brotherly notion.

"You have the knack of being friendly without creating expectations," Jack said, pausing to wind the clock on the mantel. "I'm sure when you accost Miss DeWitt beneath the mistletoe, she regards it as a charming gesture. While I…"

Jack compared the clock with his pocket watch, and moved the larger hand forward a quarter hour.

Jeremy had not dared accost the lady beneath the mistletoe. She was an enthusiastic student of the kiss, and Jeremy an all-too-enthusiastic instructor. Thanks be to the Almighty, the mistletoe would soon be taken down.

"I am charming," Jeremy said. "While you are…?"

"While I am not the friendly sort, and poor Miss DeWitt attempts to include me in all manner of social nonsense out of sheer pity."

Sheer duty, more like, which hardly seemed like the optimal motivation for marriage in these enlightened times.

"Have you considered being friendly despite your shortcomings? The ladies are charitable with us, when they know we're trying."

How odd, to be giving Sir Jack, the hero of Parrakan, advice. Clergy expected to hand out advice, but not to dashing older brothers.

Jack took the chair across from the desk, looking all too handsome and eligible in his riding attire.

"May I be honest?" Jack opened a small carved box on the desk and held it up to his nose. The soothing scent of jasmine wafted across the office.

My brother sniffs boxes. Poor Lucy Anne. "Of course you may be honest, and you may trust my discretion as well."

Jack's smile was fleeting and devilish. "Because you're ordained? I'm not confessing a sin, Jere."

Jere. Nobody else used that nickname, and to hear it was inordinately pleasing, despite the guilt it heaped on a younger brother's heart.

"You may trust my discretion because I'm your dear baby brother, and your confidences mean a lot to me." Jeremy did respect and love Jack. Always had.

"I would make Miss DeWitt miserable," Jack said. "I've been on my own for too long, and she's... she's innocent, charming, and so young. On the one hand, I'm not the man for her, but I don't want to hurt her feelings. On the other hand, if I am not receptive to Miss DeWitt's overtures, Mama will plague the poor lady relentlessly, chide her, and plant untoward ideas in her head."

"You have a point. Mama is ever so fond of untoward ideas, and considers herself something of a matchmaker." Jeremy considered Mama something of a plague, albeit dear in her own way.

Jack took another whiff of jasmine. "Mama a matchmaker? I had no idea. Poor Miss DeWitt has been put in an awful position. I think the least we can do is give the lady a puppy to keep her spirits up. I'm sure Theodosia would sell us one."

Jeremy mentally set aside his clerical collar for just a moment—the blasted thing could make being a brother far too complicated.

"What about Miss Hennessey, Jack?"

"I don't think she'd like a puppy. She spends all day looking after Mama, the household, her aunts... She's still more or less in service, and that makes a puppy difficult."

No wonder Lucy Anne was at her wits' end with Sir Hero. "I meant, what about your feelings for Miss Hennessey? Your gallantry regarding her aunt was very commendable, but mightn't Miss Hennessey develop feelings for such a considerate, generous fellow?"

Jeremy hoped this was the case, for the sake of his overtaxed conscience.

"Miss Hennessey isn't interested in marriage, to me or to anybody. She has a dim view of the male of the species, for reasons which, as gentlemen, we need not belabor."

In for a penny, or a puppy, as it were... "Jack, you carried her in from the sleigh when you came back from Theodosia's cottage yesterday afternoon. I saw you from the window of the family parlor, and I saw you pause outside the back door and kiss the lady—without benefit of mistletoe."

The great hero looked... wistful, and a bit sheepish. "Have you never longed to kiss a sleeping princess awake?"

Just as a confession might have tumbled forth, inspiration struck. "I have wanted to kiss a princess, once or twice." Or for endless moments. "One should be forgiven the occasional princely impulse, provided the lady is willing. Miss Hennessey apparently woke in a state of willingness."

For she'd kissed Jack back, and that had been something of a puzzle. The fellow kissing Miss Hennessey had known exactly what he was about. The lout who'd been the beneficiary of Lucy Anne's holiday kiss under the mistletoe had been utterly uninspired, from what Jeremy had seen.

Lucy Anne had found him uninspired, and her opinion decided the matter.

"Miss Hennessey might fancy you more than you think," Jeremy said, which was awful of him. Miss Hennessey was a lovely woman, and probably accustomed to men stealing kisses. "She did take the dog cart out last night, and I'm told her destination was that darts tournament. Perhaps she wanted to admire your deadly accuracy with Cupid's arrow, hmm?"

Jack closed the scented box with a snap. "Madeline took out the dog cart?"

"You and Pahdi took the sleigh, and it's not like the snow is fresh-fallen. We still had a foursome at whist, and Mama doesn't begrudge anybody an occasional social outing."

"The Weasel was very crowded," Jack said, rising. "I was intent on keeping the peace and leading my team, which objectives were not always in the same direction. You'll choose a puppy for Miss DeWitt?"

Jeremy stood as well. He'd come in here, thinking to sort through his situation regarding Miss DeWitt aided by recourse to Scripture, but a snippet of Ezra had gone 'round and 'round in his head, about being too ashamed and embarrassed to ask for the Lord's guidance… and that had led to recollection of the kisses engendering his embarrassment.

Such lovely, lovely kisses they'd been, though far too few in number. Lucy Anne was a quick study, also fragrant, lusciously endowed, adorably inventive with her hands, and sweet to the tongue.

"I will certainly choose a puppy for the lady," Jeremy said. "I'm your brother. It's the least I can do."

Jack clapped him on the shoulder. "I knew you'd understand. You might lurk about under the mistletoe too. Miss DeWitt is apparently a great believer in holiday traditions, and what can a few friendly kisses hurt?"

"Exactly my thinking." And Miss DeWitt's too, apparently. Praise be to the generosity of the Benevolent Creator.

"I'm off to deliver one of the little beasts to Candlewick, and my thanks, Jeremy, for being such a sympathetic ear."

"You're welcome. Any time. My pleasure."

Jack strode off in fine good humor, while Jeremy went to find Miss DeWitt. The lady should be free to choose her own puppy, after all.

* * *

"My brother thinks I should pay you my addresses," Jack said, signaling the horse to walk on. Madeline sat beside him in the dog cart, with one whining, wiggling puppy in the compartment designed for the very purpose of transporting canines. Because the little beast moved about, made noise, and pawed at the walls surrounding it, Jack felt as if he were sitting on a small riot.

"I think you should watch the road, Sir Jack."

Sir Jack. Madeline had been in this off, remote mood since Theodosia had joined the household the previous day. Mrs. Hickman's health was remarkably improved, while Madeline's mood was not. Jack's disposition wasn't much better, but he hoped he'd at least given Jeremy a nudge in Miss DeWitt's direction.

"I've been driving these lanes for years," Jack said. "I can see you and the infernal mongrel safely to our destination. Will visiting Candlewick be awkward for you?"

"Yes, but Mr. Belmont has spoken, and so I must appear. He was ever one for issuing edicts and speaking in imperatives."

The part of Jack that admitted to insecurity delighted to hear the brilliant Axel Belmont spoken of disparagingly, except that Madeline both liked and respected Belmont, and petulance was foreign to her nature.

"Madeline, what's wrong?"

For long chilly moments, she said nothing. All manner of thoughts skipped through Jack's mind while the puppy whined and fretted in his box.

Would the Candlewick staff resent that Madeline had found a better, if temporary, position? India wasn't the only place with an oppressive caste system.

Was Madeline still exhausted from her ordeal with Theodosia? The older woman seemed to be rapidly on the mend, but such a close call had doubtless given Madeline a fright.

And then, as the Candlewick lane came into view, one of those busy, March-hare thoughts came to a complete stop in the center of Jack's awareness.

"If you are with child, Madeline, we shall marry."

The look she sent him broke his heart. Incredulous, affectionate, wry, and despairing.

"You withdrew. I'm not likely to be carrying."

"If you are—"

One wheel hit a deep rut, and the dog shifted from whining to barking. No barking on earth was more vexatious than nervous-puppy barking. Jack brought the cart to a halt and passed Madeline the reins.

"This puppy won't live to see Candlewick if that noise continues." Jack climbed down and unlatched the compartment housing the dog. The little wretch was wagging his tail and trying to jump about, which resulted in knocking his head against the roof of the compartment.

"You don't like confinement," Jack said, lifting the puppy out, "and you miss your family, and that's all very understandable. Miss Hennessey will comfort you in the midst of your ordeal, but if you soil her skirts, I will have Cook turn you into sandwiches."

Madeline accepted the wiggly beast when Jack handed him to her. "You mustn't speak to him like that, Jack. They understand more than you think."

Jack understood more than Madeline thought. She was upset, for example, but also demonstrating the legendary tendency of Hennessey women to hoard their burdens.

"Vicar has agreed to accept a puppy, Jeremy is giving one to Miss DeWitt, and Dr. Higgans has already paid for his. That leaves only the one, which I will happily purchase if Theodosia is willing to part with it."

The puppy had no dignity, cuddling against Madeline's chest, and attempting to lick her chin through her scarf. His tail thumped furiously against Jack's thigh.

"You're a puppy salesman?" Madeline asked, dodging doggy kisses. "That's very kind of you. When did you accomplish this?"

"Vicar Weekes and Dr. Higgans were at the darts tournament. I accosted them both, and left them in no doubt as to their need for a dog."

Jack made the turn up the Candlewick drive and brought the horse down to the walk. Being a drive rather than a public thoroughfare, the way was snowier. Then too, his discussion with Madeline was not yet concluded.

Madeline, though, had buried her face against the dog's neck. When she looked up, her expression was furious.

"Higgans can attend a darts tournament on a winter night, but he can't treat my ailing aunt. I hope the puppy you choose for him has a contrary nature and is prone to biting and incontinence."

"I'll see what I can arrange, but I've already delivered Higgans a public tongue-lashing."

"You did what?"

"I berated Higgans in public, albeit civilly, for neglecting the care of a decent woman, a widow no less, who would have died rather than ask Higgans for help. I further informed him and the general gathering that he'd be sponsoring a darts team next year, as Tavis has decided that the proceeds will go to benefit the widows and orphans."

"Jack Fanning, you are daft." Madeline kissed him, and the puppy might have contributed to the effort as well. "You gave Higgans a birching in front of half the shire. I hope you don't fall ill in the near future."

"I enjoy reliable good health, and my own mother is a very competent nurse. I can understand why Theodosia would rather shiver herself to death than ask for help from those who refuse their charitable obligations. Which reminds me, why weren't you on hand to witness Higgans's thrashing?"

"I told you I wouldn't attend. Bad enough that my aunt is imposing on the household, but for me to have turned around and left her so I could spend the evening with a lot of drunken yeomen... no, thank you."

In India, Jack had learned to live by his wits. If the colonel's smile had looked a bit nervous, Jack had known to investigate the orders cheerfully slapped into his hand. If the guides had stopped chatting among themselves, Jack had kept his pistol loaded, and told his men to do likewise.

And still, he'd nearly died in a dank, stinking cell, forgotten by all charged with ensuring his welfare.

His instincts told him that Madeline was hiding something—an opinion, an emotion, a decision, a hurt, something.

"If you didn't attend the festivities at the Weasel, Madeline, where did you get off to?"

"I beg your pardon?"

"You took this very cart out last night, and Jeremy was under the impression you went to the Weasel. I didn't see you there, and clearly you were not in attendance. Where were you?"

"I... This is the least restful creature I have ever met. We shall call him Bounce."

As in bouncer?

"I went to visit Aunt Hattie," Madeline went on. "Hattie was very concerned for Theo, particularly when your note mentioned no call from Higgans. Hattie was pleased to hear that Theo is improving by the hour."

Jack brought the cart to a halt in the Candlewick stable yard, and a groom came forth to hold the horse as Jack climbed down.

Madeline could have sent a stable boy to Hattie's with a note, could have asked Jack to stop by on the way to the village, could have let the matter wait until this morning. She'd have him believe that—in typical Hennessey fashion—she'd seen to the matter herself, at night, in the middle of winter, without a groom to accompany her.

Further discussion was in order, but now was not the time.

Jack took the puppy, and held him with one arm while he assisted the lady from the cart. They were met at Candlewick's front door by Belmont himself.

"Ah, the promised puppy, and my prodigal Hennessey. Madeline, come in, and bring along Sir Jack if you must. Abigail, you must charm Sir Jack so he'll be distracted when Madeline admits how much she's missed me, and how badly she wants to abandon the tedium of Teak House."

Jack took the puppy from Madeline and shoved him into Belmont's arms. "His name is Beowulf. He tends to piddle where he oughtn't. He'll tear your favorite slippers to bits, and he's more flatulent than a draft horse on spring grass. Miss Hennessey chose him for you."

Mrs. Belmont came smiling down the main staircase, looking entirely too lovely for a woman with a newborn in the nursery and Belmont for a husband. Jack had known her for years, and yet, this happy, softly glowing lady was also in some regards a stranger.

"You're just jealous," Belmont whispered as the women embraced, and disappeared up the steps. "I'm wrestling with jealousy too. The little blighter in the nursery has stolen his mother's heart. You will notice, Abigail barely spared this darling puppy a pat on the head."

"I notice you have no dignity, Belmont. You and Beowulf will get on famously. I have a problem."

"Come into my study," Belmont said, leading the way down the corridor, the puppy in his arms. "All problems admit of solutions, if one is persistent and imbibes enough good liquor. I'll dower our Madeline, if that's the difficulty. Abigail expects nothing less of me. Happy wife, happy life, as the saying goes."

Jack closed the door to the study as Belmont set the puppy down. "Must you be so obnoxiously content, Belmont?"

"Yes, I must. I'm married to Abigail, after all. Brandy? Cognac? Armagnac?"

"Whatever you're having."

The libation helped settle Jack's temper, as did—oddly—Belmont's company. The puppy found a box lined with an old plaid blanket before the fire, curled up, and set his chin on his paws with a canine sigh.

"To a happy New Year," Belmont said, touching his glass to Jack's. "Now, what is this problem?"

Jack took a seat in a well-padded armchair. As magistrate, he'd extracted all manner of confessions and confidences from people with whom he'd had only a churchyard acquaintance. Belmont was a friend—a good friend—and that was all that allowed Jack to speak honestly.

"Madeline is lying to me. Prevarication is not in her gift, and even with a puppy wiggling endearingly in her arms, she could not carry off a convincing falsehood. I've never met a woman more prone to honesty, and she's lying to me."

CHAPTER TWELVE

The baby had grown in the short time Madeline had been away from Candlewick, and that emphasized her sense of having been banished from the only sanctuary she'd known.

"The staff is campaigning for your return," Abigail said, taking the infant from his bassinet and cradling him against her shoulder. "Cook pretends she can't make her Sunday scones without you. The footmen and maids are holding a mock feud. Even Mrs. Turnbull is in on the plot."

Mother and child were already a mutual admiration society. The child had got a lock of Abigail's hair free from her bun and brought it to his mouth, which larceny Abigail apparently found adorable.

"Mrs. Turnbull hasn't a deceptive bone in her body," Madeline said. "Shall we sit?"

A maid would never have asked that question, but Madeline wasn't a maid at present, and Abigail had long since become something of a friend. They took the rockers before the hearth, the soft roar of the fire punctuated by the baby's sounds of contentment.

"Mrs. Turnbull would have us believe she's grown forgetful," Abigail said, switching the child to the other shoulder. "I hope she's at least exaggerating, if not dissembling. Candlewick can't run with a forgetful housekeeper. I'm preoccupied with my little joy. Mr. Belmont's mind is on spring and plans for his glass houses."

Mr. Belmont's mind was on his wife and children, of that Madeline was certain.

"Mrs. Turnbull's eyesight is fading, and she doesn't hear as well as she used to," Madeline said. "She's not forgetful, exactly, but she sometimes can't read her own handwriting, and she doesn't always grasp what's said to her."

This had become apparent to Madeline more than a year ago, before Abigail had joined the household. Why didn't people notice the staff that looked after them day and night?

But then, Mr. and Mrs. Belmont had been very busy noticing each other, and Mrs. Turnbull was nearly as proud as a Hennessey.

"Her hearing and eyesight are troubling her? Are you sure?"

"She's complained to me many times of both problems, but I suspect she didn't want to abandon her post with your baby on the way."

Or to give up the job that meant so much to her.

"Mrs. Turnbull is being foolish," Abigail said, stroking the baby's back. He might well be red-haired, which for a man wasn't such a curse. "She will retire with a fat pension in one of the cottages on the home farm, though we couldn't possibly part with her until she's had time to train a replacement. I had hoped you might assist us to choose her successor."

The Belmonts *had* hoped Madeline might assist them? Was her assistance no longer needed or welcome?

Why wasn't Madeline, who knew the staff and the house better than she knew her family tree, the logical party to step into Mrs. Turnbull's shoes?

And why must that baby be so infernally darling? He had his papa's swooping eyebrows, even at such a tender age, and his mother's nose and chin.

"Madeline, are you well? You have a melancholy air that I do not like."

"I am in good health. Aunt Theo is at Teak House, recovering from a bout of lung fever. Her situation put me at sixes and sevens, and I'm not entirely—"

I'm not entirely sane anymore.

Madeline should not have left Teak House the previous evening, not for any reason.

Abigail's gaze was that of a friend, and worse, that of a mother. "Is Jack Fanning being impossible?"

He was impossibly dear. "Sir Jack was very kind regarding Aunt Theo's situation. The doctor would not come, and Theo was in difficulties. If not for Jack, the tale would have become dire. He's... he's an admirable man."

Madeline's chin had developed a quiver, and no matter how rapidly she blinked, she could not prevent a tear from trickling down each cheek.

"Sir Jack is being awful," Abigail said, extracting a handkerchief from a pocket, even as she held the baby. "Putting all that gentlemanly honor on display for you, and when he's been so busy hunting down coal thieves and pranksters. I do hope he's at least had the decency to linger beneath the mistletoe with you a time or two."

Madeline dissolved into open weeping, not polite, ladylike sniffles. Not since Aunt Hattie had been turned off without a character and the first undeserved beating had been delivered had such hopelessness and despair engulfed her.

"You mustn't take on so," Abigail said, patting Madeline's shoulder. "All might seem bleak, but Jack adores you. Mr. Belmont assures me this is so, and Mr. Belmont is a very observant man. I've known Jack Fanning for ages, and since you joined the staff at Teak House, Mr. Belmont claims Jack is a different person. More alive, more fierce. You're good for him."

"You are no help," Madeline said, blotting her eyes. "You are no help at all. The problem isn't Jack, it's me. It's me, and it's everything, and he's the magistrate, and I've been very, very foolish."

Abigail rose with the child, who'd begun to fret. "You are never foolish."

"That might be the problem. I was never foolish, and now, I'm foolish in every possible direction. Aunt Theodosia should not be trying to manage alone, and I suspect Aunt Hattie will soon be in the same circumstances. They are my family, and I can't look after them properly, and it's all... It's complicated, and I'm tired, and I don't want to feed chickens for the rest of my life, and Sir Jack is the magistrate."

Abigail paced the nursery, a slow, rocking walk that quieted the child and made Madeline so envious, she nearly burst into renewed weeping.

"You've mentioned twice that Jack is the magistrate. I don't see what his duties in that regard have to do with anything, much less with lying in wait for you beneath the mistletoe. Mr. Belmont is prone to diplomacy in delicate matters, while I'm not half so reticent. If Jack Fanning needs a talking-to, I'll not hesitate—"

The baby gently smacked his mama's mouth, as if even he knew that Abigail's characterization of Axel Belmont as a diplomat was far-fetched.

"Jack Fanning has acquitted himself quite competently beneath the mistletoe, as it were," Madeline said. "He's acquitted himself splendidly."

Abigail smiled radiantly. "I knew it. You fancy each other. You're intelligent, healthy adults, and all that was wanted was proximity and opportunity. Mr. Belmont will dower you, and we will stand up with you at the wedding."

"There can't be a wedding," Madeline said. "Jack is the magistrate, and he takes those duties seriously. He's a gentleman, and his honor is not to be compromised."

Abigail's smile disappeared. "But *you* are to be compromised? Madeline, explain yourself. I'm all for a woman enjoying what few freedoms she has in the blighted realm, but I didn't suggest you accept a post at Teak House so you could be ruined."

"I'm not ruined, but I've been foolish. That thief Jack is looking for so diligently, that prankster? It's me. I'm the thief, and he's the magistrate, and I cannot marry him now."

* * *

The world had gone mad.

Jack had no sooner delivered a silent and wan Madeline back to Teak House than Dr. Higgans had come rattling up the drive in his smart red-wheeled trap. Higgans was the very last person Jack wanted to see, but perhaps he'd come to claim his puppy.

"Shall we repair to the library?" Jack asked, when the doctor had surrendered his hat, gloves, and caped greatcoat to Pahdi.

"Anywhere private will do, for unlike some people, I don't air my opinions in public."

"The library is this way," Jack said. "Pahdi, we'll not need a tray just yet, but alert the kitchen that company has come to call."

When Jack and his guest were behind the closed library door, Jack took a seat at his desk, the better to maintain magisterial decorum.

"What's that odd smell?" Higgans asked.

"Sandalwood. I burn incense in here to discourage rising damp." And because the fragrance was beautiful.

Higgans took himself on an inspection tour of Jack's library, and Jack allowed it. Silence was one of a magistrate's most powerful tools, and the library spoke eloquently of education, refinement, and wisdom.

"This is teak," Higgans said, peering at the sideboard. "Don't see much teak, nor many of these fancy teapots."

"That's called a samovar." *Perhaps I should spell it for you, slowly.*

Higgans's perusal of the library had apparently modified his opinion of the deference due its owner. Books were expensive, and Jack had quite a collection. The piano was a lovely instrument from the manufactory of one Lord Valentine Windham, who'd become a neighbor. The samovar was an antique, silver, and probably worth more than Higgans's house.

"Why does a man who owns all this wealth bother playing at magistrate?"

Higgans's question came not from an arrogant, learned physician, but from a perplexed old country doctor. A *presuming*, perplexed old country doctor.

"Have a seat, Dr. Higgans. Please?"

The doctor lowered himself carefully into a chair facing Jack's desk. Sore hips, would be Jack's guess, or possibly sore knees. Maybe both, and the rosy state of Higgans's nose suggested a fondness for spirits, rather than an excess of winter air.

"I am the magistrate,"—Jack did not *play at* being magistrate—"in part because my wealth ensures I need not use my office for gain. I enjoy solving puzzles, and I have an abiding respect for the rule of law. I've dwelled where the king's justice was little more than an amusing fairy tale, and I don't care to see my own parish drift in that direction. Then too, there's the matter of honor. The law does not enforce itself."

Higgans shifted in the chair. "Theo Hickman is a tough old bird. A sniffle or a cough won't send her to her Maker."

Did Higgans seek absolution? Jack hadn't any to offer.

"I did not air my opinion at the Weasel, Higgans, I recited facts. The lady was seriously ill. You were summoned, and you received that summons in the warmth and comfort of your home. You ignored a request for your services and provided no explanation, though you were happy to brave the elements the next evening to swill indifferent winter ale and criticize the aim of every competitor. Is that what your medical training qualifies you to do?"

Jack was angry, and that wasn't helpful. Madeline had been angry too, though, and with justification.

"You needn't repeat yourself," Higgans said. "I came by Theodosia's cottage the next morning, and she'd been removed to your establishment. I was exhausted, had been on other cases all throughout the previous day, and had every intention—"

"Stop." What little sympathy Jack had had for Higgans evaporated. "Not another word, unless you're prepared to tell the truth."

Higgans tried for an indignant huff, which Jack met with a basilisk stare. He hadn't been this annoyed since—since India, and the reconnection with his temper felt *good*.

"You did not come by Theodosia's cottage the next morning," Jack said. "We were more than half the day packing her effects, arranging for the traveling coach, and accommodating my mother's various suggestions. You were not out seeing patients the previous day either, unless your groom lied to me about your schedule when I spoke with him before you arrived at the Weasel. You simply didn't care enough to look in on a sick old woman."

Worse yet, Higgans *still* hadn't asked how Theodosia fared.

Higgans rose, putting Jack in mind of a certain colonel in India. Both were portly, white-haired fellows with shrewd eyes and carefully groomed moustaches. Both had likely been handsome, spoiled youths, and both appeared distinguished in their later years.

Both were also lazy, lying cowards.

"State your business, Higgans. Though you dissemble in your own interests, if you've come to report somebody else's misbehavior, I am bound to listen and set the matter right if I can."

"You nabobs," Higgans sneered. "You think you're so superior, with your wealth and your fine airs. Will you arrest your own butler when I accuse him of stealing my medical bag? For it's gone, taken from my own home, and I saw that butler of yours skulking about town last night when everybody else was enjoying decent entertainment at the Weasel.

"You can't account for his whereabouts," Higgans went on, "because you were too busy ringing a peal over my head at the tavern. That bag holds the tools of my profession and belonged to my father. You're so keen to address wrongdoing, then send your butler to the assizes. He's the reason Berthilda Abernathy lost her post, and his larceny was at the root of her woes too."

Blast and perdition. Jack mentally counted to ten in Hindi, then again in Latin.

"The lending library is two doors down from your house," Jack said, "and Pahdi is a voracious reader. I brought him with me when I went to the Weasel, but Tavis's hospitality does not appeal to Pahdi. Pahdi transacted his business at the library and returned home on foot."

Higgans braced his hands on Jack's desk and leaned over the blotter. "As I suspected, you cannot account for his time. To nip over to my house, raise a window, and steal my bag would be the work of the moment for a fellow like him. Either find out who did take that bag, or arrest that butler. I will swear under oath that I saw him at the scene of the crime, and announce it at the Weasel too."

Jack rose, and fortunately for his temper, he had several inches of height over the doctor—also an abiding distaste for violence.

"You were *not* at the scene of the crime, if the bag was taken from your home. You were at the Weasel, imbibing heavily. If you saw Pahdi across the street at the library, it was when you stepped outside to heed nature's call and in far less than broad daylight. Say what you please, where you please, but I do not arrest people on the strength of incidental drunken observations."

"Find my bag, and find out who stole it," Higgans snapped. "If it's not returned to me, then I'll ask for another magistrate to take up the matter. It's a disgraceful man who won't arrest a criminal in his own house, and that's common knowledge, or soon will be."

Jack's temper escalated, from annoyance, to anger, to rage. He sat back down, took out a sheet of foolscap, and uncapped the ink bottle.

"I will need a list."

Higgans's brows twitched. "A list?"

"You claim to be the victim of a theft. To recover stolen property, I'll need a list of what was taken." Jack lifted a pen from the standish and inspected the point, with which he'd dearly like to stab the doctor. "Describe the bag."

* * *

"Hattie and I had the best chat this morning," Aunt Theo said, settling onto the end of the sofa nearest the fire. "I've missed that, gabbing with my sister by the hour, all else forgotten. Florrie says we haven't aged a day since last she knew us. Imagine that."

Madeline nearly stabbed herself with her embroidery needle. *"Florrie?"* And why hadn't Madeline been told Aunt Hattie had come to call?

"Florentia Hammerschmidt was the dearest girl, back in the day. I'm a few years older, of course, but Mayfair wasn't such a crowded place before I was married. The better families all knew each other, and the Hammerschmidts, while not titled, were always considered good *ton*. Florentia did well, marrying that Fanning boy, no matter he led her a dance after the vows."

Theo was at least a decade older than Mrs. Fanning.

"You know Mrs. Fanning." Which realization upset Madeline, for no discernible reason.

"Not well, of course. We never corresponded, but our families were cordial for a time."

Until the Hennessey fortunes had declined, in other words. "I'm glad you've been able to renew old acquaintances. Shall I ring for a tea tray?"

"Heavens, no! We ladies will be playing whist with Reverend Fanning, and we'll have all the biscuits and shortbread we could wish for."

We ladies apparently did not include Madeline, which left… Mrs. Fanning, Theo, and Miss DeWitt.

"I'm glad to see you feeling so much better, but you must not overdo, Aunt." Because this idyll among the memories and tea trays would come to an end, and then Theo would be back on her smallholding, counting each egg and lump of coal.

Madeline's embroidery project for the day was a summer nightgown. She was adding a border of forget-me-nots, though the decoration was pointless. When the weather moderated, she'd be gone from Teak House, and nobody would see the delicate blue and cheerful yellow chasing about her hem.

"Hattie had a splendid idea," Theo said, smoothing her hand over a velvet pillow. "When she heard I'd be accompanying dear Florrie back to Town, she said she'd speak to Mrs. Belmont about a post at Candlewick. Nadine Turnbull is getting on, and Hattie knows how to run a household. You could put in a good word for her, I'm sure."

Theo's delight at these developments nearly equaled Madeline's incredulity.

"*What are you talking about?* If you go to London, who will feed your chickens? Who will plant your garden? You haven't any proper clothes for Town, haven't even a portmanteau to put them in." And if Nadine Turnbull was *getting on*, Hattie was getting on every bit as much.

Theo set the pillow aside. "That tone is very unbecoming, Madeline Aphrodite. You should be happy for me. If you'd like to live at the farm, I'm certainly willing to discuss it, but my mind is made up. Florrie has realized how the company of another lady can brighten her days, and she's offered that post to me, once I'm well. Hattie was delighted, and you should be too."

"Damn."

"My dear girl, if that's your—"

"My French knot is off center," Madeline said, fishing in her workbox for her embroidery scissors. "You have a position as a lady's companion to Mrs. Fanning?"

This was charity, plain and simple. Theodosia Hennessey Hickman had been from good family, long, long ago, but she was hardly the sort of self-effacing, sweet, biddable creature who'd make a good lady's companion.

But then, neither was Madeline. She was managing in the role of temporary companion because it meant significant coin in a short time. She was no more a lady's companion than Theo's few acres could be called a farm.

"Florentia tires of all the young people, and the other ladies in London are a catty bunch. That will never change. I'm welcome to join her household for as long as I please. Perhaps you should buy some spectacles, dear. Embroidery can be hard on the eyes."

Family could be hard on the temper. If Madeline had spare coin for spectacles, she would have spent it on her aunts.

"If you will be happy in Mrs. Fanning's household, then I'm happy for you. I am concerned though, that a tenant will not care for your land as conscientiously as you do, and that as landlord, you will spend all of your salary making repairs and doing maintenance." Because Theo's little property was in need of much maintenance, as was Hattie's.

Theo patted Madeline's knee. "That's what a great-niece is for. With you here to keep an eye on the place, I'm sure the tenant will maintain the property adequately—assuming you don't want the cottage for yourself?"

Madeline set aside the nightgown, as any attempts to stitch a straight seam were doomed. Aunt had apparently left her common sense back among her biddies, for Madeline's ability to coerce work from a tenant or oversee repairs was non-existent.

And to think Madeline had committed crimes in the hopes her aunts' lot would be bettered.

"Aren't you forgetting something, Aunt?"

"My memory is excellent, young lady."

No, it was not. "If Hattie goes for a housekeeper at Candlewick, and you're off to London with Mrs. Fanning, that leaves two vacant properties in need of tenants and stewardship. At best I could occupy one, but I wasn't raised on the land, Aunt Theo. I was raised in London, and then went into service. What I know about running a smallholding is not sufficient for the challenge."

And that assumed Madeline escaped arrest for theft—and stupidity.

Theo's expression resembled one of her laying hens when a cat came calling at the chicken coop.

"Madeline, I cannot solve all of your problems. Hattie and I have done what we could for you, but it's time you figured a few things out for yourself. It's not as if taking over one of the farms would be a sentence to imprisonment on the hulks. Spinsters have to live somewhere, and a property of your own is a great improvement over a life in service. A fellow might marry you simply to get his hands on some good land."

Good *land?* Madeline had devoted every half day—every half day for years—to assisting her aunts with their heavier chores. Every spare penny she'd earned had gone to filling their larders or buying them seed. Every article of clothing she'd sewn late at night had been made with her aunts in mind, and half the handsome, merry men whose overtures she'd rebuffed had been sent packing because those men would not have supported Hattie and Theo.

"You've given me much to think about." Madeline stuffed her embroidery into its box and latched the lid. "But service is all I know, and I'm good at it. You'll excuse me, please. I'm supposed to review menus with Cook." And reorganize the linen closet with the head maid, and plan the next wine purchase with Pahdi.

"Away with you," Theo said, waving a casual hand. "I'll have a little nap before luncheon, so I'll be on my mettle for cards. Reverend Fanning has the best stories, and he and Miss DeWitt are a formidable pair."

Madeline left the parlor at a dignified walk when she wanted to sprint for the door.

This cheerful, selfish version of Aunt Theo was a stranger, and yet, Madeline could easily understand Theo's determination to leave the shires. But for Jack's kindness, and the visit of a passing maid from Candlewick, Theo might be coughing her life away.

Did that mean Madeline must be interred in a miserable cottage with only chickens, sheep, and an old hound for company?

Assuming she wasn't arrested for theft.

* * *

Had Jack not been battling the urge to pitch the doctor bodily from the premises, the whole situation might have been comical.

The precious medical bag turned out to be a battered black leather satchel of no particular value. Inside had been a scalpel, some patent remedies, a cracked hand mirror, and a scent-bottle containing strong vinegar.

The thief's motive had clearly not been greed.

"Do you have a spare bag?" Jack asked.

Higgans was examining a chased silver ink bottle, one of the matched pair that sat on the standish.

"Beg pardon?"

"Do you have a spare medical bag?"

"I do not. My father's bag was dear to me, and the contents served me well for decades. I place great sentimental value on that bag."

Oh, of course. Jack was nearly certain the medical bag also contained a flask or two. "What do you suppose the thief will do with it?"

"Sell it, of course. Coin is all their kind thinks about, and how to get it without working for it."

Jack tugged the bell-pull when he wanted to rip it from the ceiling. A triple tap sounded on the door a moment later, and Jack bid Pahdi enter.

"Pahdi, humor me for a moment," Jack said. "Why do you borrow books from the lending library?"

"Because, respected sir, I have read all of the books you have here in English, French, and Hindi. I also borrow books from the Candlewick library, for myself and for James Smith, whose lack of hearing makes reading a treasured consolation."

Pahdi's tone was pleasantly deferential, but clearly, he understood that more accusations were in the air.

"What books did you borrow from the lending library earlier this week?" Jack asked.

"The library was closing as I arrived, because many patrons were more interested in the darts tournament in which you participated, esteemed sir. I did not have time to choose new books, but returned an account of the life of Hannah Snell, an old tale, though interesting."

"And what story was relayed in this interesting book?" Higgans snapped.

Pahdi bowed in Higgans's direction. "Mrs. Snell, wearing man's attire, joined His Majesty's infantry in pursuit of her faithless husband, and served under the name of James Gray. She subsequently enlisted in the marines, served in India, was wounded severally at the Battle of Pondicherry, and made her way back to this most-enlightened realm, where she continued to wear her regimentals and other attire suited to men. I recommend the book to you most sincerely, revered, honored, and esteemed sir."

Three adjectives and a bow assured Jack that Pahdi was in a temper. The New Year at Teak House was off on a decidedly sore foot.

"Any other questions, Higgans?" Jack asked.

"This proves nothing."

"Thank you, Pahdi," Jack said. "You are excused."

The butler withdrew after two more obsequiously graceful bows.

"He had every opportunity to help himself to my medical bag," Higgans said. "The lending library register will verify that he was in town, and there's nothing you can say to it."

"Higgans, before I summoned Pahdi, *I* verified that he'd been in town. Even you must admit the evening was dark, without enough moon to reveal much of anything. I'll come around your house later this week and examine the premises for signs of forcible entry. Until then, I bid you good day."

To emphasize this dismissal, Jack held open the library door, until Higgans had no choice but to leave.

"A conscientious magistrate would investigate now," Higgans said, "not in his own good time."

"I'll begin my investigation this afternoon," Jack said, "and start with interviewing those who attended the darts tournament. While memories are fresh, somebody might recall a detail out of place, a snippet of conversation, and then my search of your household will be more efficient."

Higgans came to an abrupt halt in the front foyer. "Search of my household? The devil you say."

James silently passed the physician his greatcoat, a lovely wool garment that would hold up to any winter weather.

"Do you want me to find that medical bag," Jack said, "or shall I pronounce sentence on Pahdi without examination of the accused or benefit of trial right now? Perhaps treat him to a pair of thumb screws? We can reinstitute the Dark Ages right here in our little corner of Oxfordshire, and to hell with due process, the rule of law, and common decency."

Over a damned medical bag, from one perspective. Over Higgans's arrogance and indolence, from another.

Mama appeared at the top of the stairs, but she had the sense not to come down where Higgans might see her.

"You take your duties very lightly," Higgans said, yanking on his gloves.

Jack could not resist. "You've probably misplaced an old leather bag, one carrying only the barest semblance of a doctor's implements, not the Koh-I-Noor diamond. Nonetheless, I shall begin my investigation within the hour. Perhaps my example will inspire you the next time an elderly neighbor lies alone, cold, and at risk of going to her reward for want of medical care. Your puppy awaits you in the stable. We've named him Hippocrates."

Higgans jammed his hat onto his head and stormed out the door.

Slow clapping followed as the slamming of the door reverberated in the foyer. "What a disgraceful old bag of noise," Mama said, coming down the stairs. "Why did you allow him to trouble your day?"

"Because I'm the magistrate, and the rule of law matters." Or some such tripe.

Mama patted Jack's arm. "You should eat something. You get in a pet when you're peckish. Why did Mr. Patty look so thunderous?"

"His name is Pahdi." Jack had never seen Pahdi looking anything less than dignified, except perhaps when he'd failed to shoot that tiger.

"That's what I said. Patty."

"Dr. Higgans accused Pahdi of theft, the item in question has virtually no value, and Higgans has no evidence of wrongdoing other than his own offended pride."

"You're worried though," Mama said. "That awful man upset you."

She'd always been a noticing sort, but when had she grown so small? "He is an awful man, and if he has his way, I'll put Pahdi on the next ship bound for India."

"That would certainly be a relief to me."

Whatever diplomatic skill Jack had once claimed, he'd not inherited it from his dam. "Mama, I would miss Pahdi dearly." The thought of life without Pahdi's quiet presence, irreverence, and honesty left an ache in the pit of Jack's belly.

Mama drew herself up, a fierce little hen of a woman. "You would *miss* him? *Miss him dearly*? You hopeless boy, how do you think I felt when you ran off to the same jungles that seduced your father year after year? I waited months for your letters, and then that horrid colonel sent word you were presumed dead. If Mr. Patty entices you back to India, I will simply have to go with you. I cannot bear the thought of you going so far away, where you have no family, no friends, no *mama*... you—oh, drat you, you wretched, awful boy."

The world had gone beyond daft to some level of disarray Jack couldn't name. And yet, he knew his mother, his contrary, stubborn, proud mother, and he knew he loved her.

Jack wrapped his mama in a careful hug, because he didn't know what else to do.

He'd bungled, badly, and a court higher than the king's bench demanded that he attempt reparation.

"Yours was the last familiar face I saw when the ship left Portsmouth, Mama, and the first I saw when I returned. I wasn't home until I saw you again. I'm home now. I'm home to stay."

The mother who'd never before shed a tear in the presence of her prodigal son, who'd written lengthy lectures to him every month without fail, who'd doubtless prayed for Jack every night of his life, wept. She was silent and shuddery in his arms, and all manner of emotions assailed Jack while she cried.

Mortification, because he'd made his mama cry and been an insensitive lout—probably for half of his life.

Peace, because he'd spoken honestly to his mother. Teak House was his home now, and maybe someday it would be hers too. Saying the words aloud had settled the last vestige of restlessness in him.

Frustration played a role too, because had Jack's mother *asked* him, he would have told her he was done with India—but had he invited her questions? Had he done anything except avoid her matchmaking and dread her meddling?

Beside the frustration ran a welcome vein of certainty though, because Jack had had enough adventures to last a lifetime. The only treasures he needed to seek or guard were right here in Oxfordshire.

And beneath all of those shifting, fraught sentiments, Jack felt respect for his mother, for her tenacity and stoicism, and acknowledging that respect brought profound relief. Jack wanted to respect his mother, of course he did, and all he'd ever wanted was for her to respect him.

He should have known that objective was wide of the mark, for his mama didn't merely respect him. She loved him, relentlessly, and always would.

"You have turned me into a watering pot," Mama said, drawing a handkerchief from her sleeve. "You are a very naughty boy. It's well your brother is a saint, or my account with the Almighty would be in sorry condition."

Jack sneaked in one more small hug and let her go. "Perhaps if you're done scolding the son who sailed across oceans to return to your side, you might afford me a moment or two of your time?"

Mama ceased dabbing at her eyes and stuffed the handkerchief back into her cuff. "If it's about the upcoming assembly, you'll get no help from me. You are going, John Dewey Fanning, and you will dance with every wallflower who's not too tipsy to turn down the room."

And a few who were too tipsy. "Yes, Mama, of course. But before you castigate me for dances I've yet to sit out, do you suppose you could help me solve a crime or two?"

Mama took him by the arm and steered him toward the library. "I thought you'd never ask."

CHAPTER THIRTEEN

Madeline dreamed of lavender borders, great silvery billows dotted with fragrant purple sprigs. The scent brought a sense of peace and well-being, which she desperately needed.

"Madam will please wake up."

Madam did not want to leave her dream-garden, assuming Madeline was madam.

"Madam must not spend the night among the linens."

Somebody made a timid attempt to jostle Madeline's shoulder.

"Please, madam. *Wake up.*"

The urgency of the entreaty had Madeline opening her eyes to find an anxious Pahdi peering down at her. They were in the linen closet, the space illuminated by Pahdi's carrying candle and the single stub of taper left burning on Madeline's candelabrum.

"Pahdi, good evening."

"I must beg to differ with madam. If Sir Jack finds that I have allowed you to fall asleep here, at an hour when all ought to be snug in their beds, I will be instructed at great length on the proper management of a civilized English household. No matter that 'civilized' and 'English' are regarded as contradictory terms by most of the world."

Madeline's back would certainly prefer she'd sought her bed. "What time is it?"

"Nearly eleven, and yes, Sir Jack has returned."

Jack had been absent from dinner, ostensibly investigating yet another petty theft. Madeline was all too aware his investigation would not lead to the missing medical bag.

"Thank you for waking me," she said, rising. The linen closet had a wonderful scent, but the chair Madeline had occupied had lacked a cushion. She longed not for bed, but for Jack's company.

"If you would thank me, respected ma'am," Pahdi said, sweeping a hand toward the door, "seek your bed before Sir Jack comes upon you. Bad enough he must waste his time on the doctor's imbecilic allegations against me. I would not have Sir Jack worrying about your health as well."

Madeline picked up her candelabrum, and the last candle guttered. "What accusations against you?"

In the light of a single candle, Pahdi's features were fierce. "I stole Dr. Higgans's bag, of course. Though I am accounted a wealthy man by my relations in India, I must risk my liberty, bring shame on Teak House, and upon Sir Jack, by purloining some old bag of useless nostrums and dirty knives belonging to the doctor."

"You've been accused of theft—*again?*"

Madeline dropped back onto the hard chair, feeling as dumbstruck as when Theo had announced a plan to elope to London. Nothing had gone right since Madeline had agreed to join the staff at Teak House.

Or since she'd decided the parish needed a few lessons in charity.

"Of course I have been accused again," Pahdi said. "Sir Jack scolded the esteemed doctor in public for neglecting his duties, and the doctor—scurrilous varlet—could not accept a deserved rebuke. He seeks to bring dishonor to Teak House and its owner."

This was… this was a disaster that could soon veer into a tragedy, and not only for Pahdi, who was innocent of all wrongdoing. Jack would be affected by Higgans's vitriol, and possibly be asked to step down as magistrate.

The shadows shifted as the door to the linen closet opened farther.

"My staff has taken to congregating in unusual locations." Jack propped a shoulder against the doorjamb. "Somehow, that seems in keeping with the rest of the day's activities. At least it smells good in here."

"The linen needed rearranging," Madeline said, pushing back to her feet. "I fell asleep."

A look passed between Pahdi and Jack, and Jack minutely shook his head.

Of course, an evening of drinking at the Weasel hadn't revealed the latest culprit. The culprit was standing before Jack, her heart breaking.

"Find your bed, Pahdi," Jack said. "I'll light Miss Hennessey to her room."

Pahdi bowed and withdrew, passing Jack the carrying candle.

"He's worried," Madeline said. She was beyond worry, approaching blind panic, though she knew what she must do.

"I'm worried," Jack said, picking up the candelabrum. "The mood at the Weasel was hardly reflective of the good spirits which a new year should engender. Mortimer Cotton was muttering about widows who get above themselves, and the winning darts team resented giving away their tournament money."

Madeline resented that her aunt had nearly frozen to death. "Then why give it away?"

"Pride." Jack closed the linen closet door as Madeline gained the corridor. "Possibly honor."

"Honor begrudges widows and orphans a warm bed?"

On this point, Madeline was clear. If her nocturnal forays into criminal behavior had kept her aunts and those similarly situated from undeserved suffering, then she wasn't sorry for her crimes. She was sorry those crimes could result in more undeserved suffering, though.

Very sorry.

"We won't solve the moral dilemmas of the shire tonight," Jack said, as they turned the corner to the family wing. "But I'd better find that blasted bag before Pahdi is deported in chains."

Deportation in chains would be a cheery outcome, considering the alternatives.

Which, of course, Madeline could not allow. Pahdi didn't deserve the suspicion and insult that came his way, any more than Aunt Theo deserved a miserable death for want of a hundredweight of coal.

"Even if you find the bag," Madeline said, "Higgans won't look in on Theo the next time she's ill. He won't bother treating a consumptive child, unless the child's parents can pay the fee. The yeomen at the Weasel won't learn generosity. Mortimer Cotton will never stop complaining that Aunt Hattie stole a ram who weighs nearly as much as she does."

Madeline realized this now, now that she'd all but stuck her neck in a noose.

"You are tired," Jack said. "Today has been trying, and I understand our elders are hatching plots likely born of too much elderberry cordial, and not enough concern for you. I'll find that damned bag, and this will all blow over."

Somebody should find the damned bag soon, if Madeline's scheme went as planned, but that somebody would not be Jack.

"I am tired," Madeline said, stopping outside her bedroom. "I am exhausted, in fact." Tired of hoping, tired of serving, tired of wishing, tired of coping. A crime spree had created more problems than it had solved, and soon, Madeline would have to deal with those problems too.

"I missed you today," Jack said. "You have a knack for seeing what needs to be done, for honest appraisal of difficult situations. I don't suppose you'd like a go at the magistrate's position?"

His jest was a sad commentary on the limitations Madeline was sick of dealing with. She was poor, a woman, attractive, and intelligent—all of which were burdens rather than blessings.

"I do not want a go at the magistrate's position," she said, kissing Jack on the mouth. "I want a go at the magistrate. Another go, in a damned bed, uninterrupted by footsteps in the corridor, or a well-meaning butler. I want pillows, lavender-scented sheets, and privacy."

She wanted so much more than that, but Jack would be furious with her when she told him the truth. There was a limit to the memories Madeline would steal for herself.

Jack kissed her back, a sweet, lingering, answering sigh of a kiss. "You need your rest."

"I need you."

Madeline needed one night with him, for herself. He'd already been intimate with her, another encounter wouldn't make that much difference when the truth came out. But the bleak prospects awaiting her in the morning wanted some ballast, some joy to make the suffering endurable.

"I need you too," Jack said, taking her by the hand. "I do not need for your reputation to be compromised, and my quarters have greater privacy."

"I'll just get my nightgown and robe," Madeline said, hand on the door latch.

"Madeline, you won't need either of those for what I have in mind."

She would miss him terribly—starting tomorrow. "Take me to bed, and we'll just see about what I need."

* * *

Jack ought not to be having intimate relations with a decent woman to whom he was not engaged, but then, Madeline ought not to have refused his addresses.

He'd spent the afternoon interviewing various members of the lending library subscription list, all of whom confirmed Pahdi's presence in the village the night of the darts tournament—which added nothing to Jack's store of facts. Nobody had walked with Pahdi to the edge of town. Nobody had anything more to add to Jack's potential defense of his butler.

He'd also stopped by Hattie Hennessey's cottage, endured a single cup of weak tea, and heard many effusions regarding Theodosia's impending remove to London, and the possibility that Hattie would take over as housekeeper at Candlewick.

Hattie had spent the evening of the darts tournament weaving at home, just as she'd spent the majority of her winter evenings—or so she'd claimed.

"My day was mostly wasted," Jack said, as he ushered Madeline into his bedroom. "I gather you were a paragon of productivity?"

As much as he wanted her naked in his bed, he wanted even more to smooth the rough edges from his day with the sort of talk known only to couples. He wanted to learn what Madeline had done with her time, and what had put the sadness in her eyes.

"I was... I was useless," Madeline said, closing the door. "Theodosia and your mother have concocted a mad scheme to hare off to London, and Aunt Hattie has apparently decided she must become Candlewick's housekeeper, provided I'll put in a word for her. She has no idea what the job entails, and hasn't managed a household for years, but she's... she's desperate."

Jack took Madeline in his arms, famished for the feel of her. "And because you can't tell your elders what to do, you exhausted yourself counting pillowcases." Jack didn't mention that Candlewick would do far better with Madeline as its chatelaine.

Perish the notion of her returning to Belmont's household on any terms.

"I was not invited to the whist party," Madeline said. "Not the one after lunch, or the one after dinner, but that's just as well. Most of the afternoon was taken up deciding how to arrange the linens when the chambermaids cannot agree—"

She sighed and cuddled closer. "I worry about you, Sir Jack, charging around on bad roads, out until all hours in an attempt to solve petty crimes."

Madeline bore the fragrance of lavender, on her clothes, in her hair, on her skin.

"I can't help but feel that regarding our latest rash of mischief, I'm missing something obvious, a pattern that goes beyond the annoying nature of the offenses. The king's man ought not to be foiled by pranksters and miscreants."

Madeline drew away and took a seat at Jack's vanity. "If Pahdi is charged with stealing Higgans's bag, that's quite serious."

She pulled pins loose, stacking them in a neat pile on her right. A long coppery braid came free, the tip reaching below her waist. The sight was so... domestic, so free of seduction and artifice, that Jack was temporarily at a loss for words.

He shrugged out of his coat, hung it in the wardrobe, and unfastened his cufflinks.

"The law does not convict a man based on half-inebriated accusations," Jack said, sitting on the bed to pull off his boots. "Or it shouldn't. That's all Higgans has to offer—accusations."

Madeline unraveled her braid until her hair was a loose riot of curls down her back. "You know better. Pahdi can be charged on the strength of anybody's accusations, and if you're not willing to do that, Higgans will create a fuss, and demand you recuse yourself from the matter. Mr. Belmont would step in, however reluctantly. Once charges are laid, anything can happen, including a conviction and sentencing."

"Your father was taken up for debt. Your view of the king's justice is understandably grim."

"Realistic," Madeline said, examining Jack's hairbrush, which was backed with gold and nacre. "My aunt's plan to elope to London is not realistic."

Jack's plan to marry Madeline Hennessey was very—well, he didn't care if it was realistic. For the rest of his life, he wanted to end his days like this, talking with Madeline, watching Madeline prepare for bed, and sharing that bed with her.

And he'd damned well take her aunts in hand too. Madeline could devise a way for him to do that, and to keep Weekes from being so faint of heart when it came to inspiring the flock to charity.

"Mama has a kind heart," Jack said, "despite appearances to the contrary. Theodosia would fare well under Mama's roof."

Madeline set the brush down and turned on the stool to face Jack. "Fine for Theodosia, but what about her property? She's not selling it, because she's determined that I should inherit from her. I can live there, though I've no notion how to make a smallholding profitable, and neither she nor Hattie have discussed how I'm to look after two properties when I haven't the coin or ability to manage even one."

Despite Madeline's quiet tone, her words were filled with both ire and incredulity.

"I've never wanted to be a smallholder," she went on, "and they assume—without so much as asking me—that I'm thrilled to take on work that stout young men find exhausting—work I have no idea how to do, work my aunts honestly haven't been able to do. I might as well be fifteen again, learning to set a table or beat a rug."

The part of Jack that liked puzzles started manufacturing solutions: sell one property, live on the other, using the proceeds of the first to make needed improvements. Rent both and use a steward to manage the tenants. Rent one, live at the other.

The set of Madeline's shoulders warned him against that version of helpfulness. None of those schemes would work for long if the property owner was a single, young female. Her aunts were tolerated based on their widowed status, and given some financial aid from the church and neighborly assistance. Madeline would have a harder time than even her aunts had endured.

Then too, the problem wasn't the properties, but rather, the people merrily thrusting them onto Madeline's shoulders.

"You'd never set a table as a girl?"

"For the tea parties I held in the nursery." Madeline picked up Jack's boots and put them outside the door. "I never realized that every time I sat down to breakfast, everything on the table had been precisely positioned, item by item. It's silly—the food tastes the same, provided the plate and silverware are clean—but it wasn't silly when I was new to service."

Jack undid his pocket watch and hung his waistcoat over the chair at the escritoire. "Are you angry, Madeline?"

He was angry, at Higgans, who might well have hidden his own medical bag to justify making accusations against an innocent man.

"Yes." She fastened the door lock with a decisive snick. "Yes, I am angry, now that you ask. I hadn't put that label on my sentiments, but I'm furious, and hurt, and—how can my aunts assume I'll gladly step aside from everything I know, and the people I know, and take up feeding chickens? I've given them my every spare groat, keeping only a little for my own old age at their insistence. I've given up my free time, gone without... I never foresaw that they'd cast me aside."

"But you daren't tell them that, because their happiness matters to you very much."

Just as Mama had not stopped Jack from shipping out for India, though she'd probably felt awfully betrayed by his actions.

And afraid, afraid for her firstborn son. Doubtless Jeremy's decision to enter the clergy had also been a result of Jack's determination to see India firsthand.

"Can you talk to your aunts?" Could Jack talk to them? He could buy both properties, find Madeline tenants for them, and set his steward to managing them, but he could not force assistance on Madeline that she wasn't prepared to accept.

"I can't deny Theo a chance to live far more comfortably, I know that. I'm just—hold me."

That, Jack could do, happily, forever. He pulled his shirt over his head and tossed it toward the wardrobe, then wrapped his arms around his tired, bewildered, annoyed lady.

"Would you ask me for help if you needed it, Madeline?"

She yawned against his shoulder. "Do *you* ask anybody for help?"

"I asked *you* for help, and you did not fail me. My house is a happier place, my mother has seen the wisdom of having good companionship, and the year will proceed more smoothly henceforth because you have put a guiding hand on the—"

Madeline slid a guiding hand around to his backside. "You're paying me well for my time here."

Money had no place in the point Jack was making. "You could have refused me. Your position at Candlewick was comfortable, and you owe me nothing."

She had no glib retort, and she was wearing far too many clothes.

"Are you falling asleep, Madeline? My masculine pride will never recover if you prefer a nap to sampling my charms."

She turned, swept her hair up, and presented him with a row of hooks. "So be my lady's maid. A maid can get in and out of her uniform unassisted, but not so, a companion."

Her posture was trusting and alluring both. Jack made himself useful unhooking her dress and loosening her stays rather than dwell on how many ways he'd like to kiss her nape.

"You're welcome to borrow my toothpowder," Jack said, "and there's water warming by the hearth."

Madeline walked straight to the privacy screen, her undone dress and unbound hair provoking a riot behind Jack's falls.

He'd never felt this way about a woman, not even about Saras. She'd been exotic, passionate, loyal, intelligent, and beautiful, but Jack had been too young to grasp that she could also have been his friend.

And he hers. "Shall I bring you the warm water?"

"Please."

Why hadn't he lit more candles when he'd had the chance? Behind the privacy screen, Madeline stood in her shift and stockings—thin shift, much-darned stockings—twisting her hair back into a braid. Jack fetched her the tattered hair ribbon from his vanity.

"You are not shy. I like that." He hated that she hadn't even a decent pair of stockings.

"I am not sixteen, and you will soon see every treasure I possess. You might want to get out of your breeches first."

He wanted desperately to get out of his breeches, but the moment to display his wares hadn't arrived.

"I'll warm the sheets."

The bed had been turned down when Pahdi had last tended to the hearth and brought the wash water. Jack filled the warmer with coals and did a thorough job, even warming the pillows, then pulled the covers back up.

Madeline emerged from the privacy screen in Jack's dressing gown, a luxurious brown velvet article lined with blue silk. She'd probably never worn so rich a garment—and all Jack wanted was to get her out of it.

"I hope you don't mind that I've borrowed this," she said. "I like that it bears your scent."

"It will also keep you warm in a winter wind. Into bed with you. I'll be only a moment."

Jack remained before the hearth, rather than give her a moment of privacy. In this at least, he'd insist on her trust.

Madeline unbelted the robe, let it slip from her shoulders, and passed it to him.

He let the robe fall to the floor. Madeline Hennessey was... Aphrodite come to life. Her figure testified to both rigorous activity and good nutrition, and her feminine endowments made Jack ache everywhere from his hands to his breeding organs, while her trust warmed his heart.

"I'm not a girl," Madeline said, chin tipping down. "You know that."

What Jack knew, was that Madeline wasn't entirely his. Not yet. He stalked over to her, and wrapped her in his arms. The sensation of *her* against *him*, both of them naked from the waist up, was like holding the fire of life, both shocking and dangerously delightful.

"My back is scarred," Jack said. "I'm proud of those scars, because they remind me that I can fight when I have to, fight until other men with more sense would give up. You are beautiful, you don't need me to tell you that, but it's not your exquisite form that captures my regard."

He paused to kiss her, truly, properly, indecently kiss her.

"You like my form," Madeline said. "When you look at me like that and kiss me like that, I like my form too."

About damned time. "I will do far more than like your form just as soon as I join you in that bed. Don't let the sheets get cold." He managed to extricate himself from Madeline's embrace and walk to the privacy screen without stumbling, though it was a near thing.

For her, he'd get his unruly passion under control, and pleasure the lady witless as long as she allowed him to—and pleasure himself witless a time or two as well. That part, he was confident he could manage.

Jack did not know how he'd convey to Madeline that he suspected her Aunt Hattie had taken to a life of petty larceny and that his own mother agreed that such a hypothesis explained all the facts.

And Jack was in a complete quandary over what to do about it.

* * *

Of all the thefts Madeline had committed, stealing this night with Jack was the one she would not regret. Something troubled him—the missing medical bag perhaps—and yet, for her, he would put off the magistrate's role and be her lover.

As she would be his.

He emerged naked from the privacy screen, a long, lean warrior of a man, honed by life, and to Madeline's profound gratification, well past his foolish, strutting youth. When he turned to bank the fire, Madeline got her second good view of the scars on his back.

Old scars, and he was right to be proud of them. He'd not given up, against terrible odds, nor had he taken to stealing and offering silent, symbolic sermons to his betters.

But then, soldiers were permitted to fight. Their lot wasn't to black andirons, dust sideboards, and polish wainscoting until their knees screamed and their elders died of poverty and exhaustion.

Jack set the poker on its stand and replaced the fire screen. "That is a pensive expression, Miss Hennessey."

"Do you have regrets, Jack?"

"Yes," he said, climbing into the bed. "I regret that you won't marry me— yet—despite the fact that your common sense and pragmatism would greatly improve my ability to be useful to my neighbors, both as their magistrate and otherwise. Prepare yourself for a display of my legendary tenacity."

Madeline forced a smile. "That approaches a boast. Fortunately, we have all night for you to demonstrate this tenacity."

"We will talk," Jack said. "At length, and about whatever uncomfortable reasons you have for refusing the addresses of a man who esteems you beyond telling. If you fear I will dodge off to India, you're wrong. If you fear I'll grow bored and indifferent, you're in error there as well. If you fear my vows will be taken lightly, then let me put your fears—"

Madeline touched two fingers to his mouth.

She feared he'd uphold the law. A man who'd considered it his duty to stop wars wouldn't flinch at arresting his lover when she handed him a sincere confession.

"Enough talk," she said. "Tomorrow will come too soon, and we both have problems aplenty to sort out. Tonight is for pleasure."

And esteem, and—oh, why not be honest?— *for love.* Madeline loved Jack Fanning in a way a girl could not, with respect and acceptance for the man he was, and knowing that with love sometimes came disappointment.

Jack crouched over her, so she was pinned beneath the blankets. "You'll notice I sleep without bed curtains. I'm less likely to wake from a nightmare and think myself back in that cell."

"I have nightmares too, Jack."

Rather than endure his well-meant queries, Madeline resumed kissing him. Jack brought variety to kissing, unlike other men of Madeline's acquaintance. She couldn't characterize him as a nibbler, a tongue-tangler, a choir boy…

He was inventive and attentive, both, never pushing Madeline beyond the pace she was comfortable with.

"Get under the covers, Jack. I want to wrap my legs around you."

He rested his forehead on her chest. "I'm trying for some finesse here, Madeline. I must acquit myself well with you."

Daft man. She stroked his hair. "Acquit yourself under the covers. Now, please."

She felt him smile, felt him take a little taste of her cleavage. "You said please." He was under the covers in the next instant, and somehow, Madeline was straddling him. "If you are inclined to direct matters, then this position allows you more control."

So it did—at first.

Madeline plundered Jack's mouth, teased him with her sex, and generally enjoyed herself with a man more than willing to be enjoyed.

Then Jack started using his hands—free, when he lay on his back—to caress Madeline's back, her hips, her chest, her arms…

"My breasts," she muttered between kisses. "Touch my breasts."

"Manners, Miss Hennessey."

"Please, damn you."

Oh, he was a wretch, a wonderful, creative, determined wretch. His hands teased, his mouth… his mouth on Madeline's breasts was a revelation.

She'd not been properly loved before becoming intimate with Jack Fanning. He gloried in pleasuring her, elevated arousal to an art form, and had no self-consciousness about indulging his own pleasures.

His hands on her hips urged her up, as he scooted down against the pillows.

"What are you doing?"

"Being tenacious, also selfish. Grab the headboard."

"Why should I—?"

Dear God. What he did with his mouth probably had no description in English, it was so wicked and wonderful. Madeline moved minutely, riding the pleasure, until Jack used his right hand to cup her breast.

Nothing, nothing in Madeline's experience compared with the sensations that befell her in the moments that followed. She moaned, she thrashed, it was too much, and she couldn't get enough, and instant by instant, Jack knew exactly how to keep her falling endlessly from yearning into satisfaction.

When she hung over him, dazed and panting, he stroked her hip, slowly, soothingly, maintaining a connection when Madeline wanted to hide beneath the bed. She climbed off of him, and scooted under the covers.

"I can't believe that just happened." Madeline went unresisting into Jack's embrace, which seemed as good a place to hide as any. The best place, at the moment. The only place.

"I can't believe it took this long for that to happen, when you so clearly enjoy it. I do well with some direction—my skills are rusty, and leaving me to guess isn't… I want to please you, Madeline."

If that was a demonstration of rusty skills, Madeline was in bed with a terror. "How can I give direction when you're familiar with terrain I didn't know existed?"

He kissed her temple. "The landscape is beautiful. We'll explore it together."

No, they would not. Not after tonight. Rather than begin that explanation, Madeline gave in to cowardice, and let sleep claim her.

* * *

The hour was nearing midnight, and Jeremy lingered at the card table and wallowed in melancholy rounds of solitaire. *She* had touched these cards, his Lucy Anne who wasn't his.

The nasty trick about solitaire was that winning was possible, in theory. That theoretical dream of victory kept the cards turning by the hour, and hope remained, despite defeat after defeat.

The door opened with a soft click, and Jeremy anticipated a nightcap with Jack. That's what brothers did late on a winter evening—shared a drink, a hand of cards, a few observations about the politics of the day, a manly grumble about the upcoming assembly.

Jeremy was almost sure that's what brothers did, most brothers. Jack was too busy being a magistrate to indulge in much fraternal socializing. Jeremy didn't resent his brother's devotion to duty, exactly, but a fellow—

"Reverend Jeremy, I didn't expect to find you here."

Lucy Anne—to blazes with the Miss—stood near the door in a nightgown and robe, her feet clad in thick wool stockings.

Jeremy rose from the card table. "At this hour, do you suppose I might be just plain Jeremy? I'm playing solitaire, continually vanquishing my own aspirations to victory. Would you care to play a hand or two?"

She was not properly dressed, and Jeremy was fascinated with those wool stockings. Where were the lady's slippers? And yet, she was in every way modestly covered, and if she married Jack, Jeremy would have to fortify himself against future holidays spent in close proximity to his brother's wife.

Jack might not be interested in the lady, but when had the groom's preferences signified, if the groom's mama and the bride were intent on getting him to the altar? Jack was the dutiful sort, while Jeremy was the... sort to be fascinated with wool stockings.

Nowhere in the Commandments was a fascination with a lady's stockings prohibited, and yet, the way they revealed the contours of Lucy Anne's feet condemned Jeremy to purgatory. Slender feet, narrow, graceful, and Jeremy speculated that her toes—

"I came for my embroidery," she said. "We've been playing so much whist lately, I haven't had a chance to work on my stitching."

"One could say we were whist-full."

Lucy Anne stalked across the room. "One could say I'm exasperated. How am I supposed to court a man who isn't even home much of the day?"

Jeremy had wondered if Jack was avoiding Lucy Anne. What mattered an old leather satchel likely misplaced by its owner, or a few lumps of coal turning to mud?

"Lucy Anne, did Mama instruct you to court Jack?" This point had been troubling Jeremy, because Mama was not shy about hurling thunderbolts of opinion—at the servants, her friends, her matched chestnut geldings, or her children.

"She most certainly did. Mrs. Fanning said to make myself agreeable to her offspring, and she'd look with favor upon any resulting offers of marriage." Lucy Anne paced before the hearth, her hems swishing such that Jeremy was tormented with a view of more than her wool-clad feet. "I've been cheerful, I've been charming, I've been patient, I've been as perishing agreeable as I know how to be, and Jack Fanning could not be less interested."

A man who studied Scripture by the hour was attuned to the nuances of language. Nothing in Mama's edict had singled out Jack as the only eligible party. Had that been by design?

"I'm interested, Lucy Anne." Fascinated, besotted, top over tail, intrigued. Let the reputation of the great hero compete with those sentiments, or try to.

She came to an abrupt halt, her skirts swinging about her ankles. "Interested in... *me?*"

"In you." In her bare toes, her kisses, her smiles, her laughter, and her determination. Jeremy was very interested in her determination. He'd not been a monk at university, and a determined woman had a charm all her own.

"I'm not..." Lucy Anne turned toward the fire. "I'm not pious. I'm not... churchy. You're such a perfect, dear, kind, compassionate, tolerant... I'm not like you. I'm frivolous. Harmless. Your brother could use a cheering influence, but you're... you don't need a woman for that."

Harmless, she was not. Not beneath the mistletoe, and not late at night, swathed in frustration and honesty.

Jeremy came closer, the better to see her features when he was honest too. "I'm not pious either. The bit with the vestments and singing is all fine, but it's the churchyard part I truly enjoy. Hearing how people have been getting on, whose heifer had twins, which young sprout has lost his front teeth. I think you'd excel at taking an interest in people. It matters more than you'd think."

She stared into the fire, which had burned low owing to the lateness of the hour. "Friendliness isn't piety, Jeremy. I know how people can be about a vicar's wife."

What was this fixation on appearances? "May I kiss you, Lucy Anne?"

"You've kissed me before. For a man of the cloth—"

Hearing no objection, Jeremy pressed a soft kiss to the lady's cheek, and she turned into his arms with gratifying alacrity. For long, sweet moments, he explained—kiss by kiss—that love took many forms, and the love of a man for his prospective wife was one of the most enjoyable manifestations, provided the lady was similarly enthralled.

"My profession isn't complicated," Jeremy said, gathering Lucy Anne close. "I'm to help people be kind and honest, and part of that is being kind and honest myself. I like being a vicar, but it can be lonely. I will be better at my calling, and happier, if you will be my beloved companion. Will you do me the great honor of becoming my wife?"

Lucy Anne drew in a long, shuddery breath, which didn't bode well for Jeremy's future. He kept his peace, though, because no wife at all was better than a reluctant wife. Women had little enough choice in life, for the most part, and this one decision must not be wrested from them.

"I've been sick," Lucy Anne said, "sick to think that I'm supposed to resign myself to a life as Jack Fanning's invisible wife. He's all business and duty and haring about. He doesn't sit and play cards with the ladies because he enjoys our company. He tolerates us when he'd rather be on the king's business. I can't help but think he'd rather be back in India, wearing strange clothes and riding elephants. I'm boring, and he's..."

"The hero of Parrakan," Jeremy said. "You aren't being entirely fair to Jack, but don't let me stop your tirade. I hope you will consider my suit as something more than a consolation for Jack's lack of interest."

Jeremy would insist on that, for everybody's sake, including Lucy Anne's.

"You will think me wicked," Lucy Anne said, stepping back. "Do you recall when I asked you for kissing lessons?"

Jeremy would recall those kissing lessons into doddering old age. "I do."

"I sit across from you at the card table, hour after hour, trying not to stare, Jeremy Fanning. Your eyes are so kind, and your hands... I have the naughtiest thoughts about your hands. No man was ever a more perfect height. No man ever had a more charming smile or a more sonorous voice. You will love me when I'm old and querulous. You will be the sort of papa every daughter should have. You will—"

"I will be the sort of husband you've dreamed about," Jeremy said, feeling a bit heroic himself. "I promise you that. Jack can be our wealthy relation who spoils our children, but we'll be the family who treat him like family, not like some visiting nabob. I wish we could make an announcement at the assembly, but I must speak to your father."

Lucy Anne wrapped her arms about Jeremy's waist. "I wish we could be married right now."

So did Jeremy. He settled for kissing his intended, because truly, no words could come close to the sense of joy and well-being Lucy Anne's acceptance sent beating through his veins.

Jack would be happy for them, by God, or Jeremy would instruct the hero of Parrakan in the basics of brotherly love.

CHAPTER FOURTEEN

Jack held Madeline while she slept, as if keeping his arms around her might anchor him in the midst of an emotional gale. To love her to exhaustion, to show her pleasures previously denied to her, left him prouder than had any feat of diplomacy or victory in battle.

Despite her confident airs and competence in all household tasks, Madeline Hennessey was uncertain, shy, and in a sense, inexperienced.

He'd remedy *that* oversight.

Madeline stirred, her hand brushing over Jack's belly. Arousal went from simmering to boiling with that single caress.

"Go to sleep," Jack murmured. She was weary, after all.

Madeline lifted her head from his shoulder. "You don't want to go to sleep." Her insight came by virtue of her hand wrapped about his cock.

"I want you to have the rest you need, Madeline. Too many people have been selfish where you're concerned."

Madeline let go of him, and Jack mentally cursed gentlemanly scruples for the wretched inconvenience they were. Then a single finger traced his most sensitive flesh.

"I've had a lovely nap, thank you, Jack. I'm ready to conclude what you so inventively started. Shall I put my mouth on you?"

He'd last about two shakes of a lamb's tail, and have half as much finesse as Charles II on a frisky day.

"Let's save that pleasure for another time, when I'm not mad to be inside you." Though when would such a time be? Jack's interest in sex had never overly troubled him, but his interest in Madeline Hennessey was unrelenting.

"You're mad to be...?"

"Inside you," Jack said, shifting over her. "Desperate, crazy, mad. Have been for days and nights. You think I'm off chatting up the lending library patrons for my health? I see you, and I want to put my hands on you. My mouth, my anything."

Madeline wrapped her legs about his flanks. "So why don't you?"

He obliged, joyously, exuberantly, with an abandon he'd thought he'd left in India. Madeline met him kiss for kiss, sigh for sigh, and caress for caress, until Jack was nearly incoherent with need.

"Madeline?"

She rubbed her breasts against him. "Hmm?"

"Now?"

Such were her reserves of self-possession that for a moment, she traced the scars on Jack's back, an odd there-and-not-there sensation.

"You know I esteem you greatly, Jack Fanning? I've never respected a man, never liked a man, never desired a man as much as I do you. I want you to know that."

Jack eased forward, a consolatory pleasure, because respect, liking, esteem, and desire fell short of his own sentiments.

He'd been held prisoner under dire conditions. He'd walked between warring parties unarmed. He'd defied orders and risked court martial when honor demanded it. Surely, for the woman in his arms, he could show some courage?

"I love you, Madeline," he said, sinking into her heat. "With everything in me, I want to be close to you, protect you, grow old with you, raise children with you. I want to pleasure you until you scream, share your laughter, and dry your tears. *Marry me.*"

Her answer was to lift into his thrusts, to lock her ankles at the small of his back, and move with him in a harmony so close, Jack felt the lovemaking throughout his being. This wasn't simply pleasure, this was... love. The physical and the metaphysical in an oscillation of emotion and sensation that transcended time and even identity.

He wasn't Jack Fanning, he was simply Madeline's lover, the perfect complement to her, and she to him. For a sweet, luxurious eternity, he remained joined with her, until Madeline increased the pace, and asked more from him.

He gave it to her, lavishing pleasure upon her until his own control teetered, and Madeline took the initiative away from him entirely. He tried to pull back, but she was strong, and held him to her with her legs.

"Madeline, I can't—we mustn't."

"Stay with me."

Madness, but Jack hadn't the wits left to refuse her. Never had he felt such an intense *union*, of all parts of him joining with all parts of his lover, until what remained was pleasure, wonder, and a sense of having glimpsed an experience beyond the earthly realm.

When Jack could push thoughts through his mind again, he and Madeline lay cocooned beneath the covers, panting in synchrony. Madeline kissed his cheek. Jack rested his forehead on hers.

She might not be entirely his, but he was absolutely and forever hers. "Marry me, Madeline. Please."

If she refused him, he'd love her all over again, though it might kill him. Her refusal would deal a worse blow than death.

"I'll marry you," she said, easing her legs from around his waist. "But you might have to arrest me first."

* * *

Madeline could not lie to a man who made love like... like *that*. With everything in him, wholeheartedly, unreservedly. Jack didn't swive, fornicate, shake the groundsels, dance the mattress hornpipe.

He'd *made love* with Madeline. Broken her heart and mended it all at once. Now it was her turn to break his.

He lifted up enough that they slipped apart. "If you're trying to dispel the mood, Madeline, talk of arresting you is an impressive start." He kissed her nose, got off the bed, and disappeared behind the privacy screen.

When he returned to the bed, he passed Madeline a damp flannel. "Unless you'd rather..." He gestured toward the privacy screen.

Holy naked cherubs, he was bold. Madeline made do beneath the covers rather than trek across the bedroom in her natural glory. She passed the cloth back to Jack, who tossed it over the screen. The wet plop of flannel on porcelain sounded as Jack climbed back under the covers.

Her lover had good aim.

"Marrying me is not a crime," he said. "Why would I arrest you?"

Madeline was apparently to answer this question with her backside tucked intimately against Jack's... against *Jack*.

"I've committed crimes, plural. I'm not proud of that, but you're the magistrate, so it falls to you to arrest me. I'm confessing."

"Confessing? You accept my marriage proposal—and I will hold you to that acceptance—and now you confess to criminal activities. This is certainly novel. I was under the impression that cuddling and pillow talk came after the lovemaking."

He'd tucked one arm beneath Madeline's neck, and wrapped the other around her middle. She was surrounded by Jack, and nothing—not his body, not his tone of voice—suggested he was upset by what Madeline said.

"I stole the coal from McArdle and divided it between my aunts without their knowledge. I took the tournament money from the Weasel. I stole Higgans's medical bag. I was angry." Jack kissed her shoulder, which Madeline found annoying. "I solve an entire crime spree for you, and you're flirting."

"Madam, we passed flirting several raptures ago. What were you angry about?"

That question wasn't as easy to answer as Madeline might have thought. "I've been angry for years, since my father drank and gambled away all of our security, since I was beaten for offenses I hadn't committed, since my aunts were left to scrimp and starve by husbands who'd betrayed their trust."

"Those are good reasons to be angry. Are you angry with me?"

That question wasn't from the magistrate, but rather, from the lover—the brave lover.

"No, I'm not angry with you. I'm angry with myself for disappointing you. Stealing is wrong, I know that, but being good and kind and honest wouldn't keep my aunts warm through January, or make Vicar disperse the poor box funds when they were needed, rather than when he recalled to do it."

"And Higgans's medical bag?"

"Aunt Theo could have died because of his laziness. I'm not sorry I took his medical bag. In a just world, I'd leave him to shiver his way through a bad lung fever, alone in a cottage where the fire had gone out. I couldn't do that, so I took the symbol of his calling from him."

Jack started a slow kneading of Madeline's shoulders. "Stealing is a crime, you're right. I'm not sure moving the tournament money to the church qualifies as stealing, but Madeline, lying isn't considered good behavior either. Even lying to protect loved ones is still dishonest."

Madeline twisted around to peer at Jack. "What are you going on about? A confession is when one tells the truth, and that's what I've done."

She settled back into his arms, wondering if these were the last moments she'd spend in his embrace.

"Madeline," Jack said, very close to her ear, "I treasure you for your loyalty to family, but you needn't dissemble. I know Hattie helped herself to McArdle's coal, moved that money, and stole Higgans's bag. I questioned her today, and both evenings when you claimed to have visited her, she made no mention of your coming to call. She wasn't home, was she?"

God in heaven. This was worse than inadvertently incriminating Pahdi, or at least as bad.

"If Hattie were the guilty party, would you prosecute her, Jack?"

His sigh fanned past Madeline's nape. "I'm sworn to uphold the king's justice, Madeline, but prosecuting an old woman for trying to keep warm by burning what is essentially McArdle's trash is beyond me. No harm resulted from moving the tournament funds—a miraculous occurrence, if you ask

Tavis—and all we need do in Higgans's case is return his blasted bag to him."

In other words, the magistrate valued reparation over incarceration. Good to know.

Wonderful to know, in fact.

"Jack, Hattie didn't mention my visits because I was busy stealing coal, putting the darts money in the church vestibule, and nipping Higgans's bag. I did those things, and I can't plead age or poverty. I wanted... justice, I suppose, or for somebody to acknowledge that Hattie, Theo, and others like them need and deserve help."

Jack went still, stopped his stroking and caressing. Madeline couldn't even feel his breath on her shoulder.

"*You* committed these crimes?"

Oh, the incredulity in his voice. Madeline didn't know whether to be flattered or dismayed.

"Yes. My wages aren't adequate to make the repairs my aunts' cottages need. I couldn't afford Cotton's ram for Aunt Hattie. I couldn't ask Vicar to scold people into increasing their donations for the poor. I couldn't give up my position at Candlewick because without that money my aunts would be worse off than they are now. I didn't know what else to do."

"You didn't know what else to do?" His question was carefully neutral, as if verifying a translation from a foreign tongue.

"You call me competent," Madeline said, around an ache in her throat. "I'm not. I didn't know how to help my aunts, and everything I tried wasn't enough. I'm so tired of not knowing what to do."

She rolled over, and plastered herself to Jack's chest. She needed his arms around her now, and even if he ordered her from the bed, she wasn't sure she could make herself leave.

"This is the real confession," Jack said, drawing her close and resting his cheek against her temple. "You are exhausted, bewildered, and ready to drop where you stand, but you cannot give up. I know how that feels, Madeline. I do."

Madeline's tears came in noisy, undignified sobs, when a polite sniffle mortified her. Now she wanted to run from the room, but Jack's arms held her fast.

"Sometimes, I think I hate them," she said, "the pair of them. They are so stubborn, and so admirable, but they're all I have, and I can't... I don't..."

She gave up trying to explain the welter of protectiveness, need, frustration, and terror that drove her, and all the while, Jack held her. He said nothing, didn't reason with her, didn't judge or pontificate, and in his silence, Madeline heard worlds of understanding.

"You'll not arrest me?" Tears had made her voice low and raspy. "I didn't take Cotton's blasted ram, by the way, but that's what gave me the inspiration."

Jack's hand on her back paused, then resumed a slow sweep across her shoulder blades. "Charles II inspired you?"

"Not the ram, but the fact that the ram showed up when Aunt needed him. Somebody probably left a gate unlocked accidentally, and Hattie's herd was serviced. Cotton wasn't out any coin—Aunt would never have paid for the ram to visit her ewes—but Aunt's problem was solved. Her lambs will come quite late, so she'll not cost anybody else a good price at market. I know Cotton has been quietly accused of generosity, but I can't believe that to be the case."

"So you saw a victimless crime in that example."

Jack's tone was off, though his touch remained gentle.

"I saw... a way to atone for doing what I found necessary. McArdle needed to padlock his yard, and he can't sell the leavings strewn all over his lot."

"So McArdle received a valuable lesson, and a tidy yard. What about the tournament money? Another valuable lesson, to both Tavis and the vicar?"

He sounded almost admiring.

"Or Vicar's congregation. We're a fortunate parish, generally. We ought to do better by our widows, and the Weasel had a better reputation when Tavis's mother ran it."

"No argument there. What of Higgans's bag?"

"I had no higher purpose than making him look like a fool," Madeline said. "And I've got Pahdi in awful trouble. Do you believe I had nothing to do with Cotton's ram?"

This mattered to Madeline. Confessing to crimes she'd committed was difficult enough, and the business with the ram was so fortuitous, Madeline wanted to believe it was the work of kind providence.

Jack kissed her shoulder again, and this time, Madeline didn't find it annoying at all.

"You had nothing to do with Charles II paying a call on Hattie's ewes, and neither did Cotton. I know exactly who arranged that situation."

But Jack hadn't arrested anybody, or stifled the rumors that Cotton had set the ram loose himself.

"Who would do such a thing?" Madeline asked. "It was quite clever, and now everybody wonders if Cotton hasn't been hiding a latent streak of decency beneath all his bluster. I'd like to commend the thief, or ram-napper, whoever he is."

An interesting silence ensued, while Jack kissed his way from her shoulder to her ear.

Then he rolled to his back, and situated Madeline along his side. "You may commend *me*, Madeline. I put the ram in with Hattie's ewes, and I'll thank you not to peach on me. Mama has a very high opinion of the hero of Parrakan, and I'd like to stay in her good graces."

"*You*—? You put the ram in with Hattie's ewes?"

"She wouldn't take charity, and Cotton wasn't about to extend charity. Nobody wanted to meddle, and yet, something had to be done. Cost me half a night's sleep, and my dog cart will smell like ram until next summer. Stop laughing, Madeline. I thought surely you'd pick up the scent when I delivered you to Teak House from Candlewick."

She did not stop laughing. She laughed as hard as she'd cried, until Jack stopped laughing long enough to point out that all they need do is return Higgans's bag to him, and be about planning the wedding.

"That's the problem," Madeline said. "That blighted bag is not where I put it. I've looked twice, and his damned bag has somehow gone missing in truth."

* * *

Madeline had lifted the window to Higgans's study, taken his bag, and left it sitting in the muck wagon at the local livery several doors away from Higgans's house. She'd left the pony trap hitched behind the livery, an ordinary location to leave a nondescript vehicle. Nobody had remarked her crime because everybody was too intent on assembling at the Weasel, or getting home before the temperature dropped further.

Jack had searched the livery as well as he could without being obvious, and though the muck wagon had sat in its usual location—the livery was a tidy place—he'd seen no sign of Higgans's bag.

"May I interrupt?" Jeremy asked. He stood in the doorway to Jack's study, morning light from the window across the corridor gilding his hair.

"Of course," Jack said. "Need a break from the whist enthusiasts?"

Jeremy came into the study and closed the door behind him, but didn't take the seat across from Jack's desk.

"I never much cared for whist. Suppose you don't either."

Jack had been too busy for whist over the past few days. "I'm not very good at it." The one time he'd sat down with Mama, Jack, and Miss DeWitt, Mama's matchmaking innuendos had outnumbered the playing cards.

Jack kept a box of jasmine tea on this desk, the same as in the library and on the escritoire in his bedroom. Jeremy picked up the one sitting to Jack's left and peered at the carvings.

"You don't have to be good at cards, Jack. That's not the point. This is not decent."

Most people never noticed. "It's pretty. I like it. The scent of the tea soothes me."

Jeremy set it down, though his expression was a touch wistful. "I'm getting married."

Well, damn. Jack had been hoping Miss DeWitt might notice what a sterling fellow Jeremy was, and solve several problems with a single kiss, as it were.

"Congratulations. Whoever she is, she's a lucky woman."

Now Jeremy settled into the chair opposite the desk. "I haven't approached her family, though the young lady is quite willing. What are you working on?"

"I've made a list of all the people who were at the lending library. I need to speak with them again regarding the night Higgans's bag went missing."

"Don't you want to know the name of my intended?"

"Only if you want to tell me. If you're concerned her family will turn you down, don't be. We don't need anybody's money to live quite comfortably, or to see a young lady well settled after taking the Fanning name. If she's your choice, then she's deserving of our every courtesy and protection. That aside, her family would be daft to refuse you."

The list before Jack was too damned long, and beside it sat a note from Higgans demanding to know if progress had been made on "the case."

The damned case could go hang for a moment. Jeremy had chosen a bride.

"That's it?" Jeremy asked, sitting forward. "I've taken a fancy to a lady, and you're ready to start writing bank drafts and recommending me as a suitor?"

Jeremy had known their father even less than Jack had, which might explain this display of diffidence on Jeremy's part. A father might have offered advice or guidance on the choice of a bride. All Jack could offer was moral support.

"Jere, you are a fine man, and a gentleman. I'm proud to call you brother. I could not for two weeks do what you do, much less do it as well as you do. You make Mama laugh. You make Pahdi smile. I can count on my one hand the number of times I've seen that man smile, and I've known him half my life. When you walk into the room, Miss DeWitt lights up. You would have made a much better diplomat than I, but you have such genuine humility that the diplomatic corps would never occur to you."

Jeremy rose. "Miss DeWitt would agree with you. Thinks I'm a paragon. Ridiculous, but there it is."

Thank God, Lucy Anne DeWitt, and the healthy appetites of the Fanning menfolk—and their fiancées.

"Miss DeWitt has excellent taste, but now you know a bit how I felt, with all that hero nonsense, when mostly I'd managed not to bungle too badly."

"That can't be easy," Jeremy said. "Makes a fellow feel like he ought to be a hero even if he hasn't any notion how to go on. Difficult business, being a hero without a map."

Jeremy sounded only partly bewildered. The other part of him was smilingly devilishly at nothing in particular. And yet, he'd described Jack's situation exactly. Being a hero without a map was no damned fun.

"Be Miss DeWitt's hero, and the rest will sort itself out."

That was apparently the right thing to say, because Jeremy's smile became luminous. "She'll be my heroine, and then we'll have some little heroes and heroines, and you can spoil the lot of them rotten. We'll descend on you at the holidays and in summertime, and Mama will be the envy of her friends."

"Don't get started on the little heroes and heroines too soon. Unless you're thinking of a special license?"

Reverend Jeremy's ears turned a non-ecclesiastical shade of red. "My Lucy Anne can be quite... irresistible."

"So can my Madeline."

Jack had lost sleep about that, about taking risks with Madeline that might result in a child when he'd yet to put his ring on her finger.

"One suspected," Jeremy said, going to the window. "Miss Hennessey looks at you the way Mama used to look out at the sea when we summered in Brighton and you were in India."

"I've never thanked you for that," Jack said, joining his brother at the window. The weather had finally moderated, which meant the lanes were mud, the eaves dripping, and at night, everything would turn back to ice.

"Thanked me?"

"You could have bought a commission, followed me to India. Mama would not have stopped you. You stayed behind and guarded her from melancholia and bitterness. I have you to thank for the fact that my mother didn't disown me for getting captured."

"She wanted to sail after you when we heard you were presumed dead. She was ready to conquer the Bengal tribes single-handedly. My Lucy Anne will be the same sort of mama."

So will my Madeline. Though the first order of business was to find Higgans's damned bag.

"For not letting Mama take ship, you have my undying gratitude." Jack extended a hand to his brother. "Congratulations on your impending nuptials."

"I will marry her, Jack. If I have to elope to Scotland and become a Presbyterian. I gather it's the same with you and Miss Hennessey?"

Every man should have a kind, tolerant, brother who was this easy to talk to. "Madeline defies all of my preconceived notions about the institution of matrimony and its various attendant glories—let's leave it at that. Before she and I can make any announcement, I must find Higgans's damned medical bag."

Jeremy took Jack's chair behind the desk. "What has some forgetful sot of a doctor's bag to do with holy matrimony or its... attendant glories?" Jeremy rendered the term as if trying it on for later use in a sermon.

Jack had come home from India for several reasons, not the least of which was that exoticism had grown wearisome, adventure had paled, and loneliness had become his dominant experience of life. He'd missed Saras. He'd missed a land at peace that made sense to him. He'd missed seasons that offered a variety of weather instead of an annual rotation of deadly fevers.

He'd missed home. Jeremy was his brother, though only now did Jack feel as if he was being a brother to Jeremy in return.

"The situation with Higgans is complicated," Jack said, "and if you have the time to listen, I will offer you a recitation that falls under the confidential privilege of clergy."

In other words, Jeremy would not even under oath, disclose what Jack was about to tell him.

"You've been naughty," Jeremy said. "One rejoices to learn a hero can be naughty like the rest of us. I will listen with the privilege of a brother, help any way I can, and keep my handsome mouth shut about the whole of it. What have you done?"

Jack started with borrowing the ram without permission—his sin to confess, if a sin it was—and progressed to how his misdeed had inspired Madeline, but that her misbehavior had now implicated Pahdi, at least in Higgans's mind.

To talk through the sequence of events helped organize the problem in Jack's mind, but it didn't suggest any more possible locations where he might look for the damned bag.

"You could send Pahdi to London to see the sights," Jeremy suggested. "Or back to India."

"Which would confirm his guilt, and that's not right. The bag has to be somewhere."

"Have you dug through the livery's muck pit? Somebody might have simply heaped the cart full and emptied it without paying attention."

Awful—odoriferous thought. "I asked the livery to delivery me two loads of fresh manure, and... nothing. If the bag was in their muck pit, I'd have found it by now."

"Higgans won't let it go?"

"I blundered, Jere. I insulted Higgans in public, and his reaction is to shame me and my household by accusing Pahdi. He won't let it go."

"And you don't want to step aside as magistrate because the king's justice is a chancy proposition on a good day, and our Pahdi's wellbeing cannot be entrusted to chance. What if we distract people with a wedding?"

Our Pahdi. Jack would have loved his brother for those two words, if there wasn't already ample reason.

"You'd need a special license." And a fast horse for the ride to Town.

"As it happens, I have business in London with Miss DeWitt's papa, and a special license wouldn't be any extra trouble."

Jeremy was politely quivering to leave.

"Take the coach in case you have to bring Miss DeWitt's parents back with you. And Jere, about the special license?"

"I have the five pounds. Don't be insulting. I can afford my own special license."

"I've no doubt of that." Jack pulled a five-pound note from his desk drawer. "But as long as you're making the trip to get one license, how about if you get two?"

CHAPTER FIFTEEN

The groom looked... at peace, for the first time in Axel Belmont's long acquaintance with him. Sir Jack's mama was positively glowing with joy, and the bride's radiance beggared description.

Axel stood with Madeline at the door to the Candlewick library, wondering what a fellow ought to say when he'd blundered so badly—not that Madeline would hear, see, or bother with anybody save her betrothed.

"Madeline, I'm sorry."

She turned a bemused stare on him. "You're daft."

She'd asked to be married here at Candlewick so the staff with whom she'd worked for years could attend en masse. The footmen arranged chairs for the elders, Mrs. Turnbull presided from the seat nearest the hearth, and Reverend Jeremy gently countermanded half of Mrs. Turnbull's directions.

Abigail stood with Sir Jack near the piano, while Sir Jack held the baby.

And looked damned competent about it, for a man who had no offspring of his own—yet.

"I am sorry," Axel said, "because clearly you were a lady fallen on hard times, and I failed as a gentleman to grasp the situation, much less put it to rights."

She hadn't even been a lady fallen on hard times, she'd been a girl.

"Do you recall the pink roses?" Madeline asked.

Axel had myriad pink roses, but he knew exactly the ones she meant. "I tossed them out as having died en route from Persia, and three months later, my compost heap was abloom with the most magnificent specimens."

Her gaze remained on Sir Jack, "My guess is, they did better in your compost heap than they'd done in Persia. They are among your most vigorous bloomers and their scent is heavenly."

Axel lectured frequently at Oxford on botanical topics, and he knew a parable when one was handed to him.

"When I stopped watering, pruning, fussing, and fretting over those roses, and simply tossed them to the elements, they thrived. You are not a Persian rose, Madeline. I should have noticed the French, the fascination with the library, your bearing, your poise, your ability to manage a household without being seen to do it, the way you taught the boys manners without scolding them… I harbored a gently reared lady under my roof, and now that—"

Madeline kissed his cheek. "I'm the bride, I'm allowed to kiss even thorny old botanists who are made nervous by weddings."

"I'm not old." Axel was blushing though, and Abigail was enjoying his discomfort, if her smirk was any indication. Sir Jack was busy getting to know Axel's youngest, and the dratted boy was smiling so magnificently, Axel's heart ached.

"You thought you were tossing those roses to the elements, given up for dead. Instead you put them where they had warmth, nourishment, peace and quiet, and protection from the wind. Lucky roses, to be so well provided for and given a place to set down sturdy roots. I had safety here, respect, meaningful work, good mates, and time to sort myself out. I had and have friends. You will please stop troubling the bride on her wedding day over nonsense."

Reverend Jeremy caught Axel's eye.

"If ever Sir Jack gives you cause for complaint, Madeline, you will come to Candlewick for aid. I promise not to thrash him too awfully, but I can't speak for Abigail. The woman is quite fierce."

Miss Lucy Anne DeWitt took a seat at the piano, and started on a pleasant air in a major key—Bach, simplified, perhaps.

"Likewise, you and yours will come to Teak House when you're in need of aid, Mr. Belmont. I do have a request, though."

Sir Jack had passed the baby back to Abigail, and was smiling at his bride with so much naked love, that Axel… was glad for his friend. For his friends.

"Ask, Madeline. Anything I have to give, save my family, is yours."

"You already gave me your family. I'd like one of those roses, the pink ones that thrive when you think they're beyond hope. Jack's mama might like one too, and if her friends in London take a fancy to them, you will need an entire glass house to propagate more stock."

The way Madeline smiled back at Sir Jack suggested propagation had already figured on the happy couple's agenda.

Miss DeWitt—soon to be Mrs. Jeremy Fanning—brought her air to a close, and Axel winged his arm.

"I give you up reluctantly."

Madeline tucked a gloved hand around his elbow. "I give myself joyously. Stop fretting."

Axel did not fret about the bride and groom. They were so obviously besotted that spring ought to have hastened to the shire on general principles, complete with baby bunnies and warbling robins. He did, however, worry about the grumbling he'd heard over the past few days in the Wet Weasel.

Higgans was being an ass, making vague threats, and encouraging talk. Axel had hoped to draw Jack aside at some point, and warn him before the evening assembly, but no opportunity had presented itself.

"Mr. Belmont, move your feet."

"Yes, Madeline."

Axel did not flatter himself that he gave the bride away. He simply escorted Madeline to the groom's side, and took his place beside his friend. Reverend Jeremy officiated, Abigail sniffled, and the baby was very well behaved.

Such good luck could not possibly last, and the assembly—which Higgans was bound to attend—would begin in less than two hours.

* * *

"Your brother performs a beautiful wedding," Madeline said, as the coach rattled down the Candlewick lane. Jack had insisted that they be married prior to the assembly, in hopes that a wedding announcement would overshadow the mischief Dr. Higgans was bound to make.

Higgans had called twice at Teak House in the past week, demanding that Jack arrest Pahdi or produce the medical bag. Pahdi had offered to leave the shire, even knowing flight would make him look guilty, and Jack had counseled against it.

Jack claimed that if Higgans's word alone had the power to send an innocent man from his home, then justice was fleeing along with the accused. All very true, but Madeline wasn't as confident as Jack was that reason would prevail.

"You are a beautiful bride," Jack said. "I will be the envy of every bachelor present tonight and a few of the married fellows as well."

"I will be the envy of every woman on the premises, except perhaps Mrs. Belmont."

Abigail had threatened mayhem if she had to remain home with the baby while her husband and step-sons went to the assembly.

"I wasn't sure Belmont would give you away, he was so busy glowering at me. I was informed before the ceremony that if you are not ecstatically happy under my roof, Belmont will learn of it, and correct me by virtue of an application of his fists to my handsome countenance."

And yet, Mr. Belmont had patted Madeline's hand reassuringly and escorted her into the formal parlor like a doting—if somewhat fierce—cousin.

"I thanked him for his felicitations," Jack said. "Are you nervous, Madeline?"

In the strictest sense, Jack hadn't married down. His family and Madeline's had apparently been acquainted and on equal footing, albeit decades ago. As far as the neighbors were concerned, though, Madeline had married very far above herself.

"I'm nervous," she said. "I know Higgans will be underfoot, inciting trouble." Was it too much to ask that her wedding day be free from strife?

"He can incite all the trouble he pleases. He has no more evidence against Pahdi, than he does against me, for I was also in town on the night the blasted bag disappeared. Vicar and Mrs. Weekes were, and so was Belmont. Higgans has no suspicions where they're concerned."

Which added up to an admission that Jack was nervous. He had his arguments ready, if Higgans confronted him at the punchbowl. Jeremy and Lucy Anne would arrive with the Belmonts, and Mrs. Fanning and Aunt Theo were collecting Aunt Hattie in the Fanning traveling coach.

Jack would not be without allies, and Pahdi would be back at Teak House, overseeing the celebrations below stairs in honor of the wedding.

While Madeline would be... nervous.

The coach pulled up before the Weasel, and Jack assisted Madeline to alight. The street was muddy after several days of moderating temperatures, but straw had been spread to preserve the ladies' hems.

"Your presence here will cause heads to turn," Jack said, offering Madeline his arm. "People will stare, not because a former chambermaid is dancing among her supposed betters, but because Lady Fanning is stunningly lovely in her new dress."

Lady Fanning. At least some of Madeline's nerves were attributable to her new station, but most of her anxiety came from a sense that trouble was brewing—trouble she'd caused—and tonight was the logical time for that trouble to escalate.

Jack—*her husband*—was breathtakingly handsome in his evening finery, and that realization let Madeline relax a bit. He was the magistrate, wealthy, formidable, and *all hers*. If heads turned, it would be to stare at him and wonder why such an impressive man had chosen Madeline Hennessey for his wife.

Jack's first maneuver was to introduce Madeline to a dark-haired fellow standing beside a woman Madeline recognized from the occasional market day.

"Lady Valentine, may I make known to you my wife, Madeline..." Old, old lessons from girlhood struggled up from memory, and Madeline managed to get through the introductions without stumbling. To have a courtesy title, though, the man Madeline had so casually been introduced to was the son of a marquess or possibly even a duke.

"Jack, would you excuse me while I fetch a drink?" Madeline asked.

Lord Valentine looked vaguely puzzled.

"I will fetch you a drink," Jack said. "Lady Valentine, might I do the same for you?"

Her ladyship was a lovely young woman and clearly held in great affection by her husband. "No, thank you, Sir Jack. You may leave your bride in our keeping and brave the punchbowl. We'll ask her only the usual questions."

Jack winked at Madeline and sauntered off, just as Jeremy, Lucy Anne, the aunts, and Mrs. Fanning emerged from the cloakroom. Further introductions ensued as two violins and a cello tuned up in the corner.

Perhaps Higgans wouldn't come. The room was filling, and at any moment, Tavis, the informal master of ceremonies, would offer a welcome.

"Are you looking forward to dancing with your husband?" Abigail Belmont asked. "Jack cuts quite a dash on the dance floor."

"Madam," Axel Belmont muttered, "where is your spousal loyalty? *I* cut quite a dash on the dance floor. Sir Jack is competent."

Jack returned with the punch, and nearly twenty minutes of chatting, smiling, and congratulations ensued. Just when Madeline thought she'd go mad from inactivity, Tavis tapped a spoon against a glass to bring the assembly to order.

"On behalf of the Weasel, welcome friends and neighbors. I've had a special request for the first dance, in honor of nuptial vows spoken earlier today. We'll start the evening with a waltz, and the dancing will be opened by Sir Jack Fanning *and his new wife!*"

"Smile," Abigail commanded, smiling ferociously herself, while applauding madly. The clapping was slow to begin, but soon the entire room reverberated with happy thunder.

Jack led Madeline to the middle of the dance floor. He bowed, she curtseyed, and they assumed waltz position.

"I don't know how to waltz," Madeline said. The dance was a recent acquisition from the Continent, and thus hadn't been among the ones she'd learned as a girl.

"I do. Simply follow my lead, and when the rest of the crowd joins in, we'll slip away."

Jack did know how to waltz, and he knew how to explain the dance to Madeline without words. They at first moved in a conservative square of steps, then more boldly, until Jack had turned Madeline down the room, and the Belmonts had joined in along with other married couples.

For thirty-two measures in triple meter, Madeline simply danced with her husband. Regret crept close, for all the dances Madeline had been denied by her father's intemperance, all the lovely moments, but had she not been in service, she never would have joined Jack's household.

"You have an aptitude for this," Jack said, pulling Madeline close on a turn.

"Not all ladies do."

"I have an aptitude for being your wife. I forbid you to kiss me when this dance ends."

The gleam in Jack's eyes became the fire of determination, and of course, when violins lilted into the final cadence, rather than allow Madeline to sink into a curtsey, Jack held her close and gave her a kiss such as every bride ought to be given on her wedding day.

Then Jack bowed, and Madeline curtseyed, amid more applause.

Perhaps Higgans had stayed home. Perhaps the meddlesome gods who had frowned on Madeline's fortunes so often in the past were done with her. Jack offered his arm, and Madeline took it, for she had no intention of dancing her night away. Mr. Belmont would likely insist, and Jeremy was certainly entitled to a turn, but other than that—

A commotion came from the direction of the cloakroom, and Dr. Higgans emerged with two yeoman bringing up the rear.

"I've found the scoundrel!" Higgans cried. "Caught him red-handed with stolen goods!" The doctor held up a battered black satchel, and the two yeomen each had Pahdi by one arm.

* * *

Rage had sustained Jack when he was being starved, beaten, ridiculed, and threatened daily with death. He'd been determined to live, to get back to his garrison, and to his wife. For a time, he'd been insane with anger, crazy enough to dig at packed earth with a bent spoon, to drag himself through jungles teeming with predators, to push on despite starvation, fever, and despair.

That rage had been on his own behalf, and it had saved his life.

The rage he felt watching Higgans hold that damned black satchel aloft was rage on behalf of Pahdi, who would no more steal than he would denounce the king in the middle of Sunday services.

And beneath that was a cold, coiled disgust that this... this lying excuse for a physician would sully *Madeline's wedding day.*

"Dr. Higgans," Jack said, "the dancing has begun. If you have business with me, we'll take our discussion outside so our neighbors can continue to enjoy themselves."

Jack considered arresting Higgans for disturbing the peace, but that would be an abuse of the magistrate's office, more's the pity.

The room had gone silent, of course, the better to catch every word for repetition over tea or ale tomorrow.

"You'll hear what I have to say right now," Higgans said. "Before these witnesses, you'll charge this... this houseboy of yours with robbery."

"You claim the man who has been *my butler* for nearly ten years took that bag from you, by force or fear, with intent to deprive you of it permanently?"

Higgans lowered the satchel. "The rascal took it from my home."

No, he did not. "Ah, then you refer to burglary. I assume you have witnesses?"

"I did not see him take the damned bag," Higgans said.

"Language, Higgans. Ladies are present. Shall we step outside?" Jack kept his tone civil—he'd negotiated with rajas who employed assassins by the dozen—but his mind was reeling. What was Pahdi doing with the bag, and how was Jack to extricate him from being charged with a crime?

Pahdi met Jack's eye with a calm, almost apologetic gaze, and Jack *knew.*

Pahdi had seen Madeline steal the bag and leave it in the livery, and he'd hidden the bag rather than let the crime be laid at Madeline's feet. Madeline's horrified expression said she'd grasped the facts more readily than Jack had.

Jack had interviewed every patron of the lending library who'd been present on the night of the theft... except Pahdi.

Damn, blast, pox, plague, and perdition.

"I'm not about to let you talk your way out of arresting this man," Higgans said. "He had my bag, and the whole shire knows it went missing. That means he was in possession of stolen goods—a very serious crime, indeed—even if nobody saw him take the bag."

The crowd at the edges of the dance floor murmured, probably agreeing with Higgans's logic, but Jack simply didn't care.

"We have yet to establish that your bag was stolen in the first place," Jack said, which was true from an evidentiary perspective as far as Higgans was concerned. "Moreover, your bag went missing more than a week ago. In all that time, nobody has corroborated your accusations against Pahdi, and I strongly suspect that you have jumped to inexcusable conclusions. Pahdi, what were you doing with Dr. Higgans's bag?"

Pahdi bowed to Jack with punctilious courtesy. "I was returning the bag to its owner, esteemed sir. I know you have spent considerable effort this past week searching for the doctor's bag. I was visiting with John Coachman outside the livery tonight, when I saw this bag next to a pile of horse... blankets. Knowing this medical bag to be of great sentimental value to the worthy, respected, most learned, honorable, and revered doctor, I sought to bring it to him straightaway. He stopped me in the street as I approached his house. These gentlemen kindly assisted me to join this august assemblage before any explanation was sought from me."

Thank God for quick thinking, and for an ability to recite a credible version of the truth. Jack aimed a glower at Higgans's henchmen.

"Is that true? Was Pahdi approaching Higgans's house with the bag in plain sight?"

The larger of the two mumbled something.

"I beg your pardon?" Jack prompted.

"It's true, he was walking toward the house, but it was dark. From across the street—"

"Thank you," Jack said. "Higgans, what sort of thief brings the contraband to the scene of the crime?"

"My medical bag didn't take itself to the livery, Sir Jack. What was this fellow doing in town tonight, if not trying to return the item he stole? He knew I'd be at this gathering, and chose his opportunity with the cunning his kind is known for."

Jeremy put a hand on Jack's arm, as if sensing that the temptation to violence was growing irresistible. Higgans was befouling an evening that should have been special for Madeline, and he was threatening a blameless soul.

"Perhaps Pahdi was patronizing the lending—"

"The lending library is closed tonight!" Higgans bellowed. "Arrest this man, or admit that you have no more care for the king's justice than this brigand does for—"

Madeline prowled across the room and plucked the bag from Higgans's grasp.

"*Enough* of your bile." She opened the bag and spilled its contents onto the dance floor. A scalpel tumbled out—none too clean—along with two bottles of some patent remedy or other, a double-ended scent bottle, and a cracked hand mirror.

Also a sizeable silver pocket flask.

Madeline jabbed a finger toward the floor. "*That* is your stolen property. *That* is your excuse for ruining the life of a man who did nothing to harm you. *I* stole your pathetic bag. It has been returned to you by one innocent of wrongdoing. Shall you ask the magistrate to arrest his own wife?"

Oh, Madeline. No.

Higgans gazed upon the detritus on the floor, his bravado faltering. "I never meant—I only wanted my bag back. A physician needs... This is all very brave of you, Miss Hennessey—"

"*Lady* Fanning," Madeline snapped. "I stole your bag because you refused to pay a call on an old, ailing woman who had nobody else to turn to for medical assistance. You treat the wealthy, you ignore the rest of us even when we have coin. I might be a criminal, but you are a disgrace."

Higgans picked up the flask and stuffed it in his pocket. "Miss—Lady—madam, I appreciate that you're loyal to your husband's staff, and one can see, given your antecedents, that is..." Higgans pointed at Pahdi. "Enough of this posturing. I'll not be dissuaded by some female's hysterical babbling. I want that man arrested."

Jack would never cease being proud of his wife, but he'd had more than enough of Higgans.

"I agree, Higgans," Jack said. "The idea that Madeline would resort to thievery, even though you disregarded a possibly fatal situation within her family, need not concern us. I stole your bag."

Madeline blew him a kiss. Jack bowed.

"Oh, go on with the two of you," Axel Belmont scoffed. "I stole your bag, Higgans. You know how botanists are, always taking what doesn't belong to us. We go about the shire stealing plants from the very marshes and lanes. We're little more than nature's pickpockets."

"Mr. Belmont," Abigail retorted, "It's new mothers who cannot be trusted around smelly old medical bags. I took that bag while you were out in your glass house, and do not argue with a lady."

"I would never argue with a lady," Jeremy said, "but Jack ought to arrest us all, for I sense that if we didn't exactly steal that bag personally, perhaps we should have. Not the done thing, Higgans, to neglect our elders when they're in need, or to turn our backs on the sick, or the poor, or the stranger far from home."

Mortimer Cotton cleared his throat. Hector McArdle stared into his cup of punch.

Lucy Anne knelt and gathered up the mirror, bottles, and scalpel from the floor, put them into the battered satchel, and handed it to Higgans.

He took the bag and held it to his middle as he peered around a room gone silent.

"I'm sorry I took your bag," Madeline said. "I meant to return it after you'd spent a few days fretting. My aunt might have been taken from me, and I wanted you to know a little of that helplessness and upset. I should not have taken your bag. If you seek damages, I will gladly pay them, but no sum on earth could have compensated me for the loss of my aunt."

Apologize to my wife. Jack almost started forward to roar those words at Higgans, but Belmont was to Jack's left, and Jeremy to his right. They were waiting to grab Jack by the arms, and that alone prevented Jack from letting his temper loose.

Higgans shoved the bag at Madeline, turned on his heel, and stomped out.

Madeline tossed the bag aside, and barreled into Jack's arms, and still nobody said anything.

He made my wife cry. Jack was torn between anger at Higgans's rudeness, and a fierce joy, because Madeline was *Lady Fanning*, and before this group of mostly good, bewildered people, she'd defended an innocent man at cost to herself, and then turned to Jack for comfort and support.

"He's gone," Jack said. "If he comes near you, I'll arrest him for being a common nuisance and a disgrace to the species."

"If he comes near you, or Pahdi, or my aunts, I won't answer for my actions."

Madeline stepped back, but kept hold of Jack's hand. "Jack…" She nodded to her right.

Pahdi stood off to the side, looking stoic and wary. He didn't dare leave, because Higgans might well await him in the street.

Madeline had chosen the right word earlier: *enough*. Enough making excuses for rural backwardness, enough being patient, enough letting a man who'd saved Jack's life be treated as a pariah.

"Pahdi," Jack said, loudly enough to reach into every corner of the assembly room. "I should be honored if you'd stay for a cup of punch. I apologize for Higgans's behavior, and promise you it won't happen again."

"I stick to the ladies' punchbowl," Belmont said. "And not only because the ladies congregate in its vicinity."

"Or you could mix the two," Jeremy said. "A little sweetness, a little fire." He lifted a glass in Lucy Anne's direction.

"Please, Pahdi," Madeline said, extending a hand to him. "My nerves need steadying. I can't imagine yours don't as well."

Pahdi did not drink spirits. Jack cast about for a polite way to diffuse awkwardness when Pahdi smiled at Madeline. He was a handsome devil, which several of the young ladies present apparently noticed.

"The lady's punch sounds like the safer offering," Pahdi replied, "and perhaps a bite of that most delectable pear torte, or the apple cake?"

"Try some of both," Jack said. "I certainly intend to."

And then, he'd collect his wife, take her directly home, and see about giving the lady a wedding night to make her forget all about bothersome neighbors, neglected aunties, and crime sprees.

* * *

After lovemaking that had been by turns enthusiastic, tender, passionate, and inventive, Madeline had fallen asleep in her husband's arms, at peace for the first time in years. With Jack's help, she'd take the situation with Theo and Hattie in hand, whether that meant selling their properties, finding tenants for them, or adding their smallholdings to the acreage Jack farmed for his own purposes.

What mattered was that she wasn't alone with the problem.

"Don't fret," Jack said, kissing her fingers as the first streaks of pale light outlined the window curtains. "You admitted to all and sundry that you stole that dratted bag. If Higgans decides you were telling the truth, and seeks reparation, I will pay him such obscenely generous damages that he retires from the shire. Mama could not stop gushing about what a fine woman I've chosen for my bride."

Madeline linked her fingers with Jack's. "Your mama wants us to be fruitful and multiply."

"So do I, assuming you're comfortable with the notion."

Madeline had been blissfully comfortable with the notion twice during the night. She resisted the temptation to start the day with a third indulgence, and instead remained lying side by side with her husband.

"I don't want our children to have thieves for parents, Jack. I'm done skulking about in the dead of night, and I hope you are too."

"Shall I confess to borrowing Cotton's ram?"

He was asking in all seriousness. "Don't you dare. You can't stand confinement, and Mr. Belmont might arrest you out of an excess of masculine stupidity. I suggest we instead offer Cotton his pick of Hattie's tups."

Jack shifted to his side, peering at Madeline in the predawn gloom. "That is brilliant. What about McArdle?"

"We will buy considerable coal from him for distribution to the poor, but insist that he give us a discount on such a large order."

Jack kissed her cheek. "You should have been a judge. I think we should have Mr. Weekes to tea next week, and discuss his plan for managing the funds from the poor box. Jeremy tells me that letting the coins pile up until the vicar notices an urgent need is not considered a well-informed approach."

The more Madeline knew of Jeremy, the more she liked him. Lucy Anne DeWitt soon-to-be Fanning was enthralled with her fiancé, and her parents seemed very pleased with Jeremy as well.

"We'll have Weekes to tea, but not next week. Next month, please."

"Excellent notion. Did you know you talk in your sleep?"

Madeline shifted to her side as well, the better to tell if Jack was teasing. "I have vivid dreams. What did I say?"

"That I'm the most wonderful kisser and I have the most delightfully enormous—Madeline Fanning, marriage has made you bold."

"Be serious."

"If you continue to grasp that particular part of my anatomy, then conversation, much less serious talk, will be beyond me. I couldn't make out a word you said in your sleep."

Madeline let go of Jack—for now—but tucked nearer and wrapped a leg over his hip. "I used to have the same dream, over and over. I am with my mama in London on a pretty, sunny day. The streets are busy, and everybody is happy. Then it changes."

Jack wrapped her close, so Madeline could feel his heart beat against her palm, a slow, steady tattoo of reassurance.

"Tell me," he said.

"I'm holding my mother's hand one moment, and then I can't find her. I'm at a busy intersection, and I don't recognize any of the buildings. The people aren't happy, they're all harried and rushing past. I don't know which way to turn, and then I notice the crossing sweeper watching me. I'm frightened, but if I run, I know he'll chase me."

"This is not a dream, Madeline. This is a nightmare."

"Everybody knows where they're going, Jack, while I stand there, too frightened to take a single step."

Madeline loved breathing in his scent from this proximity. Loved being this close to him.

"I'll waken you, the next time I think you're dreaming. You will do the same for me."

Oh, how she loved him. "Of course I will, but the dream took a different turn last night."

A soft triple-rap interrupted Madeline's confidences.

"Go to the devil, you shameless wretch," Jack yelled. "Leave the damned tray outside the door and don't come back for it until spring."

Laughter sounded in the corridor, amid the sound of retreating footsteps.

"Remind me to turn Pahdi off without a character," Jack said.

"Just as soon as we name our firstborn after him."

"Fine notion. Now tell me the rest of your dream."

Madeline wouldn't tell him all of it—her mother had claimed to have had the sight, and Madeline was prone to strong hunches. She could tell Jack the part that mattered the most, though.

"I stood on that same terrible street corner, bewildered, battling panic, and you tooled past in the dog cart. The vehicle smelled slightly of sheep, but you had such kind eyes, that when you came around and offered me a hand up, I got in the cart, and then you drove us home to Teak House."

"You were taken with my eyes?"

Those too. "Yes. Shall I fetch the tray?"

Jack draped himself over her. "You are my bride. If you want the tea tray, you send me scampering across the room to get it for you, and you admire my form in all its natural glory, as is your right. Then I fix your tea exactly as you prefer, and meekly accept your instruction regarding the proper amount of butter for your toast."

He emphasized his point with delicate kisses to the side of Madeline's neck, and she retaliated by wrapping her legs around his waist.

Long, lovely moments later, Madeline decided that she could wait until Jack had fixed her tea to tell him that in her dream, on the bench of the dog cart, had sat three handsome little boys, all with their mama's flaming red hair and their father's devilish smile.

The fourth child, a girl older than the other three, had beckoned to Madeline, and whispered in her ear. "My name is Jacqueline, and my birthday is in October."

By the time Jack had got the tea right, Madeline had counted weeks, and started thinking up middle names. Jack noticed her distracted expression, and well… they were late to luncheon. For the next week straight, they were late for luncheon, but Madeline won the argument, and the child was christened Jacqueline Pahdi Fanning.

-THE END-

To my dear readers,

I hope you enjoyed Madeline and Jack's story, because I certainly had fun writing it. I considered making their romance a Christmas story, but didn't want to wait another four months to release it when the holiday season approaches. It's never too soon for a Happily Ever After, right?

I'm hard at work now on a story for our friend Asher Fenwick, who appeared in the **Loneliest Lords** title, **Hadrian: Lord of Hope**. Fen's tale should be published in September, so be on the lookout for a graceburrowes. com website update to that effect. The first three **Loneliest Lords** (Worth/ Trenton/Hadrian) are also available from the website as a bundle.

To keep up with all the releases and updates, you can sign up for my newsletter at graceburrowes.com/contact.php. I publish every other month or so, and I will never, no never, sell or give away my mailing list, and I only issue a newsletter when I have something worth saying.

Speaking of which…. I am very excited to be writing a new Windham family series, The Windham Brides. You may recall that Percival's brother, Lord Tony Windham, has four daughters, we all know what *that* means. The first story, **The Trouble with Dukes**, comes out December 20, 2016, and I've included a sneak peek below. The hardest thing about writing **Dukes** was keeping certain titled gentlemen from stealing scenes.

If **Jack** is your introduction to the **Jaded Gentlemen** series, you can catch up with the prequels **Thomas**, **Matthew**, and **Axel**. There's even a bundled ebook version of those first three stories available exclusively on the website. Tell 'em Jack sent you.

Happy reading!
Grace Burrowes

Stay in touch on Facebook:
Facebook.com/Grace-Burrowes-115039058572197/
Follow me on twitter:
Twitter.com/GraceBurrowes

The Trouble with Dukes by Grace Burrowes (December 20, 2016)

Miss Megan Windham is falling in love with Hamish MacHugh, the newly titled Duke of Murdoch. Megan's cousins, however, Westhaven, St. Just, and Valentine, will take an interest in her situation that closely resembles, well, meddling…

Gayle Windham, Earl of Westhaven was too self-disciplined to glance at the clock more than once every five minutes, but he could see the shadow of an oak limb start its afternoon march up the wall of his study. The remains of a beef sandwich sat on a tray at his elbow, and soon his youngest child would go down for a nap.

Westhaven brought his attention back to the pleasurable business of reviewing household expenses, though Anna's accounting was meticulous. He obliged his countess's request to look over the books because of the small insights he gained regarding his family.

They were using fewer candles, testament to Spring's arrival and longer hours of daylight.

The wine cellar had required some attention, another harbinger of the upcoming social season.

Anna had spent a bit much on Cousin Megan's birthday gift, but a music box was a perfect choice for Megan.

"You haven't moved in all the months I've been gone," said a humorous baritone. "You're like one of those statues, standing guard through the seasons, until some obliging brother comes along to demand that you join him in the park for a hack on a pretty afternoon."

Home safe. Devlin St. Just's dark hair was tousled, his clothes wrinkled, his boots dusty, but he was once again, *home safe.*

The words were an irrational product of Westhaven's memory, for his mind produced them every time he saw his older half-brother after a prolonged absence. Westhaven crossed the study with more swiftness than dignity, hand extended toward his brother.

"Good God, you stink, St. Just, and the dust of the road will befoul my carpets wherever you pass."

St. Just took Westhaven's proffered hand and yanked the earl close enough for a quick, back-thumping hug.

"I stink, you scold. Give a man a brandy while he befouls your carpets, and good day to you too."

Westhaven obliged, mostly to have something to do other than gawk at his brother. Yorkshire was too far away, the winters were too long and miserable,

and St. Just visited too infrequently, but every time he did visit, he seemed….
Lighter. More settled, more at peace.

And if ever a man was happy to smell of horse, it was St. Just.

"I have whisky," Westhaven said. "I'm told the barbarians to the north favor
it over brandy."

"If you had decent whisky, I might consider it, but you're a brandy snob, so
brandy it is. How are the children?"

Thank God for the topic of children, which allowed two men who'd missed
each other terribly to avoid admitting as much.

"The children are noisy, expensive, and a trial to any parent's nerves. Our
parents come by, dispensing falsehoods regarding my own youth along with a
surfeit of sweets. Then their graces parents swan off, leaving my kingdom in
utter disarray."

Westhaven passed St. Just a healthy portion of spirits, though being St. Just,
he waited until Westhaven was holding his own glass.

"To kingdoms in disarray," St. Just said, touching his glass to Westhaven's.
"Try uprooting your womenfolk and dragging them hundreds of miles on the
king's highway. Your realm shrinks to the proportions of one very unforgiving
saddle. Rather like being on campaign."

St. Just could do this now—make passing, halfway humorous references to
his army days. For the first two years after he'd mustered out, he'd been unable
to remain sober during a thunderstorm.

"Her ladyship is well?" Westhaven asked.

"My Emmie is a saint," St. Just countered, taking the seat behind Westhaven's
desk. "If you die, I want this chair."

"Spare me your military humor. If I die, you and Valentine are guardians of
my children."

A dusty boot thunked onto the corner of Westhaven's antique desk, the
same corner upon which Westhaven's own, much less dusty boots, were often
propped, provided the door was closed.

"Val and I? You didn't make Moreland their guardian?"

"His grace will intrude, meddle, advise, maneuver, interfere, and otherwise
orchestrate matters as he sees fit, abetted by our lovely mother in all particulars.
Putting legal authority over the children in your hands was my pathetic gesture
toward thwarting the ducal schemes. You will, of course, oblige my guilt over
this presumption by giving me a similar role in the lives of your children."

St. Just closed his eyes. He was a handsome fellow, handsomer for having
regained some of the muscle he'd had as a younger man.

"I can hear His Grace's voice when you start braying about what I shall
oblige and troweling on verbs in sextuplicate."

"Is that a word?"

"Trowel, yes, a humble verb. Probably Saxon rather than Roman in origin."

Westhaven pretended to savor his brandy, when he was in truth savoring the fact that his older brother would—in all his dirt—come to Westhaven's establishment before calling upon the ducal household.

"Where is your countess, St. Just? She's usually affixed to your side like a very pretty cocklebur."

"Where's yours?" St. Just retorted. "I dropped Emmie and the girls off at Louisa and Joseph's, though I'm to collect them—"

The door opened, and a handsome dark-haired fellow sauntered in, Westhaven's butler looking choleric on his heels.

"I come seeking asylum," Lord Valentine said.

St. Just was on his feet and across the room almost before Val had finished speaking. The oldest and youngest Windham brothers bore a resemblance, both dark-haired, and both carrying with them a physical sense of passion. Valentine loved his music, St. Just his horses, and yet the brothers were alike in a way Westhaven appreciated more than he envied—mostly.

"You come seeking my good brandy," Westhaven said, when Val had been properly embraced and thumped by St. Just. "Here."

He passed Valentine his own portion and poured another for himself.

"We were about to toast our happy state of marital pandemonium," St. Just said. "Or so Westhaven thinks. I'm in truth fortifying myself to storm the ducal citadel."

Valentine took his turn in Westhaven's chair. "I'd blow retreat if I were you."

Westhaven took one of the chairs across from the desk. "What have their graces done now?"

Valentine preferred to prop his boots—moderately dusty—on the opposite corner from his brothers. This put the sunlight over Val's left shoulder.

None of the brothers had any gray hairs yet, something of a competition in Westhaven's mind, though he wasn't sure whether first past the post would be the winner or the loser. They were only in their thirties, but they were all fathers of small children—small *Windham* children.

"His grace is sending Uncle Tony and Aunt Gladys on maneuvers in Wales directly after the ball," Valentine said, "while her grace will snatch up our cousins, doubtless in anticipation of some matchmaking."

They had four female cousins: Beth, Charlotte, Megan, and Anwen. They were lovely young women, red-haired, intelligent, and well dowered, but they were Windhams, and thus in no hurry to marry.

A situation the duchess sought to remedy.

"So that's why Megan was particularly effusive in her suggestions that I come south," St. Just mused, opening a japanned box on the mantel. "Emmie said something untoward was afoot."

A piece of marzipan disappeared down St. Just's maw.

"Goes well with brandy," he said, offering the box to Val, who took two. "Westhaven?"

"How generous of you, St. Just." He took three, though the desk held another box, which his brothers might not find. His children hadn't.

Yet.

"Beth and Megan have both been through enough seasons to know how to repel boarders," Westhaven said.

"I wondered what their graces would do when they got us all married off," Valentine mused, brandy glass held just so before his elegant mouth. "I thought they'd turn to charitable works, a rest between rounds until the grandchildren grew older."

He tossed a bit of marizipan in the air and caught it in his mouth, just he would have twenty years earlier, and the sight pleased Westhaven in a way that he might admit when all of his hair was gray.

"Beth is weakening," Westhaven said. "She's become prone to megrims, sore knees, a touch of a sniffle. Anna and I do what we can, but the children keep us busy, as does the business of the dukedom."

"And we all thank God you've taken that mare's nest in hand," St. Just said, lifting his glass. "How do matters stand, if you don't mind a soldier's blunt speech?"

"We're firmly on our financial feet," Westhaven said. "Oddly enough, Moreland is in part responsible. Because he didn't bother with wartime speculation, when the Corsican was finally buttoned up, once for all, our finances went through none of the difficult adjustments many others are still reeling from."

"If you ever do reel," Valentine said, "you will apply to me for assistance, or I'll thrash you silly, Westhaven."

"And to me," St. Just said. "Or I'll finish the job Valentine starts."

"My thanks for your violent threats," Westhaven said, hiding a smile behind his brandy glass. "Do I take it you fellows would rather establish yourselves under my roof than at the ducal mansion?"

Valentine and St. Just exchanged a look that put Westhaven in mind of their parents.

"If we're to coordinate the defense of our unmarried lady cousins," St. Just said, "then it makes sense we'd impose on your hospitality, Westhaven."

"We're agreed then," Valentine said, raiding the tin once more. "Ellen will be relieved. Noise and excitement aren't good for a woman in her condition, and this place will be only half as uproarious as Moreland House."

"We must think of our cousins," St. Just replied. "The combined might of the duke and duchess of Moreland are arrayed against the freedom of four dear and determined young ladies who will not surrender their spinsterhood lightly."

"Nor should they," Westhaven murmured, replacing the lid on the tin, only for St. Just to pry it off. "We had the right to choose as we saw fit, as did our sisters. You'd think their graces would have learned their lessons by now."

A knock sounded on the door. Valentine sat up straight, St. Just hopped to his feet to replace the tin on the mantel, and was standing, hands behind his back, when Westhaven bid the next caller to enter.

"His Grace, the Duke of Moreland, my lords," the butler announced.

In the next instant, Percival Windham stepped nimbly around the butler and marched into the study.

"Well done, well done. My boys have called a meeting of the Windham subcommittee on the disgraceful surplus of spinsters soon to be gathered into her grace's care. St. Just, you're looking well. Valentine, when did you take to wearing jam on your linen?"

Moreland swiped the tin off the mantel, opened it, took the chair next to Westhaven and set the box in the middle of the desk.

"I'm listening, gentlemen," the duke said, popping a sweet into his mouth. "Unless you want to see your old papa lose what few wits he has remaining after raising you lot, you will please tell me how to get your cousins married off post haste. The duchess has spoken, and we are her slaves in all things, are we not?"

Westhaven reached for a piece of marzipan, St. Just fetched the brandy decanter, and Valentine sent the butler for sandwiches, because what on earth could any of them say to a ducal proclamation such as that?

Order your copy of **The Trouble With Dukes**!

Made in the USA
Middletown, DE
11 June 2018